The Dragon and the Queen

ALSO BY KAITLYN DAVIS

A Dance of Dragons

The Shadow Soul ~ The Spirit Heir ~ The Phoenix Born

Leena's Story (The Novellas)

Once Upon a Curse

Gathering Frost ~ Withering Rose ~ Chasing Midnight

Parting Worlds ~ Granting Wishes

Midnight Fire

Ignite ~ Simmer ~ Blaze ~ Scorch ~ Burn

Midnight Ice

Frost ~ Freeze ~ Fracture ~ Shatter

The Dragon and the Queen

KAITLYN DAVIS

ISBN: 9781952288227

Cover Illustration: Salome Totladze

Map Illustration: Arel B. Grant

Cover & Map Typography: Kaitlyn Davis

Created with Vellum

To my family for their unconditional love,
my friends for their overwhelming support,
and my fans for their incredible enthusiasm.
Thank you from the bottom of my heart.

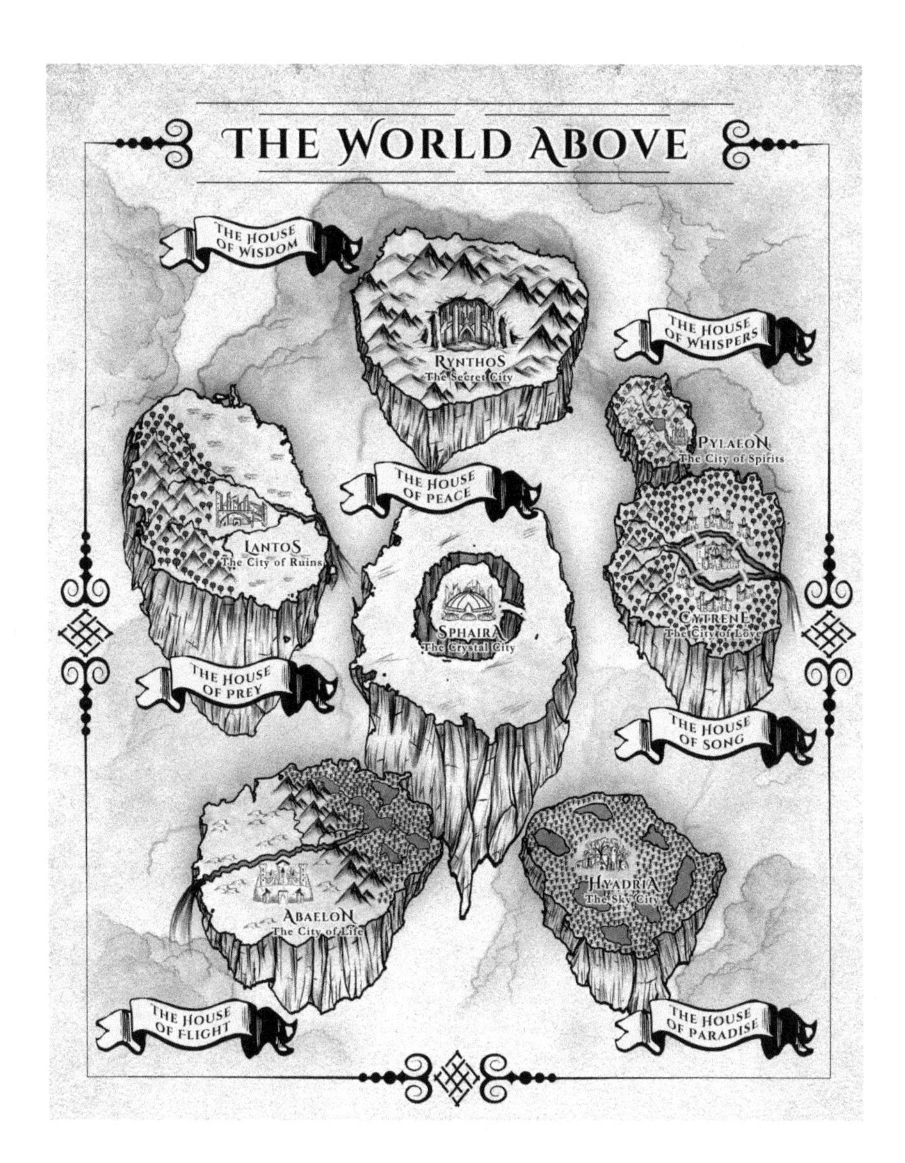
THE WORLD ABOVE
THE HOUSE OF WISDOM
RYNTHOS
The Secret City
THE HOUSE OF WHISPERS
PYLAEON
The City of Spirits
THE HOUSE OF PEACE
LANTOS
The City of Ruins
SPHAIRA
The Crystal City
CYTRENE
The City of Love
THE HOUSE OF PREY
THE HOUSE OF SONG
HYADRIA
The Sky City
ABAELON
The City of Life
THE HOUSE OF FLIGHT
THE HOUSE OF PARADISE

The Dragon and the Queen

PROLOGUE

The seer lay in bed listening to the creak of old wood and the slap of waves as the ship rolled with the ocean. The inky blackness behind her closed eyelids was her only respite from time. In here, the world was calm. In here, the days and years and centuries stood still.

"Mira."

His voice drew her back the way it always did, and she turned toward the sound. He stood in the doorway, his body lithe and strong, the golden skin of his bare arms smooth and his long hair a deep bronze. One step and everything shifted. Wrinkles marred his brow and white scruff covered his chiseled cheeks. Another step and time turned further still, leaving his skin sagging and his spine bent. Another step, another age, on and on, until he was across the room. The ship around him blurred too, the walls shifting from freshly stained grains to algae-covered planks to nothing but rot with holes. Everything stopped the moment he threaded his fingers through hers.

"Zavier?" She blinked the visions away and stared into his hazel eyes, the one constant in her ever-changing world. No matter how old her magic made him look, his gaze remained the same—steadfast and loving, her anchor in the storm. "What's going on?"

"We're here."

"Where?"

"Come. They're waiting for you."

He'd told her. If she could only just remember, but the hours bled from one to the next, leaving her unsure of what was real and what had happened only in her mind. Even as he helped her to her feet, she couldn't remember which stage of life was now and which was merely a flash of things to come. She lived a thousand lives every single second, shifting through time the way one might flip through the pages of a book, the world always in flux.

Zavier led her through the ship, keeping one of his broad eagle wings wrapped around her shoulders to fight the chill. Her homeland had been a warm place of constant sun, but this new world they found themselves in was turning gray. At least that's what he told her. As they made their way outside, the sky shifted, hazy then clear then opaque, premonitions of things to come.

"The mages have begun construction on a floating city," he explained as they walked toward the bow. "They're bringing the survivors here to begin the new world, and news of the prophecy has spread. They want to meet you. They want to hear it from your lips."

Stopping beside a damp railing, she huddled closer to his warm chest. Through the translucent mist, a jagged isle topped by thick forest came into view. Surrounding it on all sides was a vast array of ships, some old and some new, some fit for royalty and some no more than rowboats. Above them all, magic lit the skies.

But even with Zavier so close to her, out in the open like this, her power stole her sight. When she blinked, the forest was gone, replaced by an imposing castle built straight into the rock. Homes and bridges and walkways covered the seas. And there were people, so many people, looking drawn and forlorn. Suddenly, orange blazed against charcoal black. The castle was engulfed in flames as raging fires filled her gaze and cries split her ears. A deep roar made her shiver—she'd heard the terrifying sound too many times before. Golden power glittered through the air, the sort that still made her tremble in both awe and fear. The beasts were there. They were coming. This time they'd win.

That's not now, she tried to remember. *That's later—much, much later.*

"Mira," Zavier whispered, his breath tickling her cheek as his voice drew her back. She tightened her hold on his fingers and blinked the future from her eyes. The forest returned, and the odd grouping of ships, and the small force of mages trying to build a new world from the utter devastation of their old one. "Stay with me."

She was trying.

"The seer," people murmured as they neared.

"The *chrono'kine*."

"The prophetess."

The rainbow aura lighting the skies dampened as faces turned her way and the world fell silent, nothing but the subtle crashing of waves as her ship cut through the sea. There was no need to confirm who she was in a crowd of mages. The truth was clear. The rosy spark of her magic glittered across her cheeks and her arms, covering every inch of her skin. Once, in a time that felt so long ago, she'd had a certain amount of control over the power. But that was before she and Zavier had sacrificed so much, before she'd succumbed for the sake of saving them all. Now, it always simmered beneath the surface and leaked from her pores, as vital as breathing.

A man on a gilded ship stepped forward, a crown gleaming on his brow. He was no *aethi'kine*, that much she knew. They'd all been killed in the fighting. But it seemed he was a king nonetheless.

"Welcome to Da'Kin," he called across the sea, the wind

carrying his voice as yellow ignited along his fingers. "This is the start of the new world. It's not much now, but one day it will be a grand city."

Fire flashed across her sight.

She swallowed and tightened her hold on Zavier's hand, forcing the vision away. By the end of this king's lifetime, it would be a grand city, in scope if not substance. He would be long dead before the day it burned to ash. There was no point in dashing his dreams now.

"That it will," she said, keeping her voice kind.

The man grinned as his gaze swept across the ships and sea, no doubt seeing something else entirely. "We've all heard the words by now, prophetess. They travel faster than the breeze, but still, there would be no greater honor than to hear them upon your lips."

The words.

She knew exactly which ones he meant. Aside from Zavier and a few major players, they were the only other constant in her shifting world, whispered across time and sewn into the fabric of fate, laced with hope and promise. She'd written the full story down once, long ago, back when there'd been paper and ink, before the presses had crumbled and the libraries had burned and the world had split, leaving nothing but dreary ruin here below. She'd kept a diary, housing all her deepest secrets within its fragile leather binding. But it wasn't meant for this gray existence upon the sea. Deep caverns and dry underground caves would keep it preserved until the day it was meant to be found. She could see the moment now—a woman's hands reaching overhead as silvery eyes flashed across the dark.

"Mira."

She returned to the present and the many faces angled toward her, breathless with anticipation and desperate for a little bit of hope. She'd crafted her visions into a poem, something short and easy to remember, but the words had gained a life force of their own. They would exist across the ages, passed down from generation to generation, a prayer whispered not to the gods but to heavy hearts in need of lifting. The world below would remember. Despite the desolation, they would carry her visions with them until the day came to see them through.

The seer shared her prophecy.

When it was done, cheers rang across the skies, but she was somewhere else, hundreds of years ahead, her thoughts still on her diary somewhere far above. A picture formed of a man with soft lavender eyes and deep onyx wings. The space around him was hazy and in flux, not yet settled. His future was uncertain, but one thing was clear.

The fate of her diary somehow lay with him.

1

XANDER

Hidden behind the trunk of an old oak tree, Xander pulled the worn leather volume from the folds of his jacket. The binding cracked as he flipped open the pages and a musty smell wafted from the paper making him feel at home. The words scrawled across the pages, however, were anything but familiar. The language was ancient, which begged the question, why had Cassi even wanted it in the first place?

Why do I?

Just holding the book brought him back to their hours together in the libraries of Rynthos and long days filled with endless debates. No one had challenged him the way she had. No one had stimulated him so much either. But it had been a lie. Every moment they'd spent together, she'd only been pretending.

Xander sighed and dropped his head against the bark. Cassi had been born beneath the mist. She'd spied on Lyana for a foreign king. She'd coordinated the attack in the sacred nest. She'd cut off Rafe's wings.

So again he asked, why had he kept it?

He could have let the book drown alongside his homeland. He

could have let Cassi drown too. But he hadn't. As the House of Whispers had been swallowed by the sea, he and Lyana had saved her life. Were they fools? Were they idealists? Maybe those were two sides of the same coin. He didn't know. But if he closed his eyes, he could still see her lifeless body strewn across the damp planks of the ship where they'd left her, and the very thought made him ill.

"I should've known I'd find you with a book."

"Lyana!"

Xander pushed off the tree and spun to face her. His cheeks flushed and a guilty feeling stirred in his chest. If the princess noticed, she didn't show it. Amusement lit her eyes.

"Were you reading?"

"No..." He sighed and stuffed the book back beneath his jacket. No matter how much he fought the sensation, he couldn't deny that it was a comfort to have that weight against his breastbone. "Just thinking."

"Nothing good, judging by the look on your face."

He tried to refute her but found himself mute. Nothing good, indeed. What did he have to be happy about? His isle had fallen from the sky. His mother had died in the process. His people were homeless. His kingdom was ruined. Xander prided himself on his optimism, but even his well had run dry.

"I'm sorry," Lyana murmured, taking his hand.

Xander's eyes met warm green ones. "For what?"

"For not being there to help you. For not being strong enough to stop it or quick enough to save her."

His heart lurched. He knew to which *her* she referred. A scene came to life in the back of his mind, of his mother in her royal rooms as the ceiling caved in, crushing even her stubborn spirit under the rubble. Now she was entombed beneath ocean and fog, out of his reach, but hopefully her soul had found some sort of rest. His patron god, Taetanos, owed him that at least.

"We'll save the rest," he finally said and squeezed her fingers.

Now it was Lyana's turn to let doubt cloud her features. Could she be the hope their people needed? Could she convince them to trust in her magic? "Whether they believe us or not, whether they want our help or not, somehow we'll find a way to save them. Not just the ravens, but everyone."

A horn sounded through the forest.

"They're ready for us," Lyana said, pulling away.

He held on to her hand. "Are you?"

"You asked me that yesterday."

"And now I'm asking again." He dropped her fingers but didn't release her gaze. "I know we're to be mates in name only, but even that is a promise you don't need to give. I've heard the prophecy. I know you're meant for more. And sometimes a good sleep can open a person's eyes—"

"Xander," she cut in. "I wouldn't be doing this if I didn't want to—you, of all people, should know that. Does the world below need me? Yes. But so does our world. So do our people. And I won't abandon them. I refuse to believe I must choose one or the other. I'm going to help them both. And you're going to help me, whether you want to or not."

Well, he couldn't argue with that. The corner of his lip twitched, and he offered her his arm. "Then I guess I have no choice but to escort you to our coronation."

She grinned and hooked her elbow through his. "I guess not."

Together, they made their way through the nameless forest at the northern edge of the House of Song. It was, perhaps, the last place he'd ever envisioned for receiving his crown—not that there would even be a crown. The royal jewels were gone. So was the throne room…and the scepter…and the official robes. But none of it mattered. As they stepped through the trees and into the clearing filled by a sea of lost ravens, such frivolities couldn't have been further from his mind. He had his people. They had him. And in the end, that was all his kingdom needed to survive.

A path opened as they made their way to the center of the crowd, Lyana in a tattered ivory overcoat and he in a grimy, bloodstained jacket. Their trousers were covered in filth. Her braids were half-undone and his hair was a mop upon his head. Dirt smattered both their cheeks. Not even a day had passed since the House of Whispers had fallen beneath the mist, and it showed. Yet he'd never felt more like a king. His people watched them with respect, hope gleaming in their eyes.

A reverent silence settled as they came to a stop before Helen, who held two crowns made of onyx feathers in her palms. "Prince Lysander Taetanus and Princess Lyana Aethionus, I stand before you as a herald of our gods and ask you to humble yourselves before their might. No king or queen is above their power. And as you pray before them, so shall you pray before your people as you ask for their blessing on your reign."

Xander had spent the better part of the morning coaching Lyana through the ceremony, so she showed no hesitation as he took her hand. They knelt before Helen and bowed their heads. A shadow came over his face as his captain of the guards lifted the crowns. Though his hovered above his head, not touching his brow, a heaviness still settled on his shoulders—the weight of so many eyes, the weight of his heritage, the weight of the gods and the traditions and the home he wanted to honor. Even the absences were a burden, none more acute than the empty space by his side where his brother should have been. The spot Lyana filled somehow felt hollow too. She'd be his queen, but not his mate. She'd be his partner, but not in the way he had once dreamed. Before his people, they'd be a god-chosen king and queen. Behind closed doors, they'd speak of magic and dragons and a war his world would never understand. In many ways, the coronation was a lie. But it was a lie they needed.

Helen's voice drew him back. "Do you promise to honor Taetanos, God of fate and fortune and all that comes in the life that follows, and to do all in your power to shepherd lost spirits to his realm?"

"I so promise," he and Lyana said in unison.

"Do you promise to uphold the laws of our land, to rule justly and fairly, to treat each man as your brother and each woman as your sister, and to do unto them as you would your own family, keeping love, respect, and duty in your heart?"

"I so promise."

"Do you promise to protect them from all foes seen and unseen, to keep them safe from outside forces seeking corruption, and to root out all enemies who seek to burn our world in flames?"

Xander swallowed as Lyana squeezed his fingers. If he truly wanted to honor this vow as intended, he would slide the dagger from his belt and stab her in the heart right now. But magic wasn't his enemy. The dragons were, and it was them he thought of as the words slipped through his lips. "I so promise."

"Do you promise you have spoken truly, with nothing but the purest intentions to serve your people and your gods, removing all thoughts of private aspirations?"

"I so promise."

"And do the people of the House of Whispers, having borne witness to these solemn vows, entrust your lives and hearts and souls to the man and woman kneeling before you?"

The collective shout came strong, without hesitation. "We do."

"If the gods object, let them do so now."

Xander half expected a lightning bolt to flay him where he knelt. Lyana caught his eye and winked as the moment of silence passed. Where their fingers touched, her pulse raced just as quickly as his.

"Lysander Taetanus and Lyana Aethionus," Helen shouted, her voice not wavering as she placed the crowns upon their heads. "In Taetanos's name, I dub you the King and Queen of the House of Whispers. Rise and face your people."

As they stood, a cheer erupted. The sound crashed over him like a wave threatening to pull him under, their hope almost tangible. He wanted to believe. He needed to believe. But as he looked out at the crowd, all he saw were a thousand mouths he needed to feed and a thousand bodies he needed to shelter. They were refugees on foreign soil, at the mercy of a world he knew would soon come crumbling down. The isle beneath his feet would fall, and the next, and the next, on and on, taking their way of life with it. There was nothing he could do to stop it. Nothing he could do to protect them. No answer he could find in the pages of a book. Lyana would heal the rift and save the world, but what could he do against such impossible odds? A simple raven with no magic in his skin?

A deep, gurgling *caw* caught his ear.

Another sounded, and another, the calls rising and falling in a melodic rhythm that stirred the bird inside his soul. Xander looked at the sky. Between the magenta-tinted clouds, where the setting sun shone bright as gold, a dark spot emerged. Silhouettes moved like rolling shadow, heralding the night. But it wasn't an omen—it was a sign that made his spirit sing.

The ravens had returned.

Even outside the confines of the sacred nest, no bars or caverns or cages to contain them, the flock had come home. As one, they swooped into the clearing, a fluttering wave of darkness carrying Taetanos's blessing on their obsidian wings. Xander lifted his face toward the sight, breathing in their presence. Feathers made the wind swirl, and that rustling song stirred the hearts of his people. Caws and cries mixed as the House of Whispers cheered.

Lyana squeezed his fingers.

Xander found her gaze. Though the wings on her back were the pure white of a dove, the crown upon her head held the onyx feathers of a raven, and she was now their queen. A soft smile spread her lips and joy lit her eyes, matching the swelling hope inside his chest.

Maybe they *would* find a way to save them.

Through the gods or through magic, by fate or by chance, he didn't know. But he didn't care. Even a woman of prophecy needed a friend, and he could be that friend. He could be that support. And together, through forces unseen or by sheer will alone, they would find a way to save their world.

2

LYANA

There might not have been a coronation banquet or musicians or bountiful gifts to honor the gods, but there was no doubt this was a celebration. Though they dined on berries, nuts, and mushrooms foraged from the forest, it might as well have been the finest feast. Some ravens wore nightgowns and others dirty clothes, but that didn't matter, and neither did the soot still clinging to their unwashed skin. They sang with abandon and danced in scattered pockets, filling the clearing with unexpected joy. The House of Whispers had long been deemed unworthy, but Lyana saw the truth tonight. They had nothing, and yet they had everything they needed. Their spirits called out to her, not in pain or yearning, but with enough pride and perseverance to make any queen proud.

And a queen she was.

Though the crown was light, its symbol was heavy. Still, it didn't feel like the burden she'd always expected. It felt like a promise—to herself, to these people, to the world. She would save them. She would embrace her destiny and become whatever the world needed her to be.

"Enjoying yourself, raven queen?"

Lyana rolled her eyes at that teasing voice and thrust back her elbow. The resulting grunt brought a grin to her lips as she spun to face her brother. "Why yes, Luka, I am. How kind of you to ask."

Despite his wince, there was no mistaking the questions circling in his familiar honey eyes. Yesterday he'd been concerned as he soared across the clearing and nearly knocked her to the ground with his enthusiastic hug. Now he was demanding.

"I gave you a day," Luka murmured.

Lyana arched her brow. "And not one second more."

"Ana..." he groaned, as frustrated with his little sister as always. But this wasn't the crystal palace, and they weren't children anymore.

"Not here."

"You need to tell me what's going on. The last I heard from Cassi you'd run off with some raven bastard, and now you're here saying you're a herald of the gods? And you're—" He broke off and leaned closer as he flicked his gaze from side to side. Under his breath, he muttered, "And you're healing people out in the open where everyone can see!"

"I said not here," she urged, taking his large hands in hers. The familial touch was a comfort, instantly soothing some broken piece inside them both. So much had changed in the few months they'd been apart, but some things never would, their bond being one. He'd always been privy to her secrets, and even though her secrets were now far grander in scope, she hadn't intended on keeping them from him. "Please, Luka, let me find Xander first. You're right —we need to talk. And now is the perfect time, while the rest of the house is distracted by their merriment."

He held on to her fingers as she tried to turn. "You're not going to run away?"

"No," she answered truthfully. "No, my days of running are over."

Something in her tone must have convinced him. The old Luka would have put up a fight. Or maybe it wasn't he who had changed, but she. The old Lyana would have tried to use charm to skirt around the question. The new Lyana had come to realize that honesty worked just as well, if not better.

When she found Xander across the crowd minutes later, she didn't even need words. One look into her eyes and he made his excuses. The sea of ravens parted as he strode toward her, making room for their king. The smile on his lips was for show as he took her arm to lead her through the masses.

"I take it your brother demands a meeting."

"Can you blame him?"

"No." He sighed through his teeth, still nodding cordially to the people they passed. "Will he believe our story? He's already been told two different lies. I'm not sure he'll trust a third."

"Then it's a good thing we'll be telling him the truth."

Xander stopped short.

Lyana spun in his hold, turning to face him as she took his hand in both of hers. "He can help us."

"What if he doesn't understand?"

"He will." She squeezed his fingers to emphasize the words. "I've never lied to my brother before—*never*, Xander. Not about anything serious. He'll be on our side. He'll fight with us."

A shadow passed over his lavender irises as he wrestled with the news.

Before Xander could respond, a jingling caught Lyana's ear, subtle at first then louder, until the entire clearing was alive with the sound. The hairs at the back of her neck stood as the steady weight of eyes increased. A groove formed between Xander's brows and a slow breath slid through his barely parted lips. His features hardened as he tried to mask his emotions, but there was no way to hide from her. Without even using her magic, she sensed the frustration wafting off his spirit.

"They want us to kiss," he murmured, his voice strained.

With a sharp intake of breath, Lyana glanced quickly to the side. Ravens watched them warmly as they held necklaces and daggers and jewels, clanking the metals softly together to form the musical sound now filling the forest. And why not? What did they see, but their king and queen huddled close and holding hands like two lovers in a stolen moment?

"It's a silly tradition of our house," he continued softly. "For newly mated pairs. But you don't—"

"Shh," Lyana cut him off and lifted her hand to his cheek. No thrill shot down her spine at the contact. His gaze didn't burn through her. Though he was her king, they both knew he wasn't the man she wanted. And what did Xander want? Not her, not anymore. The infatuation was gone from his eyes, and for that she was grateful, but they were still back where they'd started. In matters of politics, their own wants and desires counted little. "It's all right."

She arched up on her toes, prepared to peck his lips.

At the last second, it was Xander who turned and presented her with his cheek. She pressed a kiss to his skin and held it for a beat as hurt cut across his soul, flaring like a comet through the sky. Xander pulled back, not meeting her eyes as he flushed. Their people, she was sure, found his apparent bashfulness endearing. But she knew the truth. He wasn't embarrassed. He was pained. Maybe this was the most frustrating part of her magic—she sensed his emotions, but not their roots. Did her betrayal still sting? Was he reminded of Rafe? Or was there another secret buried behind his defenses that made him hurt?

Physical wounds were so easy to heal.

Matters of the heart, however, were beyond even her formidable power.

They smiled and waved, playing their parts until the attention died down. Then Xander leaned close to whisper in her ear.

"I want to tell Helen."

Her first instinct was to object—his captain of the guards was a wild card. She knew nothing of Lyana's magic, and it was anyone's guess how she'd react. But Xander trusted the woman, and Lyana had to trust him. If not, she'd be just as bad as Malek, spitting demands without offering any concessions of her own. Xander deserved someone to confide in, someone aside from the princess who'd utterly shattered his heart.

"Meet us in the woods," she said instead. "In the spot where I found you reading. We'll be there in ten minutes."

They parted ways.

Lyana found Luka and they slipped away from the celebration into the shadows of the forest, where Xander and Helen were already waiting. Then she and Xander told them...everything. About the prophecy naming her the Queen Bred of Snow. About Malek and his magic and his world beneath the mist. About the dragons and the rift and the spell holding the isles aloft. About the coming destruction and the new world full of elemental power into which their people would soon be thrust.

"And what will you tell everyone else?" Luka asked, one of his many questions. But Lyana preferred his obvious concern and disbelief to Helen's stony silence.

"What we told the ravens last night," Xander said, flicking his gaze toward his captain before returning it to her brother. "That the gods are weakening and they can no longer fight off Vesevios's advances, which is why they gave Lyana the power to fight on their behalf. That war is coming and our people need to be prepared. That another isle will fall, then another. That more dragons will come, and they are the enemy, not magic. That we need to stop executing our own people out of fear and start understanding how they can help fight a battle we currently have no possible way to win."

"And you think the people will simply nod and go along with

what you say?" Luka asked, turning to Lyana. "With all we've been raised to believe?"

"No, of course not." She sighed. "Does that mean we shouldn't try?"

"I didn't say—"

"This is happening, Luka, whether our people believe it or not. I can feel the rift eating away at our world. I can feel the decay. The god stones are failing. The isles will fall. We can sit by and do nothing, or we can fight to preserve at least some shred of the world we've all come to love. I choose to fight. What do you choose?"

His lips pursed. After a moment, all the tension leaked from his body. "I choose to fight, Ana. Of course I choose to fight."

"And you?" She turned to Helen, meeting shrewd brown eyes that gave nothing away. "What will you do?"

"The same thing I've always done. Serve my house."

"Am I not the queen of said house?"

"For now."

Lyana glared at Xander, who proceeded to roll his eyes.

"Give us a minute, please," he said before jutting his chin to the side.

While he and his captain walked away, deep in argument, Lyana turned to her brother. "There's something else I need you to do."

He arched his brows. "I should've seen this coming."

"The House of Peace will be the last to fall, Luka," she said, her tone pleading as she threaded her dark fingers through his. "Please, I need you and your soldiers to go home. Mother and Father won't understand the truth of what I've told you, but at least you can speak on my behalf—on the world's behalf. I need you to make sure the storage rooms are filled. Make sure all the guest quarters in the outer ring are fully stocked and ready to house refugees. They won't be enough to hold everyone comfortably, or even at all, but every house will at least have some place to start. And on that note, see if we can get more shelters built. I want to stop this before

Sphaira is the last city standing, but I'm not sure how yet and I'm not sure when I'll know. We need to be prepared, and if the rest of the isles fall away, we need to make sure our frozen tundra of a home has some way to shelter the survivors."

"I'll do what I can," he answered solemnly. Lowering his gaze to their joined hands, he tenderly brushed his thumb over hers. Then, with a deep breath, he looked up. "I missed you, you know. I wasn't prepared for that. I thought it would be a relief to stop worrying about you, to stop concerning myself with the trouble you were getting into, but it didn't stop. It just got worse. And now you're here, standing before me with all the same brazen confidence you always had, but it's like I'm seeing someone else. And I like her, Ana. I can't wait to see all the glorious things you'll do."

"But?" She could hear the word in his tone.

"But I'm scared. So much is happening so fast. Do you ever wish we could go back to those carefree days as children, flying around the palace with Cassi and Elias at our heels?"

"I do, Luka." She smiled at the memories of the four of them running wild through the crystal halls. But those days were gone, and there was no way to get them back. Too much had happened, both good and bad. She wouldn't give up meeting Rafe or studying her magic or finally feeling comfortable in her own skin for anything. "We'll have them again—just a slightly more mature version."

Luka grinned.

"I'll make sure Cassi and Elias are safe. Malek won't hurt them, I swear it."

"I believe you. I always have."

"I know."

She began to pull away, but he stopped her.

"Oh, I forgot to mention. Some of the female soldiers offered to redo your braids. They said it would be an honor. I thought maybe you might miss some of the comforts of home."

She did. Oh, how she missed being among the doves, surrounded by people who knew how to properly comb through her hair and apply the right salves to her skin, who looked like her and understood the subtle differences in the way her body worked. But there was no time—at least, not tonight.

Lyana lifted her gaze toward the sky, looking not at the stars, but at the spirit hovering unseen in the branches overhead, her soul as familiar as a sister's despite everything that had happened between them. Cassi was here, and she'd been waiting long enough.

"Tomorrow, Luka. Tell them thank you, please. I'll stop by in the morning before you leave. Tonight, all I want to do is sleep."

3

CASSI

All I want to do is sleep.

Was that an invitation? A warning? Cassi had spent most of the afternoon hovering above the tree line, watching the revelry. She'd tried to ignore the little pang in her heart as Xander and Lyana were crowned. But as the day wore on, the ache only worsened. She'd tried to tell herself it was a yearning to be beside them, a yearning for her body, a yearning for her old life even if it had been a lie. But that hadn't explained her selfish flare of satisfaction when Xander had turned his cheek to Lyana's kiss.

She was a horrible friend. Maybe she'd always been a horrible friend. But right now, she was a horrible friend in possession of important information that could possibly change the fate of the world, so she was a horrible friend whom her queen would have to face.

When Lyana fell asleep, Cassi dove into her dreams.

Though her queen shared the same *aethi'kine* magic as Malek, her mind couldn't have been more different. There was no struggle for control. Cassi touched Lyana's spirit, and just like that she was welcomed inside. Rather than fighting her, Lyana's magic worked with her as a guiding force, helping to calm her friend's chaotic thoughts. As the room came into view, Cassi wasn't entirely sure which one of them had spun the image, but it fit. They were back in Lyana's old bedchambers at the crystal palace, standing beside the translucent walls and looking out at the city as it sparkled like a gemstone beneath the setting sun.

"Cass—"

"Please," she cut in hastily, taking her queen's hand and drawing her somewhat guarded gaze. "Please. I'm not sure if you want to see me, and I don't blame you, but I had to come. I *had* to. Something happened, something terrible, and no one knows about it but me. Please, just listen to what I have to tell you, and then you never need to speak to me again."

Lyana's brows drew together. "I'm listening."

"Thank you." Cassi released a heavy breath and dropped her queen's hand, not sure if she'd crossed a line. There were so many new barriers, so many new restrictions. Talking to Lyana had always been as easy as breathing, but now she found she was underwater, searching aimlessly for air. "The god stones are dragon eggs."

"Eggs?" Lyana gasped.

"I saw it with my own eyes. Do you remember that blast of magic just before the isle fell? You must've felt it. I went to find the cause, and by the time I got to the sacred nest, the god stone was already on the ground. I didn't understand, not right away. But then it split, releasing thick, inky plume. And as the shadows cleared, a creature emerged."

"A creature?"

"It was— It was—" Cassi closed her eyes, remembering the onyx scales, the gleaming white teeth, and the sharp claws soaked in crimson blood. "It was a beast, Ana. It was what Rafe would've become if his spirit hadn't won dominance during the soul joining. Part dragon and part man, with the worst of both. And it was strong—not just physically, but its power was unlike anything I've ever seen. It didn't just wield shadow magic. It *was* shadow magic, as though soaking for so long in the power of the rift had amplified its abilities. The creature murdered all the priests and priestesses with no effort at all. And when I tried to flee, it somehow sensed my spirit, then severed the tie to my body."

"That's why..." Lyana trailed off, a dozen realizations playing across her gaze.

"That's why you couldn't revive me when you found me in the dungeons of Pylaeon. The connection between my body and my spirit has been cut."

"Where is the beast now?"

"I don't know." Cassi shook her head. "I can't sense it the way I can people. I tried to find it earlier today, but I couldn't. It could be anywhere. It could be doing anything. And if there was one, I have to imagine there are six more of those things inside the god stones just waiting to hatch."

"*Beasts will emerge, filled with fury and scorn—*"

"*—fighting to recover what from their claws we have torn.*"

"We stole their children," Lyana said softly. "And we turned them into monsters." She shook her head, clearing the horrified daze, and sharpened her focus on Cassi. "Do you really think the dragons still seek revenge? After all this time?"

"I don't know." Cassi shuddered as the carnage from the sacred nest flashed through her thoughts, nothing but gleaming blood and darkness. The thing had moved with more speed than humanly possible, power leaking from its pores, and now it was on the loose, completely unchallenged. "But I'm starting to wonder if we've been worried about the wrong enemy all along. The raven god stone was full of concentrated *umbra'kine* magic, and that beast emerged like darkness incarnate. The remaining six god stones have concentrated elemental magic of their own, especially the House of Peace—"

"*Aethi'kine* magic."

She nodded. "If all seven beasts emerge, I'm not sure even our most powerful mages will be able to stop them."

"Can we destroy them before they hatch?"

"No." Her tone was final. "Malek wasn't the first mage to venture into a sacred nest. Kings before him have tried, and failed, to destroy the god stones. They thought doing so might seal the rift or force the time of prophecy forward, but something about the spell protects the eggs. I didn't think one would ever crack until I saw it with my own eyes."

Lyana pulled her lower lip between her teeth as her gaze flicked from side to side, seeing nothing yet everything. The silence between them stretched, but Cassi wouldn't break it. She'd had a day to consider all the terrifying possibilities, and still her head swam. Besides, now that her news had been shared, she didn't entirely know what to say. Could they talk like old friends? Had all the years between them been erased? Were they sisters? Strangers? The questions wrapped her tongue in knots, leaving her mute.

"Rafe," Lyana finally said into the quiet. "You mentioned Rafe? Have you seen him? Is he safe?"

Cassi released a soft breath as relief washed through her. Even if their relationship had changed, on some level her friend still needed her, and that need gave her a reason to keep going. "He's safe. I found him earlier this morning on a ship leaving Da'Kin. He's out of Malek's reach…for now."

"And you *saw* him?" Lyana swallowed. She didn't need to explain.

"I saw him." Oh, she'd seen him all right—wings and all. He'd been standing by his window with a mesh blanket over his shoulders to smother the flames, but there was no denying the change. Rafe had been soul-joined to a dragon. His spirit now burned. "He was awake, and he seemed good, all things considered."

Lyana nodded, even as concern knotted her brows. Cassi knew that look, so she stayed silent, waiting for the inevitable confession.

"I haven't told Xander," her queen whispered a few moments later. "I don't know how. I tried, but I couldn't get the words to come. He just lost his home, his mother, his entire belief system. How can I tell him his brother has turned into the very thing he most fears? It will break him."

"He's stronger than you give him credit for."

"What if he's not?" Lyana asked. "What if this is the one thing he can't handle? What will that do to Rafe?"

Cassi knew Xander's heart, and the only thing he'd feel was concern—not for himself, but for the brother he loved dearly despite everything that had passed between them. But to Lyana, Rafe would always come first. Her friend couldn't see beyond her own fears for his well-being. Then again, perhaps Cassi was the one who wasn't seeing things clearly. Words barreled up her throat to defend the raven as a protective urge twisted her gut.

"Maybe I'm not being fair," Lyana muttered.

"You're not," she said, trying her best to remove the bite from her tone. Clearly, she failed, as her queen arched a brow in question. Cassi sighed. "After everything we've both done to him, he deserves the truth. And if it makes you feel any better, when you walked away, he was still deep in argument with his closest ally and advisor, defending you. Helen will come around because Xander will convince her of the truth. And after she does, he'll expend all his energy convincing the rest of our world too. He's a good person, and he deserves for his queen, of all people, to see that. He deserves honesty from you."

"You're right." Guilt softened her expression. "I'll tell him. I promise, I'll find a way to tell him."

"Good."

"Cassi?" The edges of Lyana's lips quirked into a grin. "It almost feels like old times, standing here in these rooms listening to you chastise me. I dare say I missed it."

"Even a queen of prophecy needs to be challenged, every now and then."

"I think maybe a queen of prophecy needs it more than most."

The words were soft but heavy, making Cassi wonder what Lyana's time with Malek had taught her. Before she could ask, her queen turned toward the window and lifted a palm to the crystal. Cassi didn't know what scene she saw, but she had a feeling it wasn't the dazzling skyline of Sphaira or the vast open skies that might have once beckoned. For better or worse, they'd both changed since they had last visited these wistful halls.

Still averting her gaze, Lyana whispered, "I'm not sure I can forgive you."

The words were a dagger to Cassi's chest, and she froze. Her heart thumped wildly, but her body remained still as Lyana finally dropped her arm. When those eyes shifted toward her, they were no longer the vibrant emerald of a pampered princess, but a dull green reminiscent of the algae growing on the damp, weathered buildings of Da'Kin. Grief deepened her gaze—a grief Cassi knew she'd put there.

"I missed you—"

"I missed you too," Cassi cut in, desperate to ease the hurt written across her friend's face, but Lyana held up her hand.

"I missed you," she started again. "I missed my friend, and I miss her still, because I don't know if I'll ever get her back. But I think, maybe, I want to try. I need you, Cassi. I need your magic, yes, but I also need to know there is someone out there who isn't afraid to tell me I'm wrong, and we both know you've never been that. I'm not sure if I can ever forgive you for lying to me for so long. I'm not sure if I can forgive you for what you did to Rafe, and what you almost did to Xander. I'm not even sure if I should forgive you. But I know the world will be better off if you're at my side, so for now I hope that's enough. Fight with me. Fight with us. And maybe the rest will come later."

It was a better offer than Cassi deserved, even if it still stung. But she would find a way to make amends. She would find a way to prove herself. To Lyana. To Xander. To everyone she'd wronged. To the whole world if she had to.

Cassi straightened her shoulders, looking to her queen for orders. "What would you have me do?"

"I need eyes behind closed doors," Lyana said, sounding more like a monarch than ever before. "I need to know if Malek is planning to force me back to Da'Kin, and how he means to attack. I need to know that Elias is safe, and if he'll be used as leverage against me. I need to know that Rafe is alive and well so I'm not worried about him when I should be focused on other things. And I need to know what the kings and queens of the world above are saying about me and Xander, and the stories we'll soon be spinning."

"Done."

"Thank you."

Lyana's gaze swept over her childhood room, and Cassi's followed, landing on the bed where they'd spent countless hours braiding each other's hair, then going to the trunk where they'd hidden their outdoor gear, to the daggers neatly arranged on the vanity in preparation for a training session. As girls, they'd wrestled on these plush rugs. They'd used the bed as a springboard when they'd started learning how to fly. There were holes in the wall from the paper targets they'd snuck in from the arena, including the one to the left of the door where she'd hit her first bull's-eye. Giggles and laughter had once filled this room. Now there was only silence.

Awareness heated her cheek, and Cassi turned to meet her friend's stare. A thousand memories flickered in those piercing eyes, a lifetime of sisterhood undone by a single confession. Lyana blinked, and whatever had been there vanished.

"Only come to me during the day if it's an emergency, that way I'll know. Otherwise, my dreams will be there waiting."

"Malek might send others if your mind is too open."

"I know how to get rid of them."

"Do you?"

A sad smile played across Lyana's lips. Before Cassi could speak, a force gripped her spirit and yanked her from the dream. The crystal palace collapsed into a vortex of colors. With a snap, she was thrown into darkness. Her spirit tumbled through open air as she fought to regain control. It took her a moment to realize she was back in the forests of the House of Song, thoroughly dispelled from her queen's mind.

Cassi let the wind carry her spirit aloft.

Eventually, she'd find the courage to face Xander again, but not tonight. Tonight she had another stop to make before the sun broke over the horizon, announcing the start of a new day.

All morning she'd been musing on the same thing as she hovered above *The Wanderer*, watching the familiar woman at its helm—*why?* Why had her mother chosen now to defy Malek? Why not years before, when he'd asked her to sacrifice her daughter to the war? Why not weeks before, when he'd ordered Cassi to remove Rafe's wings? Why not during all her time spent chasing dragons and taking on crew member after crew member whom his authoritarian leadership had somehow harmed? Why now? And why for a man who wasn't even her own blood?

The questions pulled Cassi's spirit through the mist. She came upon the ship quickly, carving through fog and sea spray as she forced her way inside the wooden planks. When she burst into the captain's room, her mother wasn't asleep, and she wasn't alone either.

"We tell them nothing," Captain Rokaro ordered, her voice like iron.

The girl standing across from her didn't flinch. Cassi recognized

Brighty, the former thief from Da'Kin and the *photo'kine* who'd become Rafe's friend. Her fists were balled by her sides and a frown curved her lips, those milky eyes as unsettling as ever. Clearly, they were in the middle of something, but once a spy, always a spy, and Cassi's curiosity was undeniable.

She glided closer.

"Nothing?" the younger woman spat.

"Nothing."

"And what about Rafe? He's got a right to know. It's his—"

"Nothing, Brighty, and I mean it." Her mother's blue eyes flashed like an ice sheet in the sun, glinting with a frosty edge. "You asked for shelter, and I gave it. We're fugitives and that's enough for now. I won't court open rebellion until I have reason to believe what you told me is true. And until that day comes, we say nothing to anyone—or you might find this ship back on course for Da'Kin. Understood?"

Brighty sneered.

Captain Rokaro arched a brow as she put her hands on the desk and leaned closer. A few of her fabric-wrapped locks of hair spilled over her shoulders, colorful against the crisp white of her shirt. The expression on her weathered face was like stone. "Understood?"

"Aye, aye, Captain," the younger woman grumbled. Then she turned on her heel and marched from the room, leaving the echo of a slamming door in her wake.

Once Brighty was gone, all the strength seeped from her mother's stance. With a sigh, the captain bent to cradle her head in her hands. After a moment, she sucked in a sharp breath and dropped the rest of the way into her desk chair, turning her gaze to the maps rolled out before her. Grabbing a few utensils, she began charting a route across the seas.

Cassi watched for a few minutes, waiting for sleep to take her, but it never did. Restlessness oozed from her mother's pores.

Why? That pesky question ran through Cassi's mind again. *Why can't you sleep? What thought haunts you? And what does it have to do with Rafe? What aren't you telling him?*

She'd find out.

Maybe not today, with dawn calling and her body lost somewhere out at sea, but tomorrow, or the next day, or the day after that. For the queen who needed her and the friend who'd seen something in her worth saving, Cassi vowed to uncover even her mother's best-kept secrets.

4

RAFE

A throbbing at his temples woke Rafe. His blood pounded like fists against a locked door, the pulse pulling him from his slumber. With a groan, he rolled upright and pressed his fingers to his forehead, trying to dull the pain. But even as the ache subsided, the knocking continued, which was when he realized it was coming from the door.

"Come on, Rafe! You've been in there for a day. You can't hide forever."

He squeezed his eyes shut. *Why not?*

"Come on. The rest of the crew are starting to wonder if I killed you."

It was hardly the first time.

"I'm being kind, you know. I could pick these locks without breaking a sweat. So you might as well just let me—" Brighty cut off as he pulled open the door and a satisfied smirk widened her lips. "I knew you'd see reason."

"Go away."

He threw the door closed, but she stuck her foot out just in time and it bounced back open immediately. Not bothering to ask permission, she plowed inside the room, as he'd known she would.

"I get it," she prattled on. "You got new wings and for some reason it's thrown you into the middle of a raging identity crisis, but you can at least show your face to the people risking their lives to get you as far away from Da'Kin as possible."

"You don't—" He broke off with a growl. She was right, as usual. It was one of her most frustrating qualities.

"Don't what? Understand? Here's something you don't understand. I risked my ass pulling you from the fire last night and lugging you halfway across the city back to the ship. And when I showed up with a half-dead dragon man draped across my back, did anyone ask why? No. They took one look at your face and started raising the sails. Now, we find ourselves on the wrong side of a king with unparalleled power and it's all because of you. So the least you can do is put those flames away so as not to burn us alive and say thank you."

He swallowed and glanced to the side, finding that the leathery expanse of his wing simmered with fire. At the sight, all his pent-up rage disappeared, and a sigh racked through him. She was right again. He didn't know. His memory of that night was nothing but broken patches—walking into the warehouse, being strapped to the table beside the dragon, then burning in darkness until Lyana appeared, bright as the rising dawn to chase the shadows away. He remembered waking in her arms. He remembered watching her stop the wave threatening to drown the city beneath its might. He remembered stepping between her and the king, the man's magic somehow draining and reviving him at the same time. He remembered watching her fly away. Then…nothing. If Brighty hadn't rescued him, he didn't know where he'd be—probably locked in a dungeon somewhere, or worse. Dead.

"Thank you," he finally said.

"That's better." She crossed her arms, training those milky irises on him. Even though he had at least a foot on her, the urge to recoil raced through him. "Now, what's got you hiding out all day? And don't tell me it's just about the wings."

It was…and it wasn't.

His life had been altered in a way no one from this world beneath the mist could possibly understand. They hated dragons, and they killed them, but they didn't fear them the way the people from his homeland did. To the world below, dragons were nothing more than creatures to be hunted. To the world above, they were godly beasts, symbols of pure evil. The ravens would cry out at the sight of him and curse his name. They would call him godless and demand his head. But the crew wouldn't look at him as though he'd been tainted, and maybe that was why he couldn't face them. He didn't want their acceptance. He didn't want to feel any bit at home in this skin.

Yet it was more than that.

Nightmares haunted him. No matter what he did, he couldn't shake the visions plaguing him—of blood-soaked claws and slashed throats and silent screams. He'd spent most of the previous day staring out of his window and into the fog, seeing not the endless gray but fathomless black. Only after hours of playing and replaying the scene had he realized the truth of what it was. The screeches in the background had been ravens, and the flashes of green the ancient trees in the sacred nest. The people dying by his hands had been priests and priestesses. And it had been real. Rafe didn't know how or why or what, but he knew in his gut it hadn't been a dream. It had been a memory—one he couldn't possibly explain.

"Rafe?" Her voice made him flinch. "You need to get out of this room."

He threw her a sidelong glance, trying to cover the unease raising the hairs along the back of his neck. "Do you ever tire of being right?"

"Not around you. Now, come on."

Brighty took him by the arm and pulled him above deck. He shielded his gaze the moment they stepped through the door, the silver mist vivid enough to sting after so many hours in the dark. Though there might have been another reason too. He didn't want to feel their stares, their appraisal, their gawking eyes. None came. He lowered his arm and glanced around the ship, surprised to find everyone busily at work. They paid him no mind—Captain's doing, he was sure.

Of course, that all changed when Brighty cupped her palms around her lips and shouted, "Hey! Listen up! Rafe's got something he wants to say."

She turned to him with a grin.

Rafe's nostrils flared as a dozen eyes focused on him. There were few things he loathed more than being the center of attention. Blame a lifetime spent keeping to the shadows.

"Thanks for that." He ground the words through his teeth. Then louder, he said, "Brighty informed me of the risks you're all taking on my behalf, and I just wanted to say thank you. There's no need for you to put yourself in danger. I'm feeling much stronger now and I can take my leave as soon as—ow!"

Brighty dug the heel of her boot into his toe, just as Archer called out, "Do I need to fashion the man a muzzle?"

Before Rafe could respond, Squirrel dropped into view, dangling upside down from the sails with a bored expression across his youthful face. "Is that it?"

"You want more?" he asked.

"Well…" the boy drawled, too young to have so much attitude. "Aren't you going to *do* anything?"

"Do anything?"

"I believe the boy wants a demonstration," Brighty murmured as she leaned close, unable to hide her amusement. Squirrel's light brown eyes widened with excitement. Inwardly, Rafe groaned.

"Ignore him." Jolt glared at Squirrel. She had a motherly way about her that included the elusive skill of silencing a rebellious child with a single glance. Her nearly black eyes could cut into a person's soul—Rafe almost envied it. The boy promptly scrambled back up to where he'd been hiding in the sails, though no one missed his dramatic sigh.

"I don't know," Pyro chimed in from the other side of the deck. In the breeze, her auburn hair flared around her face like flames, accenting the wild delight in her seafoam eyes. Red glittered around her fingers as she lifted her hand. An ember peeled off Rafe's wings and sailed across the deck, igniting into a full blaze by the time it landed in her waiting palm. "I wouldn't mind a demonstration."

"I wouldn't mind a sample," Leech murmured behind him.

Rafe jumped and spun, backing away from the *agro'kine*. The man was short but stocky, and he could probably hold Rafe down just long enough to nick him if he wanted to. "Don't come anywhere near me with your needles. I mean it."

The older man's face fell as though Rafe had murdered his pet. "It would only take a minute."

"Leech."

"But—"

"Leech."

"*Achoo*!"

Rafe flinched again, this time turning to find Spout with her hands over her face, her chest already filling with more air. Framed by the dark, ruddy tone of her skin, her honey eyes shone with apology before clamping shut as another sneeze racked through her. He'd forgotten she was allergic to dragon scales. The sea exploded, showering them with salt water. The droplets sizzled as they landed on his skin. He didn't need to look to know the flames around his wings burned brighter. He could feel the livening blaze inside his chest, mirroring his mood as the crew closed in around him. Their magic simmered across the air along with their intrigue. He might have dealt with their scorn better. Disdain, at least, he was used to. Heat tickled the back of his throat. Just as he feared he might explode, a voice cut through the madness.

"Enough," Captain Rokaro shouted.

At once, everyone froze. He could almost hear their collective groan as she stepped out from behind the wheel and made her way across the deck. Patch sidled into her place, the first mate's large frame dwarfing the wheel in a way hers hadn't. But her presence commanded more respect than any other's on the ship, and the crew parted before her. Rafe didn't move as she approached. Those blue eyes pinned him to the spot, somehow both cold and warm against the backdrop of her tawny wrinkled cheeks.

"I do remember you making us one promise," she said over the slapping of waves against the hull. As she came to a stop before him, he swore he was looking not at the captain, but at the hawk who shared her spirit. Over her left shoulder, her copper feathers rippled in an invisible breeze. "You promised that when you got your wings, you'd come back to the ship so we could see a man fly."

Rafe closed his eyes in relief, his mind already going to the open air and freedom. Somehow, she knew exactly what he needed, and she was right. For all the horror of his new body, there was one benefit he couldn't deny. While the rest of the crew was bound to the sea, he was once more a creature of the sky.

Captain leaned in close, so only he could hear, and whispered, "Fly."

One pump of his leathery wings, and he was airborne. Wind ruffled the loose fabric of his untucked shirt and swirled unnaturally around his body as he took to the sky. When he opened his eyes, the mist glittered with yellow sparks of *aero'kine* magic. The captain was following him the only way she now could—with her magic and her soul. The thought propelled him onward.

I have to celebrate this one thing.

No matter the consequences, I have wings again.

Unlike so many others, I can still fly.

Rafe grinned, forgetting the ship as the breeze pressed against his cheeks and swept through his hair. These new wings were more aerodynamic, with bones he wasn't used to and a flexibility he didn't quite understand, but the dragon sharing his spirit did. Together they dove, one learning and one teaching as the leathery folds bent in and out to catch the wind. At a soar, this new body was slower, but in other ways it was as though a whole new range of the sky had been opened, allowing him to flip and spin and roll, to move with an agility he had never dreamed possible. In the solace of the impenetrable fog, no one else around to see, he quietly admitted he was enjoying himself. Part man, part dragon, entirely alone in the world, and yet he was having fun for the first time in—well, it'd been so long, he couldn't even remember.

So he didn't try.

He turned off his mind, locking away the doubts and the fears, so he could simply experience this glorious return to the sky. There was no telling how much time passed before he came to, realizing he'd lost sight of the ship and the crew entirely. Rafe widened his wings to catch the air and hovered for a beat. Glancing around, he had no sense of up or down or left or right. He was adrift in a sea of endless gray, completely and totally lost.

Gods alive! he silently cursed. *Idiot.*

A gentle current in the air made his skin tingle, lulling him closer. His stomach felt hollow. Yearning filled the vacant spaces—yearning and a hunger unlike any he'd felt before.

A brilliant blast of light suddenly sliced through the fog.

His craving flared.

Magic. Rafe sucked in a sharp breath. *I feel their magic.*

Now that he knew what it was, he closed his eyes and gave in to that newfound need. A sixth sense entirely new to him reached invisibly through the air, drawn in by their power. Captain's *aero'kine* magic searched the winds for the subtle disturbance of wings. Brighty's *photo'kine* magic cut tunnels through the mist. Pyro's *pyro'kine* magic grasped for the heat alive beneath his skin. They were looking for him. They were following him. And—

Wait.

Rafe spun in midair, his brows pushing together as another whisper of magic pulled at him from the opposite direction. It was being used with more force, creating a stronger current. The power called out, but it was something else that lured him in, another new instinct he didn't quite understand. This one formed deep in his mind rather than his stomach, unfurling like a flower in spring, drawing up thoughts of ash and fire.

It was a…dragon.

He didn't know how he knew, but he did. A dragon was close by, and judging by the powerful flares of magic pulsing across the sky, there was a ship in dire need of help.

Not thinking, he raced toward the site. The smell of smoke hit first, then the gradual darkening of the fog, until he carved through charcoal soot. Bright orange flames licked the sky, cutting through the mist, and heat struck his cheeks. By the time he reached the ship, it was already engulfed in flames. Magic lit the skies, peppering the billowing smog with bright sparks of color. Hidden within the fog, the dragon roared. The sound didn't reverberate through Rafe's soul the way it once had, filling him with fear. Instead, purpose sharpened his movements.

Letting instinct guide him, he soared closer. The people onboard probably thought he was mad or a monster as he dropped onto the ship, ignoring the flames burning his clothes. They didn't touch his skin—not anymore. And he was beyond feeling, too distracted by the new awareness burgeoning to life inside his body. Power prickled along his exposed arms. The flavor of magic saturated the air. As he breathed, he drew it in like one might consume a meal. Just out of sight, another dragon did the same, feeding on the feast that both killed and sustained it. Rafe could feel the beast. They were connected somehow. Their minds grazed.

He knew when it decided to fly closer.

He felt when it sucked in a long, full breath of air.

He sensed the heat gathering at the back of its throat.

Just as the dragon appeared through the haze and reared back its head for a killing blast, Rafe held up his hands, spread his wings to brace himself, and silently screamed, *No!*

The beast stopped.

No, Rafe thought again. *Go. Leave. Fly.*

For a moment, it did nothing. Two bulbous red eyes found his across the distance as those expansive leathery wings pumped once. The silence stretched, nothing but the crackling of flames and the smoldering of wood, as though the rest of the world held its breath. Rafe was too afraid to move, to breathe. The dragon stared and he stared right back.

Leave.

The beast dropped its head, jaws widening as they neared Rafe. Its teeth were the size of his torso, and they gleamed with the reflection of flames. Closer and closer they crawled, until the flat expanse at the front of the dragon's snout pressed gently into his open palms. Rafe sucked in a sharp breath as visions flickered behind his eyes, of barren, rocky landscapes and tangerine skies, of flames and heat and a soul-crushing absence he couldn't explain.

Fly.

The dragon retreated into the mist, its ebony wings gradually fading as it fled. Rafe lowered his hands and stared at his perfectly unblemished palms, still feeling the heat of those smoldering scales on his skin.

What in Taetanos's name was that?

5

CAPTAIN ROKARO

They arrived just in time to see Rafe stand before the dragon, surrounded by a maelstrom of billowing flames. The beast lowered its head toward the burning deck, its jaws wide. Captain Audezia'd'Rokaro leaned forward, fear gripping her throat. Beside her, Brighty gasped. No one on the ship moved. The crew's magic winked out. Even the sea seemed to still as they glided soundlessly forward, drawn in by the impossible sight. A breeze swept through, clearing the smoke to reveal Rafe unharmed, with his palms pressed against the dragon's snout. Time slowed as Zia's vision tunneled on the spot.

It wasn't possible.

It couldn't be.

He wasn't really—

"Do you believe me now?"

She snapped her face to the side, meeting Brighty's haughty gaze.

Do I?

She turned back to Rafe, but the dragon was already gone, its massive body swallowed by the mist. A cheer erupted from the distance, the sound jolting her crew back into action. Their magic cut across the sky, moving faster than the ship. Flames dampened as Pyro drew them into her skin. Steam erupted as Spout splashed water over the burning hull. Brighty didn't move. Neither did Zia, except to tighten her grip on the wheel.

"He's the King Born in Fire," the *photo'kine* whispered. "He has to be."

Zia closed her eyes, the implications of those few simple words sending a shock wave through her—reminding her of all she'd sacrificed in the name of her king, all she'd given, all she'd bled. Every fiber of her being believed Malek was the man who would save them. If not for that, she never would have done half the things she'd done. And yet, when Brighty had arrived in the middle of the night telling crazy tales of Rafe and the king and prophecy, she'd wondered. And now, she wondered even more...

"Captain—"

"Enough." The command came out harsher than Zia intended, as though Malek were there with his fist around her heart, forcing the words. "One moment does not a king of prophecy make."

Brighty snorted. "It bloody well convinced me."

"We need time," she chided. "And so does he. Look at him. He doesn't even know what happened."

"Don't mind him," the younger woman commented, as their gazes were drawn to the spot where Rafe stood staring at his hands in open amazement. "Idiotic bewilderment is his natural expression."

"I won't rush this decision, Brighty. As you so kindly reminded me two nights ago, the entire world might depend on it. So we'll wait and watch, and most of all, we'll keep our mouths shut until I say otherwise. Understood?"

The *photo'kine* sighed but slinked away without another

argument, which to be honest, Zia took as a win. The empty spot was soon filled by her first mate, his mere presence easing the tension in her weary bones. Though the others knew him as Patch, he'd always be Markos to her, especially after all they'd been through over the years. He'd been the one to fish her floundering body from the seas on that horrible night still branded into her soul. He'd been the one to teach her the beauty in her magic. He'd been the one to save her when the darker side of power had made itself abundantly clear. He'd been the one to hold her as her body seemingly split in two, delivering new life to the world. He'd been the one to help hide them, the one who consoled her in the lonely hours of the night after her daughter had been ripped away, the one who followed her to the seas in search of solace. But he was not the one who could make this decision, no matter how she wished it were so.

"Dark thoughts haunt your eyes, Zia," he whispered in that calm way of his, the deep rumble of his voice like a soothing tonic. She glanced up, running her gaze over his thick black beard and olive cheeks, the planes of his face even more familiar than those of her own blood. "You need rest. Let me take over for a little while."

Rest.

The word made her spine straighten and her fists clamp around the wheel. Sleep was the last thing she needed when it was the only way for the king to reach her. His spies would come demanding answers, and she didn't know how to face them. Or worse, Kasiandra would come. Though her daughter would never deign to question it outright, her spirit built of the same steel as her mother's, her eyes would silently ask, *Why for Rafe and not for me? Why for a stranger and not your own child? Why now and not then?*

Because he's the King Born in Fire.

The explanation would be so easy to give, but until she knew who Rafe was for certain, she couldn't risk it. Kasiandra would go running to the queen, who would come running for Rafe, and if they were wrong… Zia shivered with the possibilities.

"I'm fine," she murmured. "This is my crew and my ship, and I'll go to sleep when I damn well please."

"Aye, aye, Captain."

6

XANDER

"I need to get inside their sacred nest," Lyana said as she cut across the open skies. Xander fought to keep up.

"We need to take this slow," he urged, then glanced over his shoulder at the wave of ebony wings following them. *Slow* was a relative term. Some might say descending into a foreign house as a flock of a hundred verged on aggressive, but forcing their way into said house's sacred nest would definitely be pushing it. "We can't risk alienation. Our people need help. And it will take more than a day to get the other houses on our side."

"I told you what Cassi said," Lyana argued, stubborn to the end. Beneath them, the canopy of trees passed in a blur as her speed increased. "I need to touch the god stone. I need to know if these creatures are real."

"And *we* need time."

"We don't have any."

"Lyana—"

"Xander."

Up ahead, wooden spires broke through the carpet of green marking their destination. Xander sighed.

"Please," he tried again, his gaze boring into her cheek until she finally turned to meet it. "Please, Lyana. Let me take the lead. Let me try diplomacy first, and if it doesn't work, we'll do things your way."

A frown thinned her lips. Without responding, she free-fell into a death dive, leaving Xander no choice but to keep up.

Cytrene was commonly referred to as the City of Love, and as he first laid eyes on the sprawling metropolis through the breaks in the trees, Xander had no doubt as to why. The scene was a lover's paradise. The streets were lined with fountains powered by the river running through the center of the town. Endless trickles and shoots of water glistened beneath the sun. And where there weren't fountains, there were flowers, cascading over rooftops and running along the sidewalks, turning already lush forests into a bona fide oasis. Unlike his home of strong and sturdy stone, these houses were crafted of wood, intricately carved and ornately painted, creating an undeniably romantic atmosphere. Songbirds walked arm in arm over sculptural bridges and down winding floral roads. Laughter and music filled the air. They were a happy people, and he had come to ruin their good time.

Gasps filled the air as Xander and Lyana landed in the city center, followed by screams as the rest of the flock swooped in behind, black wings out of place in a land made of color. While the raven castle had been fortified by a massive wall, the House of Song was a peaceful place not made for war. No partition separated the palace from the populace. Nothing was there to stop Lyana and Xander from marching up the front steps and breaking down the door—nothing but decorum. He half expected Lyana to charge, but she remained by his side and slid her fingers through his, squeezing his palm once. When he turned to meet her gaze, her green eyes were filled with challenge. The message was clear. She would give him his chance for diplomacy, but if it didn't work, all bets were off.

Please work.

Xander swallowed as the massive front door of the palace swung open.

Please, please work.

A man dripping in gems and silk stepped through. Every inch of him gleamed in the sunlight. His jacket was a study in golden embroidery, his crushed velvet trousers a deep maroon. Ruby broaches and diamond studs lined the seams, and even his boots had been polished to shine. It was almost easy to overlook the crown nestled in his golden hair and the crimson cardinal wings folded behind his back. Against any other backdrop, he would have seemed garish, even to Xander, king of a house known for its mines —but before this palace, it worked. The entire façade was painted in bright hues, highlighting the window surrounds and decorative transoms, the columns and cornices, the intricate filigree and elegant spires. One could go dizzy trying to take it all in, and Xander nearly did, but he quickly covered the imbalance by dropping to one knee. By his side, Lyana settled into a reluctant curtsy. Next to this man, they looked like paupers in their ripped and dirty clothes, but royalty was a matter of blood.

"What brings the House of Whispers to my doorstep?"

"King Dominic," Xander said as he rose. "We come bearing grave news. Vesevios has gained strength, and his power sent my homeland tumbling beneath the Sea of Mist. My people have lost everything, so we came to you, the patrons of Erhea, god of the love that exists between mates and kin, to humbly beg for your compassion. The only difference between ravens and songbirds is the color of our wings. We share the same worries and the same fears. Our hearts all beat to the tune the gods create. We are one people sharing one sky, and right now, the House of Whispers needs your help. Just as we pray Taetanos will guide your souls to the life after, so too we pray Erhea will provide for our poor souls in this one. What say you?"

As the king ran his gaze over the gathering of ravens, Xander forced himself to breathe. There was a reason they hadn't come alone. It was far easier to say no to two desperate souls than to a hundred. Their destitution was shocking, especially against this lush cityscape, and this was only a small sample of his people, most of whom still waited in the forests. Erhea was known for benevolence, which was why he'd made a point to call on their god's kindness. This king would be hard-pressed to deny them, especially with the songbirds attentively listening. Still, it was a relief when a few tense moments later the man nodded.

"Thanks to Erhea, we are a house of plenty," King Dominic announced, making sure his voice carried. "I would not besmirch her name by denying anyone in need. We have more than enough to give, and give we shall. I welcome the House of Whispers to our lands, and I will see you are provided with whatever supplies you require. Please, let's discuss these matters further in the comfort of my home. Come."

In the *privacy* of his home, more like, but Xander had expected this. Once they were behind closed doors, he doubted the king would be so kind. Still, they'd gotten what they'd come for—a promise before their people and before the gods that the House of Whispers would be cared for. As he and Lyana mounted the stairs, a weight lifted.

One burden down... Countless more to go.

The interior of the palace looked much like the exterior, arrayed in tapestries and draped in silks, every wall lined with paintings and every surface saturated with color. Gilt moldings framed the cased openings and stained glass filled the windows. In the entry hall, decorated trusses arched beneath a ceiling crafted to resemble the night sky. The distant chirping of songbirds echoed down the halls, creating a backdrop of gentle music.

"It's a bit much, don't you think?" Lyana whispered as they

followed the king through the winding halls. Laughter danced in her eyes.

Xander smiled despite himself. "I'd go mad."

"We used to tease my mother for calling the crystal palace plain."

"She's a bluebird, right?"

"With the voice to match."

"Did her stories prepare you for all of this?"

"A little," Lyana murmured, something wistful in her tone. "From the few I could pry out of her. Mostly, I learned by sneaking into her room and reading her letters—a confession that I'm sure must shock you."

"I never would've guessed."

"In truth, I think it made her sad to think too much of home, a feeling I never understood or even cared to consider until I stood in her place, a princess in a foreign land."

Xander nodded, not sure what to say. If he closed his eyes, he could see Lyana standing in his library with her nose pressed to the glass, a dove out of place, a bird trapped in a cage, a woman desperate to break free. He too had failed to comprehend the pressures placed on a princess in a new home, with new duties and new burdens to replace old dreams. Maybe she'd shut him out. Maybe he hadn't tried hard enough. They'd both played a part. But now, in a way, he understood her. His own home was buried beneath the sea, and the many changes threatened to pull him under. Perhaps together they'd find a way to soar.

"Fetch the queen and the crown princess," King Dominic said to a guard as they entered his private study, a room cased in ruby silks and gold carvings, the walls lined with maps and books and paintings of royals from days gone by. They walked past the desk to a circle of oversized leather chairs. "Please, sit."

He studied them as they each took a seat, and a heavy silence descended. Xander fought the urge to drop his gaze to the floor. He was a king now, and he wouldn't be intimidated. Still, it took every ounce of patience he possessed not to squirm. Lyana remained impressively stoic by his side, a reminder that she was no longer the wayward princess he'd once known.

"You have your mother's eyes," the king finally said.

"I have her spirit too."

The man arched a brow, but before he could respond, the door to the study opened and three more people entered. The queen was decidedly more reserved than the rest of her family, wearing a cream gown with limited embroidery and keeping her chestnut owl wings tucked demurely behind her back. Rushing past her in a deep emerald gown that perfectly offset the crimson highlights of her russet cardinal wings, Princess Corrinne sped to her father's side. And following at the rear was a man Xander recognized from the trials, Prince Jayce, formerly of the House of Flight. His feathers were those of a hummingbird, but their bright orange hue matched his new home rather well.

"What's going on?" the crown princess demanded, clearly taking after the king. Their matching hazel eyes wore the same imperious expression.

"That's exactly what I'd like to know." King Dominic shifted his gaze to Xander. "Did your isle truly fall?"

"It did."

A collective gasp filled the room, followed by murmurs of, "How? When? Why?"

"It began during our mating ceremony," Xander continued, using the story he and Lyana had committed to memory the day before. "As we pressed our hands to the god stone to cement our vows before Taetanos, a wave of darkness enveloped Lyana and she disappeared. I believed it to be a trick from Vesevios until she returned two days ago with news of war."

"It wasn't Vesevios." Lyana took over, smoothly transitioning to her part of the tale. "It was Taetanos, along with all the gods. He brought me into his realm, and there I spent weeks with their spirits, learning the truth about our world and what's to come. Vesevios is gaining strength and we are partly to blame. We curse magic, and we cast it out, but the gods say we've been rash. Magic is their gift to us, a way to fight the dragons, and we've shunned it. Something needed to change, and they chose me to be the bringer of that change. They gave me unimaginable power to lead our people in the coming war, and I was still learning how to use it when Taetanos sent me back here to the world of the living. He said there was no more time. That the fall of the House of Whispers meant the war was already here."

"Vesevios corrupted our god stone, and now he's after the rest of them. We don't know which isle will be targeted next, but he's coming. And his dragons are coming. Unless we embrace Lyana, and the gifts the gods have given, we'll all be doomed."

The king and crown princess shared a look.

It told Xander everything he needed to know.

"You don't believe us," he stated softly.

"Well," the king interjected, dubious at best. "It's a rather difficult story to believe."

"Why?"

He knew the answer before King Dominic even opened his mouth. “Forgive me for being blunt, but the House of Whispers has long been deemed the least worthy among us. Your isle is the smallest. Your royal line is the most often overlooked. Your god is the last one to concern himself with matters of this realm. I find it hard to imagine why such an important message would be delivered into your hands, as opposed to, say, mine."

"Lyana is a daughter of Aethios," Xander countered.

The princess huffed. "And she showed exactly how much respect she has for her god's wishes during the trials."

Beside him, Lyana's hand tightened audibly on the leather

chair. She said nothing, but he knew her. His queen was ready to burst at the seams.

"And what do you believe, then?" he asked, genuinely curious.

"I believe your house has been losing strength for generations, and due to a lack of faith, your god stone failed you. Unfortunate, but hardly a surprise given the circumstances. Now you've come to my home to beg for shelter, knowing I could not deny you, all the while spouting grand stories reeking of self-importance to make yourselves feel better about a disaster your poor choices caused."

"I see."

Xander leaned back and folded his arms. The king and princess both dropped their gazes to his missing fingers and the rounded end of his right shirtsleeve. Then they shared another look. This time, it boiled his blood.

He knew that look.

He'd lived with it his entire life—the subtle meeting of eyes whispering he'd been found wanting. He'd seen it on his father's face. He'd seen it on his weapons master's. He'd seen it on the royals' in the crystal palace the moment Lyana had shocked them all and chosen him. Though Rafe had tried his best to shield him, Xander knew ridicule. He'd heard the other children snickering when they were younger. He'd suffered their jokes. He'd known why some little boys showed up to the training grounds with black eyes, even if magic had wiped the evidence from his brother's knuckles. He wasn't a fool. His disability made him different, and being different made him an easy mark, just as being a raven did. But he was proud of his people. He was proud of his heritage. He was no longer the boy who retreated into his library and buried his head in his books, hoping feigned ignorance would make it go away. He was a man. He was a king. And he was tired of always backing down.

"Then why don't we make a wager?" Xander said, his voice far too calm. But Lyana must have sensed his underlying rage because she cut her gaze toward him. He kept his focus on King Dominic.

The man leaned forward, intrigued. "A wager?"

"A test, if you will. Taetanos has long been known as the trickster god, and I believe he'd find this an acceptable way to restore his honor. If we pass the test, you agree to believe our so-called story and you'll share our fears with your people. If we fail, the House of Whispers will leave your isle and you'll never have to deal with us again."

The princess moved to interject, but the king held out his hand. Over his shoulder, the queen gripped his chair with a worried expression on her face. Xander had guessed right. Most kings had a hard time passing on a direct challenge, and this one was no different.

"What sort of test?" he asked.

"First, I'd like you to confirm a few important points. Can you attest that Queen Lyana has never been to the House of Song before?"

"She has not."

"Can you attest that Queen Lyana has no allies in these halls and that no one on this isle would go against your orders to offer her aid?"

"They would not."

"And finally, can you attest that you witnessed Queen Lyana's fighting skills during the trials, and though admirable, they were nothing one might describe as divine or godly?"

"I agree."

"Then the test should be simple and heavily in your favor." Xander paused to meet Lyana's gaze. A mischievous sparkle lit her eyes. For the first time, he was in on the game. In fact, it was his game, one she clearly approved. Xander turned to the king, keeping his tone casual even as he felt a wicked smile curve his lips. "I propose that Queen Lyana will be able to walk out of this room and into your sacred nest unchallenged. The moment she places her hand upon your god stone, the test is over, and we'll be declared the victors. You may use any means necessary to try to stop her, and I mean any—guardsmen, swords, arrows, and whatever other tricks you might have up your sleeve. When they fail, perhaps you'll finally understand the truth. She's been chosen by the gods, so only the gods have the power to stop her."

The man's eyes widened in disbelief, and a laugh escaped his lips. It tapered off as he realized they were deadly serious. Arrogant as any royal, he offered his hand.

"You have yourselves a deal."

7

LYANA

As Lyana stood, the king eased back in his chair and flicked his gaze toward his new son-in-law. Disgust curled her lips. Not only was he an arrogant prick, but he was an arrogant prick who let others fight his battles for him. In him she saw nothing of her mother, the determined princess who'd won Aethios's heart. Where she was shrewd, he was sloppy. Where she was strict, he was callous. To speak to them like that…to speak to Xander like that—there was nothing she wanted more than to put her uncle in his place.

But she had to be smart.

Though she could lock down the entire palace if she wanted to, the amount of magic a feat like that required was immense. The god stones already trembled precariously in the sky, and the last thing she needed was to prod them along. No, the challenge here would be to get to the sacred nest using as little magic as possible.

She needed to be precise.

She needed to be controlled.

This is just the sort of test Malek would love.

Inwardly, she groaned. Outwardly, she stepped forward, uncaring as the hummingbird to her right unsheathed his sword. He attacked swiftly, using his speed to his advantage. All Lyana wanted to do was take the king's sword and raise it in a block, to feel her muscles heat as she fought to defend herself, but Malek had been right all those days ago in the arena. She didn't need daggers or bows or weapons any longer.

She was the weapon.

And it was time to make everyone in this room understand that.

As Prince Jayce swung his rapier toward her throat, Lyana touched his soul and thought, *Stop.* The blade halted mere inches from her neck. Unable to see the horrified look in his son-in-law's eyes, the king sighed.

"As I said," he drawled. "You don't have a problem with the gods. You have a problem with self-importance."

The edge of her lip quirked in what she knew must have been an evil grin, though her voice came out as sweet as hummingbird nectar. "Do we?"

Without a backward glance, she sidestepped the sword and continued toward the door, leaving the prince frozen behind her.

"Jayce," the princess muttered. When he didn't respond, didn't even move, her voice went up an octave. "Jayce!"

Lyana didn't need her magic to know Corrinne was reaching for the delicate dagger strapped to her hip—they were cousins, after all. With a little bit of *aethi'kine* power and a silent command from Lyana, the princess stopped cold, her elbow by her ear, poised to strike. A strangled gasp escaped her lips, and the king launched to his feet.

"What is the meaning of this?"

Still seated and with a perfectly calm voice, Xander said, "I believe we are winning the test."

"Guards! Guards!"

Four came bursting into the room with their swords raised,

then stiffened. Lyana bid them step aside as she approached, and they parted smoothly down the middle. Unhurried, she strode between them and into the hall.

"Stop her!" the king shouted. "By whatever means necessary, stop her!"

Grasping on to the spirit of the wood, she slammed the door behind her and cut him off. With her magic simmering just beneath the surface, she could sense the spirits hastening toward their king's garbled cry. Compared to the mages she'd dueled against, these men and women would be easy to stop. The hard part would be finding her way to the sacred nest. As soon as they'd landed in Cytrene, Lyana had felt the subtle pulsation of power emanating from the god stone, the current growing stronger and stronger as she'd neared the castle. Once inside, she'd heard the faint chirping of birds and known the nest was close. But where? And how to find it?

Guards poured through the halls.

Lyana stopped them with a thought.

As daggers flew, she simply gripped the spirit of the metal and cast them aside. The archers started hiding along the balconies or out of sight through opened doorways. Clearly, they didn't understand the walls did little to hide them. She gripped their souls like all the rest, leaving a trail of statues in her wake. All the while, the king's voice echoed down the halls.

"Stop her! Stop her!"

Lyana was reminded of her afternoons in Da'Kin as Malek parted the crowds of excited citizens with hardly any exertion at all. At first, she'd marveled at his skill. Now she understood that human spirits, especially magicless ones, were all too easy for her to control. Of course, in Da'Kin they'd been willing and watching her with veneration as Malek gently guided them aside. Here they were lunging for her throat. But she was no longer afraid—of using her magic, of showing it to the world, of being herself—and fearlessness was a power all its own.

Lyana grinned when she stepped into the next room. The entire wall was lined with windows, and through them the location of the sacred nest became abundantly clear. It was in the courtyard, open to the elements yet shielded on all sides by the palace walls. The intricate metal cage arched in a towering dome, beneath which a peaceful grove lay, filled with trees and flowers and, most of all, birds. She stepped outside, lured by the sight and the sudden pounding of the god stone. It was as though it sensed her magic and wanted her near.

A priestess stood waiting by the gate. Her intention had probably been to guard the entrance, but Lyana reached out with her power.

Let me inside.

The woman obeyed.

Lyana stepped through the gate, forgetting the guards and the priestesses and the wager the moment her gaze landed on the subtle crimson glow sifting through the trees.

The god stone.

Ignoring decorum and throwing aside her unruffled ruse, she ran. Already, she could sense the fire magic burning inside the stone, a blaze that only grew as she neared. Just like the other two divine relics she'd beheld, it hung suspended in the air, exuding godly glory. The difference was in her. Unlike before, Lyana now sensed the power pulsing through the sacred nest—her first true sight of rift magic. A thousand rainbow strands ran through the stone in every direction, a power unlike anything she'd ever felt, a power she couldn't even begin to understand. Perhaps she should have been afraid or hesitant, but with Cassi's confession in her head, she threw caution to the wind. If they were eggs, she had to know. If they were beasts, she had to be prepared. One way or another, she needed the truth.

Ignoring the subtle prickling on her skin, Lyana pressed her palms against the radiant ruby stone. Heat stole her breath as fire magic surrounded her. She lost herself to the power. An inferno blazed, but it didn't burn. There was no pain. This was the pure, potent might of Erhea, the god of love, enveloping her in a divine embrace.

Except it wasn't.

No matter how much she wanted to believe, Lyana knew the truth. Her gods were real. Her faith was strong. But they weren't in these stones. They were watching from somewhere beyond her reach, guiding her from afar. Right now they whispered, *It's time*—time to rip off the blindfold and understand the real enemy she'd soon be facing.

Lyana reached inside the stone with her magic.

Something answered.

Flames exploded within her chest and ignited along her veins, until every inch of her body felt on fire. The pain shocked her still, her nerves so frayed she couldn't move or run, couldn't even think to break free. The spirit was unlike any she'd ever touched, human but not, forged in a furnace and fortified by an inferno that would melt even Vesevios in its blaze. This was the power of dragon blood, and she cowered before it.

"Lyana!"

Was this what Malek had withstood when he'd grasped that dragon's spirit? Was this what now shared Rafe's soul? Her chest constricted. Her skin blazed. Her blood ran like lava through her veins.

"Lyana!"

The ground trembled and she wrenched her hands from the stone, stumbling back on unsteady feet until a comforting embrace steadied her.

"Lyana," Xander murmured softly. "Are you—"

"I'm all right." She cleared the daze from her eyes as she

returned to the real world and stifled her magic. He gripped her around the shoulders, keeping her upright until her legs found the strength to hold her weight. Concern filled his eyes, but the truth would have to wait until later. She turned her attention to the king staring at her in horrified awe. "When the gods speak, not every mortal has the strength to listen. They are speaking to me now, and they say the test is done."

"What sorcery is this?" King Dominic demanded, his golden hair now disheveled from racing after her down the halls. "How did you hold back my men?"

"The divinity of the gods."

"I don't believe it."

"You don't have to," Xander said. "But you do have to keep your word. The test is done, and we passed. Now, let's make good on our wager and return to the crowd waiting outside so you can tell your people exactly what we told you. The gods will it, so who are you to stand in their way?"

"I should gut you," the king seethed.

Xander simply shrugged. "You're welcome to try."

Lyana tuned out the rest of the conversation as they made their way back through the palace. Xander was more than capable of handling the politics on his own. Her mind was still caught in the sacred nest, consumed by the god stone. Cassi had been right. They were eggs, and the creatures growing inside them were more powerful than any spirit Lyana had ever touched. They were the real enemy—and she had no idea how to stop them.

She came to in the middle of the king's speech, not entirely sure when they'd stepped back onto the front steps of the palace or how long her uncle had been speaking. The crowd listened raptly, and the fear rising from their souls had brought her back to the present. With her magic barely contained, she couldn't help but feel their panic and their fright. So, just as she had with the ravens, Lyana released a wave of her healing magic. The golden embers cascaded over the onlookers, soothing their spirits and calming their aches. With each passing moment, the tension eased. They listened. They trusted. And her magic helped them believe that somehow, she would make it okay.

A few faces among the masses looked at her magic in mystified awe, as though they could see the glittering sparks and recognized them for what they were. After spending their lives in hiding, she had no doubt the mages would keep their observations silent. But as she took note of those few knowing looks, a new idea emerged. It would be risky and challenging, but when had that ever stopped her? If she succeeded, it would be worth it, because one thing was certain—against those creatures, she would need all the help she could get.

8

CASSI

Cool detachment coursed through Cassi as she watched the ship transporting her body make port along the docks of Da'Kin. Two men carried her up from the depths of the interior, one holding her shoulders and the other her calves, leaving her wings to drag helplessly along the floor. It hardly mattered—she couldn't feel them.

In a richly adorned boat nearby, Malek waited out of sight. The entrance was heavily guarded by his favorite mages, making it clear he was onboard. People watched as she was delivered into their hold, wondering who this mysterious woman was, to be treated with such honor. If they only knew the truth, they'd understand being close to the king wasn't as glorious as they imagined. She'd do anything to dive into her body and take to the sky, to leave him and all of this behind. Instead, she continued to float mindlessly along as she was deposited belowdecks. The men arranged her flailing limbs on the pillows across from him, then quietly took their leave.

"Kasiandra." Malek sighed. "Are these dramatics really necessary?"

Dramatics?

The truth hit her so suddenly she would have laughed if it were possible. He thought she was sleeping. He thought she was being stubborn.

The king rolled his head toward where her spirit hovered in the corner of the cabin, his stormy eyes darkening as a wave of blond hair fell over his brow. "You're finally home after fifteen years, and this is how you greet me? Wake up so we can speak like adults."

Oh, we're acting like adults now?

A snort rifled through her thoughts, not reflected on her immobile lips. Malek had never wanted her to act like an adult—someone with a mind and opinions of her own. When she followed his orders, she was mature. When she disobeyed, she was childish. Little did he realize standing up to him made her feel more *adult* than heeding any of his commands.

"Kasiandra, must I do this myself?" He stood and crossed the room. "Kas—"

Months ago, it would have made her heart stop to feel his real hands upon her flesh, but now it was Malek who paused as he gripped her shoulders. A wave of confusion passed over his features. Golden magic emanated from his palms. After a moment, he snapped his face toward her hovering spirit.

"Who did this to you?"

Concern softened his tone, but it just elicited questions. Was this a ruse? A trick to lure her back into trusting him again? Could it possibly be real? Therein lay the problem. She didn't know which Malek to believe in anymore—the boy who'd once filled her dreams with wonder or the man who'd turned her life into a nightmare. Could one person truly be both? And if not, who was the lie? She'd spent her entire life learning to tell half-truths, and still she couldn't decipher this one.

Malek eased onto the cushions by her side, moving his hands to her cheeks and shutting his eyes. A shiver passed through her as she remembered how much she'd once yearned to have him so close, how many times she'd imagined a scene just like this. Now, though, the shiver was one of disgust as the magic around his fingers brightened.

"This must be why Lyana sent you to me," he murmured, still deep in his power. "She doesn't know how to fix you."

Her hope spiked at his implication.

But I do.

Truth? Lie? With him, she never knew.

Malek eased back, sliding his fingers from her temples, and just like that, whatever vulnerability she thought she saw on his face vanished. The king returned, the gaze lifting toward her as opaque as the fog.

"Come to me tonight and tell me what happened," he said, his voice like iron. "Lyana has stonewalled my attempts to communicate, but you can get through to her in a way I can't. I'd like to give you a message for her, and in return I'll do what I can to fix you."

An order.

An arrangement.

A deal.

She'd given fifteen years of her life in service to his cause, and still it wasn't enough. She'd given pieces of her soul, honest and good pieces she would never get back, and still he wanted more. But Cassi was tired of giving. For once, she wanted him to act out of the goodness she knew existed somewhere in his heart, expecting nothing in return.

She forced her spirit through his head and used her magic to grab on to his thoughts for the briefest instant.

No.

Malek flung her from his mind, but the dark look in his eyes said he'd heard. "Kasiandra, I am the King Born in Fire, and you will do as I say."

Not anymore, she thought, letting him make of her silence what he would.

"Kasiandra."

A slightly unhinged spark fired to life deep in his pupils, burning in a way that made her pause. In all the years she'd known him, he'd never lost control. But now she could almost see him teetering on the edge—the edge of what, she didn't know.

"Kasiandra!"

A knock sounded. "We're here, my liege."

Gritting his teeth, Malek released a slow breath. His fists clenched and unclenched by his sides as he cracked a bone in his neck. Two steps later, he was across the room.

"Take her to the dungeons," he said as he stepped through the door. "Leave her with the boy."

Cassi watched him go, done with his commands, and remained with her body. Soldiers carried her from the boat, up into the castle, then down into its depths. The walls turned slick with moisture and the air thickened. Outside the halo of mage light, the halls were eerily dark. In the silence, every drip of water became a rushing river and every unseen scuff a spirit. This was a place people went to disappear. Malek's message was clear—give him what he wanted, or her body might be the next to slip away.

Why? She sighed internally. *Why must you be like this?*

Images of the shadow creature flitted across her thoughts. Before meeting with Malek, she'd been fully prepared to tell him what had happened to her in the sacred nest. He needed to know, if not for her sake then for the world's. But now stubborn refusal tightened her gut. She wanted to prove a point, perhaps the same point Lyana meant to prove by leaving—he needed to learn to bend or they would all break.

If he came to her with an apology, with any sort of remorse, she would relent. But until then, he would live in his own darkness. Let him wait. Let him wallow. Let him wonder about her plans the way she had spent so much of her life wondering about his.

"Cassi!"

The name pulled her back. Elias sprang from the bed in the opposite corner of his cell and ran toward her body, which had been deposited on the cold stone floor. He was thinner than he'd been the last time she'd seen him, and his rich sepia skin was drawn and pale from too many days without the sun. His tan wings, though, were just as soft and comforting a sight as she remembered.

"What did you do to her?" he yelled as he dropped to his knees beside her still form. "What did you do?"

The resounding *bang* of the door slamming was his only response. Elias gathered her into his arms and carried her to the bed, then took the time to gently fold her speckled wings behind her back as he settled her on the lumpy mattress.

"Oh, Cassi," he murmured, grief sharpening his tone. "What did they do to you?"

The dove lifted her head onto his lap and brushed the damp hairs from her cheeks while she watched from her spot on the other side of the room. An unfamiliar burning sensation filled her spirit, hot enough to make her want to cry yet soothing enough to warm her soul. In some deep, hidden place, a thud echoed through her, as though the lost connection to her heart were trying to re-form. Memories of her former life flickered by—of days spent flying with Elias, Luka, and Lyana beneath crystal domes and nights filled dancing with them across glittering mosaics, of the hours spent beating each other in the training yards followed by the minutes spent laughing until they could no longer breathe. Luka had been the man to share her bed, but Elias had been the one to understand what living in the shade of royalty was like. He'd been a dear friend, and perhaps he still might be.

"I'll get us out of this," he whispered roughly into the silence of their prison. "Somehow, Cassi, I swear I'll get us out of this."

No, I will.

She wasn't sure how or when, but eventually, she'd help Elias escape. He didn't deserve to be here. He didn't deserve this terror. And after a lifetime of duplicity, she had a few tricks up her sleeve —with or without her body.

Tonight, though, difficult as it was to pull herself away, she had more important duties to focus on. Instead of drifting deeper into the castle, Cassi forced her spirit through the thick stone walls and into the misty air above Da'Kin. Malek could wait for her all night if he pleased. She wasn't going to visit his rooms or his dreams. Instead, she ventured out in search of news to tell her queen.

9

MALEK

Relief washed through Malek as the dream around him shifted. This was his third visit from a *dormi'kine* tonight, and it had to be Kasiandra. She'd made him wait. She'd had her fun. But she was here. She—

A sneer curled his lip as the scene solidified. Dark stone walls and damp gray skies filled his vision, lacking both the creativity and the finesse of the woman he sought.

"My liege," a man's voice said.

"What?" Malek snapped as he spun.

His spy sank into a deep bow. "Apologies for the disturbance, but I thought you would want to hear my report posthaste."

"Well..."

If they'd been anywhere but in this specific dream, the man would have toppled from straightening so quickly. "Yes, of course, my liege. My ship is currently at port in Karthe. Not an hour ago, a trade ship docked next to us, nearly burned to a crisp from a dragon attack. They barely got away with their lives."

"Not unheard of, in these waters."

"Of course not, my liege, but it's the manner of their escape that I think you'll find of interest." The spy paused to swallow, his hesitation obvious, as though he was afraid to be the bearer of this news. "They said a man with dragon wings appeared suddenly through the fog and landed on their ship. He communicated with the beast somehow. They faced off, and within moments the dragon flew away."

A frown thinned Malek's lips. "A man with dragon wings?"

"That's what they say."

"And do they say anything else?"

"Not yet, but it's past dawn in Karthe, and I wouldn't be surprised to find the gambling halls ripe with rumors by this evening."

Malek folded his hands behind his back to hide the way they clenched, keeping his face serene. "And did a ship by the name of *The Wanderer* also happen to dock in Karthe around the same time?"

"Another ship anchored just outside the city. I believe they towed the burned ship to port, but I'm not sure of its captain."

He would bet his life her name was Captain Audezia'd'Rokaro—the once-loyal leader of his best dragon-hunting ship, turned deserter by a common raven. The very thought made his blood boil. What pull did the boy have? Malek was the savior. He was the hero. He was the *aethi'kine*. So why did people keep abandoning him for a man with a power useless to everyone else? How could an *invinci* save the world? It was ludicrous, laughable even, though it made him want to scream.

"Keep an eye out tonight," Malek ordered, his voice devoid of the emotions rifling through him. "I suspect Captain Rokaro or her crew will make an appearance in the city after sundown for supplies. The man with the dragon wings is a fugitive on their ship, and he is of extreme importance to me. My top priority is to see him returned to Da'Kin. If the moment presents itself to strike, do not hesitate. Use the remaining crew as leverage if necessary, and don't worry about the use of force. The man is extremely difficult to kill."

"Yes, my liege."

The dream dissolved.

Malek rolled to his feet. The fog outside was just beginning to lighten with the sun. The hour was early, but not too early to begin the day. As he stepped before his mirror, he hardly recognized the image staring back. Dark circles stained the undersides of his eyes, and his hair stood on end as though he'd spent the night gripping it between his fingers.

This wouldn't do.

A bath first, ice cold to shock his system back into place, and with his composure restored, he'd find his mages. They needed to hear this update, and they needed to know the castle was no longer a safe place to speak. No one would mention the boy outside his presence. No one would speak of dockside rumors unless he was there to hear. These walls now had ears, and only he could sense when Kasiandra might be listening. She hadn't come to his dreams, which could only mean one thing. His *dormi'kine* had shifted her loyalties to the queen.

Lyana could never know what Malek had seen that night. The rumors would come, he was sure, now that Rafe's new body had been seen. But gossip was one thing.

By magic and by prophecy, *he* was her king.

One way or another, she'd return to *him*.

10

BRIGHTY

"What'll it be?" the dealer asked, his impatience obvious.

Brighty stared at the three kings in her hand, trying to remember tonight was not about making money. She'd snuck away from the rest of the crew for a far more nefarious purpose. Still, a winning hand was a winning hand.

Magic alive, this is painful.

"Fold," she muttered, letting the frustration ooze from her pores. The more she reeked of desperation, the more other players would want to cash in on one more sucker in the streets of Karthe trying to turn her luck around.

"You're out."

"Here's another twenty silver medallions. I've got to win eventually, right?"

The dealer offered her a sad smile but let her place the new stack of gleaming coins on the table. "Right."

As though drawn by the sight, four more patrons sat at the table, turning it half-full. Not quite enough for the fun to begin. Brighty kept her hood on and hunched over her cards, exchanging her usual mode of casual indifference for one of obvious discomfort. The more eyes she drew, the better. Despite the smoky haze infiltrating the gambling den, its regulars could spot an easy mark a mile away. A few more bad hands and another twenty silvers later, the table was full. Now she could start playing.

Brighty kept her ears perked, listening to the conversation taking place around her and biding her time. They spoke of the usual—trade, dragon hunting, the *bloody fog*, and those *damned mages* living in the wealthiest quarter of the city. A recent string of unexplained murders took up a decent part of the rumor mill, but eventually talk shifted to the topic she'd been anticipating.

"I heard he had dragon wings."

"I heard he breathed fire."

"I heard he scared the beast away with a single look."

As expected, Rafe's reputation preceded him. *Actually, he's bloody clumsy at times and a downright grump, but he's all we've got.*

Captain had expressly forbidden Brighty from revealing her suspicions to anyone—that Rafe, and not Malek, was somehow the King Born in Fire. Magic strike her if she knew how *that* was possible, but she knew what she'd seen on the outskirts of Da'Kin—Queen Lyana and Rafe standing face-to-face, framed by ashy snowfall and burning flame, like a portrait painted by fate's own hands. If she was the Queen Bred of Snow, then he was the King Born in Fire. Brighty would bet her life on it, and despite the evidence presented this evening, she almost always won.

"Did he come from the rift?"

"They say he just appeared through the mist."

"An old friend of mine is on the crew, and he said the man spoke to the beast. He said the dragon bowed to him, like one of us would to a king."

There.

She bit back her grin. It was the perfect in.

"Well," Brighty drawled, as she tossed a handful of coins into the pot, drawing their gazes. Money spoke, and it was time to start winning. Maybe then, they'd believe her. "It does make you wonder."

Two more gamblers folded, leaving only Brighty and one man in the hand. He met her eyes across the table and matched her bid. "Wonder?"

She placed another stack of coins into the heap. So did he.

"The man has dragon wings. He can breathe fire. He can talk to them. They're afraid of him. We've been told again and again the time of prophecy is upon us, and, well, it makes you wonder..." She trailed off, letting the crumbs lead where they might, and raised the bid.

Her opponent glanced briefly at his cards, a tell if she'd ever seen one. Despite the confident way he dropped the coins into the center, one by one in a smug cascade, he was nervous. So was she—her hand was a total flop. But no one else needed to know it. And her conservative bids earlier in the night suggested that if she was going all in, it was because she had something great.

"What are you implying?" he asked, taking another second to look at his cards.

Brighty kept her eyes on him and raised again. "What do you think I'm implying?"

"You don't really believe he might be the King Born in Fire?"

Behind her, someone gasped.

"You said it." She shrugged. "Not me."

"He could be working for them."

"What if he's working for us?" She sat back in her chair and laid her cards facedown on the table, then covered them protectively with her palms. "Your bid."

"He's been spotted!" someone shouted across the gambling hall. "Someone just saw a man with flaming wings through a break in the fog!"

Blasted idiot, Brighty cursed internally, careful not to move.

What part of "stay on the ship and stay out of sight" did you not understand?

Half the people who'd been watching her game turned toward the door, and a swarm of patrons ran outside. If her opponent wanted to fold, it was now or never, with the room distracted and no one paying attention to his defeat.

Come on. Come on.

"Well?" she said and arched her brow.

The man sighed and tossed his cards onto the table. "I'm out."

"Excellent," Brighty chirped. With a swish of her arm, she brushed the pot into her coin purse and jumped to her feet. "It's been a pleasure."

One hand tipped her imaginary hat. The other deftly flipped her cards to reveal her bluff. The man shot to his feet.

"You son of a—"

His cry was lost in the din of the hall as she cut swiftly through the crowd. What she'd come to accomplish was done. By morning, Karthe would be alive with the question of who exactly this mysterious dragon man might be, and Karthe was only the beginning. Sailors were notorious gossips. Half the seas would be bubbling with the news within the week.

Would Captain Rokaro be happy? No. But technically —*technically*—Brighty hadn't broken any of her rules. So, really, how could she complain?

She'll find a way.

With a sigh, Brighty slipped into the shadows of the city and crept along the edges of the dock, all the while keeping her gaze on the sky. There was nothing she wanted more than hot food and her bed. Instead, she needed to track down a runaway dragon man before anyone else found him.

All right, Rafe, she thought as she scaled the side of a building to crouch atop the nearest roof. *Where the hell are you?*

11

RAFE

That might've been too low.

Rafe cursed and angled his body higher into the skies. But how else was he supposed to see through this blasted fog if he didn't dive beneath it? Yes, he'd promised the captain he wouldn't leave the ship. And yes, he'd promised to stay out of sight. But no, he hadn't listened. And now...he was pretty sure he'd been spotted.

Great. Just great.

When they arrived at port, he'd agreed to remain on the ship while the rest of the crew slipped into the dark streets to gather supplies. But that had been before he peeked through the porthole to find a familiar skyline staring back. He'd been to Karthe before, not in body, but in a dream the night before. The docks had been just as full, bustling with magic and mage light despite the late hour, the sort of place where it was easy to go unseen—at least for anyone without flaming wings. In the memory, he'd stuck to the shadows, moving through liquid pools of inky black and staying out of sight. Then he'd caught a scent in the air, too intoxicating to ignore. He'd followed it until he'd found the source—a young girl with silver magic glittering along her fingers. She oozed spirit and life. He'd wrapped a scaled claw around her throat and drained the power from her skin until he was dizzy with it. Someone had come. It didn't matter. All he remembered from then on were flashes of blood and gore and death.

Rafe shook his head to clear the nightmare.

Gods alive.

It had been so real. Too real. When he'd glanced through the window to find the same city staring back, one he was certain he'd never stepped foot in before, he'd taken to the skies without a second thought. If the dreams were real, he needed proof. Was he doing these things? Had the dragon inside of him found a way to gain control? The possibilities were too terrifying to consider, but imagining the worst was making him crazy.

Oh, screw it.

He couldn't see anything through the fog. He needed to be closer. And if the people saw him, so what? His magic made him unbreakable, and now he was half-dragon too. If anyone in the streets of Karthe wanted a fight, they could have one. It might be just the outlet his restless energy needed.

Rafe dove.

The fog dissipated as he neared the tops of the buildings, scattering just enough for him to see. Magic glittered along the busy streets, but the farther from the docks he flew, the quieter the city became. The scene from his dream had been a dead-end street, circled by buildings and edged by a deep canal, stuffed full of empty crates and boxes. When he reached the richly ornate buildings near the center of town, he knew he'd gone too far and circled back, scanning the passing sectors for any hint of familiarity.

There.

A façade painted in fading teals and yellows caught his eye. Rafe plummeted from the sky and landed easily on his feet to press his fingers against the chipped wood. He'd been in this spot before.

He'd touched this siding. Just around the corner, a dark alley waited. He ran down it, the shadows just as thick as he remembered. Left, then right, then left again, he moved on instinct, until finally he stopped in the center of a small clearing at the edge of a canal.

It was real.

His chest tightened as he turned slowly, taking in the broken crates and the scattered glass, evidence of a fight. The girl had been playing just over there, beside that door. He kicked debris to the side with his foot—and froze. Dark stains marred the wood.

No. No. No.

Rafe knelt and pressed his fingers to the spot. The firelight from his wings caught the edge of the sticky liquid. It flashed with a crimson sheen.

Blood.

The alley was real. The girl had been real. The nightmare was real.

He'd lived it.

No!

He stumbled back. Behind him, a tile crashed to the wood. Rafe gripped his swords and pulled them from their sheaths as he spun.

"Whoa!" Brighty jumped out of reach. "Put those things away before you hurt yourself."

The tips of his blades dropped with two *thunks* to the wood as all the breath left his lungs. "It's you."

"Who'd you expect?"

"I really don't know." He stared into the shadows, unable to fight the feeling of being watched. "How'd you find me?"

"How do you think?" she growled, then punched him in the arm. "I followed you across the rooftops, and I'm not the only one. What part of *stay on the ship* don't you understand? I mean, magic alive, Rafe! Half the city is out looking for you right now, and no offense, you aren't exactly incognito with those things."

She pointedly eyed his fiery wings.

Rafe tucked them casually behind his back. "I'm sorry. I know. It's just, something's been going on, something's happened, and—"

"Tell me later," she cut him off and glanced over her shoulder. "We've got to go."

"Why?"

Before she could answer, a wave of pine-green sparks spilled through the alley and surrounded them in a neon glow.

Brighty sighed and shook her head. "Too late."

His swords chose that moment to jerk free of his hands. One swung for his neck. The other sliced toward Brighty's gut. She rolled to the side while he ducked, and their foreheads banged together.

"Ow."

"Watch out!"

He shoved her aside and caught the blade in his hand before it struck. Blood spilled down his forearm. Rafe gritted his teeth and strengthened his grip as the sword lashed from side to side. Silver magic pooled beneath his skin. Beside him, Brighty brandished a broken slab of wood and whacked the other sword away.

"I told you these things were a bloody hazard!"

"Don't give me a lecture."

"I should've given you a leash!"

The sword attacking Brighty lodged in the wood. For a moment, she grinned triumphantly. Then the blade started spinning, whipping the shard of wood around like a floating wheel of death. She bared her teeth as Rafe leapt in front of her, using his body as a shield. Reaching back, he tried to get a grip around her waist.

"Let me carry you."

"No."

"We'll be safe—"

"No."

"Would you just—"

"Look out!"

A metal grate lifted from the scattered shards and flew toward them. Rafe took it in the chest, grunting as he felt a rib crack. Brighty steadied him from behind. Three mages walked into the alley, their leader clearly the *ferro'kine* wreaking havoc on Rafe's pride. The other two weren't using their magic, but he could smell it on their skin.

"What do you want?"

"The king sent us to retrieve you," the metal mage warned.

I bet he did. The mere mention of the king made Rafe's blood burn. Heat filled the air as the flames along his wings blazed, turning the mage's pupils orange with the reflection.

"Come with us, and we won't hurt your friend."

"Touch her, and I'll kill you."

"No one's going to die tonight," Brighty drawled as she stepped out from behind him with a swagger to her hips. "Least of all me. I'm sure we can come to some sort of arrangement."

She darted her milky eyes toward him, and Rafe slammed his shut just as magic exploded from her palms. The light was so piercing even he felt the sting as the darkness fled. He expected screams, or at least some heavy groaning. Instead, a moment later, it dimmed.

"Oh, for magic's sake," Brighty grumbled under her breath.

Rafe peeked to the side. A wave of shadow rolled from another mage's hands, meeting her power head-on, so the two clashed in a battle of penetrating white and fathomless black, neither gaining the upper hand.

Well, damn.

It had been worth a shot.

His swords sprang from the floor again, both aimed toward

Brighty's heart, and Rafe lunged to intervene. Yellow streaks of *aero'kine* magic flooded his sight as a windstorm swept through the alley, knocking him aside. He dug his heels into the wooden planks, his feet slipping with the moisture.

"Brighty!"

Locked in battle with the shadow mage, she didn't hear his cry. The sharp points flew closer to her chest as gusts whipped at him from all sides. Rafe tried to barrel his way through.

"Brighty!"

She glanced toward him, her eyes widening upon seeing the blades, and stumbled back. But it was too late. The metal was a foot away, then inches, then—

The swords clanged to the ground at her feet as the *ferro'kine* gasped in pain. Rafe jerked his head toward the sound. The man clutched his shoulder, a wince digging into his brow as he hissed. Blood spilled over his fingers, pouring down his arm and soaking his clothes. The mage found Rafe's gaze, a mixture of fear and renewed determination shining in his eyes.

It wasn't me, he wanted to say. *I didn't do it.*

But what did?

A brilliant wave of green flooded the alley before Rafe had time to guess. Dozens of shards of metal rose into the air, light enough to be swept into the tunneling winds. A maelstrom of sharp edges and dust spun toward them. Rafe glanced at Brighty, then at the sky, then back at Brighty. She bit her lip, all her concentration on the shadow mage. Rafe would survive the onslaught, he was sure. It'd be painful, but not fatal. His friend, however, would be butchered alive.

As if hearing his thoughts, the *aero'kine* sent another gust into his chest, and he stumbled back. Surrounded by green glitter, two metal bars rose before him like a moving cage, preventing him from crossing the distance. The spinning vortex of doom glided closer.

"Surrender and we'll spare her," the metal mage ordered.

Like hell.

The fire in his chest stirred, but Rafe clamped down on that instinct. It would burn Brighty just as easily as it burned the rest of them. There had to be something else, something—

His raven cry.

Was he still…? Could he still…?

He had to try.

As wind and metal barreled down on him, Rafe thought of Brighty and of the raven he prayed still lived somewhere inside his battered soul, and he screamed.

The piercing screech echoed down the alley, reverberating off the wooden walls like the sweetest music. Everyone stopped. Wind died and metal dropped to the ground like soft rain. Both light and shadow winked out. Brighty stood slack-jawed, prompting the corner of his lip to quirk as he raced toward her, ready to flee to the sky.

A tickle at the back of his neck stopped him.

Dread slipped down his spine.

Drawn by something out of his control, Rafe slowly turned. The air was still. The metal mage and the wind mage both stood frozen, their eyes blank and unseeing. Behind them, though, the darkness rippled. A creature emerged from the ebony folds, its skin covered in scales. Shadows wafted off its onyx wings. The only bright spots on it were the pointed teeth visible between slightly parted lips.

"You…" Rafe's whisper fell away to nothing.

The demon cocked its head to the side as though curious. Then it reached a hand around the metal mage's throat, the pointed claws of its fingers creating indents in his tan skin. The mage blinked. His gaze sharpened as the power of the raven cry fled. For a moment, his eyes widened. With a sudden jerk, he dropped dead.

"No!" Rafe shouted.

The creature was already gone, disappearing into the shadows as though it had never existed in the first place. But it had. He'd seen it. And not just moments ago—he'd seen it in his dreams. Impossible, yet true.

The *aero'kine* screamed and dropped to the ground beside her dead companion. Before Brighty had a moment to complain, Rafe grabbed her by the waist and launched into the sky, every fiber of his being alight with the desire to flee.

"Put me down!"

Rafe ignored her and carved a path deeper into the fog, rising high above the city.

"Rafe, put me down now!"

He loosened his grip, and she screamed loudly enough to wake the gods. "You said—"

"Not *right* now, you bloody idiot!"

He grinned as she wrapped her arms around his throat, nearly choking the life out of him in her desperation to hold on.

"I thought you weren't afraid of heights."

She grumbled unintelligibly and buried her head in his chest. He shook his and reached out with his senses, using the subtle pull of magic to guide him closer to the docks. Only, it wasn't subtle. The port was ablaze with power, and as they neared, rainbow explosions broke through the mist. He dove beneath the fog bank, not surprised in the least to find the crew of *The Wanderer* at the center of the fray. A group of mages on the dock were attempting to come aboard. The crew held them off. Magic crashed and collided, nearby ships and buildings getting pulled into the destruction. A furious storm brewed across the sky, spun by the captain's hands as Pyro burned the sails of a nearby ship and Jolt rained lightning on the empty deck. His friends were clearly stronger, holding the other mages off and careful not to inflict any permanent damage—on the people, anyway.

"Go!" Rafe tried to shout. They'd been waiting for them. It was obvious. Rather than flee, they'd stood their ground, but he'd never forgive himself if anyone got hurt. "Go!"

Above the blistering winds, he knew he had no chance of being heard. But against the charcoal skies, his wings were hard to miss. Patch grabbed Captain by the arm and pointed. Immediately, the air shifted and the sails of the ship puffed. Rafe cut back into the fog before the mages on the ground spotted him. He'd meet the ship out at sea.

"Did you see their faces?" Brighty groaned against his chest. "I'll never hear the end of this, being carted around like some damsel in distress... *blech*."

The shadow creature's sharp onyx claws flashed through Rafe's mind and a shiver pulsed down his spine. He tightened the grip on his friend. "At least you'll be alive."

THE DIARY

Eleventh Day of the Third Moon

I don't know why I still do this. Perhaps because it's the last thing I remember my mother telling me before she passed into the aether. Write down your visions, Miralee. Write them down so you'll always remember. One day, they might save everything.

Unlikely.

My mother wasn't a chrono'kine. She didn't see into the future as I do. She was a cryo'kine, and I've missed her magic in the many years that she's been gone. Our lands always burn with a constant summer sun. She used to plop frozen pellets in my drinks to keep them cool. She used to press her palm to my brow and freeze the sweat upon my skin. She used to dip her fingers into the shallow fountain at the base of the palace then take my hands so we could slip together across the ice. Sometimes when it rained, she tossed her frosty power into the air and the droplets would turn to snow. If I close my eyes, I can still taste the chill upon my tongue.

Father always thought her magic frivolous, as he does mine. All he ever wanted was a son, an aethi'kine same as him, someone to inherit the throne. Power speaks in our world, and no power speaks louder than his. But I don't mind being quiet.

Father tells me he has no use for my magic. He calls my visions pretty pictures with nothing to say. I don't tell him I've seen his death, and it isn't pretty at all.

It happened for the first time two moons ago. We were eating supper and he was droning on about my marriage prospects—my least favorite topic. I was staring at my food when the back of my neck started tickling, the prickle of my magic. Where my fingers held the fork, a subtle rosy shimmer danced beneath my skin, the stirring of my power. When I looked up, my father was still before me, but he was no longer the man I recognized. His olive skin resembled melted wax, his cheeks dripping from some unseen heat, blood vessels strung red and boils oozing with puss. His eyes ran like liquid down his face. His thick black beard was gone, and the top of his head was bald, still smoking where his hair had burned to ash.

I blinked and it was gone.

My father was so used to the blush of my magic, so unmoved by it, he didn't bother to ask what I'd seen, and I didn't say. The vision was clearer than most, but still fuzzy around the edges, offering no details of time or place. That's the problem with seeing into the future—it's always in flux. Sometimes I see things that will never come to pass. Sometimes I don't realize what I've seen until it's already too late, as with my mother. I had visions of her on her deathbed, face peaceful with flowers woven through her ebony hair. I'd always thought she'd been sleeping. It wasn't until I stood over her, watching the final breath leave her body, that I realized my mistake. My father had been visiting another kingdom when the accident happened. She fell from her horse and broke her spine. We sent a hummingbird avian with a message, but it was too late. She was dead by the time he returned, and within the hour, the hummingbird and the horse had joined her. I've never been to the stables again.

I'm not sure why I never saw the accident. That's maybe the most frustrating thing about my magic—I have no control. The visions come to me with no explanation, no meaning. I can't draw them out. I can't call upon them. They change from day to day, sometimes little more than blurred colors of uncertainty, sometimes with the sharpest clarity but still opaque in meaning. They frightened me when I was small, but I've since learned my father disapproves of such weakness. Maybe he'd be proud to know I saw his face melted off and hardly batted an eye.

Maybe I'm more my father's daughter than I thought.

Fourteen Day of the Third Moon

I just saw another vision. At least, I think I did. I was staring outside my window, watching the avians soar above the city streets, carrying messages and running patrols, when suddenly the bright blue, cloudless sky turned an angry, hazy orange. The clouds went gray. The streets turned black. In a moment, it was gone, hardly more than a flash, too quickly for me to tell what exactly it had been. A blood dawn, perhaps? I've never seen one, but every hundred years it's said a red sun rises, an ill omen.

The very thought makes me shiver.

There was something else, too, something I just realized. In my vision, the skies were empty. Never once have I glanced out my window to a sky unmarked by swiftly moving wings, some black, some white, some hardly more than a rainbow blur dashing beneath the clouds. The avians are as much a part of this life as magic. They're our messengers. Our warriors. Our servants. Our subjects. They flock to my father and the other kings like him because aethi'kine power is the only thing that can give them wings. They're loyal to us, and in turn my father keeps their way of life alive.

No one knows for sure how the avian race began, just as no one knows how our civilization ended up here, on a peninsula on the other side of a towering mountain range, impassable without magic or wings. There are myths, of course. I've been told people with magic were once hunted and killed. People believed our blood and bodies could be used as talismans. Others believed we were dangerous. Still more thought we were loyal to an evil god who lived in a burning realm deep within the earth. Even with all our power, we lived in fear until an aethi'kine leader rose. He thought himself a god, so he forged an army fit for a god. In that age, the people believed in a single deity who ruled the skies. Thus he gave his warriors wings and the avians were born. Some people prayed to him. More cursed him. The mages united behind him, free for once from persecution. And though they could have destroyed that world, more death wasn't what they'd wanted, just peace. So they pilgrimaged to this peninsula, then used their magic to raise the mountains and roughen the seas, until the world forgot we even existed. Now those with magic rule, and those without, well…live, I guess.

If there's one thing my magic has shown me, it's that time is cyclical. Power too. Paupers become princes who become paupers again. Someday, though I'm not sure how or when, maybe mages will once again be the ones begging for scraps. It's hard for me to imagine that ever being so, sitting here in the fine rooms of the palace, my father's scarlet banners whipping in the breeze, his strength so absolute none would dare question it. But I think of the empty skies in my vision, and —I don't know.

If the future is one thing, it's uncertain, even through my all-seeing eyes.

Nineteenth Day of the Third Moon

My father has found me a husband. At least, he thinks so. I should be rejoicing—households rise and fall like the sun in our lands. With my power as it is, we've been prepared for doom should anything happen to him. Lacking an aethi'kine heir, the avians would flee to new lands and we'd be exposed, ripe for the taking, no army to protect us. Even with all the magic in the world, one of the neighboring kings would come and claim our home for his own. I saw it happen five years ago. A kingdom in the far north fell not even a year after losing its aethi'kine queen. But if my father secured my marriage to an aethi'kine, our kingdom would be safe, and our people would prosper for another generation.

So, I should be rejoicing.

But I'm not.

There are only two eligible aethi'kine men that I'm aware of at the moment, unless another has recently come into power. One is a five-year-old boy, just a child, and the other an unabashed bachelor. He's a few years older than me, and I'm told quite handsome, but that matters little. All I know is that he had a chance five years ago to claim a kingdom, and instead he watched from the sideline as the city was torn apart, its people ripped from their homes and its royal family slaughtered. He claimed he had no interest in being a king. Well, people with no sense of duty are of little interest to me.

Though I guess I'm being harsh.

Everything I've just written shows my own reluctance to perform my duty. I will, of course, when the time comes. I would never let my home fall because of my own selfish desires. But here, in the safety of these pages I pray no one else will ever read, perhaps I can be honest.

I've lived under the unrelenting rule of an aethi'kine man my entire life.

I don't relish the thought of surviving the rest of my days under yet another.

Their power can be as cruel as it is kind. They can save a life just as easily as they take it. Even under the most honorable aethi'kine, freedom is a ruse. It can be stolen at a moment's notice with a single stray thought. Being so powerful must do something to their minds—men and women alike. Though I have more experience with aethi'kine kings and princes, I'm sure the queens are just the same. They command spirits, and yet their own feel broken, as though being so entrenched in humanity has somehow made them less human.

Or maybe my father has left me jaded.

One way or another, I'll see—whether it be with a ring on my finger or a sword at my throat. I don't need my magic to know that.

Twenty-First Day of the Third Moon

I can't breathe as I write this. My heart pounds in my chest. My pulse races. I ran back to my room to record every detail of the vision before it faded, though I doubt it ever will. Those hazel eyes seem burned into my thoughts like a brand, brighter each time I close my eyes.

But I'm getting ahead of myself.

I was on my way to dinner when I felt the tingle at the back of my neck, signaling the onset of my magic. A strong breeze blew in from the window, so I turned to face it. My slipper caught on my skirts and I stumbled back. As soon as my shoulder blades struck stone, he was there. A warm hand encased my cheek, and his face was close, so close I could see nothing else. His tan skin held a warm summer glow and his long hair fell around his cheeks in waves, like bronze curtains streaked with sunlight. But his eyes are what still pierce, even now, long after the vision faded. They were so deep I felt as though I might drown within them, copper at the edges, then jade in the center, flecked with spots of gold. He looked at me as though he never wanted to look away, something fierce and protective in his gaze. He stroked my face once with his thumb, the rough edge of a callus scratching my skin, before he disappeared. I still feel the mark. I still feel his eyes. Within me something stirs, something I've never felt before.

Who was he?

My husband?

I fear not. The vision showed me nothing else, but the danger lingering in my heart promises his is a touch I'm never supposed to feel in real time.

The future, though, is mine to do with what I will.

Third Day of the Fourth Moon

I haven't written in days, and it's because there's nothing to report. My eyes are so filled with visions of him, I see nothing else. Not magic visions. Not visions of the future. These are the sort weaved by my mind, not my power.

I can't stop seeing him.

Every time I close my eyes, I wonder who he is and where he lives and when I'll finally find him. Why is he important? Why did my magic show me his face? What is it trying to say?

Chrono'kine power is maddening.

No one else understands what it's like to see something that may never come to pass, to want so badly for it to be real, but to know it might be little more than a dream. What if I never meet him? What if he's forever just a face to haunt my thoughts, a reminder of what could have been? I see the future, but I have such little power to affect it—to keep it the same, to bring it closer, to change it. One person may live who was meant to die, one person may die who was meant to live, and just like that, the fate of the whole world changes, taking all my visions with it.

But he'll come.

I just need patience.

His face was too clear. His eyes too knowing. His touch too real. He's a certain future. It was everything else around him that was hazy.

Or maybe I was just too bespelled to look.

Eighth Day of the Fourth Moon

Nothing.

Nothing. Nothing. Nothing. Nothing!

Nothing.

Twelfth Day of the Fourth Moon

My father complains that I've been in a daze these past weeks. He thinks I'm moping over the prospect of getting married.

Let him.

The aethi'kine he is speaking with is the one I suspected, who stood by while another kingdom perished, who's shown no interest in ruling and no understanding of what it means to be a true king. For all my father's faults, I do believe that deep down he wants what is best for his people, though I don't always approve of his methods. My mother was the only one who ever managed to question him, and ever since her death, he's reigned unchecked.

Will my husband be like that?

Will he do as he wants, when he wants, knowing full well there will be no one around to stop him? Or will he listen to reason?

I'll know soon enough.

I'm to meet him in a few days' time.

Thirteenth Day of the Fourth Moon

As if my freedoms weren't limited enough, my father is putting more guards outside my rooms in anticipation of my potential betrothed's visit. He's afraid and it's unsettling. I've never seen him nervous before. Unlike bodies that age, magic doesn't weaken with time, so I should think he has nothing to fear at the prospect of a younger man's arrival, even if he is an aethi'kine, but maybe his fear is of the more traditional sort. I live so often in the future, I forget that so many dread it. Time is the one thing no one can stop, no one can control, and one day, it will claim even my father. I've been considering this new arrival as my possible husband so often, I forget he is also my father's possible replacement, a thought I don't believe any king relishes.

Is it wrong that makes me more eager to meet him?

Oh, there's a knock on my door. I had best go welcome my new chaperones. With luck, I'll be able to bribe them into turning a blind eye when I wish to go walk the gardens at night. There's nothing quite like the glow of moonlight on a bed of roses or the shimmering carpet of an uninterrupted starry sky.

Worst comes to worst, I'll use my old route out the window. It's been a long time since I've had to shimmy down the trellis to escape my nanny, but some tricks are never quite forgotten.

Thirteenth Day of the Fourth Moon

I met him.

No, not my husband. Him, him. The man from my vision. His skin was just as golden and his eyes just as deep, though they didn't regard me with passion. Not yet. They were carefully blank, measured by control, a flimsy shield hiding the breath of emotion I already saw in them.

He's one of my new avian guards—an eagle with glorious golden wings.

12

XANDER

The door to the palace of Cytrene closed behind Xander and Lyana with a resounding *bang*. Thankfully, the dark night hid his flinch.

"They'll never help us with the other houses," he murmured as he took her arm and led her down the front steps. "King Dominic will never forgive us for making him the fool."

"I believe he did that all on his own."

"I doubt that's how he sees it."

Lyana sighed. "Do you regret making the wager, then?"

"No," Xander answered honestly.

The edge of her lip lifted, prompting his to do the same. No, he didn't regret putting the man in his place even a little bit, and the King of the House of Song had made good on his word. He'd shared their proclamation with his people, he'd sent food to the ravens, and he'd welcomed them to his home, providing supplies for the House of Whispers to build more permanent housing. However, his good will had ended there. No matter how many times Lyana and Xander had come to his door in the following days, he refused to hear them. He refused to order an end to the execution of mages on his isle. He refused to send letters of support to the other houses. He refused them any further access to the sacred nest. Short of Lyana using her magic to break her way inside, they'd reached an impasse. To Xander, a man of diplomacy, there was no bigger frustration. "All I mean is we need to consider other ways to convince the rest of the houses, ones with more amicable outcomes."

His queen huffed—not an outright disagreement, which he'd take as a win. They were silent the rest of the way down the steps.

"Xander?" she finally asked as they reached the bottom. His wings had started to spread in anticipation of the sky, but they fell still at the sound of her voice. "I know we have so much to do, and so little time, but do you think, maybe, we could take a short walk?"

The expression on her face spoke of wonder, all her attention on the ornate bridge lit by soft lantern light leading deeper into the city. He'd been ready to say no—there was too much to do, too much to plan—but the twinkle in her eyes made him swallow the refusal. For the first time since they'd landed in the House of Song, she looked a bit like the princess he remembered, full of awe and curiosity, not weighed down by responsibility. The sight brought a warm tingle to his skin.

"I suppose we have time for a walk," he conceded.

Lyana smiled up at him. The look no longer brought a flutter to his heart, but it did smooth the tension from his frame. Maybe they both needed a break, no matter how small. And he had to admit, he, too, was curious about this foreign city neither of them had taken the opportunity to explore.

They walked arm in arm over the bridge, marveling at a scene that was beautiful by day, but glorious by night. Since the city was composed almost entirely of wood, Cytrene was lit by contained colonies of firebugs instead of flame lanterns. Their muted glow softened the evening ambience—a mood enhanced by the fountains cascading along and arching across nearly every street, the water sparkling like starlight descended from the sky. Soothing splashes mixed with tingling chimes to create a musical backdrop. Everywhere Xander looked, bright colors weaved through the shadows, a mixture of floral carpets and sculptural accents. The City of Love lived up to its name, a romantic paradise, though the very thought made his chest tighten.

Strolling among the songbirds, he and Lyana looked every part the mates they pretended to be. No one here would guess the raven king and queen slept in different beds, that they dreamed of holding other lovers in their arms, that their union was just as flimsy as this world around them, suspended in air and held aloft by shredding threads, as temporary as a fleeting thought. But Xander knew, and with each passing day it was becoming harder to maintain the ruse.

"Lyana?"

"Xander?"

Nervous laughter spilled from their lips.

"You first," he said, not even sure what he'd been going to ask anyway. "Please."

She stopped halfway across the next bridge and put her hands against the banister, looking down at the flowing water as an expression he couldn't read passed over her face, there then gone. He took the spot by her side and leaned his forearms on the wooden rail. Shadows darted and danced beneath the surface of the river, flashing as iridescent scales caught the light.

"I like those, by the way," she murmured, indicating his arm guards. He'd been rubbing the polished metal with his thumb subconsciously. "They suit you. Are they new?"

Xander stood and tucked his arms behind his back, removing the weapons from sight as the memory of Cassi's knife at his throat stirred. He didn't know why he still wore them, just as he didn't know why he still had that leather-bound diary tucked against his breastbone, hidden beneath the folds of his jacket. They were a comfort and a curse—things from which he couldn't be freed.

He cleared his throat before answering, "They were a gift."

"Oh?" Her curiosity was piqued. "From who?"

Xander held back a grimace. *I should've known that would happen.* The name scratched its way up his throat, coming out strangled. "Cassi."

"Oh."

An uncomfortable silence stretched, the sort he couldn't help but note he never experienced with her friend. The problem with Cassi had been losing himself to their conversations, until time and duty both seemed distant ideals, a fact he now knew had been the point all along. She'd been lying and leading him in circles, all the while plotting his demise.

Was he so different?

Now, Xander was the liar—to his people, to his world. He didn't want the avians to live in fear. He didn't want the houses to crumble. But the isles were going to fall, no matter what they did, and every passing day he lived without confessing that ugly truth the guilt thickened. His every proclamation was drenched in false hope, and it ate away at his soul.

How had Cassi lived like this?

How did Lyana?

Maybe that was what he'd been going to ask before—how she kept a smile on her face and the wonder in her eyes, how she carried on, knowing the doom that lay ahead.

"I've been speaking to her," Lyana confessed softly and Xander's heart lurched inside his chest. "That's what I was trying to say earlier. I've been speaking to Cassi, and I'm not sure why I didn't tell you sooner, but I should've. I asked her to spy for us, and she's been giving me information about what's happening on the other isles and down beneath the mist."

On some level, he must have known. How else had she been

getting the information she'd been sharing at their meetings? Obviously, Cassi was the source. Yet upon his hearing it, disappointment carved a hollow inside his chest, a feeling he'd been trying to ignore every morning since first waking from a dreamless sleep in the House of Song. It was better this way—seeing her would only bring him pain—but if he were honest, it was an ache he welcomed.

"Is she...?"

"She's in Da'Kin with Malek," Lyana answered, sensing the question he couldn't complete. "Her body is, at least. He's not sure how to heal her yet, or maybe he's not willing. I don't know. But I do know she's doing everything she can to help our cause."

"So you've forgiven her?"

"No." The word was adamant, yet a moment later, the harsh lines of her face softened. "No. I don't know. I guess I understand her, knowing Malek, knowing the prophecy, knowing the impossible choice placed before her. But every time I look at her it stings, and I can't quite erase the hurt. I suppose it's probably how you feel every time you look at me."

"What?" Xander frowned. "I don't—"

"It's all right," she interrupted. "I deserve it. I lied to you, in the worst way possible. I wasn't thinking about you or about him, or about the relationship you both share. I was thinking about myself. And I don't know if I ever told you how sorry I am for treating you the way I did, but I am, Xander. From the bottom of my heart, I'm so very sorry."

"I know."

"And he is too."

Xander lifted his face to the sky, searching the forest canopy for the bright spot of the moon. His cheek burned beneath the weight of her stare, and his voice was hardly louder than a whisper as he said, "I know."

That didn't stop it from hurting.

He'd forgiven Lyana, and she was wrong—it didn't hurt every time he saw her. But the ache was there whenever he thought of Rafe, a blow far deeper than the one she'd struck, sharpened by time. For all Xander knew, his brother carried the same scar from how quickly he'd been banished, with no thought for his defense. They'd cut each other, and the wounds were still bleeding. He wasn't sure when they'd heal.

"There's one more thing I should probably tell you before I lose my courage," Lyana started. "Rafe—"

"Your Majesties!"

They spun, wings slapping together in their surprise. A raven guard landed behind them, his feathers inky as he offered a deep bow.

"What happened?" Xander asked, all personal thoughts fleeing at the worry written across the man's face. The role of king settled on him like a mantle.

"A letter arrived while you were gone, and Helen insisted you be informed of the news immediately." The man paused to swallow, and Xander felt his stomach drop all the way to his toes. "There's been an earthquake in the House of Paradise."

The gods, he silently cursed and lifted his fist to his mouth to cover his frown. Beside him, Lyana tensed. Whatever time they thought they had was gone. Mnesme's god stone would be the next to fall.

Visions flashed across his mind—of his people crying, of their screams, of his city engulfed by mist and his isle sinking beneath the waves. Soon, the House of Paradise would experience the same terror. Soon, they'd lose everything. And if there was even a shred of comfort he could provide, an ounce of solace, any lie was worth it. He would say and do whatever he needed to ease the pain headed their way.

Resolve hardened around his heart like a shield.

"Go, find Helen and tell her we'll be there shortly," Xander ordered. When the man disappeared into the shadows of the trees, he returned his attention to Lyana. "What were you saying? About Rafe?"

"Huh?" She shook her head as though clearing her thoughts. Clarity sparked like green fire in her eyes, then quickly dampened. "It was nothing. It's not important."

Xander took her hand, studying her face. "You're sure?"

"Yes. He's safe. He's with friends."

"Friends?"

The word popped out drenched in unintentional shock. The brother he remembered was a brooding recluse who pushed everyone away, and now he had friends? Who? How? What had happened to him beneath the mist? Questions Xander had been suppressing for days bubbled from the depths, a topic he'd been avoiding now more intriguing than ever, as though Lyana's apology had opened a door he hadn't realized he'd locked.

"Later," Lyana pleaded, the word carrying the weight of a promise as she tilted her chin toward the sky. Moonlight spilled through a break in the trees, casting her skin in a luminescent glow and reminding him she was more than just his queen. She was a servant of the gods, and right now her power was needed elsewhere.

"Let's go," Xander agreed, pushing all the selfish desires of his heart aside. "Helen's waiting."

13

LYANA

The raven camp was still beneath the moonlight as Lyana crept through hastily erected tents, leaving the royal quarters behind. The meeting with Helen had been quick. They were leaving for the House of Paradise tomorrow, which meant she had one final night to enact the plan she'd been concocting for days, the one she'd conceived as she used her magic to calm the House of Song and spotted a handful of knowing eyes among the crowd. Unlike in the past, she'd already filled Xander in and acquired his approval. Not that his disapproval would have stopped her, but still—she was trying to be better, fairer, more open than the king she'd left to stew in the mist.

"I have an idea, Xander," she'd told him after Helen left their spacious canvas palace. The sight of a space far too large for just two people had left them feeling guilty when ravens were still sleeping beneath open skies, not even a pillow to rest their heads upon. "I'm not sure it's one you'll like, but I want to be honest and I don't want to go behind your back anymore."

His brow had furrowed. "What?"

"I want to put a personal guard together."

"That sounds wise."

"...formed of mages."

He'd gone rigid.

"Hear me out. No one needs to know they're mages—not yet, anyway. But I want ravens with magic to understand we support them. And we're going to need every soldier we can get as more of the eggs hatch and the rift widens. I can help train them. I can—"

"Do it," he'd cut in, no ounce of doubt in his tone.

"Really?"

"Yes. If you're able to find a mage among our people, do whatever you can to help them."

"I'm glad you said that." She'd paused, pulling her lower lip into her mouth in a moment of hesitation before blurting, "Because I already identified five."

His eyes had about fallen from their sockets with disbelief. Lyana explained how she could sense the power in their spirits, and how she'd spent the past few days quietly using bits of magic around camp and searching for awareness in people's eyes. He didn't understand what she meant until she described the secret beauty of magic and the golden sparks dancing around her fingers, invisible to him, yet so clear to her—so clear to any mage, including the woman who would be her first visit of the night.

Lyana stopped beside a tent near the outskirts of the clearing and called upon her magic, letting it simmer beneath her skin. A single soul rested at peace on the other side of the canvas, alone and sleeping, exactly as she'd hoped. Pushing her hand through the flaps, she ducked inside. The woman woke immediately, her heart leaping in her chest as her spirit filled with fear. Recognition sparked in her deep brown eyes and she stumbled from her cot. Waves of ebony hair spilled over her shoulders, blending with her wings, as she swept into a deep curtsy.

"My queen."

"Please don't be frightened," Lyana hastily whispered. "I'm not here to hurt you. What's your name?"

The woman swallowed, her lips pursed and her throat tight. She was older than Lyana by a few years, but age didn't matter when speaking to a monarch. Despite her obvious reluctance, she answered. "Amara, my queen."

"Amara," Lyana said as she stepped farther into the shadows of the small tent, letting the flap fall behind her. The sounds of the forest slipped away, replaced by tense silence. "Do you know why I'm here?"

Awareness sparked in the corners of the woman's eyes, like diamonds in the dark, but she shook her head in a silent *no*.

"I know you've seen my power." Lyana lifted her palm and released the smallest tendril of her magic. Brilliant gold sparks flared to life, illuminating the space between them and casting a sunlit glow upon Amara's pale skin. The raven dropped her gaze to the display, then jerked it back up, alarm written across her face. "I know you have magic, too."

"Your Majesty, please. I don't—"

"It's all right," Lyana crooned, aching to use her power to calm Amara's spirit. The woman's hands trembled. Her dread dug into Lyana's soul like claws. But unlike Malek, she would give people a choice, and if they chose terror, the fault lay in her. "You don't need to say anything. You don't need to explain. I won't even ask what type of magic you have, though I sense the earth in your spirit. Unlike most people in our world, I didn't come here to hurt you. I know the terror of living with our secret, but I also know magic is a gift from the gods, and I don't want the mages of our world to live in fear any longer."

She waited for Amara to relax, but her body remained as tense as a bow held taut, one second from snapping. It had been her intention to sit with the woman and practice some magic, to prove she meant no harm, but it was clear that would be too much for tonight. Instead, she made her offer, hoping the hours alone would change Amara's mind.

"I came here tonight to ask you a question, and if you say no, then I will never bother you again. Your secret will be safe, and no one will learn the truth of your power from me. You'll be able to go on living the way you always have been. But if you are tired of living in fear, if you are tired of hiding something that feels as much a part of you as the raven who shares your soul, if you are tired of wondering what you could do once freed of the chains that bind you, then please consider my words. I'm looking to form a personal guard, and I'll be visiting four others tonight who share our secret. If you want to learn how to use your magic, if you want to unleash your power, if you want to fight at my side to save our world, then come to my tent at dawn and pledge your allegiance. We'll be flying to the House of Paradise at midday, and I would be thrilled to have you by my side. I know the idea of discovering who you really are and what you're truly capable of might be terrifying, but embracing my magic is the best thing I've ever done, and I want to give every mage I can the opportunity to find their inner strength as well. It may be a while before our people understand, but I assure you, the gods are on our side."

While she spoke, Lyana's power filled the tent, spreading more and more, so that when she finished they were surrounded by the shimmering beauty of her magic. It was the sun and the stars. It was Aethios come to life. And even after all she'd experienced, the sight of it left her breathless with pride.

But that was her journey.

This was Amara's.

Difficult as it was, Lyana pulled the power back beneath her skin, snuffing out the light. Amara studied her as the glow faded, those dark eyes missing nothing yet giving even less away.

"If I don't see you in the morning, please know you can always change your mind and I'll be there waiting whenever you're ready."

Then she departed, leaving the woman to her thoughts. The hour was late, and she had four more souls to visit before dawn broke, chasing all her time away.

Despite her best efforts, the meetings all passed in similar fashions. The older man she visited next held his cards even closer to his chest than Amara had. The older woman was intrigued, but just as quiet, her gaze darting almost constantly to the corner of the room where her toddler slept. The youngest of the night, a boy of fifteen was the most eager, perhaps through the folly of youth, though Lyana sensed in him a kindred spirit. He was the only one to confess to his magic, revealing himself as a *hydro'kine*. And her final stop, a man around the same age as Amara, still young enough not to be mated, had been calmer than the others. She wasn't sure if that was better or worse.

All in all, the night had gone less well than she'd hoped, yet better than she'd expected. By the time she crawled back into the royal tent, she was ready to collapse for a few short hours of sleep, but the gods had other plans.

Cassi's spirit hovered invisibly over the bed.

With a sigh, Lyana stepped quietly around the edge of the room, careful to avoid Xander's slumbering form. Just as every night before, he'd left her the large cot in the corner and stretched out upon the hard floor, forgoing comfort for propriety no matter how many times she told him not to. The bed was big enough to share, but their past loomed larger for him. Or perhaps he really was just that polite. In truth, she couldn't tell.

"I hope you have good news," Lyana muttered as she curled on her side and dropped her head upon the pillow. She couldn't see it, but she could feel a snort riffle through Cassi's spirit, and it brought a smile to her lips as sleep took her.

The dream formed quickly. One moment, she was in the makeshift raven camp on the outskirts of the House of Song, and the next she was back in the crystal palace of Sphaira, overlooking the ivory landscape of her icy homeland. Longing panged deep in her chest, but she stifled it as she turned to her spy.

"Please tell me you have good news."

Cassi crossed her arms. "Only if your idea of good is an earthquake in the House of Paradise."

Lyana groaned. "No. Definitely not."

"Too bad."

"Tell me anyway."

Cassi launched into the tale, recounting the terror that betook the citizens of Hyadria as their isle trembled beneath them. The damage to the city wasn't severe, but it was an omen of things to come. Now that the earthquakes had started, they'd continue until the House of Paradise fell from the sky.

Lyana asked questions, Cassi supplied answers, and when the topic was exhausted, they moved on to the rest of the isles and the world below, same as they had every meeting before. Turned out the relationship between a queen and her spy was much the same as the one between a princess and her best friend—sarcastic, teasing, and most of all, comfortable. So comfortable, there were moments Lyana could almost forget everything that had happened, everything Cassi had done, as though these translucent walls weren't a dream, but real, and they were two girls back home on some grand adventure.

Then she remembered, and the truth of Cassi's betrayal cut anew, stealing her breath until she had to look away to escape the pain. Forgiveness was a fickle thing, swinging like a pendulum, so close one moment and so very far the next. As a single name spilled from Cassi's lips, a burning ache cleaved Lyana's chest in two, sending all thoughts of reconciliation into the stratosphere.

"I have news of Rafe."

Rafe, whom Cassi had maimed. Rafe, whom Cassi delivered into Malek's fiendish hands. Rafe, who was now his own worst nightmare come to life, all because of the woman standing before her.

Lyana spun and pressed her palm against the crystal wall for balance. Her world swayed as flames danced before her eyes. Deep within the inferno, she imagined his face, and the determination in his vibrant blue eyes pulled her back, freeing her the way he always did.

"Is he all right?"

"I'm worried for him."

"Why?" Lyana swallowed her pain and turned back to Cassi. "What's happened?"

"Malek is closing in. He's had people following them ever since the ship left Karthe, and they can only evade his mages for so long. Eventually they'll run out of supplies. Eventually someone will get hurt. And though it won't be Rafe, I'm not sure what the loss, what the guilt, will do to him."

It would destroy him.

"What can we do?"

"I don't know."

"Where can he go?"

"I don't know."

"Then why—" Lyana froze as an idea sparked like metal to the flint, a bright flame flaring in the deepest dark. "What's the one place Malek would never send his mages? What's the one place he wouldn't dare bring this fight?"

Cassi knitted her brows, her silvery eyes as vacant as the fog. In an instant, they sharpened into blades. "The world above."

"Exactly."

A laugh escaped her spy's lips at the sheer audacity of Lyana's newest plot—to bring a man who was half-dragon to a world entrenched in their fear of the beasts, to bring a ship of mages to a land riddled with a hatred of magic. It was ludicrous. It was absurd.

Cassi grinned. "It's brilliant."

"I know."

"But where—"

"To the raven guest quarters on the outer isle of the House of Peace," Lyana interjected, her thoughts already racing ahead. Meant only as a rest stop for traders and diplomatic convoys, the guest quarters weren't large enough to house an entire populace, which was why she and Xander had brought the ravens to the House of Song. There was, however, more than enough space for a small crew of mages to reside in. "Malek wouldn't dare bring another magic fight so close to the god stones, especially against a crew of experienced mages, and with trade come to a standstill now that the House of Whispers has fallen, the rooms will be empty. I asked Luka to have the guest quarters for all the houses stocked before he left, just in case, so there should be plenty of food. Rafe will be safe there."

"Assuming he goes along with it."

"Well, yes," Lyana muttered, plummeting back down to earth. "There's that."

To a ship full of wingless mages, escaping to lands floating precariously among the clouds might not be ideal. If they didn't go, Rafe wouldn't either. He was too loyal to leave them to face Malek's wrath alone.

"You'll just have to convince him."

"Right." The hesitant edge to the word made the hairs at the back of Lyana's neck stand on end. Her spy was hiding something. She was hedging.

"Cassi, you *have* spoken to Rafe, haven't you?"

Silence.

"You spoke to him days ago, right? When I ordered you to go to him immediately and tell him about the shadow beast, and the eggs, and the truth of the god stones. You did as I said, didn't you?"

The owl opened her mouth, then wordlessly closed it.

"Didn't you?"

"I— I—" Panic drained the color from Cassi's cheeks. She darted her gaze about the room as though searching for any way to delay, and then a molten streak in her irises flared. Cocking her hip to the side, she jutted out her chin in a stubborn look Lyana recognized. "Have *you* told Xander the truth about Rafe, the way I asked you?"

I tried, sort of... Lyana bristled. "That's different."

"How?"

"Because the fate of the world doesn't depend on my honesty."

"Doesn't it?"

"Cassi!" She growled and flailed her arms in frustration. "That thing could be after him, and he's totally unaware. I'd be far more afraid of that than of Malek's mages. You need to tell him everything. Now. That's an order from your queen."

"Oh, is—"

Before Cassi had time to finish her snappy retort, Lyana snatched her spy's spirit and flung it from her mind. The dream ripped apart and she jolted awake, sucking in a sharp breath as she jerked to a seated position. Her heart thundered, but she ignored the pounding and lifted her face toward the spirit cowering in the shadows.

"Now," she demanded.

Cassi fled and Lyana dropped her head into her palms.

"Now, what?"

"Xander!"

She leapt about five feet in the air at the sound of his voice. If not for her wings, she would have fallen over. As it was, while she righted herself a wind stirred in the tent, rustling their meager supplies. Her king was no longer on the floor, but hunched over his desk, a finger saving his place in the middle of an unrolled scroll. One of his brows lifted.

"What are you doing awake?" she asked, her voice still breathy with shock.

"It's past dawn."

"It is?"

Forgetting Xander, and Cassi, and the dream that wasn't really a dream, Lyana darted across the room to fling open the tent flaps. Peach light chased the darkness away and cast the canvas sea in a rosy glow, the trees around the meadow silhouetted by the sun. Standing in the grass before her, their feet wet with morning dew and their eyes wary, were three of the mages she'd met what felt like days and not hours before.

A wave of relief washed through her.

They'd come.

Not all, but enough—the beginning of her army.

14

CASSI

D*on't be awake*, Cassi thought as she cut through the ever-lightening fog, urgency fueling her speed. *Please, don't be awake.*

Lyana was right. It was time to face Rafe and her guilt, and the brutal truth of what she'd done. He deserved to know whatever information she could provide, especially when she was the one responsible for bringing him into this fight in the first place.

The dark outline of a ship broke through the haze and Cassi dove for *The Wanderer*, not pausing to hover over her mother's bed or listen to crew gossip, instead oozing through wooden planks into the room she'd been avoiding for days. Rafe slept beneath a mesh blanket, the fire in his wings stifled by the metal, but his spirit still blazed. Harsh lines cut into his brow and sweat dampened his skin. Unintelligible protests spilled from his lips as he thrashed back and forth, wrestling with his nightmares. Before she lost her courage, Cassi pressed a phantom palm to his brow and sank into his dreams.

They were black.

A violent storm of shadow and heat swept her away, pulling her deeper into the vortex. No up. No down. No color. No light. It was ebony chaos. Cassi had never experienced anything like it, as though she were fighting with a demon and not a man for control of his mind. The spirit didn't feel like Rafe. It was dark and deadly, foreign in a way she couldn't explain. Every time she tried to grab it, the force slithered away like a snake in the night, slipping through her fingers, gone.

Come on, she silently cursed, flailing in the abyss like a bird caught in a winter storm, helpless against the furious winds. Her magic flared. She sank deeper into Rafe's mind, fighting to find the human within the beast. *Come on.*

All at once, the darkness imploded.

Cassi reeled, digging her power like anchors into any foothold she could find. Color and light burst into dazzling life. The sudden clarity stung her eyes. But she recognized Rafe in this madness and latched on to his spirit. Control came easily. The bedlam calmed. The swirling hues slowed. Cassi warped his thoughts and twisted his dreams into a scene they both recognized—the practice yards outside the raven castle. Same golden dirt. Same blue skies. Same still air. They'd spent many afternoons there sparring beneath the sun, Rafe as her unaware teacher while she'd categorized his every strategy, his every move, saving each morsel of information for the fight when she would need it most. When that horrible day finally came, she'd won the battle, but at the cost of her soul.

Dispelling the memories, Cassi placed her finishing touches on the dream. Rafe appeared across from her, brandishing his twin swords, made not of practice wood but of steel. The wings at his back were raven black, soft and feathered, no longer simmering with flame. But the wild look in his eyes burned. Before she could open her mouth to speak, he charged. She could have raised her weapon. She could have taken to the skies. She could have done any number of things, but she didn't.

She froze.

Rafe closed the distance. With a yell, he raised his weapon. Time seemed to slow. The metal edge flashed in the sun and a bronze lock of hair swirled before her eyes. The sneer on his lips flattened as the anger drained from his face. But it was too late to stop. In that split second, all either of them could do was watch as the blade sank deep beneath her skin.

With a gasp, Rafe released the hilt and jerked away. Cassi stared at the sword protruding from her chest. Blood soaked through her clothes, spreading like a spilled drink down her stomach, a flowing river of red. She dropped to her knees, woozy and light-headed. The agony stole her breath. Dots spotted her vision. Her body swayed in an invisible breeze.

"Cassi?" Rafe whispered.

The horror in his eyes broke her from the trance. On some level she'd wanted this to be real, and her mind let it be so. But she couldn't let him dwell in his remorse, no matter how much she welcomed the pain.

"I deserved that," she groaned as she gripped the leather-wrapped hilt and pulled the sword from her chest, rising to her feet. With a thought, the blood vanished and the wound disappeared. She flipped the blade, gripping it by the metal edge as she offered it to him. "And maybe I deserve to die, but unfortunately, I can't die here. Though if it makes you feel better, you can stab me again. This is, after all, your dream."

"I didn't— I wasn't—"

He shook his head, fighting the confusion that so often struck the first time someone experienced her peculiar magic. As he took the sword and slid his twin blades back into the scabbard crisscrossing between his wings, relief flooded his gaze—relief, she assumed, at not becoming a murderer. It was quickly followed by awareness, then anger, then grief as drop by drop his memories fell back into place. A storm gathered in his blue eyes. By the time he returned his attention to her, his guard was fully raised.

"Why are you here?" The words were sharp and demanding.

Because Lyana ordered me to come. Because she finally called me out. Because I only just found the strength to face you after everything I've done.

Cassi swallowed. "Because you're in danger."

Dark laughter escaped his lips. "That's funny, coming from you."

The blow hit harder than the blade he'd just put through her chest.

"I—" Cassi broke off as a knot tightened in her throat. *I'm sorry.* He wouldn't want to hear it, not after everything he'd been through. "I did what I thought I had to do."

The wings at his back transformed into those of a dragon, drenched in fire, the heat enough to sting her cheeks. His lips curled as he growled, "Get the hell out of my mind."

"I have a message from Lyana."

The fire shrank as his brows furrowed. A moment later, his jaw clenched and the blaze returned. "I don't believe you."

"I'm telling the truth," Cassi implored. "Malek ordered me to kill Xander, but I couldn't do it. I let him capture me, and I confessed. He locked me in the dungeons, and I would have died there when the House of Whispers fell if he and Lyana hadn't come to save my life. I owe them everything, and I've pledged my life and loyalty to their cause. You might not believe me, but all I've ever wanted to do is help save the world. For the longest time, I thought Malek's way was the only way to see that through, but I know better now. Lyana is going to save everyone. I know she will, as long as she stays focused. But if she's distracted, if all her thoughts are set on worrying about you, she'll never seal the rift."

A muscle in his jaw ticked. "Where is she now?"

"In the House of Song with Xander. They've been crowned

King and Queen of the House of Whispers, and they're using their positions to try to prepare the isles for what's to come."

Rafe closed his eyes, inhaling a long slow breath as pain cut deep grooves along his brow.

"They're mates in name only," she tried to explain.

His eyelids flew open as his fists clenched. "I don't need comfort from you. You say you have a message from Lyana? Well, what is it?"

"I have two," Cassi said before taking a deep breath to calm the nerves racing across her chest. He was so angry, and he had every right to be, but this was so much worse than facing Lyana, than facing Xander. The worst she'd done to them was lie, but the man before her had been undone by her actions, completely destroyed by them. She deserved another stab wound to the heart. In fact, she welcomed it. "The first she thought I gave you days ago, so please don't blame her for being out of contact. It's my own fault it took me so long to come. I was in the sacred nest the day the House of Whispers fell from the sky and I saw something you won't believe. The god stone didn't fail. It broke open. It was an egg, and the creature inside was unlike any I've seen before, covered in black scales and oozing shadow, as though formed of darkness—"

"I've seen it."

"You've seen it?" She straightened her spine in surprise. "And you lived?"

"I don't think it wants to hurt me," he said slowly, as though trying to process his thoughts while he spoke them. "I think it—I think it tried to help me."

"Tell me everything."

He scoffed at the demand.

Cassi's nostrils flared. "So I can tell Lyana. So we can save the world."

"How do I know you won't go running back to your king?"

"You don't."

The sun beat down harder on the practice fields but neither of them moved. The sky was cloudless, the air thick, as though sensing the unspoken challenge. There was no proof Cassi could provide to show her loyalty. He had to decide what mattered more —his fury or the risk he was taking with Lyana's life, with all their lives, if she were telling the truth and he refused to believe her.

Rafe sighed. His sensitive side won out, and he reluctantly told her of his one night in Karthe and his run-in with Malek's mages. Cassi's jaw dropped open in disbelief as he described the creature who'd slipped from the shadows to snap his attacker's neck, giving him the opening to run.

"And that's not all," Rafe finished softly. "It comes to me at night, in my dreams, and shows me horrible visions."

She sucked in a sharp breath, remembering the impenetrable darkness that had devoured her the second she'd sunk into his mind. "Was it here? Tonight?"

"I had a nightmare, yes." He shrugged. "As to whether it was here, you would know better than me. Did you see it?"

A frown turned her lips. Rafe had been alone when she'd entered his rooms, not another man or beast in sight, and yet, something had been there, in his thoughts. She'd felt it. "No," she murmured. "But I wonder..."

The creature was part man, part dragon.

Rafe was part man, part dragon.

All that separated them was a split-second victory during the soul joining, one of the beast and one of the human. In manner, in attitude, in outward appearance, the two were a thousand miles apart. Yet maybe, they were far more similar than she'd ever realized.

"We've never been able to figure out how dragons communicate," she offered into the silence. "We've never understood what called them to this world, what force lured them through the rift—our magic or something more. What if they can communicate with their minds?"

"What's that got to do with anything? I'm trying to figure out what that thing is doing inside my head. What—" He broke off suddenly, alarm making the flames at his back erupt. Understanding settled like a heavy mantle on his shoulders. "When you said the god stones were eggs, you meant dragon eggs, didn't you?"

She nodded slowly.

Rafe stumbled back as though struck.

"It's communicating with me mentally," he murmured, as though so many pieces he'd been trying to force together had suddenly fallen into place. "It thinks I'm one of them."

"You're not," she hastened to say.

The broken look in his eyes made her heart tear in two.

"Are you so sure?"

"Yes." She gripped his shoulders, ignoring the fact that he hated her, and ignoring the fact that she'd done this to him, pretending for a moment that they were those two people back in the practice yards in the House of Whispers who'd almost felt like friends. "You're nothing like that thing. It kills without remorse. It has no soul. It wants to destroy us. For all my faults, I know your heart, Rafe, and though this world has given you nothing but pain, there isn't anything you wouldn't do to save it."

He swallowed as a grim determination lit his eyes. Cassi stepped back, dropping her hands from his jacket, aware that in the heat of the moment she'd crossed a line.

"What was your second message?" he finally said, his tone emotionless as he drew the conversation back to neutral ground.

All she wanted to do was pester him with questions, but he needed time to consider this new revelation for himself. And she was quickly losing control of his mind. Awareness pressed in at all edges as time sped forward, carrying him into the new day. She wouldn't be able to force his spirit to continue sleeping for much longer.

"Lyana's worried for you. I know you've evaded three of Malek's ships since leaving Karthe, but he's closing in. He's using *dormi'kine* mages to follow you, and he has armies waiting at every port. Eventually your supplies will run out. Eventually he'll catch you—"

"What's your point?"

"We figured out a place where you can hide safely, a place he wouldn't dare try to attack you."

"Where?"

"The raven guest quarters in the outer isle of the House of Peace."

A grimace passed over his face.

"They're empty," she pressed before he had the chance to refuse outright. "And they're fully stocked with supplies. Think on it. Before you say no, please, just take the time to think on it."

The castle beside them vanished into a swirling vortex of color. The edges of the practice fields grew fuzzy, the wall disappearing as the sky overhead flared with a rainbow hue. All around them, the dream collapsed. Cassi took Rafe's hands, trying to hold on.

"Is there anything you want me to tell Lyana?" she shouted as pressure pushed against her chest, lifting her feet from the ground and forcing her to pump her wings. The chaos swallowed her ankles, creeping up her legs, her body slowly dissolving into the maelstrom.

"Tell her—" Rafe clutched her fingers as his gaze ticked from side to side, uncertain. "Tell her—"

Cassi's control broke.

Rafe woke, throwing her from his mind, and she careened back into the world. On the bed, he gasped and jerked upright. His head snapped toward the ceiling. Though he searched the empty room for any sign of her spirit, he couldn't sense her hovering in the air above his head.

I'm here, she wanted to scream. *Just tell me.*

Instead, a dejected sigh escaped his lips, and he dropped his head into his palms. Cassi groaned, as much as an invisible specter could groan. For better or worse, her work here was done. She'd lost him.

15

RAFE

Rafe sat on the bed, his mind reeling. The shadow creature was half-dragon. The shadow creature was what he would have become if his soul hadn't won dominance in the joining. The shadow creature was communicating with him through his dreams.

That day on the ship...

When Rafe had faced that dragon and screamed at it to stop, the beast had actually heard him. It wasn't a coincidence. It wasn't an accident or a fluke. He'd sent a command, and the dragon had listened.

I can speak to them...with my mind.

He inhaled sharply and ran his fingers through his hair, jolting to his feet, the information too much to process. With a soft *thud*, the mesh blanket fell from his shoulders and the room around him glowed orange, illuminated by the fire in his wings. Rafe shoved on his boots, then paced, the steady drum of his steps calming his racing heart.

What does this mean?

What does this mean?

There was only one way to find out. After turning on his heels, Rafe stomped to the door and jerked it open. One look at his face and Jolt sidled up to the wall as he stormed past. Within moments, he emerged on deck.

"Rafe!" Brighty immediately called, as though she'd been waiting all morning for him to walk through that door. "Just the man I— Hey!"

He nudged her aside, ignoring the affronted expression on her face, and took to the sky, soaring up to the crow's nest on the main deck, surrounded by nothing but fog.

"Good morning to you too!" she shouted.

I'll deal with that later. He sighed as he perched on the small wooden platform and closed his eyes. How exactly did one go about mental communication with a dragon? Did he just send the thought out into the world and hope it stuck? Could he sense them? Would they answer him?

Hello? he silently shouted.

Are you there?

Can anyone hear me?

A frown curved his lips. He felt utterly ridiculous.

Breathing deeply, Rafe tried to clear his mind. Letting the sway of the ship pull him into a meditative state, he reached out with his newfound senses. Immediately, the crew's magic stimulated a hunger deep in his stomach, their power an alluring scent on the breeze. Rafe pushed past it, extending himself farther, imagining he was soaring on the winds, not crouched atop a ship, his spirit one with the air.

Heat tickled at the edge of awareness.

Rafe dove into that sensation, the subtle burn grazing his thoughts almost like a touch, stirring up images of smoke and fire. He reached out, moving on instinct, not really sure what he was doing. A force reached back.

Where?

He sent the word through the connection.

There was no response—of course not. They didn't know his language. The creature hadn't spoken to him in words, but in images and thoughts, in memories. Switching tactics, Rafe imagined himself lost and wandering, no sense of place. He pushed that unsettled, aimless sensation down the bond, along with thoughts of fog too thick for his sight to penetrate.

Then he waited.

And waited.

Hunger flashed across his mind, acute and yearning, making his stomach ache with a hollowness he knew couldn't be his own. The sweet tang of magic made his mouth water. A sense of intention, of direction, pulsed from the dragon's mind, almost as if it were inviting him to follow. There were mages close by, and the beast intended on paying them a visit.

Rafe severed the connection and leapt from the crow's nest, his wings catching him before he crashed into the deck. Two quick beats and he landed beside the captain. His sudden appearance did little to rattle her. She kept her hands on the wheel and her feet braced, not bothering to turn her head.

"Is there a city close by?" he demanded, an urgency to his voice. "Any place with concentrated magic?"

Captain Rokaro offered a sidelong glance. "Why?"

"Please, I can't explain now. I just need to know."

She shrugged and returned her gaze to the sea. "Depends on which direction you mean."

"West," he said, closing his eyes and trying to remember where the pull of the dragon's mind had led him. "Southwest, maybe, but mostly west."

"Then there's no city."

Dejection coursed through him. He'd been so sure.

"But," the captain continued, "there's a trading outpost, maybe a day's sail away by natural means, a few hours if we really pushed with our magic."

Rafe cursed under his breath.

The dragon was already on its way. They'd be too late to stop it, too late to help. Unless…

"Why, Rafe?" Captain asked again.

There was no time.

"I'll be back," he muttered as he turned on his heels.

"Rafe."

His wings were already pumping as he ran to the side of the ship and jumped, pushing off the banister as he launched into the sky.

"Rafe!"

The wind quickly swallowed the sound of Captain Rokaro's voice. Yellow currents cut through the fog, her magic chasing where her body couldn't. The snapping of sails and groaning of wood carried across the sea. He didn't turn to watch the ship careen in his direction. He disappeared into the mist.

In the bright silver nothingness, Rafe had to rely on his inhuman senses. The bird still deep inside his soul navigated not visually but instinctually, aware of north and south and east and west despite the opaque haze. And the dragon followed still another intuition, one new to him, but just as innate.

Connecting with the other beast came easier the second time, as if, once established, the mental bond could never quite be severed. Its spirit still smelled of hunger and fire, determination shooting down the current as it chased the scent of magic. Deep in their shared thoughts, Rafe lost all awareness of time. Hours might have passed, perhaps minutes. As he closed the distance, the images came sharper and the feelings stronger. He knew the moment the dragon arrived at the outpost. Satisfaction hurtled like a spear into his mind, making the beast in him hungry and the human in him pained.

How many were dying?

How many were wounded?

Was he too late?

Magic saturated the sky, close enough that he could pick up the sweetness with his own nose, the rumble in his gut not from his mind but from his own need. The oppressive stench of smoke hit next, stirring a cough as the air grew thin.

He was close.

So close.

Just as the shapes of ships broke through the mist, topped by plumes of black and bursting with orange flares, a wail pierced his ears. Pain infiltrated his thoughts, so immense he nearly dropped from the sky. Fire hurled across the sea, the heat simmering with anger. Desperation clawed at him as the distressed dragon pleaded for his aid.

As Rafe darted around sails, the outpost came into view—a small collection of buildings surrounded by a handful of ships. The spot was meant as a temporary meeting place, no grand castles or sprawling homes, just a few ramshackle gambling halls and warehouses for trade. But the sailors parked there were made of magic, and their power lit the skies. Through the bubbling flame, glittering sparks of every color dove for the same target—bright shoots of light and dark swirls of shadow, crashing waves and tempered fire, blustering winds and, most of all, sharp metals glowing green. Through a break in the flames, he saw the dragon release another stream of fire as a screeching cry bellowed from its throat. Rafe's attention went not to its snout, but to the arrow protruding from its chest and the chain secured by steady *ferro'kine* power, ensuring the beast didn't fly away.

There'd be no escaping now.

The dragon was as good as dead, and though the idea might have once filled him with pleasure, the circumstances were no longer black and white. The human in him cheered. The dragon in him mourned. Agony seared his thoughts, but underneath the hurt, there was a drive and a desire to live he couldn't deny.

Give up, he wanted to say. *It's over.*

But it couldn't. It would fight to the bitter end, not knowing any better, flames flying and wings beating, struggling to change the inevitable.

So close to the battle, yet outside of it, Rafe saw the dragon for exactly what it was—an animal, like any other, running on drives it didn't fully understand. It didn't have ill intent. It didn't mean any harm. It wasn't plotting to destroy the world. It was hungry and hurt, chasing food and resources, fighting to survive in the hostile world it had found itself in—which raised the question, *why?* Why was it here in the first place? From everything he'd learned, the beasts came here chasing magic, and maybe that was true, but it wasn't the complete story.

The dragon collapsed, setting flame to a sail and crushing the roof of a warehouse as it slammed against the outpost. Another arrow punctured its chest, but this time it didn't wail. Steam slipped through its nostrils as its body shuddered. Those blood-red eyes found his through the smoke.

Peace, Rafe thought, sending not the word but his memories of it down their mental connection. Warmth stirred in his chest as he imagined his mother's laughter while they twirled around her rooms, and the soothing quality of her voice as she sang him to sleep. He thought of Lyana, her hands upon his chest and her magic diving into his skin as they lay surrounded by rubble. They'd been on the brink of death, yet he'd been calm and unafraid as her breath washed over his cheeks. The dragon wouldn't understand the scenes, but it might still understand the message. *Be at peace.*

Its eyes slipped closed.

Its body fell still.

Their connection vanished.

Before he was seen, Rafe turned to leave. A tickle at the back of his mind stopped him still. He frowned, hovering in midair. Murmurs rose from the ship deck beneath him, spreading as arms pointed toward him. But it wasn't the people who concerned him. Heat seeped into his thoughts, an invisible scorching that drew his eyes back to the sky.

Another dragon was there.

"The battle isn't done," he cried and sped over the outpost. Skidding to a stop on the moist planks, he landed before the lifeless beast. Mages eyed him warily, not sure what he meant. "There's another—"

A piercing roar cut him off.

Where? Where?

Rafe opened himself up to the dragon, letting the mental bond steal his thoughts.

There.

He looked up just in time to see an avalanche of fire descend from the sky. The inferno crashed upon him, drenching him in waves of flame. His clothes burned. Ash filled his nose. But there was no pain. The heat sank harmlessly into his skin, the blaze not burning him but igniting something within.

The mages around him weren't so lucky. Another blast of fire stole his sight, the flaming tempest as thick as the fog and impossible to see through. But above the sizzle, cries punctuated the attack, some in fear and pain, others in gritty determination.

Stop!

He wasn't sure if the message was for the dragon or the mages. He wanted both to stop. No more destruction. No more killing. But there was only one creature he might force to listen.

Stop, he thought again, this time gripping the mental bond as though with talons. *Go*, he ordered, flooding the connection with thoughts of open skies and freedom and places far, far from here. *Leave. Go. Save yourself.*

Hesitation raced down the line.

Rafe beat his wings, flying up and up and up, until razor-sharp teeth and smoldering scales broke through the raging flames. No longer afraid, he pressed his palms to the dragon's immense chest, its heartbeat thundering against his skin.

Magic prickled the air.

They were running out of time.

Go, he roared, now filling the bond with the awareness of everything the dead beast below had suffered so as to frighten this one into submission. *Go!*

The air stirred as the dragon pumped its wings, once, twice, retreating into the fog. With it gone, the fire drained away, snuffed out by glittering red sparks of *pyro'kine* magic. The smoke cleared, leaving Rafe acutely aware of his position as the only creature left suspended in the sky. Not a sound stirred as he descended, the crunch of his boots on burnt debris loud above the soft sizzle of the water spilling across the outpost to douse the few remaining flames. His clothes still burned, cloth melting away to reveal untainted flesh. Countless eyes watched on as he drew that singing heat beneath his skin. The last thing he needed to be in this crowd was buck naked, though he supposed they might find that sight less shocking than the one currently before them.

Despite the tension, the corners of his lips quirked into a smile.

Let them make of it what they will.

Before the mages could react, in happiness or horror, Rafe fled from the outpost, completely oblivious to the rumors that would soon be churning in his wake.

16

MALEK

"My liege?"

Malek tore open his eyes and stifled his magic, breaking from his meditation. It was a useless exercise anyway. No matter how often he reached out with his power, Lyana refused to respond. No matter how much time he spent visiting the rift, it wouldn't close—not without her help.

Fighting back a sneer, Malek turned. His *ferro'kine* stood in the doorway of the study, her thin lips a grim line. Her black hair hung about her shoulders, unbrushed and unkempt. Only half of the buttons on her jacket were secured. She'd come in haste, which meant this wouldn't be good.

"Jacinta."

"I was visited by a *dormi'kine* this afternoon."

"Who?"

Her gaze darted about the room. "Is it safe to speak?"

"She's not here." Kasiandra, his darling little traitor, the thorn in his side. There was no telling when her haunting spirit might decide to drop in for a visit, but she was, for the moment, absent. "Proceed."

"There's been another incident with the raven."

He clasped his fingers behind his back and squeezed them until his arms began to tremble. If his mage noticed, she didn't say. Though he prided himself on control, he wasn't able to keep the bite from his voice as he asked, "What?"

"It happened not an hour ago. A dragon attacked one of the trading outposts and was brought down. The traders thought they'd won, until the raven appeared from the mist, shouting that the battle wasn't over. Moments later, a second dragon attacked from above. The *dormi'kine* was there, on one of the ships. He said the fire devoured the raven, burning half the outpost before the mages had time to react. Then the beast, for no rhyme or reason, simply disappeared. By the time the flames cleared, the raven stood alone, unscathed among the wreckage."

"Did no one think to catch him?"

"He retreated too quickly."

Fools, Malek seethed, yet deep down he knew it was his own fault. The man was invincible, and on top of that, he'd given him wings. He should have known better. He should have just killed him when he'd had the chance. No amount of information was worth all this, and now the very fate of the world was in jeopardy.

"Say it," he commanded, noting the hesitation in Jacinta's deep brown eyes.

"There were rumors…" she offered slowly.

Of course there were. Every ship in his kingdom was rife with them, and now, nearly every city too. Just last night, he'd received reports of the gossip finally reaching Da'Kin. With his presence so close, only the boldest sailors dared question his position as the King Born in Fire—but in a way that made it worse, giving weight to the words, making them even more alluring. Meanwhile, he could do nothing. To speak out would only feed the flames.

Malek was stuck, and the position left him fuming.

If not for one simple fact, he'd fly into a rage right now—

Kasiandra didn't know. He was sure of it. The owl had spent too much of her life among the royals above the clouds. She wouldn't think to go to the gambling halls for information. She wouldn't dare step foot inside a brothel, not even as a spirit. While she was shrewd in some regards, she was naive in others, exactly as he'd crafted her to be. Though born beneath the mist, she had no idea how this world within the fog truly functioned, and he had to keep it that way.

Lyana could never know what people whispered. But with each passing day the raven remained free, Malek's time ran out. A few more daring feats, and the gossip might grow too large to contain.

"Go on."

"More of the same, but there was one thing I thought might catch your interest. The *dormi'kine* overheard two men suggesting the raven might somehow speak to the beasts. They said he appeared to know of the second dragon's presence before anyone else, as though he'd sensed it, as though, somehow, he was connected to them, perhaps mentally."

Now that *was* intriguing.

It wasn't the first time the thought had entered his mind. They could sense magic across great distances, suggesting some sort of connection to the spirits, but he'd never had proof. Was that why they kept coming through the rift? Were they calling to each other? Calling for help? And if so, could he silence them?

This might be the key to ending the war—or at the very least, to delaying it. He needed more information. For that and so many other reasons, he needed to catch the raven. And if none of his mages were up to the task, then maybe he needed to do it himself.

"Anything else?"

"No, my liege."

"Good. Find Viktor and tell him to prepare my ship. We leave tonight."

"For where?"
Malek's lips twisted into a grin. "For a hunt."

17

LYANA

Hyadria was a notoriously difficult place to locate. It was commonly referred to as the Sky City, but in truth, the famed floating homes and walkways were buried beneath a thick rainforest canopy, nearly impossible to spot from above. The hollowed-out trees fit perfectly into the landscape, the wooden platforms blended with the branches, and the rope bridges looked like little more than vines. Or so she'd been told.

Luckily for Lyana, eyesight wasn't the only sense at her disposal. She would have been able to find the city even without the help of the two escorts who'd been waiting for them at the edge of the House of Paradise. Its inhabitants called out to her, their spirits loud and yearning. Fear, accusation, and anger saturated the air, twisting her gut. Something was terribly wrong.

"How much farther?" she called to their guides.

"We're close, Queen Lyana. Only a few minutes more."

Xander eyed her curiously, then dipped his left wing to swerve closer. "What's wrong?"

"Nothing, yet," she told him, keeping her voice low as they slowed, moving to the back of the flock where their conversation wouldn't carry on the wind. "But something's off. The people—their unrest is palpable."

"From the earthquake, surely?"

"No." Lyana bit her lip to hide her frown. "No, this is something else. They're too united. Their feelings are too similar, as though turned on the same target. Whatever it is, it's happening now."

A horn sounded, announcing their arrival. The raven flock followed the birds of paradise through a narrow break in the foliage, easy to overlook. As soon as they dipped under the tree line, the city emerged. Suspended walkways hung as far as the eye could see, connecting the intricate network of hollowed-out trees housing homes and shops. Terraces circled the wide trunks, stacked at every level, some so low they could barely be seen through the leaves. The ground waited somewhere out of sight, wet and swampy. Under normal circumstances, Lyana wouldn't have been able to take her eyes from the oversized vegetation, some of the vibrant flower petals below as large as her wings. As it was, she could only focus on one thing.

There were no people.

Despite the spirits clinging to her like beggars, not a single soul was visible. The bridges and verandas were vacant.

"Where is everyone?" Lyana asked as soon as they landed behind their escorts on a large wooden platform at the outer edge of the city. An eerie tingle scratched up her spine.

"I'm not sure, Queen Lyana," one of the escorts said, her bewilderment evident. "Perhaps the queen called everyone to the city center."

"Why?"

The two escorts shared a look.

An ominous pit formed in her stomach. "Take us there immediately."

"Queen Lyana," the man beseeched. "We were told to wait here until—"

Uninterested in hearing more, Lyana leapt from the platform. Her magic flared to life beneath her skin, guiding her through the unfamiliar city. Spirits clawed for the power. A buzz charged the air, building and building, toward what she didn't know. There was so much anger, so much hate, all she wanted to do was smother the ugly feelings.

This isn't good.

This definitely isn't good.

The distant drum of an authoritative voice hammered at her ears, but it took a few seconds for her to understand.

"...carries the penalty of death."

No!

Her stomach dropped to her toes. Suddenly, the truth became clear. An execution. That was the charged sensation, the cause for all the rage, and there was only one known reason for executions in the world above.

Please don't let me be too late.

The city center slipped into view. A sprawling platform connected five different tree trunks, each seeming to house a different sector of the palace if the ornate suspended walkways and buildings were anything to go by. Above the crowd, on a balcony carved from gleaming white stone, the royal family presided—Queen Zara in deep amethyst silks, her honey-russet wings tucked behind her sandy shoulders; King Arie in a matching violet coat, his iridescent citrine hummingbird wings blending with the leaves; Crown Prince Milo in more subdued evergreen leathers, his emerald neck plumage glistening; and finally Princess Elodie in a jade gown as the newest member of the family, her blue-and-orange songbird wings not quite blending with the scene. Beneath them, the entire population of Hyadria had gathered. Their faces were turned toward a raised dais where a boy sat with his head against a block. His bright red-and-brown wings tipped with a spot of hot yellow were a beacon to her eyes.

"Stop!" Lyana shouted.

The executioner hitched his sword.

"Stop!"

Faces turned toward her, but it was too late. The metal fell.

Stop! she shouted a final time, but instead of using her voice, she used her magic, reaching for the executioner's soul and bidding his body to freeze.

The blade halted an inch from the mage's throat.

The crowd gasped.

Lyana swept over their heads and landed at a furious stride. In one move, she ripped the sword from the executioner's hands and drove it into the wooden platform with enough force to make the shaft vibrate. The subtle ring of metal was loud across the shocked silence. Ignoring everyone except for the terrified child, Lyana knelt by his side. Even with the bag over his head, she could tell he was young by the small size of his body. She removed the covering to reveal a boy of no more than ten, his only crime the fact that he existed. Heart breaking for him, she pressed her palm to his cheek and slid her magic under his skin to still his trembling. At her touch, he finally opened his eyes, a spark of marvel within his pitch-black irises. Light and dark magic were the most difficult to hide. Their eyes gave the mages away, turning either as milky as a pearl or as shrouded as onyx as soon as the magic made itself known. The shift was visible even to those without power.

"Shh," she whispered. "No one will hurt you today. I promise."

"What is the meaning of this?" The queen's sharp voice cut through the crowd.

The boy tensed.

Lyana stood and whipped around to face the queen, wearing a look cold enough to smother fire. "I should be asking you the same question, Queen Zara. What is the meaning of this? Surely you got the missive I sent. Our world is dying, and the gods have given us one gift with the power to save it. Yet you defy their generosity. You throw it to the wind."

"Magic is an affront to the gods," the queen answered calmly, placing her hands on the rail. Murmurs of agreement rose from the crowd as she leaned forward, spreading her wings with an inscrutable expression on her round face. "One letter from a newly crowned queen with no kingdom is not enough to change my mind on that."

If Xander were there, he'd bid caution.

Too bad he hadn't caught up yet.

"Is that so?" Lyana asked.

"Yes."

"Fine, then I call upon Mnesme, god of arts and medicine, patron of the House of Paradise, to give us a sign." Gasps rose. The queen's upturned eyes widened. The sight only fueled Lyana's ire. "If magic is evil, if this boy should die for possession of it, may she choose her murderer now. Step forward, and I will not stand in your way. Step forward and see your god's will done."

While she spoke, Lyana flooded the platform with her power. A wave of gold descended over the crowd, wrapping them in unbreakable binds. Behind her, the boy drew in a sharp, wonder-filled breath. He could see her magic. He could, and possibly a few others, but to the rest, the scene was unchanged—eerily unchanged, as though frozen in time.

Stay, she commanded their spirits. *Do not move.*

A breeze swept through the trees, ruffling their skirts and shifting their feathers, but their bodies were stuck.

"Come. If Mnesme wills his death, will none of you step forward? Will none of you devout servants carry out her wishes?"

The queen gestured to the king, and he vaulted over the edge of their balcony, his hummingbird wings carrying him swiftly across the distance. Lyana let him get as far as to tug the sword free from where she'd stuck it and lift it over his head before she stopped him.

Distantly, she felt the god stone thrum.

It was close, she knew, housed somewhere near the palace. The power of the rift called out to her, an urgent beat to match the rapid pounding of her heart. She was using too much magic by holding this many souls for so long. Yet she couldn't let go. She refused to back down. The people needed to understand. They needed to believe her.

The stone wavered.

The rift spell weakened.

"I invoke all the gods," she shouted, hoping her panic didn't show. "If you want magic destroyed, send someone forward to kill this boy. Now. Show us your will."

Still, no one moved. But their spirits shifted. With their bodies caught within her grasp, their fury diffused, turning instead to uncertainty, to confusion. One more moment, one more second, and she'd have them. Just one more—

The ground trembled.

It dropped.

The trees groaned and branches swayed. Rigid floorboards shuddered and snapped. Glass shattered and flaming oil caught rope, shooting a blaze across the clearing. In the back of her mind, Lyana heard squawking ravens and creaking metal, her own screams as the sacred nest of her former home threatened to collapse beneath the might of her new magic.

The memory snapped her from her daze.

She pulled her power beneath her skin, releasing the crowd at once. Screams lit the air. Several people took to the sky. But with her magic doused, the god stone stopped quaking. After a long moment, the earth fell still, leaving a deafening silence in its wake. Not a soul moved, this time of their own volition.

"You see who answered our call," Lyana stated just as Xander and the rest of the ravens finally arrived at the scene, their two escorts trailing behind. He stared at her beneath furrowed brows. Lyana gestured, not to her flock but to the fire now cutting up the ropes, the sizzle loud in the quiet. "Vesevios is the only god who wants magic erased, because he knows it is our only weapon against him."

Even from this distance, she swore she could hear Xander's groan. He'd left her alone for a few minutes, and look what happened.

But Lyana held no regrets.

"By the power of Aethios, Taetanos, and all our patron gods," she cried, "I cast you out, Vesevios! Be gone!"

Beneath the command of her magic, the flames retreated. Lyana gripped the wild spirit of the fire, taming it until every last spark burned out. Then she knelt and gathered the boy in her arms, helping him stand. Holding his hand, she led him above the crowd to where the ravens hovered, and then she turned back to the queen, now at her eye level.

"The boy is free—the gods will it so—and he is coming with me. When you're ready to hear what else the gods command, when you're finally ready to listen, you know where to find me."

With that she spun and caught the eye of one of the escorts. Understanding the unspoken command, he jolted, glancing once between Lyana and his queen before leading their party away.

18

XANDER

"They're not coming," Xander muttered.

"They *are*," Lyana insisted. "They're coming. Trust me."

"They're not."

"They're—"

A knock at the door cut her off, and she grinned triumphantly.

Inwardly, Xander groaned. He knew why she'd done what she'd done, and he couldn't fault her. A boy's life had been on the line. Swift action had been needed. Yet he'd had such high hopes for their negotiations with the House of Paradise—high hopes of getting at least one house on their side, an important first step in changing the tide of people's minds. Queen Zara had reached out to them for help. She'd told them about the earthquake. She'd asked them to come. And the first thing they'd done was challenge her before the entire city, immediately putting her on the defensive.

Still, on the other side of the door, two guards and an escort stood with an invitation to meet with the royal family. Xander and Lyana quickly took them up on the offer, following the trio back toward the city center. The sun had started to set, casting Hyadria in a golden glow as soft beams cut through the trees, flickering with the movement of the leaves. The people had gone back to their daily routines, the constant flutter of colorful wings a comfort compared to the unnerving absence of it during his first flight through the city. Little more than an hour had passed since the stalled execution, but perhaps an hour was all they'd needed for tempers to calm. Queen Zara was waiting for them on a wide balcony, her dark brown eyes unreadable in the dying light as she welcomed them inside her home.

In stark contrast to the gaudy halls of the House of Song, the palace here was built directly into the trees, in hollowed cores and carved stairs and rooms suspended off the bark, relying on little more than natural beauty for its decor. Views of the forest greeted them at every turn. Flowers descended from the ceilings. Polished wood grains swirled along the walls and across the floors, giving an almost painterly effect. Every inch of the space had been meticulously designed, and yet the overall effect was soothing, as though the palace were one with the forest, a tribute to Mnesme and the fine arts.

They settled in a room balanced on the highest branches, where the rest of the royal family sat waiting on plush floor cushions, no longer in formal garb but in relaxed silken robes. A warm floral scent filled the air, emanating from the kettle set in the center of a low table. It was unlike any meeting space he'd been in before, nothing like the heavy wooden chairs and table in the castle where he'd grown up. Servants poured him and Lyana cups of herbal tea before disappearing through the door. The flavor instantly soothed him as he took his place upon the floor, his leather pants a bit restrictive as he tried to fold his legs. Lyana's lips twitched with a grin when his clothes groaned in protest. With a sigh, he simply stretched his long legs before him, trying to hide them beneath the table.

The silence lengthened, four sets of eyes watching him and Lyana over steaming rims, until the queen finally broke the quiet.

"You're so young," she said softly.

His chest squeezed painfully tight, as though a searing rod of iron had been pressed to his skin, stealing his breath. His mother's violet eyes flashed across his thoughts, but he buried the image. Now was not the time to show weakness, to show vulnerability. "We're not the first to have been crowned too soon, and I doubt we'll be the last. But our age matters little—"

"I think it matters a great deal," she interrupted, her tone holding no anger or chiding, but rather a pensiveness he'd never expected. "There's a boldness to youth, an invincibility and an openness so often whittled away by time. Perhaps that's why the gods chose you—they knew you would be the most likely to believe. My mind has been molded by the years. The clay is no longer malleable. Try to change me, and a crack appears, as it did today. We got off on the wrong foot, I believe, King and Queen of the House of Whispers. For my house's sake, I should like to start over."

So, they did. They started from the beginning. Xander and Lyana launched into their rehearsed tale, explaining their mating day, her disappearance, and his isle's fall. The royal family listened raptly, sometimes interrupting with questions, but showing far more interest than the songbirds ever had. And as their story came to a close, Xander ended with a soft, "You need to be prepared."

"Can it not be stopped?" King Arie asked.

Lyana released a heavy breath. "I'm going to try."

"How much time do we have?"

"I don't know," she said, her frustration evident. "I need access to your god stone. Take me to your sacred nest, now, and I might be able to give you an answer."

As their feathers bristled, Xander hurried to soften her demands. "What my queen means is she needs to touch the god stone to sense the havoc Vesevios has wrought and see how much Mnesme's spirit has been tainted. The closer she is to the gods, the better she can communicate with them. If you'll honor us with access to your holiest place, it might be possible to slow the spread and gather more time."

"Done," Queen Zara agreed, her tone final. It was the first she'd spoken since the start of the conversation. All through their tale, she'd simply sat, sipped her drink, and studied them with her soulful eyes. Now she gently placed her cup on the table and gestured to her son. "The crown prince and princess will escort Queen Lyana to the sacred nest immediately. King Lysander, I hope you might stay and answer a few more of my questions while my mate returns to the business of our house."

"Nothing would please me more."

"Good."

Lyana caught his eye on her way out the door and nodded subtly. So far, so good. An almost odd sense of optimism warmed his heart, out of place among the doom and gloom he'd been drowning in. The spark faded as quickly as it came.

"She's too rash," Queen Zara said the moment the door closed, leaving the two of them alone.

He sighed. "I'm aware."

"She doesn't ask. She demands."

"I'm aware of that, too."

"Had the gods not spoken so clearly this evening, I might never have listened."

Xander paused, his pulse skipping a beat. "But?"

"But I find you intriguing, King Lysander," she continued. He furrowed his brow. *Me?* "The prince I remember from the trials was just as rash as the queen I met today, relying on instincts instead of intellect. I'm not sure what's changed you, but it's as though losing your hand made you gain a new sense, or perhaps so much hardship and responsibility so soon has simply forced you to grow up. When I got your letter, I was thinking of the prince and princess I'd once met. I had my doubts, but seeing you as King and Queen has made me understand why the gods have chosen you. The queen has all the passion of a natural-born leader. She's the sort of woman who can rouse an army, but how would that army be fed? Where would they live? Who would clothe them and care for them long after the rallying cry has faded? She is the storm, but you, King Lysander, are the shelter. You are the one I trust."

Lyana was the chosen one.

Lyana was the queen of prophecy.

He was… He was…no one.

"I'm not sure I understand what you're asking me."

"For the truth," she said simply.

He sucked in a strangled breath. "The truth?"

"Come."

She stood from her floor cushion, walked to a wide veranda, and placed her forearms along the rail. Xander took the place by her side, following the path of her eyes. Night had fallen while they spoke, and Hyadria had been born anew. Lanterns blazed across the forest, but none so bright as the bonfire upon the dais where only hours before a boy had nearly lost his life. Around the flames, the people danced, bodies fluid as they leapt and spun, swaying toward the blaze and retreating, moving as one unit as though the song lived in their blood. And perhaps it did. There was no music aside from the pounding of feet, the humming of insects, and the rustling of leaves.

"They're praying," Queen Zara explained, reading the wonder in his gaze. She was clearly intuitive. "This is how our house gives honor to Mnesme—we dance with the fire to show we're not afraid of it, to show our faith that she will protect us and keep us safe. And we won't stop until the fire has died. Oh, some will sleep and some will tire, but others will take their place for as long as is needed to see Vesevios conquered. So I ask again, King Lysander, for the truth. Do my people dance in vain?"

"No," he murmured, his voice low.

The queen studied him. His pulse pounded beneath her scrutiny, the rhythm in the forest filling his heart until it beat to the same tune. His spirit moved as one with the bodies below, demanding and forgiving, believing and wanting, pleading with him the way these people pleaded with their god.

He couldn't tell her the full truth.

He couldn't lie either.

"No, they don't dance in vain," he continued, staring into those bright flames as though they held the answers. "Because time spent praying to our gods is never wasted. They've sheltered us and protected us for hundreds of years, long before these isles rose into the sky, and they'll continue to do so long after our time in the clouds has ended. Vesevios will never destroy our faith, but our homes…" Xander took a deep breath and turned to face her. The flames flickered across her unblemished cheeks. "They are going to fall."

"You're sure?"

"Yes."

"If we can't prevent it, why do you need my help?"

"Because the people need to be prepared." He closed his eyes, memories drawing him back to the night he would never forget. "My kingdom plummeted in a flash of terrified confusion, marked by screams. It happened so quickly. There was hardly time to take to the sky before the isle was falling. Many ravens died, and I don't want the other houses to suffer the same fate. Start moving your people to the House of Peace. Start packing your supplies. Start preserving what you can of this way of life. The gods have given Lyana the power to buy us time. We cannot save our palaces. We cannot save our cities. But we can save our citizens. And as long as they still have breath, our cultures and our gods will live on."

He didn't know if he'd said too much, if he'd pushed too hard. The world wouldn't change in a night, but it would never change if he and Lyana didn't have help.

Queen Zara placed her hand upon his arm and squeezed gently as she watched her people dance. They stood like that for a few moments, side by side, listening to the rhythm, two monarchs with the weight of their subjects on their shoulders, until a cough interrupted.

"My queen," a soft voice said, "Queen Lyana waits for King Lysander in the entrance hall. Shall I escort him out?"

"Yes."

A sigh escaped his lips. He'd failed. His plea hadn't been enough. He'd tried honesty. He'd tried lies. He'd tried action. He'd tried diplomacy. It seemed no matter what he did, he was destined to fall short.

Xander turned to the door.

The queen dug her fingers into his jacket sleeve, and he froze, his body, heart, and spirit all hanging on her breath.

"I'll stop the executions," she said, tone low but not a whisper, full of authority. "The gods have chosen Lyana to save us. Her power can't be denied. But perhaps they've chosen you to lead us, raven king. Come tomorrow. Help me plan a future for my people. Let me see what you can offer above public displays and pretty speeches. Then, maybe, I'll plead your case to the other houses. Convince me, and I'll help you get the other rulers on your side."

He nodded, but her attention remained on her people, so he left her to her thoughts. The servant escorted him through the palace. With his every step toward the door, her words echoed across the silent halls.

Convince me.

Unlike Lyana, he had no magic, no godly displays, no irrefutable power. But he had his heart. He had his conviction. And he prayed they would be enough.

19

CASSI

Their swords crashed together, the sound echoing off the crystal dome and reverberating around the empty arena. When Lyana attacked again, Cassi rolled to the side and sliced her blade toward her queen's calf. Lyana jumped and took to the air. Cassi pursued, her speedy owl wings gaining ground, but her friend darted left, then right, shooting up and then plummeting down, her dove wings far more agile in flight. Frustrated, Cassi tossed the sword aside. With a single thought from her, a bow filled her hands and the weight of arrows nestled against her spine. She grinned as she sent one flying.

"Hey!" Lyana shouted as she swerved out of its path. "No fair!"

"Who said anything about fair?"

Cassi released another arrow. Lyana widened her eyes indignantly, her power churning in the background of the dream. She took control of the scene and a belt of daggers appeared around her waist. With a wicked grin, she flung one toward Cassi.

I probably deserved that.

Arching her wings back, she plunged to the ground and skidded to a stop. By the time she pulled the bowstring taut, Lyana had landed. Halfway to her mark, the arrow transformed into a feather and drifted harmlessly to the ground.

Cassi frowned. *Two can play at that game.*

Snatching back command of the dream, she set her sights on the dagger in Lyana's hand. The metal tip sprouted a tail, then four limbs, finally emerging as a small monkey that darted up her queen's arm and leapt into her hair.

"Hey!" Lyana said again, her voice thick with laughter this time as she swatted at the little beast. Cassi made it vanish with a thought.

"Swords?" she asked.

Lyana nodded. "Swords."

A blade appeared in each of their hands and they crashed together again, needing an outlet for all the energy their waking lives provided no way to expend. They were restless, and in that restlessness, they'd come here for the third night in a row. Saving the world made one a lot more stir crazy than Cassi had thought possible.

"Is Malek still sailing?"

"Yes," she grunted as she parried Lyana's attack, her teeth clenching at the mention of the king. Spying on him was *not* going according to plan. The man had his castle on lockdown. No one spoke outside of his presence, at least not about anything interesting. And every time she got within earshot of his meetings, they fell silent. He could sense her within moments, perfectly attuned to her spirit after so many years of shared dreams. And as much as she wanted to confront him and scream at him and beg him to put her body right, she refused to be the one to break. Unfortunately, it didn't seem as though her king had plans to relent or apologize anytime soon. "He's been in the open ocean for days. I have no idea where he's going, and he can sense my spirit before I even see his ship through the fog. It's infuriating."

Lyana sighed.

Cassi used the opening to swing for her exposed left side, but Lyana spun away, refocusing on the fight in an instant. She advanced. Cassi blocked. They traded blows.

"What about Rafe?"

"Also still on the open ocean. Last I saw he was still trying to figure out how the whole communicating-with-dragons thing works, but he hasn't run into one again. I would've heard the crew talking."

Lyana ducked and sliced with her blade. Cassi jumped over it. They met back in the middle, metal ringing.

"He won't go to the House of Peace?"

"Not yet."

"His shipmates?"

"Let's just say they aren't exactly enthused about the idea of fleeing to a place where magic is forbidden. Oh—or a place that's fifteen thousand feet in the air and ready to crumble."

"It's not..." Lyana protested weakly.

Cassi arched a brow.

In a burst of frustration, Lyana surged forward on the attack. Knowing exactly how to mentally and physically put Cassi on the defensive, she then asked, "Have you spoken to your mother?"

Low blow.

Cassi lifted her foot and kicked Lyana in the breastbone, forcing her back as she took to the sky. In an effort at honesty, she'd confessed to Captain Rokaro's true identity, and not a day went by when she wished she hadn't. Their relationship was complicated, now more than ever, and while she might have been able to ignore her mother's obvious avoidance, Lyana wouldn't let her. Captain Rokaro wasn't sleeping—at least not during any of the times Cassi had tried to pay her a visit. She was hiding something, something big, and it was driving her daughter mad with curiosity.

"Obviously not, or I would've told you," Cassi said, the words coming out in short bursts between quick breaths as her body grew labored with the fight. "How go things with Queen Zara?"

It was Lyana's turn to groan. "Fine."

"Fine?"

"In truth, I've stopped attending the meetings. There's no point in just sitting there as she and Xander review logs and take notes and talk endlessly about any number of subjects I don't care about when all I can focus on is the rift, and the magic, and the countdown running in the back of my mind."

"Xander's well?" Cassi asked, doing her best to keep her voice even, though just the sound of his name on her lips made her heart thunder.

Lyana rolled her eyes, unaware. "If the House of Whispers weren't lying somewhere beneath the ocean right now, I'd say he was having the time of his life."

For some reason, that made her chest twinge. "Oh, good."

"Great," her queen said, the tone implying anything but. "Except we're not here to plan every little movement of the House of Paradise. We're here to prevent a war. We're here to open people's eyes to the beauty of magic. We're here to try to figure out how to close the rift and seal off the dragons and save the world, but no matter how much time I spend in their sacred nest with my hands pressed against the stone, I can't figure out a gods-damned thing."

That last word turned into a yell as she charged.

Cassi sidestepped easily. "Training is going that well, then?"

"I don't know how to teach them." Lyana spoke through heavy breathing, dejection evident in her tone and in her person as her blows weakened. She was, of course, talking about her *army*—though Cassi wasn't sure three ravens and one bird of paradise with absolutely no experience really counted as such. "I only just learned how to use my own magic. I have no idea how to help other mages use theirs. I mean, I'm trying. Don't get me wrong, I'm doing everything I can. But they need someone else. They need Malek and his mages. And we both know that will never happen."

No.

Definitely not.

"And I sensed two more mages in the House of Paradise, but I'm not sure what I can do for them even if they will join me. I'm going to speak to them, if for no other reason than to lessen their fear, but I wish I could do more. With all my magic and all my power, I'm so tired of not being able to do more."

You and me both.

The uselessness was driving her insane. Sure, she kept Lyana informed. Sure, she tried to spy and gather intel. Sure, she acted as messenger, even though the messages had lately been few and far between. But there was only so much aimlessly floating around the sky a spirit could do before one went mad, and she was part bird for crying out loud.

She missed her body.

She missed being alive.

She missed feeling, even if all she remembered feeling lately was pain.

She missed being able to move and do and act and run and fly.

She missed having true wind beneath her wings.

As their anger grew and their muscles weakened, their attacks turned sloppy. Cassi's body burned, but not in the way that counted. This was all in her mind, in their minds—the sweat, the exhaustion, even the pounding of her blood. And knowing that somehow made it all as useless as everything else.

Tired in more ways than one, Cassi feinted left and Lyana lunged, falling for the ruse. She hooked her sword underneath her queen's and twisted, flinging it across the practice yard. Before she could right herself, Lyana wrapped an arm around her waist and pulled them both to the ground. They lay there, panting, as they stared at the blue sky through the crystal ceiling overhead. Another lie. They weren't back home, just as they weren't best friends, not anymore, as the silence stretching between them seemed to whisper.

"Lyana?" Cassi finally murmured.

"Hmm?"

"Can I ask for your blessing on something?"

Her queen dropped her head to the side. "What?"

"I'd like to try to free Elias," she said, not giving Lyana the chance to respond as she hastily continued. "I know we said it was too dangerous before, with Malek there watching. But he's gone now, and I just— I just— I need to *do* something."

A moment passed, then, "Do it, Cassi. Do it so—"

Lyana broke off. She jolted to a seated position, tilting her head as though she'd heard a troubling noise. Cassi had seen Malek behave similarly. It immediately put her on edge.

"What?"

Before she fully got the question out, the dream shattered. Lyana grabbed her spirit and flung it from her mind. She catapulted into the waking world, unable to find her balance, the scene chaotic and loud and refusing to settle. It took a moment for her to understand the truth.

An earthquake.

Lyana jumped from the bed as Xander sat up on the floor. As soon as their eyes met, they launched out the door of their guest quarters and into Hyadria. Cassi followed like a swiftly moving breeze. The trees shook. Rope bridges swayed. All around, wood splintered and groaned, drowned out only by the screams as the citizens took flight, fighting for an avenue through the thick canopy of the forest and into the open sky.

A few minutes passed.

They seemed an eternity before the isle finally fell still.

Cassi didn't miss how her queen's hands curled to fists by her sides or the frustration, like the desperation of a caged animal, she exuded. But there was nothing she could do either. As the King and Queen of the House of Whispers flew to help these people, Cassi abandoned them to soar over the edge and back to the room where her body lay as immobile as a corpse upon the floor.

Elias was asleep on his cot.

I'm going to get you out of here, she silently whispered. *If it's the last thing I do, I'm going to get you out of here, so at least one of us will be free.*

20

RAFE

Rafe woke from the nightmare as he always did, sweat dripping down his forehead, pulse racing. The shadow monster was close. At least, its spirit was. Rafe bolted out of the bed and ran to the window, reaching out with his mind.

Don't leave.

Don't go.

There was no response.

He stared into the fog until his vision grew fuzzy and the world faded. Reaching for the darkness, he touched the part of him deep inside that seemed to pull the creature, the tiniest bit of raven magic still lingering beneath his skin. Entrenched in that sliver of power, Rafe sensed a shadowy presence across the fog. It was flying… somewhere. It was looking for…something. An almost childlike curiosity filled its thoughts, at odds with the fully grown monster Rafe had seen in the streets of Karthe.

Come back.

He sent the image of his ship and his face into the connection, then the memory of waking up alone in his cabin, hoping to lure the creature back. The nightmare had been another massacre—four bodies this time, in the back alleys of a city he'd never seen. And while Rafe wanted nothing more than to keep this monster far, far away from his friends, he felt responsible somehow, as though the dead had fallen at his hands. The dreams weren't his memories. Logically, he knew he'd played no part. But he was also the only person alive who might be able to stop the monster, so he had to try, or the guilt would destroy him.

Please, come back.

Unlike the dragons, the creature wouldn't listen. Rafe had been trying to get through to it for days, and nothing. It heeded no commands. They were equals, except that the shadow demon flew with the stealth of a breeze, moving unseen, leaving Rafe with no way to catch him.

"Rafe!"

Brighty's voice snapped him back to the ship. He spun just as she crashed through the door, a look of panic in her milky eyes.

"Come quick."

"What's going on?"

"No time!" she shouted over her shoulder as she disappeared back into the hallway.

Rafe chased after her, following her up the stairs. Halfway to the top, she stopped dead. He nearly ran her over.

"Brighty, what the—" He cut himself short.

Golden magic glittered across the air, shimmering in the dark shadows of the hull as warm as sunlight while it grazed his skin. The sight of it made his heart turn cold. Fire flooded his veins, fighting the power as it crept into his soul.

King Malek was here.

"Brighty, come on! Brighty!"

She didn't move.

She didn't respond.

She was stone.

Gods alive! Rafe cursed as he grabbed her biceps, picked her up, and moved her a foot to the right, out of his way. Under the king's thrall, her body didn't shift an inch, stiff as a board, her spirit tight in his grip.

"You can yell at me for that later," Rafe muttered as he sprinted past her and emerged above deck.

The skies were lit by magic. Waves of gold crashed against the ship, dampening the yellow streaks of *aero'kine* power whipping into the sails and the flood of *hydro'kine* power sinking into the sea. Not a soul moved. The entire crew was frozen in time. Captain held the wheel, her lips in a grim line. Beside her, Patch's mouth hung open as though calling out an alarm. Squirrel lay curled on his side by the main mast, his body fallen from the ropes. Leech knelt over his plants. Pyro stood at the bow, flames still dancing around her raised hand. Jolt, with Archer by her side, had been caught in the middle of a laugh while telling a story. Spout stood beside them, her forearms resting casually on the rails as she turned to glance behind her. Magic swirled about their fingertips, the only clue they were still alive, still conscious, still fighting against the king they had no hope to best. Though he couldn't see them, Rafe had no doubt Shadow and Cook had also been detained. *Aethi'kine* power couldn't be stopped by walls.

He should have known this would happen.

He should have forced them to take Lyana's advice. The crew would be safe now, if they'd just gone to the House of Peace. Instead, the most powerful man in the world was breathing down their necks, and it was all his fault.

Rafe flew the rest of the distance to the captain, the king's power burning away the moment it touched his body, and landed before her. "I'm going to get us out of this."

She gave no indication that she heard. He flicked his gaze to Patch, then back to her, biting his tongue. He hadn't exactly been honest these past few days, but there was no time like the present.

So what if the first mate knew? On this ship, nothing remained a secret for long.

"I'm going to call a dragon for help," he said in a rush, the words flowing together in one continuous sound. "I know it sounds insane, but they listen to me. They heed my orders. I'll command it to attack the king's ship, and in the chaos, I'll distract the king. He can't touch me. When you have an opening, take it, even if I'm not here. I'll get away. I'll meet you on the sea."

Nothing.

No bother. He'd get an earful later, he was sure. For now, it was his plan or, well, he didn't even want to think about what the king might have in store. The crew had spent their lives hunting dragons —it was high time one came to their rescue instead.

Rafe soared to the crow's nest where he found it easier to think, surrounded by wind and fog. Then he sent his mind searching the mist for the scent of fire and smoke.

There.

The connection was faint, but unmistakable. Rafe held on to that line, the way he'd been practicing ever since that day at the outpost. The bond strengthened.

Come.

He pushed the command toward the dragon, along with images of the ship and the memory of the king's *aethi'kine* magic. Hunger twisted his stomach and he forced that down the line too, stirring up a mix of craving and emptiness, luring the beast closer.

Come.

Voices carried on the wind. Rafe snapped open his eyes just in time to see the outline of a ship cutting through the fog. The king was close.

Come!

Lightning crackled, exploding in the air above the oncoming ship, turning the fog lavender as it splintered down from the sky. Before touching the sails it froze, and the king's crew sailed harmlessly underneath. Stirred by Spout's magic, the seas turned choppy, waves rising and crashing with an angry zeal, until blue sparks cut across the mist and dove into the water, urging it to calm. Winds clashed, opposite forces swirling, laced with yellow flares, but no side gained the upper hand.

The king's ship closed in. Like a living figurehead, Malek stood at the bow, his hands gripping the rails. Golden power exploded from him, so bright it nearly stung the eyes. On either flank his mages stood, waiting with stoic faces.

Rafe felt for the dragon.

It was close—but not close enough.

The king was minutes away.

No concern for himself, thinking only of his crew, Rafe dove off the crow's nest and took to the sky, making a beeline for Malek. If he were honest, he'd been waiting for this meeting since the moment these fiery wings had been forced onto his back. Maybe even earlier, since the moment Captain first told him of the king, the moment he'd seen his raven wings bundled on Malek's desk, or earlier still, the moment Cassi had cut them from his back. Revenge blazed like its own fire in his heart, coming entirely from the man and not the beast sharing his soul.

The sea erupted.

Rafe swerved around the spout as droplets sizzled against his wings. Another exploded, then another and another, not quick enough to slow him as his wings carved deftly through the air. A blast of pure light stole his sight. He gritted his teeth against the burn, using his dragon senses to follow the magic, not needing his eyes to see. Winds surged, but he was a creature of the sky, and no gale was strong enough to stop him.

Malek.

Malek.

Malek.

That single name was his war cry. The king would regret

hunting down his friends. The king would regret not leaving him free. The king would regret turning him into this monster.

Knives shot across the sky.

Rafe ducked underneath the first one and released his raven cry. The shriek bounded across the waves and smashed into the ship with a force no mage could stop. The blades dropped harmlessly into the sea. The ocean calmed. The winds died. All the magic lighting the skies blinked out of existence. The king widened his eyes in surprise the second before they went blank, and then Rafe was there.

He grabbed Malek by his jacket, lifted him from the deck, and flew across the wooden planks to slam the king's spine into the mast. The man gasped. Rafe punched his cheek and Malek's face snapped to the side. Blood dribbled from the corner of his lip. As the magic of the raven cry faded, the king's gaze sharpened and golden power emanated from his skin, but it was useless. Rafe drank the spirit magic in, absorbing the power as though it were an elixir of life revitalizing his every aching muscle and providing newfound strength. Malek hissed, his body failing as the connection to Rafe's spirit burned him from the inside out. The golden aura vanished, but Rafe didn't stop fighting. He had the king right where he'd wanted him for so long. Without his power, Malek was weak. And Rafe intended to show him exactly what it felt like to be the one without control.

He slammed his fist into the man's stomach, satisfied when he heard him grunt, and kneed him in the groin. Catching him before he fell, Rafe then tossed Malek across the deck. His body rolled helplessly over the wood. Just as he started to rise, Rafe pumped his wings and sailed into his chest, knocking him back to the floor. His fist found the king's face, again and again, his knuckles turning bloody.

So consumed, Rafe forgot about the other mages—a mistake that cost him dearly. As he reeled back for another punch, a strip of metal latched over his mouth, blocking his raven cry. Then chains wrapped around his torso, securing his arms to his chest. The metal jerked and he stumbled back. Rafe beat his wings, struggling against his binds. On the floor, the king eased onto his elbow, his skin already swelling as he wiped the blood from his chin. Hatred darkened his eyes.

"Jacinta," he seethed. "If you would—"

A roar thundered across the sky, making the air itself tremble. A wave of fire rained down from the fog, casting the ship in an orange blaze. Malek looked up, shooting out his golden magic just in time to catch the flames before they touched his skin.

The rest of the ship wasn't so lucky.

The sails caught, turning to an inferno. The wood crackled and popped as the masts burned. Shouts cut across the chaos, but not of pain, thank the gods. Rafe didn't want them hurt, just distracted, which they were. Chutes of water rose from the sea while the fire swirled toward a single figure to his left. Already, the blackened wood was regenerating, sparks of green simmering around the damage. The mages worked on securing the ship, all but the one he most needed off his back.

Reaching for the bond, he sent the metal mage's face into the dragon's mind, not needing to see her to remember the harsh line of her cheekbones, the severe angle of her chin, the deep onyx of her hair. He'd never forget the woman's face, and deep down a part of him he couldn't deny wanted her to feel just a little bit of the terror he'd felt as she'd dragged him helplessly across the warehouse to his doom.

Descending through the mist, the dragon dove into the ship and gripped the main mast in its claws, snapping the wood in half. It roared and another blaze flooded the deck. The king kept most of the flames from getting too close, but hidden within the bubbling orange, the beast spun. Its tail slammed into the metal mage's gut, and she flew backward, disappearing over the side of the ship. The metal end of a rope sparked green and rushed after her, but not before Rafe heard a splash. The chains fell from his torso and landed with a *thunk* on the wood. The muzzle slipped harmlessly from his lips.

Rafe turned on the king.

Fear flashed in the man's eyes.

He could end him right now. He could destroy him.

The very thought made Rafe pause.

He was a man, not a monster—at least, he didn't want to be. And refusing to murder was the only thing keeping him on the human side of the line. A memory stirred, of Lyana on those long-ago nights in Pylaeon, healing the injured in their sleep. He didn't want to be like that shadow creature, a thing of fear. He wanted to be like her, a symbol of hope. And maybe he could be, but not if he destroyed the man whom the rest of the world viewed as their savior.

Malek was the king of prophecy and Lyana needed him.

For that alone, he would live.

Go, Rafe thought, sending thoughts of danger and fear into the bond to the dragon. *Go and save yourself.*

The beast didn't listen. The magic in the air was too potent, too alluring for a creature of pure instinct to ignore. But Rafe still had his wits. So before the *ferro'kine* came back from the sea, he launched into the sky, leaving the king behind him.

21

CAPTAIN ROKARO

Rafe emerged from the flames, a black spot in a flood of orange, seemingly unharmed as he cut across the fog.

"Did you see?" Brighty whispered by her side. "Did you see?"

Oh, she'd seen.

Rafe, totally unaffected by the king's magic. Rafe, beating Malek to a pulp. Rafe, calling upon a dragon. Rafe, escaping unharmed. He was either the King Born in Fire or the destruction of them all, but one thing was certain—this wasn't a decision that should rest in her hands any longer. He needed to know, and so did the queen.

Zia turned to Brighty, meeting her pleading eyes. "We tell him tonight."

"Tonight? But—"

"Silence."

Brighty growled but sealed her lips, unprepared to defy a direct order from her captain. At least for now. Zia knew she was pushing the mage's loyalty, but she had no other choice. Rafe landed beside them, his chest puffed with all the words he ached to say. The boy had no poker face. His every desire was written in his eyes, his every fear too. He was afraid of himself. Good. She was starting to fear him too.

"We need to go to the House of Peace, now," he said in a rush, placing his hands on the wheel to gain her full attention. Dried blood covered his knuckles, gruesome against his pale skin. Under her scrutiny, Rafe swallowed and dropped his arms, softening his tone as the fire along his wings dampened. "The king will keep coming and I'm not sure if that trick with the raven cry will work a second time. He'll be more prepared. We need to get away. We need to go somewhere he won't follow."

"Rafe," Brighty chided, rolling her eyes. "We talked about this. The isles are falling. None of us have wings. You see how those two facts don't really—"

"I agree," Zia interrupted.

Rafe grinned.

Brighty dropped her jaw. "You what?"

"We go to the House of Peace. Now."

"Captain—"

"Enough, Brighty."

Zia sensed the presence of her first mate nearby, always there watching her back, the support she so dearly needed. When she stepped to the side, Markos took her place at the wheel, his thick olive hands gripping the spokes.

"Listen up," she shouted, cupping her hands around her lips.

The crew stopped what they were doing and turned. She'd earned their respect. She'd earned their trust. Every last soul on this ship had come to her at the lowest point in their lives, when there was nowhere else to turn, and she'd been their guide ever since—through storms and rough seas, against dragons and against the sort of demons that couldn't be seen. She was steady. She was sure. She was their captain. So she stifled the nerves fluttering beneath her skin and hardened her tone.

"The sea is no longer safe, so we only have one choice—it's time to take to the sky. Spout, carry us as high as we can go. Leech and Archer, push with every ounce of magic you possess. It's going to take everything we've got to lift this hulk of wood above the fog, but I'm not leaving her behind. Patch, stay with me. Everyone else, stay out of our way."

Not giving them a moment to argue, Zia released her magic into the sky and a gust blew across the deck. The snapping sails whipped them to attention. A wave of green *agro'kine* magic erupted from Leech's palms, flooding the deck and wrapping around the ship as he urged the wood up. Deeper pine sparks cut through the haze as Archer did the same with the metal. Spout stood at the rail, *hydro'kine* magic pouring from her arms and diving into the sea. The ship shuddered, boards groaning. They pushed harder.

The ocean swelled, rising in a churning column. The wind cut underneath the hull, swirling into a vortex. Zia stepped back until she was shoulder to shoulder with Markos, both of them shooting their *aero'kine* magic into the mist.

"Are you sure about this, Zia?" he murmured, leaning down so no one else would hear.

She swallowed. They'd make it—of that she had no doubt. And for the time being, they'd be safe. She was sure of that too. But was she ready to return to the world she'd left behind? A world that had cast her out? A world that loathed magic? A world about to come crashing down?

"No," she whispered. "But we've no other choice."

"Hmm." He took a deep breath, then nudged her with his elbow. His deep brown eyes held the smile his lips wouldn't show. "At least I'll finally see the sun."

A soft laugh escaped her lips as she turned her face up. The fog was thick. Gray vapors swirled with the breeze, lit by their combined magic. But soon, it would break. Soon, the sky would be blue. Soon, they would all feel a warm caress like no other, a kiss she hadn't felt in over three decades, the soul-reviving touch of the sun.

The bird within her soared.

For a moment, it almost felt like flying.

THE DIARY

Fourteenth Day of the Fourth Moon

I meant to write more in my last entry, but my father came to my rooms, so I had to quickly hide this journal. Could you even imagine if he found it? If he read it? I shudder at the very thought.

Back to the man from the vision.

I heard a knock at my door and opened it to receive the Master of Arms, a ferro'kine and one of my father's closest advisors.

"Princess," he said, then gestured from one side to another. While I'm sure there were men hiding somewhere on either side of the door, all I saw were two feathery curtains framing the opening, one honey golden and the other ashen gray. "I've brought your new guards. They'll remain outside your door during the day, and will escort you as needed."

I nodded along as he spoke. I'd heard it all earlier that morning as my father announced the additional security measures. When he finished, I asked a simple question, one I was surprised he hadn't yet addressed. "And do they have names?"

"Mikhail," he said, pointing to the left where the smoky gray feathers jutted out from the edge of the doorway. Then he shifted to the

right, where the seemingly sunlit brown wings curved beside the frame. "And Zavier."

"And can they speak?" I teased, a smile on my lips and a hint of laughter in my voice.

The Master of Arms frowned. I fear I'm the only one in the palace who still maintains a sense of humor—I'm sure I can blame my mother for that. The halls were lighter when she lived within them. Still, he took a step back and jutted out his chin, giving them space to move. The dove soldier turned around first, his skin a deep umber and his eyes a warm caramel—a false sense of sweetness since they hardened upon seeing me.

"Princess," he said, sharp and quick, jaw clenching as soon as he was done. With his hands folded behind his back, he offered a deep bow.

I curtsied when he stood, unbothered by his obvious discomfort. This was only the beginning of my seeing him every day, and I refused to be unnerved in my own home. Perhaps I'd win him over. "Greetings, Soldier Mikhail. Thank you for your service."

Then the other man turned.

Oh, I must have looked a fool!

My jaw dropped to the floor as those elongated eagle feathers shifted out of sight, replaced by the man from my vision. Those same hazel eyes. That same sun-kissed skin. His hair was pulled into a tight knot atop his head, but I remembered it flowing around his cheeks, so soft I yearned to put my fingers through it. He must have spoken, but I didn't hear. I was too shocked, too entranced. I could curse myself now for missing the soft timbre of his voice. I imagine it deep and soothing, like the melodic churning of waves.

The Master of Arms coughed.

I started.

My legs trembled as I hastily dipped into a curtsy, murmuring a greeting though I can't be sure what I said. Even now, thinking back, my thoughts are a jumble, those few minutes lost to the pounding of my heart and the drumming of my ears. What I wouldn't give to see into the past just once, just to relive this moment—I could do it so much better if given the chance.

Then again, maybe not.

He stood outside my door the rest of the evening, escorted me to dinner and back. I couldn't sleep knowing he stood just a few walls away, my chest aflutter with the very thought. Now, in the bright morning sun, I'm too afraid to open my door. What does he think of me? What will he say? What will I say? My mind spins.

That's enough.

I'm not a frightened little girl anymore. If I want this man to be mine, if I want the future I've seen to be true, then I must make it happen.

I must do something.

And I will.

Sixteenth Day of the Fourth Moon

I'm a coward. I've done nothing.

For two days, Zavier and Mikhail have escorted me everywhere, and for two days, I've been mute, barely glancing up from the floor, too scared to say a word.

It ends tomorrow.

I don't care what I say, I must say something. What happened to all my courage? All my strength? What would my mother say if she saw me now?

Seventeenth Day of the Fourth Moon

I did it!

Well, I tried, at the very least. This morning as Zavier and Mikhail brought me to the dining room for breakfast, I paused to look out the window and said, "It's a beautiful day, isn't it?"

They replied, "Yes, Princess."

Oh, his voice. So warm and rich. A tingle shot down my spine at the sound, as though I could feel his phantom touch upon my cheek. Even now, I shiver just thinking about it. I practically jumped out of my slippers from the excitement!

Of course, the weather is as banal a topic as I could have possibly chosen, but it was something. I broke through my fear, and like a river unleashed, I couldn't stop for the rest of the day. I chattered on and on. I'm sure I was more of an annoyance than anything else, but it's a start. Here are a few examples:

"Where do you live?"

"With the other birds of prey, Princess," he said politely.

Of course! I knew that. All the avians live in segregated villages outside the city. The eagles, hawks, and falcons all group together, though I'm told having so many predators in close quarters isn't the most peaceful existence. And Mikhail lives with the rest of the doves, a more serene part of the neighborhood, I'm sure. Still, though, I prattled on like a fool.

"And do you like it?"

"Of course, Princess."

"And who do you live with?"

"My mother, Princess."

With that, my heart pinched with a jealousy I quickly stifled. Oh, to be free of this palace and somewhere safe with my own mother. What I wouldn't give for that to be true.

"No siblings?"

"No, Princess."

"You don't need to end every sentence with my title."

"I do, Princess."

"Very well... Soldier Zavier."

If I could only describe how delicious it was to feel his name roll through my lips, even if it was in a mocking manner. I smiled after, to show I was only teasing, and I swear, the golden sparkles in his eyes brightened.

Mikhail continued frowning. I asked him all the same questions in probably a lame attempt to make my infatuation less obvious. But his answers were even gruffer and quicker, though I'm not sure what exactly it is I've done to earn his ire.

Oh well.

Better luck tomorrow.

Eighteenth Day of the Fourth Moon

My aethi'kine suitor arrives tomorrow, which, I'll admit, has put a damper on my mood. Even still, I managed to learn a few more things about Zavier.

He likes lemon tarts, or at least he pretended to when I offered him one, unlike Mikhail. He prefers a crossbow, though in the palace he wears only a sword. He is twenty-two, a few years older than me. I was too afraid to ask if he had a mate yet, as the avians call their spouses, but he couldn't possibly. He doesn't. He can't.

Moving on.

He and Mikhail went through training together, though this is their first time working in a pair, as I suspected. Avians usually remain with their own kind—the ravens with the ravens, the songbirds with the songbirds. Avians of prey are often elite soldiers and guards, as I'm sure Zavier is, to have been given this post. Doves are more often militia, though Mikhail must be an excellent fighter to be working in the palace. Songbirds more often serve as maids or cooks. Hummingbirds are our messengers, because of their speed. Ravens are our spies, since they blend so well into the night. Owls often work as secretaries or the stronger as night watchmen. Avians of paradise are our entertainers. And when I say 'our,' I don't mean just my father and me —the palace would be overflowing! All the powerful mages in the kingdom have avian help. We live together and work together—mages, avians, and the poor souls with neither magic nor wings, the ones who most need my father's protection.

Aether help me, I don't even know what I'm writing about anymore. My mind fills with the image of his face and my hand keeps scrawling brainlessly on.

Time for bed.

Tomorrow, I meet my future husband. I doubt his gaze will leave a mark on my skin the way Zavier's does. His burns so hot even my mother's magic would melt beneath the blaze.

Nineteenth Day of the Fourth Moon

I was right. The aethi'kine has cool eyes filled with secrets, their gray-blue color as chilly as ice, even though his hair flames red. I should've known he would be just like my father, and I did, but still, I never expected him to—

I'm getting ahead of myself.

He arrived early in the afternoon with a small group of men and women, mages no doubt, the beginnings of his future council. We greeted him in the throne room. My father looked impressive surrounded by shimmering gilt and crimson velvet, the crown gleaming atop his head, the ceremonial weapons at his waist—but mostly the glittering aura of magic resting above his clasped palms. Beside him, I probably looked rather mousy, petite in my own throne, swallowed by the red silks of my gown, a golden tiara nestled into my brow, though I kept my back straight and my chin proud as Mother taught me. I've become too at home alone in my rooms, nothing but this journal, my sewing, and my often-wandering mind to keep me company. Displays of power just make me feel all the meeker.

I knew the moment he stepped in the room that my father's fears were not unfounded. The way he walked, strong and straight, without a care in the world. The subtle grin upon his lips, one end twisted as though caught in a private joke. The sweep of his eyes, commanding and possessive, as though already taking stock of what would one day be his. We needed him more than he needed us, and he knew it. He bowed, and though he did everything by the book, I couldn't shake the sense that his every move was a mockery.

My father launched into a welcome speech, but I admit, I tuned most of it out. Magic tickled my skin, first a subtle prickle at the back of my neck, growing and growing, to a tingle that spread to the very ends of my fingers and toes. I could almost feel time rearranging before my eyes, this meeting and this moment shifting the gears of fate, the future narrowing toward a certain point, no longer full of a thousand different possibilities. The aethi'kine was changing something. He was at the center of something.

I waited for the vision.

Waited and waited.

Then, after I don't know how long, the aethi'kine stepped up to my throne, offering a deep bow. As he rose, that cold-as-ice gaze swept over me. It was all I could do not to shiver. The fascination in his eyes was impossible to ignore. It was not directed at me, I knew, but at the subtle rosy sheen emanating from my skin. Perhaps the greatest downside of magic is that it's impossible to hide from one of our own.

"Princess Miralee," he said, extending his arm.

"Lord Bastiant," I replied, digging through the depths of my memory for his name as I offered him my hand.

The moment our fingers touched, the vision took over. At first it was pure chaos, nothing but the sound of screams in my ears as a sense of dread enveloped my body, making my hairs stand on end. I blinked to clear the darkness from my eyes, and when I opened them, the throne room was burning. Fire swooped in an arc across the floor, catching the curtains, which erupted in flames. A deafening roar shook the very foundations of the palace, the ground quaking in the aftermath, a sound unlike any I've heard an animal of this world make. Before the monster stepped into view, the vision fell away, fire and madness replaced by polished walls and heavy silence. Bastiant pressed a soft kiss to my palm, his gaze never leaving my face. I've enough experience with visions, and I've learned not to give the game away. I'm certain my expression was stone, carefully blanked by a lifetime of practice, but his eyes still swirled with questions.

I should have known he'd come looking for answers.

I should have, and yet it was still a surprise when he cornered me on my way back from what was an uneventful dinner filled with polite if ostentatious conversation—a show if I've ever seen one. No, later that night, the aethi'kine revealed his true form, and it was not the sociable, well-mannered man on display in the banquet hall.

He stepped from the shadows as I neared the entrance to my room, golden power swirling around his palms. Even if I had noticed the shimmer of magic in the air, there was little I could do anyway. Before me, Zavier reached for his sword. Behind me, I was sure Mikhail did the same. I appreciated the effort, but we all knew it was useless. At a flick of his fingers, Zavier and Mikhail stumbled to the other side of the hall. Part of me yearned to run, but the better part of me stood strong. If my father taught me anything, it's that fear is a weakness. Bastiant's power crept along my limbs, but he didn't need to use it to hold me still. I faced him with my head held proud, defiant in a way I hadn't felt in a long while.

"Princess." His voice slithered like a snake across the hall.

"Lord Bastiant."

"You had a vision in the throne room. I'd like to know what it was."

"I'm sure you would."

"It was about me."

"Perhaps."

"What did you see?"

His fingers gripped my chin at that point, his chilling eyes staring straight through mine, seeing me, I knew, not as a person but as a possession. He wasn't the first aethi'kine to look at me like that, noticing not who I was, but what I could be to him.

"Tell me, Lord Bastiant," I replied absently, my voice steady and calm despite the pounding of my heart. "Do you always get your way?"

"Yes."

"Then I'm afraid our marriage will be a disappointment. My visions are mine, and mine alone. And no matter your power, even aethi'kine magic isn't strong enough to force a woman to disclose her secrets. Not everyone is meant to know the future."

He dropped his hand from my chin in disgust.

Behind me, the ringing of a sword slipping free of its scabbard filled the silence. Zavier stepped forward, a sorry look in his eyes as he raised his weapon, my neck at the other end of one graceful swing.

"I'm not afraid to die," I told Lord Bastiant, my voice bored. "At least then I'd have the security of knowing I took my secrets to the grave."

"And what of pain?"

His golden magic shot across the room, and before I could move, Zavier acted with all the grace and speed of a predator. The tip of his sword cut through my cheek, deep enough to draw blood, but his eyes revealed silent horror. I cried out. How could I not? The burn was immense. And though I wish I didn't, I couldn't help but lift my hand to my cheek as a whimper escaped my lips. But no words passed. And they never would. Though I'm sure he never meant to, my father had taught me one important lesson—how to keep my secrets.

Zavier attacked again.

I didn't even try to fight back. His sword sliced through my arm, carefully missing my sleeve as another line of red erupted on my skin. This time I bit my lips to keep from making a sound as I met Bastiant's eyes, my own, I'm sure, filled with fire. It took all the strength I had to arch my brows at him, as though to say, 'Is that all you've got?'

His lip curled.

Zavier stumbled back to where Mikhail stood, both watching with strained muscles, fighting what I knew was an impossible fight for freedom.

"I could heal you," Bastiant said, his voice now shifting to sickly sweet.

A laugh escaped my lips. "I suspect you will regardless, unless you want my father asking questions tomorrow morning. It would hardly be the first time aethi'kine magic has been used to cover up my abuse."

He stepped forward, and this time his power was the only thing to keep me from stepping away as he lifted his hand to my cheek. Warmth sank beneath my skin, sealing my cuts before the blood evidence could reach the fabric of my gown, though against the crimson, I'm not sure it would have been seen.

"You forget something about my magic," he whispered as his thumb grazed my skin, almost lovingly if I didn't know better. Then he leaned even closer, until his scarlet hair brushed my cheek and his lips were close enough I could feel his breath against my neck. "I don't just control spirits. I see through them. Your walls may be made of iron to everyone else, but to me, they're glass. You're a she-wolf with a soft heart—all bark, and no bite."

He stepped back and a golden arc of power shot across the hall. Metal clinked as Zavier and Mikhail stepped forward, facing one another with their weapons raised. Bastiant arched his brow in my direction, his power sizzling above his palm, one fatal command away. I'd like to think my reaction would have been the same no matter who stood before me, that I would always value life before my own stubborn pride, but I can't deny that as I stared at those swords poised to strike, my mind flashed back to the vision in which Zavier's hazel eyes looked at me as though I were his whole world, and I acted.

"Stop."

Bastiant's mouth curled into a smile that could make even the sun go back into hiding. "Your vision?"

"Not nearly so interesting as to cause all of this. I saw the throne room on fire. People were screaming and a roar shook the earth, then nothing."

"That's all?"

"My magic is a little more unwieldy than yours. It does what it wants, and all I can do is bear witness."

"Well, at least I learned one thing tonight."

"And what's that?"

"Our marriage might not be so disappointing after all."

I don't think I breathed as he walked away, dread like a vice around my throat. Even after the shimmer of his power left the air, I stood frozen by the fear. It wasn't until I felt a warm hand on my forearm that I finally snapped from the trance.

"Princess?" Zavier asked, his voice like a fire on a cool winter's night, instantly fighting off the chill. "Are you all right?"

"Of course."

I nodded and turned toward my rooms. He hurried ahead to get the door while Mikhail lingered behind, his sword at the ready. There was no need. The danger had passed. Still, I didn't argue as Zavier led me inside, through my quarters, all the way to my bedroom, his hunter's eyes scanning the shadows for hidden threats. When it was clear the area was safe, he strode quickly to the exit to give me my peace. Before he left, he paused in the doorway, drawing my gaze.

"I'm sorry, Princess" he murmured, focused on the ground, though I could see the grooves etched into his forehead from his frown.

"For what?" I asked.

He turned to me with surprise. "For hurting you."

It did not go unnoticed that for the first time he forgot to end the sentence with my title. His guard was down, and his hazel eyes were as deep as undiscovered forest pools. I held them, feeling my own walls crumble. "That wasn't your fault."

"It was my sword."

"You're not the first unwilling participant to lay a hand on me, and I doubt you will be the last. Please, don't feel guilty on my account. I know better than most how aethi'kine power works."

The golden highlights in his eyes flashed with unmasked sadness. But I wanted his pity even less than his disregard. I'm a princess of the realm. My suffering is small compared to some of the other suffering I've seen.

"Thank you," he finally said.

I knew what he meant—thank you for sparing him and Mikhail both, for choosing their lives above my secrets. The cost tonight was small, a simple vision, but we both knew that with time, revealing my weakness would exact a greater price. Oh well, Bastiant was right. I have a soft heart. If he didn't discover it tonight, I doubt I would have been able to hide it for very long.

"Good night, Soldier Zavier."

"Good night, Princess."

He stayed for one more moment and we held each other's gazes across the distance. For the first time, despite the title, I think maybe he saw me as a woman. A charge filled the air, spreading a heat across my skin, and then he was gone. The feeling remained, though. Even now, as I write, my cheeks are flushed.

Something changed tonight.

And if that's the case, my sacrifice was most definitely worth it.

Twenty-Third Day of the Fourth Moon

Bastiant is still here, but the days have been uneventful. He's agreed to our marriage. To my father, he is ever the charming soon-to-be son-in-law. He hasn't cornered me in the halls again, though I get the sense he's just biding his time. Soon enough, I'll be his to do with as he wills.

The very thought makes me queasy.

So I try to focus on other things—my people, my kingdom, all the lives that will be saved by securing this alliance so none of the neighboring aethi'kine will dare attack us.

Mostly, though, I concentrate on Zavier.

My attention slides to him as though by strings, and lately I've felt his gaze upon my skin as well. I study the way the light falls across his bare biceps, the way it plays along his sun-kissed skin, the way his muscles flex and coil as he moves. I trace the outline of his wings and imagine what it might feel like to brush my fingers over his feathers, to watch them ripple at my touch. Sometimes, I wonder what it might be like to fly. Not myself, of course, but in his arms, the ground a blur below me as I huddle against his warm chest, the breeze swirling around us. In the privacy of my room, I envision more intimate things, the sort that make me blush to even write—what it would be like to press my lips against his, to kiss my way down his throat, to feel the deep rumble of a sigh beneath skin.

Do avians make love the way we do? I never thought to wonder, but now I do. As my marriage night goes from a far-off future to a very real possibility, I can't help but dream of my first time with a noble warrior instead of a cruel mage. I doubt even my mother would fault me. What did she think on the eve of her union with my father? Did she have a lover first to show her the way? Or was she a proper lady, honored to be chosen as queen?

I suspect the first.

But perhaps it's just my own selfish desires that wish it might be so, that if she were alive she might understand me. It makes me feel a little less alone.

Tomorrow is my last day with my future husband. He'll return in a few moons for our wedding, and though I'm not experienced in seduction, I think it would be a rather enjoyable way to spend my time in the interim.

Twenty-Fourth Day of the Fourth Moon

Something is about to happen. Something big is coming. I don't know what, but I know when—tonight. Which is why I'm writing this down in case I don't get the chance.

I had a vision this morning.

After breakfast, I took a walk in the gardens to clear my head, Zavier and Mikhail following me dutifully. I paused to smell some of the jasmine newly bloomed after the cool winter and plucked a bud. As I crushed the petals and lifted them to my nose, I felt the tingle at the back of my neck. Before I could blink, I was deep in the future.

Wind rushed against my cheeks. Warm arms held me close. My forehead was pressed against a solid chest and my eyes shut as I trembled with fear. The air prickled with magic, crashes and booms so loud they made me jump.

"I've got you," a man whispered in my ear. Zavier. I would know his deep voice anywhere, and instantly the sound calmed me. "We're almost—"

He broke off and my eyes shot open.

The window he flew toward disappeared behind a cascade of falling stone, but I recognized our location by the richly painted archways—the banquet hall. The starry pendants on the ceiling caved in and the room collapsed around us. He dove, to where I'm still not sure. All I saw were the flowing violet skirts of my gown as they rose to cover my face. I tried to swat them away, but before I knew it, the screaming chaos was replaced by perfect silence.

Then, "Zavier!"

Not me, someone else. Someone older, a voice filled with fear.

The vision ended.

I still don't understand what it means. How did we escape so quickly? Where did we go? Who did that voice belong to?

I dropped my hand from the jasmine and turned to face him. I'm not sure what gave me away, but understanding lit his gaze. Somehow, he knew I had a vision. Somehow, he sensed my magic. And by the look in my eyes, he must have known I'd seen him.

When I returned to my rooms, my maid was there with my evening dress already laid upon the bed, the same deep violet silks from my vision. Whatever I saw, it's happening tonight. It's happening now, as soon as I finish writing this and I leave my room for dinner. Bastiant is going to act. My father, I'm sure, will stop him. I could try to warn him, but I don't want to change the future I've seen—I want to fly. I want Zavier to whisk me away. I want to know this secret of his that waits just out of reach. But the future, even from visions so clear, can be fickle, which is why I wrote this down.

Just in case I don't come back: I love you, Mother.

I'll see you in the aether.

22

CASSI

The *pyro'kine* circled down the steps, a dinner tray balanced in one hand while the other sizzled before him like a torch, lighting the way through the dark halls at the base of Malek's castle. The moisture along the walls sparkled. In the darkness outside that moving halo, Cassi hovered unseen.

She'd been planning Elias's escape for days, neglecting all her other duties, and the time to act was finally here. There was no telling how soon Malek would return, but when he did, she'd lose her chance. His mages were vulnerable without him, and she planned to capitalize on that weakness. Elias, of course, had no idea. He feared magic far too much. Though she'd whispered subtle suggestions through his dreams, trying to make him understand the entire plan would have been more than he could handle. Besides, he was a warrior. When he saw the opening, he'd take it. At least, she hoped he would.

The *pyro'kine* stopped outside their cell and set down the tray. The keys jingled loudly in the silence as he tugged them free of his belt and lifted them to the lock.

Please hear that, Elias.

Please be ready.

The door to the cell swung open. In the back corner of the room, Elias stood protectively before her immobile body, his sandy wings spread to either side like a shield. Suspicion shone in his deep brown eyes as he watched the man push the tray deeper into their room. The flames around the fire mage's hand brightened. Elias stepped back involuntarily, his sharp intake of breath loud against the silence. In her spirit form, Cassi could feel the mage's amusement. It made her want to scream.

Elias bent his knees, shifting subconsciously into the stance of a soldier at the ready. The tray scraped against the stone, inching farther and farther into the room, until finally it was beyond the door. The mage straightened and reached for the knob.

Cassi acted.

Shooting through the shadows, she forced her spirit inside his mind and took hold of his thoughts. The mage rebelled against her. While dreams were easy, Cassi had to claw and scrape and dig with her magic to hold on to his waking mind. He expelled her within moments.

A satisfying *crack* split the air.

By the time Cassi righted herself, the mage was unconscious on the floor. Elias stood above him with the water jug in his hand, the gray stone bright with blood. He tossed it to the side, the remaining liquid splashing as it fell.

Go, she thought. *Go.*

But he didn't. He stood frozen before the open door, his jaw clenched. Then in one fell swoop, he spun on his heels and knelt before her bed.

"Come on, Cassi," he murmured as he shoved his hands beneath her back and knees, then scooped her into his arms. "Time to go."

No, she wanted to scream, but it was useless. *Leave me, Elias. Forget about me. Save yourself!*

He didn't. He wouldn't. The sight warmed her heart, affection and annoyance both ripe and burning. It was her curse in life to be surrounded by noble idiots—her curse and her blessing.

The light from their cell only extended so far, and after moments of running, they were enshrouded in darkness. Elias used his wings to feel along the walls, his feathers scraping painfully against the uneven stones as he searched for the opening. Luckily, the stairs weren't far, and he found them quickly. The climbing was slow in the narrow, circular passage, the cramped space too tight for their wings. He moved gingerly to avoid crushing her feathers, which dragged along the floor.

Idiot, she silently cursed the entire time. *Beautiful idiot.*

They reached the top and he braced her against the wall as he slid open the door, blinking away the sudden brightness. No one waited on the other side. They were alone, as she'd known they would be at this late hour of night.

Go, she thought. *Go.*

Excitement fluttered through her spirit. The plan was actually working. He was going to make it.

Elias ran down the hall, his bare feet silent on the rug. If she had breath, she would have held it, waiting for some sort of alarm to sound. But they weren't used to housing prisoners in the castle, and they'd underestimated him, seeing only his lack of power and not his other skills. He took the corners slowly, checking for guards before dashing around the bends. Cassi knew exactly where they were, but he didn't—he couldn't.

Go right, she silently urged. *Turn right.*

At the next fork, he cut right as though he'd heard her voice in his thoughts. At the end of the hall, a balcony waited, the heavy curtains stirring in the breeze. His spirit lifted. So did hers. Elias ran, no longer worrying about caution. His wings began to beat. His feet barely touched the ground. They soared, closer, closer, closer, and—

A spout of water shot through the opening and slammed into Elias's chest, knocking him backward. As her body spilled across the floor, Cassi's spirit spun. A mage stood behind them, blue simmering at her fingertips while she tunneled water in from the outside. Despite the flood, Elias jumped to his feet, ripped a torch from the walls, and hefted it like a club. Before he could take a swing, a liquid sphere encircled his face, churning around his mouth and nose to cut off air.

Stop!

No one heard her scream. She lay useless on the floor, her mouth open and unmoving, even as her spirit cried.

Stop!

Elias's body twitched. His arms dropped as he swayed unsteadily on his feet. The water kept cycling, kept spinning.

Stop!

Cassi slammed into the mage's mind. Same as the last time, within moments she was expelled, unable to hold on. Elias knelt on his hands and knees, coughing as the breath rushed to his lungs. The *hydro'kine* glanced suspiciously around the hall, a knowing look in her eyes. A whistle rose to her lips. Elias scrambled toward Cassi's body as two more mages rushed into the hall.

Leave me, she whimpered. *Go. Go.*

He grabbed her by the armpits and tried to drag her toward the balcony. Wind rushed through the opening, pressing against his chest like a living wall. Still, Elias fought, gritting his teeth as he battled for just one more inch. The metal torch on the ground rose into the air, surrounded by flecks of green. His eyes widened in fear one moment before it whipped into his stomach, knocking the breath from his lungs. He stumbled backward. The torch swung, swiping his legs out from underneath him. Elias dropped. Once more, the torch came down, this time into the center of his chest. Her friend groaned in pain.

Cassi crashed into the *ferro'kine*, all the while knowing it was no use. He swatted her from his mind as though swatting a bug from the air, and by the time she emerged, Elias was already bound at the wrists.

Against three mages, they had no hope. At least not like this—her body splayed across the soaked carpet, her limbs motionless. All she wanted to do was sink into her skin, rise from the floor, and defend him—but she couldn't. She could do nothing as they hauled him through the castle and back into the cell. The slamming of the door reverberated through the darkness.

She was useless.

No—less than useless. She was a burden. A liability. If not for her limp body, he might have made it to freedom. He would have moved faster, flown more swiftly. He could have been halfway home by now.

"I'm sorry, Cassi," he whispered over her body after the mages had hauled her back into the cell. "I'm so sorry. I tried. I tried."

It's not your fault.

It was me.

I failed you.

She wanted to scream. She wanted to kick over a barrel. She wanted to punch a wall. She wanted to throw and tear and rip and pull until the entire castle was in shambles. She wanted to knock it down stone by stone. This had been her one shot to *do* something, something tangible, not sharing messages or eavesdropping or spying, but something that made her feel good, something that made her feel alive. She couldn't remember the last time she'd felt alive.

Except she could.

It had been in the dark hall of the owl archives, her body pressed against Xander's, her lips grazing his throat, his hand digging into her waist as his breath washed over her skin. That was the last time she remembered feeling that potent spark of life, that unique burn of being perfectly in a moment, of being awake in every sense of the word.

She wanted to feel that way again.

She needed to feel that way again.

By the time her mind caught up with her spirit, she was already racing through the mist. Cassi burst through the fog, the moon and stars goading her on as they twinkled defiantly in the darkness. The House of Paradise loomed like a shadow overhead. This was a bad idea. A terrible one. A mistake.

She couldn't stop.

She didn't—not until she pushed through the tree trunk to find him peacefully asleep, a soft smile on his lips. He was stretched across the floor, one arm flung casually above his head while the other rested across his abdomen, hand hidden beneath the sheets. His wings unfurled, taking up most of the floor. Lyana slept soundly on the bed, her dove wings acting the cocoon as she turned away from Xander toward the wall. The King and Queen of the House of Whispers. It was a sham, but the thought still stopped her cold.

He was a king. She was a traitor.

He was honest. She was a spy.

He was undeniably good. She was irrevocably damned.

They would never be, which was why she hadn't visited his dreams. It would be too painful to spend even a moment inside his beautiful mind, remembering the night they'd flown through imagined worlds together, knowing it would never be the same now that he knew the truth of who she was. She didn't want to taint that single perfect memory—that one stolen night.

Cassi retreated, shrinking back across the room. She was halfway through the wood when his voice stopped her.

"Cassi."

It was hardly more than a mumble, but she froze.

"Cassi."

The word was half air, softer than a whisper. Xander shifted in his sleep, his shoulders writhing as his legs twitched. His eyelids fluttered with movement, a sign he was deep within a dream. But what dream?

She inched closer.

A soft sigh escaped his lips.

If curiosity was her downfall, let her be doomed. Before she could second-guess, Cassi pressed her spirit to his body and dove inside his mind. Instead of trying to tame the chaos, she let it envelop her, allowing Xander to lead so she might follow, down and down and down the vortex, until she settled in his dream.

The room was silent aside from the crackle of fire. Book spines pressed into her back. A hand cupped her face, thumb gently caressing her cheek. She couldn't breathe. She couldn't move. Slowly, Cassi opened her eyes, waiting for the trick—the knife to cut into her side, the fingers to stiffen around her throat, the anger, the pain.

Nothing came.

As she met his lavender gaze, time seemed to stop. Then Xander leaned forward, closing the distance between them, and kissed her.

23

XANDER

Xander pressed his lips to hers, not sure what she would think. Cassi was Lyana's best friend. Lyana was missing. He was breaking every one of his rules, all sense of decorum. The only thing he knew was that if he spent one more moment in his library beside her but not touching her, he'd go mad. So he took his chance. He kissed her.

Cassi fell still.

He caught her gasp in his mouth as her face arched up to meet his. Then he pulled back, studying her molten eyes in the moonlight. Did she want this? Was this all right? His blood pounded in his ears, every one of his muscles straining not to pounce until he knew for certain.

"Ca—"

She grabbed him by the jacket and pulled. Their lips crashed together once more, frantic this time, as though all the walls had crumbled, leaving nothing but a raging river of desire to swallow them whole. Her kisses were hungry, almost feral, the she-cat in her spirit bringing out a wildness he didn't know he possessed. When she moaned, he dug his fingers into her hair, something within him coming undone. His arm wrapped around her waist, drawing her closer. She arched into his chest. He leaned into her weight, pressing her back against the shelves as he grabbed her fingers and held their clasped fists above her head.

Cassi was a fighter. She could have broken free at any moment, if she wanted to. But she didn't. She slid her hand up his chest and around his neck, drawing him in until they molded together. A groan escaped his lips and he shifted his mouth to create a trail of kisses down her throat. She sighed, a sound that made the fire beneath his skin blaze. One of her legs moved up his thigh to hook around his waist as a frustrated growl purred through her.

All at once, the shelves dissolved and they fell together, landing on the soft pillows of a bed. Cassi pushed his shoulders, rolling him over so she straddled his hips. His shirt disappeared. Xander inhaled sharply as her hands roved over his bare chest and down his abdomen, his every nerve aflame. He reached for the buttons on her jacket—and paused.

He only had one hand.

His right one was gone, which meant…

Xander tore his mouth free of hers. "Cassi."

"Xander," she sighed his name, her lips tracing the curve of his jaw as she writhed against him.

"No, Cas—"

Her mouth came upon his and he lost himself in the feel of her, in the heat rising between them, in the hands still trailing down his torso, skimming the edge of his belt. Then he remembered the knife at his throat, the brother he'd lost, the game she'd played.

"Cassi, stop!"

He pushed her back and rolled out from under her, breathing heavy as he fought the instincts screaming at him to just let go, to give in to this moment, to fall for the dream. Behind him, Cassi sighed. Unlike before, this one was full of dejection, not passion.

"How did you know?" she asked simply.

He swallowed, his throat tight, and then he balled his fingers into fists, all ten of them, both real and imagined. "My hand."

"What about it?"

"I only have one."

The mattress dipped as she shifted on the bed, her gaze on his back as tangible as any touch, hot and burning. She didn't speak. She just waited, the silence stretching between them, the air so thick he couldn't breathe. He knew her. She was stubborn enough to wait all night if she must. So was he, but the words simmered on his tongue regardless.

Closing his eyes, as though somehow it made him less vulnerable, he murmured, "In *my* dreams, I touch you with two hands."

There was no pity, no sympathy, no concern, all of which he'd feared. Instead, she simply ran her fingers over the edge of his wing, a shiver rippling across his feathers, and said, "You've only ever needed one."

He stood, the words too much to bear. They were everything he'd ever wanted to hear, spoken by the one person he knew he shouldn't crave but did.

"What are you doing here, Cassi? Or should I say Kasiandra?"

"Don't."

"Why? It's your name, isn't it?"

"Please, Xander. I didn't— I mean, I— Just...please."

She sounded so tired, his body turned of its own accord. He'd never seen her so fragile, sitting in the center of an empty bed, her feet tucked beneath her, staring down at the hands clasped loosely on her lap. Her wings hung around her shoulders like a cape. For a moment, he couldn't help but wonder if it was an act. But the truth was out. She had no more reason to lie, to pretend, at least not with him.

"Are you all right?"

She looked up, surprise softening her features.

"Your body, I mean. That man, that king, he's not hurting you, is he?"

"No," she whispered, releasing a long breath. "No, he's not hurting me. He's not helping me. He's not doing anything with me, really, which would normally thrill me, except he's the only person in the world who can fix me."

Xander nodded as though he understood, though he didn't, not really. Even after his spending these past few weeks with Lyana, the magic was beyond him.

"And you?" Cassi asked. "Are you well?"

He was mated to the woman in love with his brother. He was lying to his people. He was fighting a war he couldn't win. He was struggling at almost every second of the day not to scream. "As well as can be expected."

"That's good."

He studied the floor, the conversation between them almost embarrassingly stilted when he considered all the nights they'd forgotten to sleep in the libraries of Rynthos, too absorbed in their discussions to notice time passing. Now it inched along, painfully slow.

"I should leave," she mumbled.

The very thought made his chest tight. "No, wait."

A hopeful glint lit her eyes. His mouth went dry. He needed a reason, anything aside from the pathetic truth that despite her lies and her actions and her deception, he was happy to see her, and he didn't want to be alone with his problems just yet. Only one option remained, but even that choice contained a revelation of its own, one he hadn't fully deciphered.

"There's something I should tell you," he said, the words coming slowly, part of him whispering, *Just let her go, just let her go*, but he couldn't. "I haven't told Lyana. I'm not sure why—maybe I didn't think it was my secret to tell. But it might help her, and you, and all of us. You just need to promise me something first. Promise you won't ask me why."

A knot formed in her brow. "Why, what?"

"Just why." He shrugged noncommittally. "Promise you won't ask."

"I promise."

"The diary you stole in Rynthos? I have it. I kept it."

"Wh—" She stopped herself as her torso rose and her wings slid back, her curiosity obvious. After licking her lips, she amended, "When did you take it?"

"The night you… The night I…" Xander swallowed, the pinprick of her blade suddenly sharp on his throat. Yet when he remembered that moment, he thought of the pleading in her eyes and the way the tension had left her body in surrender. She could have killed him, but she hadn't, and that fact was stuck on his mind like honey that couldn't be wiped clean, leaving a residue full of unresolved feelings. He cleared his throat. "That night, we searched your rooms and found the diary in your trunks. I knew you'd taken it from Rynthos, and I was going to ask you why, but, well, obviously other things happened first. I had it tucked in my jacket when the isle fell."

"And where is it now?"

"Still tucked in my jacket."

A smile fluttered over her mouth, there then gone. "What are you planning to do with it?"

"Whatever you were planning to do with it. I can't read it and asking the owls for help deciphering the language isn't exactly an option. Who did it belong to?"

"I don't know." She shifted on the bed, uncurling her legs and crossing them instead, the concentrated expression on her face one he recognized. The vulnerable girl was gone, replaced by the strategist. "There's a type of mage called a *skryr* who can pull memories out of objects. One still lives in Da'Kin. I was going to bring the diary to him, to see if there was any useful information he could pull."

"And you think there might be?"

She nodded eagerly. "This might sound crazy, but when I touched the diary in Rynthos, it was like I could feel the threads of fate sewn within its pages. It's important somehow. I'm sure."

"I believe you, which begs the question, how—"

Xander broke off as his fingers touched the bare skin of his chest. He'd been reaching for the diary in his jacket, forgetting for a moment that they were in a dream…and that he was half-naked…and that Cassi was still perched far too alluringly in his bed.

He swallowed.

Amusement danced across her eyes like starlight on a river as her lips twisted into a rueful smile. She'd read every thought in his mind, which was great. Just great. In an instant, the scene around them transformed, the walls of his room at the palace blurring then sharpening to overflowing bookshelves. Cassi lounged in one of the leather chairs before the fireplace, eying him expectantly. The sound of her passionate sigh as he pressed her against those same shelves flashed across his mind, sending a flush to his cheeks. Xander hastily took the empty chair across from her, grateful for the space, and even more grateful she'd returned his shirt, as his skin was aflame.

"Anyway, how do we—"

"Get the diary to Da'Kin?" she interrupted. He nodded. "I was going to take it myself, after I…well…"

It was her turn to squirm. A devious part of him he hadn't realized existed reveled just a little in her discomfort. "After you killed me?"

She tossed him a hard look.

Xander offered the same look right back.

"Fine, yes, after I killed you," she huffed, then took a deep breath. "I was going to take it with me when I returned to my king. Obviously, that's out of the question now."

"Maybe Lyana—"

"She shouldn't go anywhere near Malek. He's… Well, if I'm honest, I think he's becoming somewhat unhinged."

Based on what Xander had heard of the man, Malek had been unhinged for quite some time, but he kept that thought to himself. "Well, I could—"

"No, we can't risk you."

"I'm hardly—"

"Enough, Xander. Enough thinking you're dispensable, please. I can't hear it anymore. You're the King of the House of Whispers. Lyana needs you by her side. You ground her. You balance her. No one would believe her if you weren't there repackaging her demands as requests and making peace when her mind is focused on war. Enough."

Her words were so similar to Queen Zara's, they silenced him.

"Besides," Cassi continued in a softer tone, her gaze flicking to him before darting away. "*I* won't risk you. And if Malek saw you, if he caught you, I don't want to even think of the havoc it might cause."

His heart thudded painfully in his chest. *Business. Stick to business.* "So where does that leave us? No one else would dare fly beneath the mist."

"It leaves us at an impasse." She frowned. "But give me time. I'll come up with something."

"You always do."

She winced.

He hadn't meant the words as a jab, or maybe he had. He wasn't sure anymore, not with her. Nothing between them was simple, not like before, when he could look at her and see the studious owl leaning over library books or the skilled warrior amused as she attacked him by surprise or the lonely woman kissing his neck in the dark. She'd been a study in contradictions, but it had been a puzzle he'd enjoyed piecing together. Now, when he looked at her, he saw her king as the man plunged a knife in his chest during the ambush she'd helped plan, or the fear in Lyana's eyes as she'd ordered him to go, or worse still, his brother, alone somewhere, no wings at his back and a haunted expression on his face, a shell of the bird he'd once been. Things would never be easy or carefree between the two of them again.

"Xander, I—" She sighed, her wings drooping to the floor. "Thank you for saving my life. The day when the isle fell? You and Lyana didn't need to rescue my body, but you did. And I can't thank you enough for that."

"I wasn't going to just let you die, Cassi."

"You could have," she whispered, her voice and person small. "You could have, and I wouldn't have blamed you."

His chest swelled with all the things he wanted to say—that he'd missed her, that he couldn't stop thinking about her, that just having the diary close, knowing it had touched her hands before his, gave him strength. But he couldn't.

He shrank away. "Good night, Cassi."

"Goodbye."

She vanished and his consciousness slipped away. By the time he woke, light seeped through the flaps in the tent, signaling morning. He had no idea how long Cassi had been gone, or whether maybe she was still there, lingering unseen. The thought both calmed and unnerved him.

Scrubbing his palm through his hair, Xander rolled to his feet. The night was over and the time for dreaming gone. Now he needed to prepare for his next meeting with the queen.

24

RAFE

"All right, I'm just going to say it." Brighty's voice trickled down from above, nearly lost to the wind. "Your wings are a pain in my ass."

Rafe looked up from where he was perched on the cliffs, struggling to keep a smile off his face as Brighty hugged a rope to her chest, limbs trembling from the cold. At least, that's what she'd claim. But it couldn't be easy to dangle over the edge of an isle floating thousands of feet in the air when one lacked the ability to fly.

"What are you doing here?" he asked, dropping his head back against the rocks as she continued to descend into his field of view.

"What am I..." She shook her head, a sneer on her lips. "What are *you* doing here? Captain and I have been trying to talk to you ever since we landed in this frozen hellhole, and all you've done is sulk down here for hours."

"It's...complicated," he said, unable to explain the emotion stirring beneath his skin. Being back in his world as this *thing*, being back in the House of Peace again, Rafe didn't know what to feel. The last time he'd been here had been the beginning of the end

—meeting Lyana, participating in the trials, winning his brother a mate, then telling her goodbye. Every bit of him longed for those hours the two of them had spent in the cave reveling in their magic, yet every bit of him wished to forget, to go back to that fateful morning on the bridge and tell his brother no.

That was a lie.

He wouldn't change anything. Even with these flaming wings on his back and the inferno simmering beneath his skin, a heat not even this frozen landscape could subdue, he wouldn't change his past. The few bright sparks had been worth all the pain.

"Rafe, get your head out of your ass."

He frowned at her.

"There's something important Captain and I need to tell you, and we've waited long enough. Trust me."

"What? What do you need to tell me?"

Brighty pointedly eyed the rope cinched around her waist and the misty sea far, far below. Then she glared at him. "I'll tell you when I'm back on solid ground… Well, relatively solid ground." She wrinkled her nose. "Just, come on."

"Fine."

With a sigh, he fell forward and tumbled through the air. As his wings snapped open, they caught the wind, and with a few quick beats he raced past her.

"Show off!" Brighty shouted, followed by some mumbled curses he couldn't quite make out as the crew hauled her back up to the edge. By the time she'd clawed her way over the icy precipice, he was there waiting with his arms crossed. One glance, and she stomped toward the crystal dome to their left. Captain Rokaro stood on the other side of the translucent wall, watching them with a grim expression on her face.

"Do you have any idea what this is about?" he asked his shipmates, a sense of impending dread making his chest tighten.

They collectively looked at him, then at each other, then at their boots.

"I'm freezing my bloody balls off out here," Archer announced, hugging his arms, his teeth chattering. "I thought a world bathed in sunlight would be warmer. I'm going inside."

"Me too," Jolt added.

"Me three," Pyro chimed in. Rafe glared at her accusingly as he took in the flames simmering around her palms. She was a creature of fire just like him, and there was no chance she was cold. "What?" She shrugged. "Cook's making a stew."

"A word of advice," Patch's deep voice boomed in his ear as a meaty hand came down on his shoulder. "Whatever it is, Captain won't drop it. Neither of them will. So I'd get it over with if I were you."

The first mate, along with the rest of the crew, trudged across the ice to a different building in the raven guest quarters, leaving Rafe very much alone. Well, aside from the two women glaring at him from the other side of the crystals. He cast a longing gaze at the blue skies overhead, then sighed. Patch was right. Whatever it was, he couldn't put it off any longer.

"Brighty said you were looking for me?" he asked as he stepped through the door, keeping his focus on Captain Rokaro and not the *photo'kine* practically bouncing by her side.

"I was."

"Well, here I am. What's going on?"

"You should sit."

Every muscle in his body tensed. "I'm fine."

"Rafe, there's something we need to tell you." Captain Rokaro paused, shifting her weight from one foot to the other, the feathers of her copper wing rippling as her shoulders writhed. "Something you have a right to know."

The gods.

Was it Lyana? Was it Xander? Had Captain heard something?

Were they injured? His heart hammered against his ribs. With each second she delayed, the pounding only intensified, until Rafe could no longer hear anything except the drumming of his blood.

"Rafe…"

Brighty glanced at the captain, rolled her eyes, and stepped forward. "Rafe, we think you're the King Born in Fire."

"What?" All the air left his lungs as though he'd been punched in the gut.

"The King Born in Fire?" Brighty said slowly, as though talking to a child. "The king of prophecy? The one destined to save the world? We think you're him."

"Brighty, you can't— Come on, Captain— I mean—" He broke off, shaking his head. Was this some sort of a joke? His lips spread in a smile as laughter spilled up his throat, loud against the heavy silence. They had to be kidding. This had to be some twisted game. Yet as he stared into their unflinchingly somber expressions, his mirth died. "You can't be serious."

"Deadly," Captain Rokaro replied.

Rafe gulped. "But that's ridiculous. I'm not a king. Gods alive, I'm as far from a king as anyone can get. I'm a bastard. I'm half-dragon. I'm not some hero from a storybook come to save the day."

"That remains to be seen."

"Rafe," Brighty said, drawing his attention. For once in her life, there was no teasing grin on her lips or sarcastic retort on her tongue. Her voice churned with sympathy, an almost reverent edge to her tone. He wanted to puke. "We always thought the King Born in Fire would be an *aethi'kine* because the prophecy mentions healing, and they're the most powerful mages in the world, but what if we read it wrong? I saw the queen stop that tidal wave from crashing over Da'Kin. She's powerful enough on her own. She doesn't need Malek. She doesn't need another *aethi'kine*. But she might need you."

Rafe staggered back.

It was everything he wanted to hear—that he was destined for more, that he had a purpose, that he and Lyana had been drawn together by forces outside their control.

But it wasn't possible.

It couldn't be real.

"Brighty, I—"

"You can *speak* to them, Rafe. You commanded a dragon to come to our aid. You saved a ship full of sailors by sending one away. They listen to you. They heed your orders. Dragons are the only creatures in the world that can kill an *aethi'kine*, the only creatures in the world that can prevent the queen from fulfilling the prophecy, and you can control them. Don't you see what this means?"

The room began to spin. His thoughts flooded back to that night after the earthquake when Lyana had snuck into his room to heal his wings. Her golden magic had flooded his skin, and his silver power had risen to meet it, and they had crashed together, two opposite forces meeting as though made for one another.

I don't think what we have is magic, Rafe, Lyana had said as her silken fingers trailed across his bare shoulders, her gaze burning his skin. *At least, not the kind our ancestors feared. I think we were chosen—by Aethios, by Taetanos, by all the gods even. We were chosen for something more.*

He'd wanted to believe her.

He'd wanted nothing more than to take her hand, kiss her lips, and soar into the night, following whatever path destiny had created for them. Then he'd remembered Xander, and the dream had fallen apart. But what if it was real?

What if they *were* meant for something more?

The two of them—together?

"You can keep her safe," Brighty whispered as she placed her hand on his arm, something tender in the touch. He'd never spoken to her about his feelings, but she knew. She'd read the emotion on his face, the torture of wanting someone he could never have. Maybe it was a pain she herself understood. "You were made to protect her."

Rafe froze.

Protect?

His spine straightened as a gasp fled his lips and he turned toward the wall, seeing not the blue skies and snowy landscape on the other side but a dark alley and a beast of shadow made to blend into the night. His nightmares flashed, one after another after another, visions of gore and slaughter. He'd never mentioned the creature to Brighty, nor to the captain or the crew. He hadn't wanted to terrify them. Now, horror ran through his blood, turning his body cold.

Dragons weren't the only beings capable of killing an *aethi'kine.*

Just the day before Rafe had been one good punch from ending the king, a man no one else could get close enough to touch. If he could, the shadow creature could. And if the shadow creature could, so could the six others just like him waiting to hatch.

"I have to go."

Rafe spun for the door as Brighty reached for his hand. "Rafe, wait—"

"No, I have to go. I have to find her."

A wind cut across the room, slamming into his wings and drawing him back.

"We didn't tell you so you could storm off like a lovesick fool," the captain reprimanded. "Did you forget your wings? What they look like in this world? How your presence might affect everything the queen has been trying to build?"

"You don't understand," Rafe shouted.

All day, he'd been sitting on those cliffs. All day, there had been a nagging sensation at the back of his mind, a gentle tug he couldn't quite place. Brighty and the captain thought he'd been sulking, and in truth so had he. He'd felt off ever since they'd broken through the clouds, moving closer and closer to the House of Peace. From the memories, he'd thought. From the pain of his past.

Now, he realized the truth. Coming to the House of Peace hadn't unsettled him. It was coming to the rift, coming closer to the eggs. The subtle pulse in the air hadn't been a headache, but an awakening, the presence of another mind reaching out for his.

I'm here, I'm here, I'm here, the drumming seemed to say.

I'm awake.

I'm alive.

I'm here.

"The House of Paradise," he murmured to himself, turning south toward the isle as the voice in his head grew louder. "It's falling."

"What?" Brighty and Captain Rokaro asked in unison.

"It's falling!"

He ran, tearing through the guest quarters and emerging into the frozen landscape at a sprint before taking to the sky. Another of those creatures was about to hatch, and if he knew Lyana, she would be right there waiting when it did.

25

LYANA

The earthquake started at midnight. Lyana had known it was coming. All day, she'd felt the rattle in the air, the thrum of the rift, as though the spell was holding on for one final, gasping breath before it snapped. At the first shudder, she jolted out of bed. Xander was already awake, shoving his feet into his boots.

"This is it, Xander," she said hastily as she looked for her shoes.

He froze. "You're sure?"

"The isle is falling. Grab whatever you don't want to lose, then go find Queen Zara and tell her to evacuate anyone still left in the city. Get her assurance that when she arrives in the House of Peace, she'll send letters and messengers to the rest of the isles, telling them what happened here and giving us her full support. I don't know which house will fall next, so they all need to be ready. I'll meet you back at the raven camp in the House of Song as soon as I can."

"Lyana." He took her by the arm, stilling her for a moment. "Come with me."

Her heart softened. "You know I can't."

"Cassi told you what happened to the raven priests. Those creatures are dangerous. You don't know—"

"I have to see for myself, Xander. I have to see what they are, or I'll never know how to fight them. And I need to touch the rift. I need to at least try to use my magic to slow the spread, to do something."

He stared at her for a moment, then nodded, as though he'd known the argument was futile before he even made it. She loved him for trying.

"I'll be fine." She squeezed his fingers. "Trust me."

On her way to the sacred nest, she hastily stopped to warn her burgeoning army. They'd increased by four members during their time here, but their magic was still untested and timid. In this fight, they'd do more harm than good, so she told them to travel with Xander to the House of Song and wait for her there.

The palace was in chaos when she arrived. Most of the city had already been evacuated, but those who remained were clustered around the royal family. These halls, once foreign, were now familiar and no one tried to stop Lyana as she made her way into their most holy place. The priests and priestesses had, weeks before, pledged to remain with the stone until the very end, and none of her convincing could change their minds. By the time she arrived, they were already holding hands, chanting, and dancing around the floating orb which glowed emerald in the moonlight. They were determined not to abandon their god. Unless she could slow the isle's fall, they'd be dead before dawn with no wings to save them.

"Let me through," Lyana murmured as she pushed past them, magic already simmering at her fingertips. Rainbow swirls spiraled across her spirit vision, the power of the rift, growing dimmer and dimmer as the tremors intensified. The spell was fading quickly. Only minutes and the anchor would fail, but the egg hadn't cracked yet.

Lyana pressed her hands to the god stone.

The spirit within shoved back.

She reeled, releasing her magic even as she stumbled away. Golden power sank into the egg, searching for a foothold, but there was none. The creature was a rock in a riverbed, and her magic flowed around it without breaking through.

Come on.

Green flares oozed from the orb and the ground lurched. Earth magic. The human lost somewhere inside the beast must have once been a *geo'kine.* Lyana reached for the spirit in the soil, trying to calm the tremors, but with the earthquake already rattling the isle, it was useless. Her wings held her upright even as half the priests and priestesses fell to their knees. Deep within the palace, someone screamed.

Come on.

She reached for the creature's spirit again, but even with her magic, there was no way to command it, at least not for long. The briefest graze burned, its soul too hot to touch, like trying to hold a fire in her hand. It blazed. The dragon inside fought back, as though it knew she wanted to keep it caged, but the beast was too wild to tame.

Lyana switched tactics, focusing not on the egg vibrating ferociously in the air, but on the rainbow threads laced through it. The rift spell was nearly gone, the lingering traces of power hardly more than shimmers in the air, not the bright, buzzing weave she remembered from her last visit to the sacred nest. She dove into the magic. Like the creature, it slipped through her fingers, oil on water, too slippery to grasp.

How am I supposed to seal it if I can't even hold it?

What am I supposed to do?

If Malek were here, he would know. Not for the first time, she wondered if she'd done the right thing in leaving him—if it was her stubborn streak, and not his, that would cause the end of the world.

Malek wouldn't be here anyway. He abandoned this world a long time ago, but I won't abandon them too.

The god stone dropped to the ground with a resounding *thud.*

The priests gasped.

"Step back!" Lyana ordered, using her magic to shove them away. They were humans, and their souls were like butter in her grasp, malleable and soft.

Go, go, she silently ordered, uncaring of their devotion to Mnesme and the protests spilling from their lips. Any moment, the creature would emerge, and they couldn't be there when it did. Cassi had described the scene in the House of Whispers as pure slaughter, over before it had even begun. The same would not happen today. *Go!*

They scattered.

A crack appeared in the egg, fine at first then spreading like slow-moving lightning, fracturing across the shell, until *snap*. The stone split, falling open into two halves. Jade smoke oozed from the cavity, spilling across the floor like an earthen fog. From the center of the haze, the creature emerged, its leathery wings unfurling like a cocoon. Dark pine scales glistened over every inch of its body. The edges caught the light, sharp as knives. In place of fingers, it had claws, menacing and deadly. When it opened its eyes, turning toward her, there were no pupils, no white corners, nothing but deep, impenetrable green. A pink tongue darted through its lips, licking once as it stretched its head from side to side.

Lyana stepped back involuntarily.

The creature moved forward, each placement of its foot reverberating through the floor and making the walls of the sacred nest shake with renewed vigor. Rift magic crashed across the air, no longer set in place, struggling to remain connected to the anchor now on the move. If she could just keep the beast in the sacred nest, maybe that would give them more time. If she could just hold on to it for a moment.

The creature roared as she dug her magic beneath its skin, snapping its head toward her with new focus. Her heart burned. Fire bubbled through her veins, scorching her from the inside out. Hardly more than a second passed before she let go with a gasp, stumbling back as she clutched at her chest, surprised to find smooth skin instead of melted, swollen flesh. The beast was on her in a heartbeat. Its hand latched around her arm, the touch making her inhale sharply as its spirit penetrated deep as a blade, like a claw digging into her soul instead of her body. It pulled. Her power lurched, flooding down her arm and seeping through her pores against her will.

What?

Lyana jerked her arm, but the creature's grip was relentless. A spark lit the corners of its eyes, gleaming almost like pleasure as her magic continued to sink beneath its scales, the golden aura completely absorbed by the green. In the world below, Malek had cautioned her not to rely on weapons, but Lyana had never quite been able to give them up, thank the gods. The creature was so consumed it didn't notice as she gripped the dagger at her waist and slashed. It let go, more from shock than from pain, no cry upon its lips. Her blade had barely pierced the tough hide of its wrist, but the reprieve was all she needed.

Lyana reached for the spirit of the nearest tree and yanked, a *crack* splitting the air as the trunk broke in half. The wood slammed into the creature's chest, tossing it backward. She flipped the tree end over end and twisted the branches around the beast like a cage. It sank a fist into the ground, and the soil crumbled into a cavernous ravine. Lyana launched into the sky as the ground beneath her gave out. The creature disappeared in the shadows of the crevice. Green shimmers flooded the air. Boulders of mud and rock shot from the opening, speeding toward her. Lyana batted them away, one after another, branches snapping as the grove took the brunt of the damage. Birds fled, squawking as they took to the sky. But there was nowhere to go. They were trapped in the hollowed-out core, same as she, unless…

High overhead, metal glinted in the starlight.

Lyana reached for the cage with her magic and yanked on the grating until she felt it pull free. The creature materialized from the shadows, soaring toward her, arm outstretched. A foot from her body, the metal slammed into the beast, sending it to the ground. The creature writhed beneath the bars, which held it flat against the dirt. Lyana landed by its side and pulled another dagger free, eying the soft flesh around its neck. The scales there were finer, more rounded, vulnerable. Arching her arm behind her head, she aimed the weapon down and—

A hand grabbed her around the throat.

No—not a hand. A claw with five sharp points dug into her flesh until she felt beads of blood drip down her neck and soil her collar. A creature dark as night stood before her, like a phantom appearing from thin air. Its eyes were fathomless black, its scales liquid ink. Everything about it promised death.

Lyana choked.

Her magic rushed from her spirit, useless as it fled into the creature's skin. Her toes scraped along the floor as the beast drew her closer, cutting off air. Its mouth opened, fangs stark white against the ebony.

This is it, she thought, her vision spotting. *This is how the world ends.*

"Ana!" Rafe's voice filled the sacred nest, quiet against the rumbling of the earthquake, surely a dream. "Ana!"

A blade flashed.

The creature wailed.

Lyana dropped to the ground as an inferno stormed to life before her.

26

RAFE

Flames seeped from Rafe's wings to match the fury raging in his gut. Onyx blood dripped from the edge of his blade as he whirled the sword around for another attack. This time, the shadow beast caught the steel in its palm and held it steady. Shock poured from its mind, flooding Rafe's, the confusion thick and overwhelming. It looked at the black fluid oozing between its scales, then back up.

Rafe dug his boot into the creature's chest, pushing it away as the second one slowly rose from the ground, earthen magic pouring from its frame. They stared at each other for a beat, the same and yet different. He realized with perfect clarity what the shadow monster had been doing these past weeks—studying him, testing him, trying to figure out if he was friend or foe. Those obsidian eyes watched him now, calculating and intense.

The onyx creature stepped forward.

Rafe moved to block.

It ticked its head, then stepped to the other side.

Rafe leveled his blade at its throat, his message clear.

She's mine.

Possessiveness oozed from his pores, sinking into the mental bond with undeniable authority. They wouldn't be allowed to pass. The line was drawn, Lyana on one side and these creatures on the other—and Rafe knew exactly where he stood.

Go, he ordered. *Leave now.*

The shadow beast hissed, baring its teeth. Beside him, the earthen creature did the same. They moved together, communicating with their thoughts, a conversation he couldn't hear as one slid left and the other right. Rafe yanked his other sword from his back and menacingly whirled the twin blades before his face. Behind him, magic stirred.

"Rafe?" Lyana murmured, stunned.

"Stay back, Ana."

"I can help."

Golden power flooded the air. Immediately, both creatures snapped their heads toward her. Hunger flared deep in Rafe's stomach, a yearning so intense he could hardly breathe for want of her magic. It oozed with life and spirit, like air to a drowning man, promising vitality. One touch and he could drink in her power. A yawning abyss opened deep inside him, a darkness and a need only her magic could fill. It took every ounce of strength he possessed not to spin toward her and lunge, to remember who he was, the human and not the beast, his love for her like a tether in the storm, keeping him anchored.

"Ana, no—"

It was too late.

The creatures attacked.

"Cover your ears!"

Rafe lunged for them and released his raven cry. The green creature stopped cold, frozen by the power in his call. Made of shadow magic, the onyx one didn't even pause. They crashed together, flames and darkness, claws and swords. Rafe stabbed. The creature dodged. He swung. It rolled. Sparks flashed on steel as his blade scratched razor-sharp scales. The beast was fast, but so was Rafe, and unlike its other victims, he always knew where it was thanks to their mental bond. Even though the creature was made of smoke, Rafe followed it through the night, neither gaining ground. As the green one started to stand, he released another raven cry.

"Rafe!"

He couldn't stop to look at her. It took everything he had to stay on top of the shadow monster, to stay between them.

"Rafe!"

Her magic swelled, the golden sheen so thick he could hardly see the trees of the sacred grove. The creature became nothing more than an onyx wisp darting between rays of sunlight, her power turning midnight to midday. The sky glittered.

"Rafe! It's fall—"

The ground gave out and her voice turned into a yell. Branches, bark, and wood grain rushed by as he snapped his wings to catch the air. The isle dropped out from under him, the canopy of the rainforest giving way to a canvas of stars. The shadow beast hovered beside him, but no one else. Lyana was alone with the earthen creature.

Rafe dove.

The monster dove after him.

Below, the forest shimmered, a golden aura spreading across the trees, wider and wider, until the whole isle glowed like a comet falling in the night.

All at once, the light blinked out.

"Ana!"

Rafe collapsed his wings, not bothering to dive or aim or fly, but rather plummeting with as much speed as possible toward the ground far below. The shadow beast kept pace. They fell, faster and faster, the wind a whistle in his ears. Against the backdrop of the dark forest, a glint of metal caught his eye. The spot grew, surging toward them, surrounded by flecks of gold. Rafe grinned as the cage flew past him, golden bars warped and twisted in an uneven circle holding the green creature inside.

Lyana was all right.

She was alive.

The isle slipped between the folds of fog, disappearing into the Sea of Mist, but not before the golden aura returned. Twice as bright as before, the spirit magic was fueled by a heart more determined than any other he'd ever encountered. Whatever she was trying to do, she would succeed. Somehow, she'd find a way. All he had to do was give her time.

Rafe flipped in midair, turning to face the onyx creature trailing him. In one deft move, he opened his wings and held out his swords. The beast plummeted into the blades before it could stop, taken by surprise. A wail filled the air, more anger than pain. Rafe sent an image through the mental bond—his sword plunging into the heart of the earthen creature. Exactly as he'd hoped, a roar surged up from below.

Darting skyward, Rafe searched for the glow of the cage in the air. It was falling now, no longer suspended by Lyana's magic. The beast was still trapped inside, but it wouldn't be for long. The bars were bending beneath its strength, stretching wider and wider. Rafe cut across the sky, smooth as a sharpened blade through flesh, holding his sword aloft.

Claws dug into his ankle.

His skin tore open.

Healing magic rushed to the spot as he kicked the shadow monster free. A moment later, those same talons raked across his calf, then dug into his thigh. Rafe hissed against the pain. The creature climbed him like a tree, claws taking root in his spine then his shoulders as a hand came around his neck. Rafe flipped his sword and drove the blade backward. The metal met resistance. He forced it deeper, then twisted the hilt, satisfied when he heard a crunch.

The shadow beast released him.

Rafe ripped his weapon free and spun to face the creature. It clutched its midsection, ebony blood seeping through its fingers. Hurt struck his mind, sharp and piercing, deeper than any physical pain, strung through with betrayal.

This wasn't over.

Far from it.

Deep down, Rafe understood this battle was only just beginning. But tonight, he'd won. The demon retreated, fleeing back into the dark folds of night, and the green one raced to follow, still new to this world and willing to go where led. They'd be back. They'd never stop coming for him or for Lyana, not now.

Let them.

Rafe collapsed his wings and let the fog envelop him, happy to leave the moon and the stars behind as he raced toward the piercing pull of Lyana's magic, still a potent elixir gnawing at his gut. By the time he reached the isle, her power was little more than a dull shimmer in the air, fading more and more with each passing moment. The land was no longer falling, which meant it must have reached the sea. He had to find her before it sank.

Hold on, Ana. Please, hold on.

He cut through the trees, passing broken branches and severed trunks, the destruction unmistakable. As he neared the city, her magic gave out. That last bit of light disappeared, leaving him blind and without the hunger to lead him forward. Wisps of vapor curled around the trees, turning the forest dark and gloomy. An eerie tingle itched up his spine as he flew past rope bridges swaying and creaking loudly in the silence. Homes were destroyed. Once-sturdy platforms were little more than splintered fragments. A few gentle cries echoed across the air, in pain and fear, their desperation obvious. Looming ahead was the familiar entrance to the massive tree containing the sacred nest of the House of Paradise, now little more than a hollow core of wood, empty of all that had once made it holy.

He found Lyana in the spot where he'd left her, white wings drooping to the ground as she swayed unsteadily on her feet. When she fell, he caught her.

"Rafe."

She said his name as though everything good in the world were contained within the sound. He melted, the fire in his blood replaced with something just as warm, just as potent, yet infinitely more powerful. Love.

"Ana, I'm here."

He stroked her cheek as she lifted her palm to his face and ran her fingers along the edge of his jaw. No magic lit her skin, but her touch was electric just the same.

"I did it, Rafe," she murmured, a smile widening her lips, even as her eyes grew dazed. "I did it."

He had no idea what she was talking about, so he just brushed his thumb across her skin and threaded his hand through her braids, holding her head up as her muscles weakened. They dropped to the ground together, Lyana's body failing as he cradled her to his chest.

"They'll have an isle to come back to," she whispered, voice growing softer with each word. "When all this is over, they'll have a place to call home."

The last bits of her energy gave out and she went limp in his arms. Breath slid evenly between her lips as her chest rose and fell in a soothing rhythm. She was exhausted and spent but alive, and that was all that mattered. Rafe shifted them into a more comfortable position, content to let her sleep across his lap however long it took for her to wake. There was no place in the world he'd rather be and no one in the world he'd rather be with.

Maybe he was the King Born in Fire.

Maybe not.

Either way, he would never leave her side again, not unless she asked, and maybe not even then. Brighty had been right. Protecting her was what he'd been born to do. From now on, where she went, he would follow. Nothing would break them apart again.

27

LYANA

The gentle thud of a heartbeat stirred Lyana from her slumber. Warm arms held her close, leaving her calmer and more peaceful than she could ever remember. She didn't need to open her eyes to know who it was. His spirit called out to hers, steadfast and true. The fingers gently stroking her cheek were as familiar as her own, she'd felt them so often in her dreams. The gentle scratching of his rough knuckles lured her back to the world.

"Rafe."

"I'm here," he murmured, the deep timbre of his voice sending a shiver down her spine. "You're safe."

His blue eyes held more promise than the vast open sky as she lifted her hand to trace the chiseled curve of his jaw. "I told you I'd come back for you," she said, a smile tugging at her lips. "But I guess you beat me to it. How did you know?"

"That you'd be in the most dangerous place possible?" His mouth twisted into a grin. "Experience."

She rolled her eyes. "I meant that the isle was falling."

"I—" The humor vanished from his face, leaving dark shadows

in its place. Shame burned at the edges of his soul, a stain she wished she could wipe clean. "I heard it." He swallowed the knot in his throat. "I heard it waking up."

The creature.

Cassi had told her about his nightmares, about his communication with the dragons, about his interaction with the shadow beast. He was connected to them somehow, a fact that clearly grated at his thoughts.

"Good," she said simply, not giving his discomfort space to thrive. "If you hadn't, I'd be dead. Where are they?"

"Gone…for now."

Lyana nodded, understanding the unspoken implication—they'd be back. Though she wanted to remain in his arms all day, there was no time for her own desires. Already, the souls of the injured called out to her from across the city, their pain and yearning too great to ignore. She was a queen first and a woman second, no matter how much she wished it could be different. Dropping her hand from his cheek, she pushed off his lap with a sigh.

"How long have I been asleep?"

"Not long," he said, following her to his feet. "Half an hour, maybe."

"And the isle's been steady?"

He knitted his brows. "What?"

"The ground hasn't moved? It's been stable?"

Rafe glanced around, as though only just realizing the truth in the statement, and nodded, more confused than before. "How?"

"When the House of Whispers fell, I was too weak after the tidal wave, and I got there too late to stop it from sinking into the sea. But this time…" The walls of the sacred nest were fissured, the trees broken, the birds once housed within long gone, but the ground was steady under her feet. It didn't sway. It didn't shake. The isle was level—set. "I think I saved the House of

Paradise. Instead of thinking it was falling into the sea, I tried to envision it returning to the soil beneath the water. This land once belonged here, before our homes were lifted into the sky. I focused on that. I thought of the cliffs as tears and breaks, I thought of the deep-sea floor as a vacant cavity, and I healed them, like I would a person. I healed the earth, and I think it worked. Now the isle is just that—an island, surrounded by water instead of air."

Laughter, full of pride and marvel, spilled from her lips. If she could preserve the isles, then maybe her people's way of life wouldn't die. Sure, she still had to figure out how to prevent a war from breaking out between the avians and the mages, how to ease their fear of the world within the mist, how to seal the rift, and how to stop the eggs from hatching, but it was a start. Maybe she could do this. Maybe she truly would save the world.

"Ana."

The hesitant scratch to his voice brought her back. Worry coiled like unruly threads in her gut. "What? What is it?"

"There's something I think I should tell you."

"Are you injured? Is someone hurt?"

"No, no," he rushed to say, taking a step closer. "It's nothing like that. It's something my captain told me this morning, something I'm not sure how to believe."

She tilted her head, studying him. "What?"

"She said— She said—" He turned his face to the side as a breath escaped his lips. Lyana reached for his hand. Their fingers danced across the silence, his every move making her heart flutter. The flames along his wings dampened, the light growing softer, almost romantic against the darkness of the night. When he finally looked back at her, his eyes smoldered. "She thinks I'm the King Born in Fire."

A gasp escaped her lips.

"I know it sounds ridiculous," he said, shaking his head as he tightened his grip on her hand. "But it also, somehow, might be true."

Before she could answer, he launched into an explanation, reviewing his time beneath the mist and his interactions with the dragons, his nightmares and his experiments, his conversation with his captain. Lyana half listened, but the other half of her mind was spiraling back, back, back to that morning on the sky bridge. Meeting him had felt like fate, like destiny. The dragon being there. His being alone. Her watching. And later in the caves, as their magic merged in the firelight, their spirits had grazed, the touch like two halves of one whole finally rejoining. He'd been a stranger, yet at the same time a soul mate, no matter how insane it had seemed. They'd been drawn together, time and time again, no obstacles able to stand in their way, almost as though a force outside of their control had willed it.

"I don't believe it. I can't believe it," he murmured, his voice softening. "But they were right. Against those monsters, I'm the only person in the world who can protect you."

And he would.

Lyana could feel the promise in his touch, could hear it simmering in the back of his throat, could see it churning in his gaze. No matter what she said, no matter how she answered, he would spend the rest of his life keeping her safe. Because he loved her. Because he believed in her. Because despite all that had come between them, he'd never once turned away. He'd been her prince in the dark, her raven in the night, her dragon in the mist—why couldn't he be her king, too?

"Rafe." She took his hand in both of hers and pressed it to her chest, so he could feel the steady beating of her heart. "What if you *are* the King Born in Fire?"

He sucked in a sharp breath.

For a split second, all his walls came crashing down, and behind them was the boy who'd lost his mother, his father, and his very place in the world all in one devastating night, the man who'd been content to live in his brother's shadow because at least it was somewhere to call home, the bird who had been a phantom among his own kind, and the beast who knew he would never again blend in. Hope burned like a fire amid so much darkness, shining with the belief that maybe, just maybe, he'd finally found the place where he belonged—by her side.

A blink, and it was gone.

"What if I'm not?"

He stepped back, removing his hand from hers as his jaw clenched. His hooded brows furrowed, with torment, with regret. She stepped forward.

"Rafe—"

"Ana," he pleaded.

The tone made her freeze. Suddenly, they were no longer in the fog-enshrouded grove at the heart of the fallen House of Paradise, but back in a room now buried beneath the sea, with heavy curtains and thick stone walls, the air full of secrets and sin. They weren't a king and a queen, but a raven and a dove surrendering to one stolen night that had destroyed so much. She wouldn't have taken it back, and she knew he wouldn't either, but there was no denying what their passion had cost them. His relationship with his brother. Her future with her mate. Nearly an entire kingdom.

Now the stakes were even higher.

If they were wrong, if in their desire for each other they allowed themselves to believe in something that might not be true, this time it would cost them the world.

"What should we do?" she asked, helpless and unsure.

"We don't need to decide anything tonight, but I do know one thing. I'm not leaving you again."

"But your wings—"

"I don't care. I'll keep to the outskirts of the cities. I'll stay out of sight. I'll live on the cliffs if I have to. Whatever it takes. I need to be there. I need to be close when they come again."

That wasn't what she wanted, for him to hide like some outcast, like some criminal. He was a hero. He deserved dignity, not shame and shadows and solitude. "Rafe, no—"

"Ana, I won't risk it."

"I know," she cooed gently, closing the distance between them as she lifted her hand to his cheek and rubbed his skin once before sliding her fingers through his silken onyx hair. His head dipped into her touch, worry in the lines of his face. "That wasn't what I meant. I'll come with you."

Confusion clouded his features, but she'd never thought more clearly. For weeks in the House of Paradise, she'd felt useless. As Xander had spent hours in discussion with the queen, as he'd ordered shipments and evacuations, as he'd helped them prepare for the inevitable, she'd lingered in the sacred nest, hovering by the god stone, waiting futilely for the answers to come. But they never had. She hadn't stopped the rift from breaking, or the egg from cracking, or the isle from falling, and she was starting to think no matter how much time she spent in the other houses, the outcome would be the same.

Xander didn't need her help convincing the rest of the royal families. In fact, he might have better luck without her. But the mages she'd gathered into her small army, they needed her. And Rafe, he needed her. And somewhere within the fog was a man she wasn't ready to face who needed her too.

"I'll come with you," she said again. For once the answer was clear. "I'll go to the House of Song and gather my mages, and we'll come with you to the House of Peace. They can learn magic from your crew. We can figure out the meaning of the prophecy together. I don't want to leave you either."

He reached up to grip her hand and threaded their fingers together, then paused. "What about Xander?"

"He'll do better without me. We can tell him together—"

"No." He stepped back and turned to the side, disentangling their palms as a haunted look passed over his face. The fire in his wings flared, spurred by an inner demon she didn't know how to cast out. "You should do it alone."

"Rafe, he—"

"Does he know, Ana? Does he know what I am?"

"No," she whispered, silently cursing herself. Cassi had been right. She should have told Xander—right away, she should have told him, if for no other reason than to avoid this moment with Rafe and the humiliation burning in his eyes. "He loves you. He won't care."

"I don't want him to see me like this." The words were gruff and jagged, as though ripped from somewhere deep inside his chest. They made her heart pang.

"All right, Rafe." It was his body, his brother, and his choice, no matter how wrong she thought that choice might be. "All right. He won't. I'll go to him. I'll explain. And then I'll meet you in the House of Peace. Those creatures are gone for now—you said so yourself. They'll be back, but not right away. We have time. Wait here while I search for survivors, while I explain what's happened, and then we'll fly to the world above together. You can drop me off at the House of Song. We won't be apart for very long."

He nodded, still choked up and torn.

She leaned forward. As though drawn by magic, so did he, until their foreheads dropped together, and they stayed like that a few moments, just breathing in each other's presence.

Lyana rose to the tips of her toes and pressed a soft kiss on his cheek, wishing to do so much more. For now, the simple touch would have to do. He remained behind, her faithful guardian, as she flew into the wreckage of Hyadria to search for wounded souls to heal.

28

CASSI

Lingering high above the broken branches of the sacred nest, Cassi watched Lyana leave, unsure if her queen had even noticed her presence. She and Rafe had been consumed by each other, as they always seemed to be, the rest of the world fading whenever they were close.

Maybe there was a reason for that.

She thinks I'm the King Born in Fire.

His words crashed across Cassi's mind like a boulder through glass, shattering her every belief, leaving nothing but broken shards behind. He'd been speaking of her mother, Captain Rokaro. It explained so much. Why she'd turned her back on Malek to ferret Rafe from Da'Kin in the dead of night. Why she'd been avoiding Cassi for weeks. Why she'd risked so much for a man who wasn't even blood.

She must believe it.

Cassi knew her mother. She wouldn't have told Rafe unless she thought it was true, not when it was obvious he'd tell Lyana and both of them would hope beyond all else for it to be real.

And I don't think she's the only one.

Malek knew or at least suspected. He'd been crazed the past few weeks, manic even, not like himself, losing his composure and letting his emotions take him. Cassi had thought Lyana's absence had been his undoing, but this was a far more convincing reason. Everything he'd ever done, every order he'd ever given, every ruthless mission he'd ever carried out had been in the name of saving the world. He believed without a doubt he was the King Born in Fire. It was his foundation. His rock. The role upon which he'd built his entire life.

And now, maybe, he'd been wrong.

I have to know.

Cassi shot out of the sacred nest, up and into the misty sky, her spirit cutting through the fog with haste. She'd told herself she wouldn't be the first to break, not this time, but she had to know, and one look into Malek's eyes would tell her the truth. It was time to face him. It was time to dive inside his dreams and turn his waking world to a nightmare.

Last she'd seen him, he'd been on his ship in the middle of the sea—but as she followed the tug of his soul, she found herself back above the familiar streets of Da'Kin, making for the stony castle in the center of the city. He was asleep when she soared into his bedchamber, his face cast in shadow. Shock tore through her as she neared. If not for the familiar scent of his spirit, he'd be unrecognizable.

Bruises marred his pale skin. Bloody red lines were carved across his face. One of his eyes was completely swollen shut, and his lower lip was twice the normal size. And that was just his face. Buried beneath clothes and sheets, the rest of him, she had to imagine, looked the same. He'd been beaten—but how? He was an *aethi'kine*. He was untouchable. No one could even get close.

No one except Rafe.

Cassi retreated as the realization burned through her. In all the time spent focusing on freeing Elias, it seemed she'd missed a lot.

That was why Malek had been out to sea. That was why her mother had finally fled to the House of Peace.

Malek had gone after Rafe…and he'd lost.

Was that proof enough?

No, she thought. *Lyana deserves the truth. The world deserves the truth. And I can uncover the truth. All I need to do is face him.*

Determined and unafraid, Cassi dove into his dream. She didn't know what propelled her, but as the scene came together, they were standing on the outskirts of the House of Whispers. Howling winds whipped over the edge of the isle, riffling through the forest. Her clothes were moist and sticky, her hands stained red. His cheeks held a spattering of freckles and his skin shone golden in the sunlight. They were back in the place where they'd last faced off, in the moment right before he'd stolen her sky.

Maybe it was Cassi's way of trying to change her past.

Maybe it was just a message—this time, don't back down.

"Kasiandra."

He addressed her with his arms crossed, smug as always, as though they weren't fully aware that outside this dream his body and spirit were broken. Cassi didn't give him time to say anything else. She marched across the distance between them until their noses almost touched and his midnight eyes were all she could see, giving him no space to hide.

"Is Rafe the King Born in Fire?"

Malek flinched. His walls crumbled, revealing the terrified, lonely man underneath the royal title. It was all she needed to see to know the truth. A sound escaped her lips, half a gasp, half a laugh, as she stepped back, knocked off balance by the revelation. "He is."

"Don't be ridiculous," Malek snapped, trying to recover, but it was too late.

"He is," she repeated, voice airy with shock. "Rafe is the King Born in Fire."

"Kasiandra—"

She snapped her attention back to him, a sneer pulling at her lips. "How could you try to hide this, Malek? How could you try to cover this up?"

"It's not—"

The *smack* of her palm against his cheek rang through the forest. A red imprint stained his sun-kissed skin, lingering as he lifted his fingers to the spot, his eyes wide.

"You who ordered me to cut off his wings, who ordered me to kill a man, who let countless people suffer and die all in the name of saving the world—you knew this, and kept it to yourself? Why? Because you might not be the hero of the story anymore?" She spat at his feet, her anger like a dragon unleashed, making her want to spew flames across the sky. "I followed you because I thought you would do anything to save the world. I believed in you. I trusted you. I gave you everything—"

"Not everything," he cut in, matching her fury with his own. "If you'd given me everything, if you'd done what I said, Lyana would be with *me* right now."

"To what? Stand by your side as you watched the world burn?"

He opened his mouth, the veins in his neck thick and pulsing. No sound came out because he had nothing. No excuse. No explanation. His words were as empty as his soul.

"You're a fraud," she seethed. "You've spent your entire life claiming you want to save the world, and now, when you have information that might do that very thing, you throw a tantrum like a scared little boy whose favorite toy got stolen away. Well, now I know the truth, Malek. I'm going to tell Lyana. And for once in my life, there's absolutely nothing you can do to stop me."

"Kasiandra."

He dug his fingers into her forearm, holding her as a golden shimmer rose to his skin, seeping into the air. But this was her dream, and his magic held no power here.

"Goodbye, Malek. Good riddance."

Cassi tore out of his mind, leaving him sputtering on his bed as he bolted awake, a groan escaping his lips as his body no doubt cried out in pain.

"Kasiandra," he wheezed. "Kasiandra!"

Not pausing to glance behind, she fled into the fog, only one thought in her mind.

Lyana.

Lyana.

Lyana.

The queen was still in the House of Paradise. Cassi found her kneeling over an injured priest, his green robes stained red with blood as he shivered in her arms. The broken end of a severed branch protruded from his leg.

"Shh," Lyana whispered as she pressed her palms to the man's chest, letting her magic do its work before she removed the blockage from the wound. "Shh. I'm here. The gods are here. They're with us. They never left."

His trembling eased.

In that brief moment of relief, she yanked the branch out. He screamed, the sound ripping through the forest and echoing across the trees. Cassi sank lower as golden light filled the air, blindingly bright against the gloomy midnight fog. The man passed out, going limp in Lyana's arms even as she fought to heal him.

"Not now, Cassi," her queen finally said, sparing a glance in her direction. "Can't you see I'm busy?"

She felt for the priest, for the injured, she really did, but this was too important to wait. Shooting like an arrow across a battlefield, Cassi flung herself into Lyana's mind, a single demand blaring so loudly from her spirit she had no doubt her queen would hear.

Now!

Magic dug into her soul and tossed her away. Lyana frowned and glared toward where her spirit hovered in the sky.

"Not now," she repeated, a tone Cassi recognized from so many years of being bossed around by a princess who had more stubbornness than sense. There would be no getting through to her tonight, not while the injured still cried out for help.

Spirit groaning, Cassi spun toward the next closest soul and shot across the forest toward Rafe. He sat in the sacred nest, his eyes closed and his breath even, but he wasn't sleeping. The flames on his wings simmered. She tried to sink into his thoughts, to take control, but his mind was like steel, impossible to penetrate. His focus was so acute there was no way to break through. He was speaking to the dragons, she realized upon sensing the presence of something else inside his head, something foreign.

This was hopeless.

Xander, then.

Cassi changed tactics. That's where Lyana said she would go next. If Cassi couldn't give her queen the message, or her new king, then telling Xander was the next best thing.

Magic carrying her faster than wings ever could, Cassi catapulted through the sky, a weapon unleashed as she broke through the fog and into the clear expanse of the world above. Within moments, she was racing above the House of Song toward the raven camp. The night was silent, hardly any movement between the tents erected across the clearing, the only light the silvery glow of the moon.

Yes, she thought. *Yes.*

Yet when she burst into the royal tent, Xander was nowhere to be found, not in the bed, not on the floor, not even huddled over his desk. She followed the trail of his spirit back into the woods, seeing the subtle orange glow of firelight long before she saw him. Xander stood with ten others in whispered conversation, Helen and Lyana's small army listening raptly as he told them of the House of Paradise's fall. Trapped in her spirit form, Cassi cursed—a silent thing no one else could hear.

Gods alive! Doesn't anyone sleep anymore?

The ship. The crew. They were her last hope. Surely at least one of them would be dreaming. There were nearly a dozen mages in the group. All she needed was one measly soul to bear witness to her confession. One person, and she'd save the world.

Come on, Cassi urged as she raced across the sky. *Come on.*

When she burst through the crystal walls of the raven guest quarters, relief surged through her. Captain Rokaro lay in bed, a caramel wing arched back as if in flight, her eyes closed in slumber. After weeks of evasion, her mother was finally there waiting, as though somehow she'd known that tonight of all nights her daughter would need her.

Cassi raced across the room, reached out with her magic, and—

She froze.

Awareness burned at the edges of her soul, like the dawning of a new day. Somewhere far away, water splashed cold and damp across her cheek. Screaming filled her ears, words she couldn't quite make out. Pain flared, the sting of nerves firing up after a long, corpse-like absence of life.

He healed me.

No. No. No!

That bastard healed me.

Cassi reached for her mother, clawing at the air with her magic, uselessly trying to grab hold of the captain's mind. As if she were a puppet on a string, her master pulled and she had no choice but to follow. Her spirit slipped back and back and back, no matter how she fought to move forward, until she oozed through crystal and into the frigid air of the House of Peace.

No!

The next thing she knew, she was back in Da'Kin, groaning on a wet floor as her body spasmed, her mind sputtering awake despite her magic as another icy blast of liquid shocked her skin.

"Leave her alone!" Elias shouted, his voice raw, as though he'd been screaming for a while. "Don't hurt her!"

Cassi blinked, the world a blur through eyes unused to seeing. A warm finger trailed a path down her cheek, making her wince. She knew who it was before he even spoke.

"Welcome back, Kasiandra," Malek crooned, the sinister sound eliciting a shiver. "Welcome home."

Cassi tried to yell, to shout, to scream, but her protests came out as garbled sounds, her vocal cords weak from little use, her body and mind slow to reconnect after such a long separation.

Malek stood, the heat of his skin retreating as the shadowy outline of his face disappeared. His boots clicked loudly against the stone as he walked away.

"Keep her awake," he ordered, his voice growing softer with the added distance. "Whatever you have to do, for however long it takes, don't you dare let this prisoner fall asleep."

THE DIARY

Twenty-Fifth Day of the Fourth Moon

So much has happened, I don't even know where to begin. Can it truly have only been a day since my last entry? Since I wrote of that vision in Zavier's arms? I never dreamed what would come to pass. Even seeing the future, I never imagined this.

I was right—Bastiant made his move at dinner.

As the meal ended, we all stood to make our formal farewells. While I smoothed the wrinkles from my skirt, out of the corner of my eye I caught sight of a subtle white shimmer in the air—magic. Magic of a color I'd never seen before.

I whipped my head toward my father to sound an alarm, but before I could speak, a wave of Bastiant's golden magic arced across the room, leaving me mute and the others frozen in place before it slammed into my father's chest. He stumbled back, but recovered quickly, mounting an attack of his own. It's nearly impossible for one aethi'kine to best another, so I didn't see the purpose behind the display, until one of Bastiant's friends stepped forward, his ivory magic spiraling wider and wider, spinning and folding and shifting until a tear appeared in the aether. The very essence of the world split, and behind my father a new scene formed in the hollow, that of fire and rock and barren wasteland, nothing but gray skies filled with white steam and charcoal smoke.

I gasped.

At least, I think I did.

The mage was a spatio'kine, a riftmaker who could bend space to his will. I'd heard of the magic before, but I'd never seen it with my own eyes, and suddenly Bastiant's plan became clear. He didn't need to kill my father. He didn't even need to beat him. He just needed one good strike, and he'd send my father to a place where no one would ever find him again.

My father's attacks intensified as he realized the truth. So did Bastiant's. The banquet hall filled with a maelstrom of aethi'kine power, the rest of us nothing but pawns in the chaos. My father's mages joined the fight, but Bastiant's ferro'kine sent knives to their throats. My father caught them, but it left Bastiant an opening, and a blast of power sent my father sliding closer to the rift. Aethi'kine magic pulsed with orders, mages acting on silent commands, their power hardly their own as my father and Bastiant pulled them into the fray.

I, of course, was forgotten, my magic useless in this sort of war. I wondered what it said about my father's spirit that Bastiant didn't even attempt to use me as a bargaining chip, my life for my father's surrender, though I didn't dwell on the thought. Truth be told, I knew long ago that my father would always choose himself.

Soon, the room began to tremble beneath the strain of so much power. That's when Mikhail and Zavier acted. The battle must have looked silly to them before that, the power invisible to their magicless eyes, nothing but men and women bending to unseen forces. But as the stone walls groaned and fissures snaked their way across the ceiling, even the avians realized the severity of what was happening.

Zavier grabbed my hand. "Come with me, Princess."

Together we ran for the door, but as we neared, a marble column snapped and crashed to the floor. Zavier skidded to a stop, using his body as my shield. Dust fell from the ceiling, whispering of instability. He glanced to Mikhail. They spoke without needing words, the sort of companionship I envy, and together turned toward the opposite end of the banquet hall, to the massive rose window revealing the dying light of the sun.

"I'll go first," was all Mikhail said before he took to the air.

Zavier scooped me into his arms, and we were flying. Unlike in my vision, I didn't tremble with fear or shut my eyes. I did, however, curl into the warmth of his chest to breathe in his soothing essence. The muscles around me were firm and comforting, his strength undeniable, his prowess too as we cut across the room. The ties at the top of his shirt came loose and I pressed my cheek to the hollow of his throat, unable to deny the yearning to feel the heat of his skin.

I'm terrible, I know.

My father was a few steps from doom. My kingdom on the brink of disaster. My future husband the cause of it all. And yet I hardly cared, protected as I was in the circle of Zavier's arms. Perhaps I knew that nothing would ever be the same, and I needed to take those few moments of calm before the storm. Perhaps I'm what my father always feared, a foolish girl. Perhaps I'm just like so many other lonely souls, desperate for the barest hint of connection. I drank those few moments in, waiting for the inevitable.

Mikhail crashed through the window, shattering the glass and clearing a path to safety. But I already knew it wouldn't be enough. Before we reached the window, the ceiling collapsed, just like in my vision. Zavier dove with all the grace of an eagle on the kill. My skirts flew into my face, but having predicted that, I clutched them to my chest, clearing my eyes. A blast of energy surged into our sides, tossing us off course, directly under the falling debris. Zavier was fast, but not fast enough. We were going to be crushed. I heard him mutter a soft curse, and then, just as we were about to slam into the floor, the world glittered white. It was the same white I'd seen for the first time only minutes before—the ivory sparks of spatio'kine magic.

Zavier landed hard on a mud-packed floor, dropping to one knee as he set me down. The world was eerily peaceful compared to the chaos we'd left behind, but his body oozed tension, thickening the air between us. And then the same scream from my vision broke the silence.

"Zavier!"

I rolled to the side before he could stop me, my gaze going toward the woman. In an instant, her identity became clear—the same hazel eyes, the same sun-kissed skin. Her wavy hair was streaked with ivory highlights, and wrinkles hinted at her age, but there was no mistaking his mother. Anger and fear built in her gaze as it shifted between me and her son.

"What have you done?" she demanded.

"What I had to," he said softly, tossing me a lingering glance, one I could feel as easily as a touch though I kept my eyes on her, wondering at her reaction as a derisive snort escaped her lips. "She spared my life when she could've sacrificed it. I was duty bound to save hers."

He had magic.

I didn't think avians could have magic. I'd never heard of it before, never seen it. This was wonderful. Elation grew like a tide within me, until I finally turned to meet his shattered expression. Confusion punctured my excitement.

"You saw?" he asked.

I nodded.

"You understand?"

I swallowed, looking back and forth between him and his mother. "You're a spatio'kine." A bit of the light seeped from his eyes and his jaw clenched. "It's marvelous. My father will be thrilled. We don't—"

"You can't tell him," Zavier said, his voice louder as he reached out to clutch my hand. "It's forbidden."

I glanced down at our entwined fingers, his golden skin against my olive, wanting more than anything to rub my thumb across his palm, but he snatched his hand away.

"Forgive me, Princess."

He seemed to remember himself, who I was and who he was, and he jumped to his feet, offering to help me rise. I glanced around the room, taking in the clay walls and the simple furnishings, the kettle over the fire and the smoke hole in the ceiling. I'd never been to an avian home, and I'd never felt more out of place, used to gilt moldings, ornate carvings, and mural-covered walls. Our lives couldn't have been more different, but in one simple way we were the same—magic.

"Forbidden?" I finally asked, turning back to him.

"My kind aren't allowed to possess magic."

"Allowed?" I wrinkled my nose, shaking my head. "But I thought you couldn't?"

"We're born the same as you," he offered, a new spark igniting in his eyes, taking me in as though seeing me anew. "It's your father who gives us wings, but other than that, we're no different. I assure you, we have magic. The only difference is that for us, it's a death sentence."

"You mean..." My voice caught and I turned toward his mother. I'm not sure why. She would never pick my side against her son's, and she stared at me with hard, unbending eyes. "Surely they wouldn't..."

I couldn't even finish the sentence. My father would. Bastiant too. Any aethi'kine would do whatever was necessary to keep their kingdom and their power, to maintain the balance. Avians are already stronger than us, better fighters, faster and more agile. If they had magic too—if one of them was ever born with aethi'kine power—they wouldn't need mages like my father any longer.

The truth dropped like a weight inside my chest, making me stumble. How many deaths? How many lives? Of what other horrors had I been ignorant? Worse, what did they think of me? A princess in her palace, spending her days bent over a journal, reaping the benefits of her station and foolish enough to think they didn't come at dire costs? Even now, my stomach rolls with nausea. What other secrets has my father kept from me?

A pounding at the door broke the silence.

All three of us jumped, even Zavier.

And then a deep voice called, "Zavi, let me in."

With a curse, he opened the door to reveal Mikhail's furious face. The dove spared a moment to cast a disgusted look at me before closing in on his friend. "How could you be so foolish? You did, didn't you? In the palace? With the princess? There's no other way you could've beaten me here."

"I did."

Mikhail lifted his hands, his fingers curling into fists. His arms hovered as though he was unsure whether to punch his friend or pull him close.

"I won't tell."

I meant to sound strong, but the words came out weak as all three avians in the room turned toward me, their wings making them seem so large and imposing. My own petite frame had never felt so small.

I tried again.

"I promise you, all of you, I won't tell a soul. Your secret is safe with me."

They didn't believe me, which was fine. I understood. But I made the promise to myself as much as to them, and I knew deep in my heart that I would never break it.

"We have to get her back to the palace before they come looking," Mikhail said. "All three of us fled through the window for safety and then we brought her to her rooms to wait for the battle to end. I went there before coming here, and they're empty. The halls were clear. I don't think anyone will come for a while—"

"My bedroom," I cut in, understanding what he was hinting at. "The curtains were shut when I left, and no one will be in there at this hour."

Zavier nodded, a frown curving his lips. But still, he lifted his palms and a white glow pulsed from his fingers. Mikhail and his mother didn't notice, but I did. I could see his power, and as our eyes met above the glittering haze of the forming rift, I hoped he understood I found it beautiful. A tear cut through the room, just like the one that had formed behind my father, but in the center of this one were familiar embroidered silks and my ornate four-poster bed.

"Let me go first, just in case," I said, then stepped through.

The room was empty. Zavier and Mikhail followed, and then he closed the rift. An awkward silence filled the air.

"I'll guard the door," Mikhail said, leaving us alone.

We tried to speak at the same time.

"I won't—"

"I'm sorry—"

I laughed softly, surprised to find the hint of a smile gracing his lips. He inclined his head.

"I won't tell anyone," I said, finishing the sentence this time. "I promise. And I don't know why you're apologizing, but please don't. You saved my life at great risk to your own, and I'll be forever in your debt. I know you have no reason to trust me, but no one will learn of your magic from me. I swear it."

"Thank you, Princess."

I nearly sighed upon hearing my title—not that again—but there was something different in the tone, in the way the word rolled through his lips, no longer empty, but full of something I don't yet know how to place. All I know is it brought a flush to my cheeks.

He turned to leave, but I had one question left to ask.

"Why your house?"

He paused and glanced over his shoulder, those piercing eyes finding mine just above the curve of his wing. "It was the only place I knew would be safe."

Safe for him, I realized, not for me.

Safe from prying eyes.

Safe from discovery.

"Good night, Soldier Zavier."

"Good night, Princess."

He left, but it would be a lie to say I slept. I couldn't. Not with the day's events spinning circles around my mind. I threw open the curtains and watched the sky shift from deep midnight to soft lavender to vibrant pink to clearest blue. It was a beautiful day, but it would bring nothing but terrible news.

One of Bastiant's advisors fetched me from my room and brought me to the throne room, where my future husband sat on his newly acquired perch. I'm too tired to write of all the details now, so I'll just say this: My father is gone, banished to some barren wasteland from which there will be no return. Bastiant has laid claim to the kingdom and has already placed the crown upon his head. We're to be wed to quiet any naysayers, and the ceremony will take place in one moon cycle, giving the royal families across the peninsula enough time to send witnesses.

I'm going to be queen far earlier than I ever imagined, and though I've been naive, I refuse to live in ignorance any longer. My father has been hiding things from me—but my father is no longer here. It's time I learn the truth about the kingdom I was born to rule, and all the people housed within it. It's time I pay attention to the world outside my window, instead of the one inside my head.

First Day of the Fifth Moon

As it turns out, information is not so easy to come by—at least for a woman in a position of power whom so many people have a vested interest in silencing. Bastiant doesn't want me to have a voice, just as my father didn't. He doesn't want a partner. He wants a puppet, something I've vowed to never be. So my quest has been slow, but not altogether unfruitful.

I started with my father's advisors, going down the line one by one, but they're weak and afraid. My father was hardly gone a day, and already they'd fallen over themselves, bowing to their new king, hoping not to lose their lofty place in the kingdom. One thing I will say for Bastiant—I believe he was as disgusted with the display as I was. So, while I got small bits of information, it was nothing worth reporting.

After that I tried to be subtler, speaking casually to my maids as they dressed me in the morning, but they were also too afraid to speak, though I don't blame them. I went to speak to some of my old tutors, but the answers they gave were the same from my youth, too polished to be real. So I tried the cooks, the groundsmen, the soldiers, but none would talk to their princess. Never had I wanted to throw open the palace gates more, to run through the streets and beg for a willing ear, to shed these skirts and this crown and escape for a few hours. But my home is as much a prison as a palace, and I gave up dreams of sneaking beyond its walls long ago.

Then, an idea struck—Zavier.

I'm not sure why I didn't think of him before, perhaps my own girlish nervousness about getting too close, perhaps my fears about not wanting him to get hurt. The less involved he was, the safer he and his secret would be. But that should be his choice, right? He'd spoken to me freely before, why not again? Especially if I made it worth his while…

Which is how I got to the library.

My father's collection holds endless tomes on magic, so I pulled as many as I could, concentrating on those with mentions of spatio'kine magic, hoping any spying eyes would assume my sudden interest was fueled by my father's disappearance, though that was hardly the case. I'm sure wherever he is, it is as much as he deserved. Though sometimes I do wonder if the death I saw for him is the one he'll soon find. The idea makes me sadder than I thought it would.

But I digress.

Dinners have been canceled until the banquet hall is repaired. Bastiant is too busy building his new kingdom and shows little concern for his queen. I'm just as happy to eat in my rooms, especially when Zavier brings me my meal, as he did tonight.

I daresay I cornered him when he walked into the room. The poor man had no chance! Before he even set the tray on the table, I was on my feet, nerves racing as I leapt across the room to close the distance.

"Soldier Zavier?"

"Yes, Princess?"

I could sense the wary edge of his tone as his gaze swept quickly across my face, then dropped back to the floor. It wasn't proper for him to meet my eyes, especially not when we were alone in my rooms. It definitely wasn't proper for me to take his hand, but I did so anyway.

"I have a proposition for you."

He arched a brow but said nothing. It took a moment for the full implications of my words to land, and when they did, I just know my face flamed red, but I pressed on.

"What you told me the other day, about certain things being forbidden—I had no idea. But I'm to be queen soon, and ignorance is no longer an excuse. I want to know what truly goes on in my own kingdom. I need to. And I've tried all week to search for answers, but no one will tell me. No one except you."

He licked his lips, swallowing once in an agonizingly slow way that drew my gaze to his throat, a bit of heat pooling in my stomach as his muscles clenched. I glanced back at his face before my focus failed me.

"I would like you to tell me the truth of what happens outside these walls, no matter how ugly, and in return, if you're interested, I thought I might try to teach you about your magic."

His eyes found mine then, though not another inch of him moved.

"My magic works differently than most, but I've still been trained by the best mages in the kingdom. I know their rules and their lessons. I can show you. And I brought books so that we might learn about your magic together. What you did the other day was impressive, and I imagine what little you've learned has been in secret midnight sessions huddled in the quiet of your own rooms. But there is so much more you could accomplish given the chance. I want to give you that chance."

He stared at me for I don't know how long. Our breath mingled in the silence. Outside my window, the breeze rustled through the trees, muffled voices spoke, life continued—but inside, time stood still. My magic prickled, not with a vision, but as it did sometimes in important moments, ones that balance on a precipice, whose outcome might change everything.

A knock broke the moment, curt and demanding.

We flinched apart.

Zavier dipped into a deep bow as the door swung open to reveal one of Bastiant's advisors, no doubt bringing with him a long list of my future husband's demands for our wedding ceremony.

"Thank you, Soldier Zavier. That will be all," I said with a bored voice as I turned to the advisor. "Am I to be given no moment's peace? My dinner just arrived, and I'd like to eat it before it grows cold. What does the king want?"

Zavier left.

My heart went with him.

I was hollow as I ate my food, not tasting a single bite. Hopefully, tomorrow he will give me an answer, a sign. If I believed in gods, I would pray to them that he would.

Second Day of the Fifth Moon

A note sat crumpled with my breakfast when I woke to find it already laid out in my sitting rooms. It was only two words long. "I'm in."

Twelfth Day of the Fifth Moon

Ten days have passed, and my, what days they've been. I haven't had time to breathe, let alone write in my journal, though I've missed these few peaceful moments to myself. As the wedding plans race ahead, I'm pulled into fittings and meetings. Bastiant doesn't seem to care as long as his power is on full display, so naturally, the burden of the decisions has fallen on me, as though ceremonies and flower arrangements and dining options and dressing gowns are all a queen is good for! But I play along and do my part, at least during the day.

At night, I've begun a little rebellion of my own.

Zavier has slipped into my rooms every evening while the rest of the castle sleeps, and in the darkness of my bedroom, behind my closed curtains, we do all sorts of forbidden things. Not quite the ones I'm truly looking forward to, though I have more hope than ever that eventually the moment in my vision will come to pass, but with each day we grow closer.

I've learned more than I ever imagined about the avian culture, and the many ways my own kind work to suppress it. As he told me before, avians with magic are prone to disappearing as soon as their powers make themselves known, but it is so much worse than that. Everything from where they live, to whom they marry, to what jobs they get must be carefully approved by the royal household, and if they step a toe out of line, the threat doesn't fall on them, but on their future children—children who depend on the king's magic for their wings.

Their villages aren't broken up by species for no reason—Zavier says it's a way to keep them separated. Doves can only mate with doves, owls with owls, ravens with ravens. They work in different fields as another method of division, which is why it's so rare for an eagle and a dove to be paired as Zavier and Mikhail are. He says it's because there are far more avians than there are powerful mages, so it's in the king's best interests to keep them from joining forces.

I never thought about it like that before.

I just assumed, perhaps as most do, that they preferred to live that way, apart and with their own kind. I'm embarrassed to say I never put much thought into it, or into why they always worked very specified jobs.

I should have, but at least I'm doing all I can now to open my eyes, just as Zavier is doing all he can to learn his magic. Rift magic is so much more than I ever realized. Untrained as he is, Zavier has limited range and limited strength but with every day and every session his power is growing. We've read of the things his magic can do, and I see the eagerness in his eyes to try them—to carve doorways to the other kingdoms, to create portals to new worlds, to master single-way windows meant for spying. We're a long way from those endeavors, I fear, but maybe someday. His power works through anchors, so it helps to know someone on the other side or have seen it before or have some sense of the space to grasp. Right now, we focus just between my room and his on the other side of the castle walls, enough distance to hold meaning, but both safe. I'm trying to think of other places we might try, but what if we're seen?

I'll wait for him to say the risk is worth it.

Until then, I'm content with our heads bent over my books, his body so close I can feel his warmth. Sometimes our knees brush, and a thrill shoots through me. Sometimes it's our fingers, pointing for the same sentence on a page. Sometimes it's just our eyes that meet, and though it's not a physical caress, I feel those glances the most, burning deep inside of me.

I'm beginning to think he feels them too.

Twenty-Second Day of the Fifth Moon

Another ten days gone in a blink, much the same to report as the last. Wedding by day, rebellion by night. Zavier tells me more about the kingdom I didn't know before. Avians are not allowed to learn to read, though some (such as his mother) have carried on the practice in private, teaching their young. Avians are not supposed to believe in anything but magic and the all-powerful aether, as we mages believe, but they have an entire system of gods they honor behind closed doors. They are not supposed to communicate with the others of their kind, but they've created secret messages through wing shapes and movement across the skies that no mages could hope to understand.

He doesn't know much about life in the other parts of the kingdom, though he tells me, from what he's heard, the hierarchy of magic isn't kind to those with little power, or worse yet, none at all. I've known this, of course, in theory. Powerful mages get the biggest households, the most servants, the most prestige, but I always thought my father took care of the rest. But there are sectors of the city that grow hungry and weak, and with fields tended by agro'kine magic yielding unending crops, for that there is no excuse.

I asked him what he once thought of me, and he grew quiet.

"That I was a spoiled princess, no doubt," I teased, laughter in my voice, though it didn't quite cover the hurt. Not at his thoughts, but that they were true. "Up here in my palace, uncaring of the horrors the outside world faced."

He placed his palm over mine and squeezed gently. "It wasn't true."

"Wasn't it?"

I met his eyes as he rubbed his thumb across my skin, making me shiver. We were close, our faces no more than a few inches apart, close enough I could just feel the brush of his breath on my cheek. He tilted his head to the side, moving our lips closer in the process, but he didn't drop my gaze. The golden speckles in his eyes brightened, the green depths shifting wider as though opening to let me in. There was no judgment and no anger, only sympathy.

"I admit, I thought that, yes," he said slowly. "But just as you had no knowledge of what happened in my home, I had no knowledge of what happened in yours. The palace has thick walls, not just to keep enemies out but to keep its secrets in. And there are things that happen here, Princess, things I've seen happen to you that would make even your enemies shudder."

I thought of my soon-to-be husband.

There was no telling what he would unleash on me once the ceremony was through, though I tried not to think on that too often, and especially not in moments like these, with Zavier close and the rest of the world so far away.

He seemed to sense my shift.

We pulled apart. I didn't want to think of Bastiant with Zavier's hand upon me—it felt wrong. Not to my future husband, but to this gentle man who didn't deserve to share space in my thoughts with that monster.

Only six days until my wedding.

Six days.

What would my mother say if she were here?

I guess I'll never know.

Twenty-Fifth Day of the Fifth Moon

As I look out my window, the first of the bannermen are approaching the castle walls. All along the main streets, colorful fabrics fly, the symbols of all the kingdoms, their most powerful mages coming to bear witness to the end of my youth, the end of my freedom, but not the end of my life. I'll find a way to power through.

Tomorrow, the festivities begin.

On the twenty-eighth, I'll be wed.

After that, who knows? But I'll find a way to keep meeting with Zavier. No matter what, I won't let him go, not when he and our time together are the only things that have ever been mine.

We—

I've just had a vision while looking out my window. The same one from so many weeks before, with orange lighting the skies, only now I realize it wasn't a blood dawn. It was fire.

My kingdom is going to burn.

When and how, I have no idea, but even as the scene fades from my eyes, replaced with fluffy clouds and endless blue, I see the flames. They were thick, spitting ash into the sky, and angry, as though with a spirit of their own, swallowing the city whole. There were no avians in the skies, but there was something else—some sort of beast I didn't recognize, sifting like a shadow through the haze, as monstrous as it was graceful, too far away for my eyes to clearly see. I have to know what it was. Somehow, I need to see.

The vision was clearer this time, which means we're moving closer to this future. How do I stop it? How can I? And the more nagging question—do I want to?

29

XANDER

The sun was nearly at its peak by the time Lyana finally arrived at the raven camp. The sound of shouts and cheers lured Xander from the royal tent just in time to see her white wings flash against the tree line before she disappeared into the crowd. The knot in his chest loosened, all the worry he'd been trying to ignore draining away in an instant.

She was all right.

She was alive.

Though he wanted to rush across the camp and bombard her with questions, he remained where he was, waiting patiently for her to reach him. Kings needed to be confident. The last thing he wanted to reveal was the doubts plaguing him all night, keeping him awake—the fear that she might not return. When she approached the royal tent, he took the hand she offered and kissed the tops of her fingers before leading her inside.

The moment the tent flap closed, he dropped her hand and spun. "What happened?"

"I was going to ask you the same thing." She grinned and stepped past him toward the basin of water in the corner. Her leathers were covered in blood, though he knew by her gait none of it was her own. "What did Queen Zara say?"

"She agreed to send letters to the remaining houses," he said, turning his back to give her privacy. "When she reaches Sphaira, she vows to take our cause directly to your parents. Once they're on our side, the other royals will have to listen."

"They'll be on our side," Lyana said, utterly sure in a way he almost envied. Her voice grew muffled by clothes as she changed behind him. "I'm their daughter. My father, especially, has never been able to tell me no. And Luka has been speaking to them. They were already on the verge of making a proclamation on our behalf, but now, with Queen Zara's support, I've no doubt they will."

"Good." He nodded, mulling over the information for a moment. "So, what happened in the sacred nest?"

"Exactly what we feared." She sighed, the sound drowned out by the splashing of water. "I was powerless, Xander, absolutely powerless. The rift broke. The creature hatched. My magic couldn't touch either of them. I wouldn't have made it out alive if not for—"

She broke off suddenly.

He knitted his brows. "If not for what?"

"If not for Rafe."

"What?" He turned before he could stop himself, propelled by surprise, then promptly covered his eyes with his arm, finding her in her underclothes. Once, the sight might have brought a blush to his cheeks or made his heart drum. Now he just felt uncomfortable. "Sorry, I just— What do you mean, Rafe?"

"There's something I haven't told you," she said, not at all bothered by his intrusion. Clothes ruffled in the silence. He waited a few moments before peeking through his fingers, relieved to find her in trousers and a fresh shirt. "Something I should have told you right away, but I was too afraid of how you'd react when we'd only just started learning to work together again. I realize now that wasn't fair of me, to you or to him, and

I'm sorry, but I just didn't know how to tell you or what to say…"

The longer she rambled, the quicker his pulse raced. Fear lit his veins, sharp and acute, something he wasn't used to feeling when it came to Rafe—his warrior brother always ready with a smile, untouchable, especially with his healing magic.

"Lyana, what is it?"

"Rafe is a dragon."

A claw seemed to clutch his throat, cutting off air, and then a moment later laughter full of relief and denial spilled through his lips. "The gods, don't tell me you believe that nonsense, too? I've been dealing with these rumors my entire life, and I can assure you, Rafe—"

"No, Xander, listen to me," she cut in, her voice so deadly serious he stopped cold. "You know how we're all taken to the sacred nest as children to get our wings? It's not a gift from the gods. It's magic, somehow wielded by the rift spell, but the same power runs in my veins. It's called soul joining, and birds aren't the only creatures we can be united with. Malek has the same magic as me, and he—he soul-joined Rafe with a dragon."

"I don't—" Xander stumbled as his knees went weak. "He can't—"

"It's true," she murmured, those intense eyes studying him, her face puckered with concern. "His wings are made of fire. His spirit burns. He's the same man he's always been, but he's no longer a raven. At least, not visibly."

"Rafe. Oh, Rafe."

Xander collapsed on his desk chair, all his muscles giving out as a lifetime of memories flashed before his eyes—wrestling with his brother as children, spending countless nights talking in his rooms, exploring the isle, playing games in the castle halls, every moment of his youth made brighter by the presence of his sibling. Then the other memories came—classmates teasing, people whispering, the looks, the gossip.

Fire cursed.

Bastard.

Son of Vesevios.

Xander remembered how the names struck like knives, carving wounds his brother tried to hide, but how could he? No one deserved what Rafe had grown up hearing. No one deserved to be an outcast among his own kind, hated and reviled through no fault of his own. Despite it all, he'd been loyal to his house and his people. He'd won them a queen. He'd done anything Xander ever asked of him. He'd sacrificed everything.

And I banished him.

I banished him and led him to this fate.

Xander raised his fist to his lips to stop the sob from spilling out, a plug forming in the back of his throat as his eyes burned.

Taetanos, help me.

What was Rafe thinking right now? What was he feeling? His worst fears had come to life. His every horrible thought had been confirmed.

It wasn't true.

He had to know it wasn't true.

Xander didn't care what wings his brother possessed or who shared his soul. Though Rafe had spent his life pushing people away, trying not to let them see, Xander knew exactly who he was —noble and kind, softhearted despite his walls, a hero. His hero. A man he'd been able to rely on, and lean on, and admire, not just for his physical strength but for his heart too.

"I have to see him," Xander murmured, the decision shooting through him like lightning as soon as it was spoken, prompting him to his feet. "I have to see him. I have to speak to him. I have to tell him I don't care—I don't care about any of it."

"Xander."

"No, Lyana. He thinks I hate him. You don't know. You weren't there. He left, and I let him, and now, now… Where is he? Please, where is he?"

She grabbed him by the shoulders, drawing him back to the world. His chest heaved. His breath came in wild spurts. The room spun, everything aside from her face swirling about him as his thoughts whirled.

"Xander, listen to me," she commanded, staring at him hard. "You need to stay here. I *need* you to stay here, because I'm leaving."

"What?"

"I'm leaving," she repeated, more softly this time. "The creatures saw what I am, and though I got away last night, they'll be back. I don't know how to fight them, but Rafe does. He'll protect me. And though I would love nothing more than for him to come to us, we both know that with his wings, that's not possible. It'll undermine everything we've fought to achieve. So I need to go to him, and you need to stay here to carry out the rest of our mission with the remaining houses."

"But what will I say? How will I explain?"

Those weren't the real questions he wanted to ask. Lyana had the magic. Lyana was the queen of prophecy. Lyana was the storm. How would he do this without her?

"Tell them the gods called me back. Tell them I went somewhere private to pray. You're better with stories than me, Xander. I'm sure you'll come up with something. I believe in you, and there's no other way. I think—" She paused, biting her lower lip as she dropped her hands from his shoulders. The edges of her lips curved, revealing the smile she was trying to hide. When she spoke, her voice held awe. "I think Rafe might be the King Born in Fire, so I have no choice but to go to him."

"You think Rafe…"

His voice faded as the information sank in. His brother, the

King Born in Fire. His brother, the hero of prophecy. His brother, the savior of worlds.

The description fit.

For their whole lives, he'd had the sense that Rafe had been destined for something more—more than rejection, more than a life in his shadow, more than a sword, and an empty practice yard, and simply getting by. He'd always been a warrior, and now, maybe, the world would see it too.

"Go to him," Xander murmured, giving the blessing he hadn't been able to give before. Lyana and Rafe had been drawn together, time and time again, through fate, through love, through choice, perhaps through a mix of all three, but one thing was clear—he would no longer stand between them. "Go to him, Lyana, and when you do, please give him this."

He slid the dagger at his waistband free, then balanced the blade on his palm as he held it out to her. The hilt was carved to resemble a raven in flight, two wings unfurled, while at its base rested a polished obsidian stone. It was a gift from his father, and its twin now lay at the base of the sea, lost forever, but their meaning endured. Once upon a time, he and Rafe had made a promise to each other, a promise to always remember what it meant to be brothers, to be blood, to be bound by a trust so deep it could never be broken. Their father had been a man of many mistakes, but instilling that lesson had been his greatest success.

They'd forgotten that promise.

Now Xander intended to see it through.

Lyana took the dagger and tested the balance before finding his face, a question in her gaze. She knew there was more to this request, but it was a matter between brothers, and it would stay that way.

"Rafe will know what it means," he said instead, pushing away the memories. "But you can tell him I love him, and I'm sorry, and as far as I'm concerned, there's nothing left to forgive."

"I will." She curled her fingers around the hilt and tucked the blade safely at her side. "I'm going to ask Cassi to act as our go-between, but in case you need me for any reason, I'll be at the raven guest quarters in the House of Peace. And I'm taking my mages with me. There are people there who can help them learn their magic—people with far more experience than me."

A lopsided grin pulled at his cheek. "The raven guest quarters?"

"I figured they were available." She shrugged, a spark lighting her green eyes. "Besides, where else would the Queen of the House of Whispers stay?"

"Our people will miss you."

"They won't," she answered softly as she took his hand and gently squeezed his fingers. "They've always had exactly what they needed. They've always had you."

A warmth gathered in his heart, lingering as he watched her pack a few items in a small bag. She paused at the tent flaps before she left, but there was nothing left to say. Instead, they nodded to each other, a leader to a leader, a friend to a friend, understanding passing between them. Then she was on her way.

By the time Helen came running through the same opening, he was already bent over his desk, fingers covered in black ink as he hastily drafted a letter to Queen Zara, requesting an update.

"The queen! She's gone!"

"I know," he said simply, glancing up from the paper. "And she won't be coming back."

"But the isles, and the magic, and everything she told us—"

"Sit, Helen."

Xander kicked the chair to his left and it slid toward his captain of the guards. She eyed it, her expression torn between concern and control. If this was how she reacted, he certainly had his work cut out for him. But Lyana believed in him, and so did Cassi, and so did Rafe—maybe it was time he started believing in himself too.

Oh, there was doubt and worry and fear, but instead of pushing it away, instead of funneling it into his invisible fist to fester and grow, Xander embraced the uncertainty. He embraced the challenge. He let it fill him until all that was left was the burning desire to prove his every insecurity wrong, to show the world exactly what a raven king could do.

"You've been my top advisor ever since I came of age," he said, authority oozing from his tone. "And I need you to keep it together for me now. The prophecy has pulled Lyana away, which means it behooves us to convince the remaining houses to prepare for the worst. Our entire way of life is on the brink of extinction. If there was ever a battle we needed to win, this is it. So…" He motioned to the chair with his chin. "Have a seat, take a breath, and help me figure out a plan."

30

LYANA

In all Lyana's years spent wondering what the edge of her house might hold, she never imagined finding a seafaring ship buried among the snow. Though the crew had done their best to camouflage the wood, in the soft light of dusk shadows crawled across the barren landscape, leaving the mast and nets to stretch like fingers upon the ice. Bits of glass caught the sun, reflecting brilliant gold against the darkening gray. Beside her, her army gasped, though Lyana suspected their awe might be directed more toward the shoots of glitter spiraling into the air behind the hidden courtyard and less toward the ship. Magic lit the skies of the House of Peace, a sight she'd been sure she'd never see.

The very thought made her smile.

Or maybe it was the series of crystal domes gleaming beneath the sunset that made her chest feel warm despite the cold.

She was home.

"Follow me."

Lyana landed with grace and marched confidently across the frozen ground, her mages following, their spirits thrumming with interest. She remembered the way inside from her last time at the guest quarters, and she slipped around the wall with no problem. A circle of wingless mages waited in the center courtyard, all their focus split between a woman with auburn hair whose palm simmered with crackling flames and a second woman with rosy cheeks who oozed tendrils of darkness.

Lyana held out her hand and her army paused. They hovered in the shadows of a crystal building, waiting and watching. Like the others, she was curious to know what would happen next. Unlike the others, she recognized a magic duel when she saw one.

The *pyro'kine* acted first.

Flames blazed across the sky, shooting toward the *umbra'kine* with deadly precision. For her part, the blonde mage dove, limber and quick. Shadow shot from her palm as she rolled across the snow. The onyx coils wrapped around the fire mage's head, blocking her sight. The flames blazed brighter, dropping toward the ground, trained on a spot in the center of the circle that clearly held meaning. The shadow mage cursed and bit her lip. Another blast of fire flared across the circle.

"Hey!" a third woman said, blue simmering at her fingertips as she pulled at the snow. The frozen fractals turned to liquid as they rose to shield against the blaze. "Watch out!"

The fire mage shrugged, still blinded by darkness. "Sorry."

While they spoke, the *umbra'kine* crept around the outer edge of the circle. One of the men elbowed another as she tiptoed behind them, a grin on his lips.

"Shadow," the fire mage muttered, caution in her tone as she braced her legs. "I know what you're doing."

The blonde woman just grinned.

"Shadow—"

She lunged, catching the *pyro'kine* around the midsection as she tackled her to the ground. Fire exploded in a bulbous cloud that was quickly swallowed by darkness. The entire courtyard went black, the sky and ground disappearing as an onyx wave shrouded the light. As quickly as it came, it was gone.

The *umbra'kine* sat in the center of the circle with a smug smile on her lips as she tossed a pair of dice in the air. "I win."

The fire mage slammed her fists into the ground, the ice immediately turning to a puddle upon impact. She grumbled something unintelligible as she jumped to her feet, but smiled when another woman bumped her hip, her magic a soft lavender as it crackled like lightning between her fingers. They whispered to each other. The redhead laughed, a loud, throaty sound.

A mix of jealousy and joy twisted Lyana's stomach. These mages were perfectly at ease. They were comfortable with each other and their magic in a way the birds around her would never be. But that was why they were here—to learn, not just how to use their power, but how to accept it as well.

She cleared her throat and emerged from her hiding spot. A few of the mages spared a moment to glance in her direction, but it was the shout from the other end of the courtyard that left them jumping to attention.

"Is that how you greet a queen?"

Lyana guessed the owner of that sharp voice before she rounded the corner, her single hawk's wing on full display. If there was any doubt, her expression washed it away. Though her skin had weathered from a lifetime spent on the sea, her icy eyes were just as cunning as her daughter's, the resemblance between them undeniable.

"Well?" Captain Rokaro crossed her arms, staring down her nose at her crew. "Look alive!"

At her bidding, the mages scrambled, hastily falling into a single-file line as they offered a mix of haphazard bows and curtsies. Lyana folded her lips between her teeth, fighting the urge to laugh. Captain Rokaro didn't bother. A derisive snarl blew through her lips, the sound somehow affectionate, regardless. In the world above, their attempts were pathetic, but a life spent chasing dragons hardly prepared one for a royal audience. To be honest, Lyana preferred their informal greeting. It had been nice to be treated the same as anyone else for a moment.

"Thank you, Captain." She stepped forward, trying to hide her sigh. "I hope Rafe mentioned I'd be coming."

"He did."

"And he told you why?"

"He did."

Lyana swallowed, feeling more like a child than she had in weeks. Cassi had warned that her mother could be tough, but the captain oozed authority in a way that was almost unnerving. It was enviable. "Excellent. I've been putting together an army—"

A loud snort made her stop short. Lyana's brows drew together as she located the source of the noise. The petite woman was familiar, her face round and her ebony hair cut short, her milky eyes aimed at the sky as though looking away might prevent her from being seen.

"I know you."

The mage winced.

"You were in my room in Da'Kin," Lyana continued, piecing together the memory. All the mages in the line leaned forward to peer at their friend, amusement flaring. "You said you were a servant. You pulled on my feathers."

"I don't think that was me," the woman muttered as she scratched at the back of her neck, looking everywhere but at Lyana. "I have a very common face."

The man to her left, his hair a mix of gray and black, lifted his fist to his mouth to stifle his laugh. The woman elbowed him in the gut. Lyana simply stepped closer.

"You were asking me all sorts of questions, about my life, about —" Her eyes widened as realization hit. The woman had been asking if there was anyone she missed from her world, someone special she might care about. She'd been asking about Rafe, but Lyana had answered with Xander's name, and the next thing she'd known, the mage had vanished. Her heart immediately softened. "You're friends with Rafe."

"It depends who you ask," the same man from before interjected. Pine-green magic simmered around his fingertips, identifying him as a *ferro'kine*. "Rafe would probably call her a thorn in his side."

The woman made a face.

"Ah, then they must be great friends," Lyana teased, liking these people already. "Rafe only reserves that term of endearment for his favorite people. I should know—I've been called the same."

"Her name is Brighty," Captain Rokaro interjected. "And she's a pain in all of our asses. What were you saying about an army?"

"Well..." Lyana swallowed, glancing at the mages behind her. Their expressions were uncertain, their souls wary yet tinged with the slightest bit of interest. "We're not much right now, but it's a start. All of these people have magic, and I was hoping you could teach them how to use it."

The captain's gaze cut to her companions, the feathers on her single wing ruffling, as though brushed by an invisible wind. Shadows marred pale eyes haunted by dark memories. Lyana remembered the rumors. Mages in the House of Prey weren't killed outright but tossed over the side of their isle while still alive. Whatever had happened to the captain, it hadn't been good. And it was a fate her companions well understood.

"I'm trying to put an end to the executions," she said softly, drawing the captain's attention. "And in the meantime, I'm rescuing everyone I can. All these people want is to learn how to use their power, an incredible, innate part of themselves they've always been forbidden from exploring."

The captain swallowed, then sighed, the tension in her back releasing as her wing dipped. "I suppose we have nothing better to do. How about some introductions, and you—" She spun, staring at her crew, taking the time to look every single one of them in the eye. "No games of dice until I say they're ready."

A collective groan filled the air.

"I mean it. You're a bunch of thieves and cheats, and I won't have these people taken advantage of, understood?"

No one even tried to deny it. As one, they grumbled, "Fine."

"Good. Let's start with you." Captain Rokaro pointed to the raven at Lyana's left. "Name and type of magic."

"Amara," she said, nervously shifting her feet. "And I can grow plants."

"You're an *agro'kine*. You'll partner up with Leech. What about you?"

Down the line they went, with the captain dividing Lyana's army among her crew. By the time they were done, voices filled the courtyard, some eager and some sarcastic, but the sight of burgeoning magic still filled Lyana with a joy she'd never known. The future she was working so hard for was here. It was happening right before her eyes. People from two different worlds, working together, finding common ground.

Maybe this wasn't hopeless.

They were all mages, so not everyone would be this simple, but hope sparked deep in her chest. If she could find a way to close the rift and defeat the monsters, maybe she could also stop a war between two cultures so vastly different she never imagined they might find a way to live together until now.

While they practiced and mingled, Lyana stepped around the perimeter of the courtyard, making for the *photo'kine* all alone in the corner, her arms tucked tightly around her chest as she shivered quietly in the cold.

"Brighty."

The mage offered a sidelong glance. "You want to know where he is?"

"I do. Please."

"Stupid idiot," she grumbled, though the sadness in her tone was unmistakable.

Sympathy simmered across the girl's spirit, revealing the warm heart she tried to hide. They were close, clearly. To Lyana's surprise, no jealousy tightened her stomach. Instead, she was grateful he'd had someone to confide in all these weeks they'd been apart. He deserved loyalty. He deserved a friend.

The *photo'kine* kicked at the dirt, then continued, "He was worried they'd take one look at his wings and run. I told him good riddance, and we didn't need people like that around anyway. He, of course, muttered that I didn't understand. But what's to understand? It's not like he did that to himself. And if he *is* the King Born in Fire, it was bound to happen anyway. I just—"

She cut herself short, wrinkling her nose as she cast a hard look at the birds filling the courtyard around her, tentatively using their magic.

Lyana put a hand on her arm.

"Give them time," she murmured. Rafe had been right. Brighty didn't understand, but it wasn't her fault. No one from the world below would understand the hold their gods had over her people or their deep-set fear of Vesevios. As much as it pained Lyana to admit, he'd been right to hide, at least for this first day. "Where is he?"

"A room at the back of that building. He said you'd know which one."

Lyana followed the path of Brighty's finger to the crystal building across the way, the largest and most prominent one, meant to house the royal family. She'd spent a single night in those halls, every moment burned in her memory. She knew exactly where he was.

"Thank you."

Her heart pounded as she made her way across the courtyard and inside the crystal building, same as it had all those months before. Back then, the halls had been dark and quiet, the hour late and the night still. Their meeting had been illicit, a stolen exchange between two lost souls. She'd cursed at him for lying. He'd coldly cast her out. Both their actions were a cover for the truth—that their hearts were aching.

For some reason, despite the soft light of sunset streaming through the windows and the new roles they'd come to play, this moment felt just as forbidden.

Was he her king or simply her protector?

Had fate drawn them together or was a darker force at work?

Would their love save the world or doom it?

Lyana swallowed her fears and knocked. "Rafe? It's me."

Footsteps padded softly across a rug. He paused on the other side of the door, long enough she could almost hear the deep breath he must have drawn into his lungs and the heavy sigh as he let it slowly out. A second later, the knob turned, and he welcomed her inside.

31

RAFE

"You found me," Rafe murmured as Lyana swept into the room.

As always, the sight of her stole his breath away, making his chest burn with both pleasure and pain. She tossed him a look over her shoulder, her eyes gleaming mischievously above the edge of her ivory wing.

"Brighty ratted you out."

He snorted. "Of course she did."

"I'm sorry you felt the need to hide."

"Don't be." He shrugged, stepping farther into the room, pulled toward her by something outside of his control. "It's hardly the first time my presence could be classified as unwanted."

"Rafe," she chided in a whisper as she ran her fingers along the back of a chair. Her gaze swept across the room, pausing momentarily on his bed before snapping to the window. Yet no argument came, because they both knew the truth. Today the sight of his wings would have done far more harm than good. Lyana sighed. A shiver ran visibly down her spine, rippling her wings as she hugged herself.

"Are you cold?" He hadn't felt a chill in weeks. In fact, he'd forgotten what it felt like to live without fire running through his veins.

"No." She spun to him with soft laughter on her lips. "No. I guess I just— It's strange to be back here, in these rooms, with you..."

"Ahh." His mouth quirked into a lopsided grin. "You mean talking and not fighting?"

"I've been told I can be unreasonably demanding."

"I've been told I can be irrationally stubborn."

"By who? No, wait. Let me guess."

As one, they said, "Xander."

Strange how for the first time in her presence, the thought of his brother didn't sting. Instead, laughter simmered at the back of his throat, only slightly bittersweet. "I believe you stormed in demanding to know my real name."

"And I don't think I ever got the true answer to my question."

She hadn't.

At the time, he'd been afraid that if he gave her even one more piece of himself, he'd never get it back. Little did he realize he was already too far gone. Now, the thought was almost freeing. He loved her. No matter what he did, he couldn't stop loving her. So why fight it? The truth didn't scare him anymore. He'd follow her to the end of the world, if that's where they were headed. She need only point the way.

"It's Aleksander."

She drew her brows in. "What?"

"My name. My *real* name. It's Aleksander Ravenson."

"Aleksander," she murmured. The flames reflected in her eyes brightened as a tremor ran through him. They were standing so close their thighs nearly touched. He didn't remember moving toward her, but he must have, or she to him, drawn together by an innate yearning he no longer cared to stifle. "I like it."

"I don't."

It reminded him too much of his father, a man he both loved and loathed, depending on which person he remembered—the crownless falcon who'd spun him and his mother about their modest room at the very base of the castle, or the king who'd turned his back on his vows and the heir who'd loved him.

"Aleksander," Lyana whispered again, her voice seductive, making him want to forget the world and everyone in it. She lifted her hand, fingers skimming his chest until they found the bare skin of his throat, then sliding into his hair, her touch tingling with magic. The ache in his soul eased, as it always did when she was near, from her power or simply from her presence, he wasn't sure. In truth, he didn't care.

"You asked me to apologize," Rafe said as he ran his fingers up her arm, watching her body respond to him, her muscles flexing as she leaned closer. "Do you remember that?"

"Actually, I ordered it, but you refused."

"I couldn't," he confessed, not meeting her eyes, because he knew the second he did, he'd give in. He'd let everything melt away until nothing existed outside of him and her and whatever this was between them—no magic, no monsters, no prophecy. It had become his new deepest fear. Not loving her, but the awareness that in his love he might let the world burn. "At the time, I told myself it was because I wanted you to be angry with me, to hate me, but the truth is, I wasn't sorry. I've never been sorry for a single moment we've spent together."

He was only ever sorry for all the times they'd had to say goodbye—like now. The apology stuck in his throat as he ripped his hand away from her and stepped back, turning his face to the side. Lyana let him retreat, because she knew, same as he, that though the stakes had changed and the players were different, the game remained the same. They were two souls on a crash course, ready to combust, but their collision might set the world aflame.

If he wasn't the King Born in Fire, then he was a distraction.

If he was, they couldn't lose themselves to passion, the way they had once before. It would cost them too much.

Rafe ran his hand through his hair, pulling in a deep breath as he searched for a distraction, any distraction, from the heat coursing through his veins. A spot of glimmering onyx caught his eye, dousing his rising desire as thoroughly as a cold shower. An icy chill struck him.

"Where'd you get that?" he asked, already reaching for the dagger at her waist. He hadn't seen it in years, but the hilt formed by open raven wings was unmistakable.

"Oh." She jumped and grabbed the weapon before he did, then pulled it from her belt and offered it to him immediately. "I should've started with this, Rafe. I'm sorry. Xander gave it to me, to give to you."

His throat tightened with emotion as he lifted the weapon from her hand. "He did?"

"He said he loves you, and he's sorry, and there's nothing to forgive."

"He said that?"

She nodded, curiosity sparking like golden highlights in her eyes. But she didn't ask. She didn't intrude, even as he collapsed into a nearby seat, his legs no longer strong enough to hold him, the enormity of the gesture leaving him overwhelmed.

"It was a gift from our father," he said anyway, the words so insufficient they almost made him want to laugh.

The dagger felt different from what he remembered, more balanced in his hands, lighter, less awkward. Then again, he hadn't held it since he was a boy. It probably wasn't the dagger that had changed, but him. If memory served, he and Xander had been fighting when their father cornered them in the practice yards to present the gift, a matching set, one for each of them. He'd made them promise to remain true to one another, to put blood above all else, to remember they were brothers no matter how the world tried to come between them.

He forgives me.

For not being truthful. For sneaking around with Lyana. For running away.

And he's sorry.

There was only one thing Xander could have been apologizing for—allowing him to leave.

And he loves me.

Rafe drew in a shuddering breath and tightened his grip on the hilt. "Did you tell him what I am?"

"You're the same Rafe you've always been, thinking the worst about yourself despite all the evidence to the contrary."

"Lyana," he murmured, no humor in his tone. "Did you tell him what I am?"

She sighed. "I did."

"And he gave you the dagger after?"

"He did."

He doesn't care. The realization pulsed through him like a shock wave. *He knows about my wings. He knows about my soul. He knows, and he doesn't care.*

A thousand pounds seemed to lift from his shoulders, but instead of feeling invigorated, Rafe slumped forward in exhaustion until his now-flameless leathery wings dragged along the floor. He felt as though he'd been fighting for months, straining and struggling to carry this burden, and now that it was gone, he could breathe, yes, but he could finally rest too.

"Rafe." Lyana took his free hand, wrapping their fingers together. "You look tired. When's the last time you slept?"

"I'm not sure."

The past few days were a blur—fighting Malek, retreating to the House of Peace, and racing to the House of Paradise, then battling in the sacred nest and waiting endless hours for Lyana to return. All his focus had been on connecting with the creatures to make sure they remained far away, to ensure they wouldn't touch her while she was gone. He couldn't remember the last time he'd closed his eyes or the last time he'd truly slept a whole night not plagued by nightmares.

"You should rest," she said.

There was so much to do. "I'm fine."

"Well, I'm not," she bit back, the arch to her brow promising an argument if he didn't relent. Rafe remembered the look well, yet he couldn't find the will to fight. She always seemed to push him whenever he needed it most. "We'll be of no use to anyone if we're exhausted and delirious. Come on."

Lyana pulled him toward the bed, not giving him the opportunity to say no as she dragged him across the room. Rafe stumbled behind her, his heart heavy. The pillows and blankets were as inviting as ever, especially after Lyana released him to crawl across the mattress and lie down. He stopped with his shins against the frame, frozen in place. There was nothing he wanted more than to take the spot by her side and wrap his arms around her, but what—

"It's just a bed, Rafe." Lyana sighed, reading every tumultuous thought in his mind. "And we're just going to sleep. I promise, the world will still be there when we wake up."

She was right.

Still, nerves tightened in his chest as he reached for the mesh blanket folded at the end of the bed, the one Brighty had stolen. It was made to stifle fire, and he never went anywhere without it, not anymore. Lyana watched him silently as he tossed the heavy drape over his side of the bed, putting a barrier between his wings and the highly flammable blankets, just in case. Awareness lit her eyes, tinged with an edge of sadness, as she ran her fingers over the material, recognizing what it was. Rafe swallowed the knot in his throat and sank into the spot beside her, careful to keep his arms to himself, but Lyana had different plans. The second he put his head upon the pillow, she rolled closer, wrapping an arm around his torso and pressing her cheek to the hollow of his neck. As their legs tangled together, he stopped trying to resist and slid an arm behind her back to pull her closer. He buried his face in her hair and breathed in her scent. Everything about the two of them felt so right. The way their bodies fit. The way their spirits calmed. The way their heartbeats slowed, coming together until they thumped softly to the same rhythm, almost as though made for one another.

Within moments, they both fell asleep.

He flew across a frozen landscape, the snow glowing cerulean in the moonlight, glistening with the reflection of the stars. The night was quiet. Ahead, a cluster of crystal domes marred the otherwise barren landscape, resting along the edge where ice and rock gave way to sky.

They were there.

He could feel them.

One of the buildings shone bright white against the night, a group of people visible through the translucent walls, laughing and talking. He stuck to the shadows, keeping out of sight. No one noticed him. Few ever did.

They were somewhere else.

He crept across the darkness, following the connection at the back of his mind, whispering of nearness. A dark dome loomed ahead, larger than the rest but absolutely still. He pressed his nose to the crystals, unfazed by the cold, and peered inside. Even without the assistance of the moon upon her luminous wings, he would have seen them. They curled together on the bed, fused from head to toe, no sense of where one started or the other ended, just limbs and feathers and fire. His wings simmered, casting a subtle orange glow about the room. Their bodies rose and fell to the same cadence.

An unfamiliar feeling stirred deep within, making his hands curl into fists as his every muscle tensed. Thus far, he'd been living in this world based on instinct, moving from one meal to the next, but now the human bits within him rose to the surface, promising retribution.

He'd left them for her.

He'd cut them for her.

Someday, he'd regret that decision.

Claws scratched upon crystal, carving deep grooves into the rock. The squeal mirrored the cry inside his heart, his newly awakened emotions wreaking havoc as he—

Rafe gasped and sat up, his pulse hammering like thunder as he turned toward the crystal wall, but no one was there. Moonlight and shadow danced across the frozen land, unbroken and unblemished, nothing but endless tundra and empty air. The fire upon his wings intensified, chasing the darkness of the room away. He searched the corners, the crevices, every hollow, but the night was still.

"Rafe?" Lyana murmured sleepily by his side, her body protesting his absence. "Is everything okay?"

"It's fine," he whispered as he settled back down, pulling her into his arms. "Shh."

Within moments, she was fast asleep.

Rafe rested his head upon hers, trying to let the brush of her breath and the steady pulse beneath his hands calm him, but it was futile. Every shift in the shadows drew his eye. Every sound stirred his thoughts. He stared ahead, not entirely sure what he was searching for until the starlight caught the crystal just right, illuminating five jagged grooves—a message drawn for his eyes alone.

They were coming.

For him.

For Lyana.

For the world.

And he had better not be asleep when they did.

32

CASSI

Time passed in a blur, the minutes, hours, and days blending together until Cassi had no sense of how long she'd been trapped. The room was a haze. Her vision had long since gone bleary, and her mind was too strained to focus. The world passed in shades of shadow and light, in splashes of cold water and pricks of hot spears, in loud shouts and blissful oblivion. She could no longer feel her legs or her arms, was unsure if she stood or lay down, was unaware if she slept or remained awake or hovered somewhere in between.

"Cassi," Lyana called, appearing as if from a dream. "Cassi, hold on. Be strong."

Heal me, she tried to say. *Help me.*

The golden magic never came.

"It's what you deserve," Rafe spat as he hovered over her. "You did this to yourself."

I didn't, she tried to argue. *I want to help.*

He was gone before he could listen, replaced by his brother, the two of them so very similar and yet so different.

Xander! she called. *Xander!*

He couldn't hear. No matter how she shouted, he just stood there, absent-eyed, as though he didn't see her, or worse, didn't care.

I have something I need to tell you! Something important!

But what?

She couldn't remember anymore.

Malek's voice was the loudest and the most frequent, but his requests were nonsense. "How's the prisoner? Has she slept? Is she conscious? Don't do that again unless I'm here to heal her. Use the water instead. Has the boy stopped fighting? Did she say anything? Did you hear anything? Leave us. Tell me if her condition changes. Again."

Other times, he threaded his fingers through her hair and leaned so close she could feel his lips upon her skin as he whispered, "I'm sorry, Kasiandra. There's no other way. I don't want to hurt you. You forced my hand. You'll feel better soon. I'll help you."

Power flooded into her veins, just enough for her to make out his tumultuous blue eyes, and then the storm would crash over her again, the waves dragging her under, until sounds and sights and smells faded, lost to the oblivion.

Come back! Come back!

Silence.

33

XANDER

The desert stretched before Xander in rolling hills of endless orange. Sweat dripped from his brow, the sun blazing against his black wings. A lone river cut through the monotony, flanked by vibrant patches of green. Far in the distance, along its bank, a bustling metropolis bloomed, bursting with color and buzzing with movement. It was no mirage. Though the heat and the sand had played tricks on him earlier, there was no mistaking Abaelon, the City of Life, the capital of the House of Flight.

Xander swallowed, his pulse hitching with the awareness of how exposed he'd soon be. The plan he and Helen had devised was risky, but he didn't see another way. Lyana had never sent Cassi to his dreams, so he'd never been able to inform her of the earthquakes on the hummingbird isle. Helen was the only person he trusted to carry the message, so he'd sent her to the House of Peace and traveled to the House of Flight alone. Sure, he could have brought guards or advisors or any other sort of entourage, and now, as the city loomed, he was starting to question his sanity, but the truth was he needed to prove himself—to the hummingbirds, to the other houses, and even to himself.

This is going to work. He silently tried to convince himself. *You have no choice but to make it work.*

The bad blood between the House of Whispers and the House of Flight was undeniable. Prince Damien had been Lyana's intended mate before she pulled her stunt at the matching ceremony. He'd been snubbed, forced to pair with the owl princess instead. Even before that, the prince and Rafe had butted heads. And the poor relationship continued. The royal family hadn't sent for Xander when the earthquakes began. In fact, they seemed to go above and beyond to ensure he wouldn't find out. If not for a letter from Queen Zara informing him of the news, he might never have known. They clearly didn't wish for his or Lyana's help, despite how obviously they needed it. Yet hummingbirds were notoriously loud and boastful, quick to anger but also quick to defuse, given the right circumstances. They were a house more ready for a celebration than a confrontation, so if he played his cards right, he could convince them.

At least, that was what he told himself as he soared into Abaelon.

Gardens covered towering sandstone buildings, green foliage brilliant against the honey backdrop. Flowers of every color spilled over the edges of the tiered levels, while rows upon rows of columns stood wrapped in various vines. An endless supply of water trickled like music in the background, flowing through the intricate network of aqueducts spread across the vast city. Fountains and layered streams twinkled in the sun. The winds from the desert howled, making the palm trees sway. Against that movement, darting faster than the eye could follow, hummingbirds zipped through the sky, their wings little more than blurred swathes of color at their backs as they raced from terrace to terrace, cultivating their crops, delivering messages, and just living life at a speed ten times faster than everybody else.

In comparison, Xander clambered slowly through the air, his black wings standing out not just for their color, but for their seemingly lazy flight. If not for the crown of onyx feathers nestled on his brow, he was sure someone would have stopped him. Instead, they waited and watched as he made his way to the palace looming in the center of the city.

The building was at least twenty stories high, shaped like a pyramid, the tiers growing smaller and smaller as they stretched into the sky. Unlike the rest of the city, it shone brilliantly white against the cloudless blue sky, the sandstone covered in marble quarried from the mountains. The effect would have been blinding if not for the hanging plants and foliage draped over every inch of the exterior, as though the palace were alive. Two enormous waterfalls framed the front entrance, the central lifeline of the irrigation system, pumped directly from the river itself. Xander had read all about the engineering, but the drawings in his books hadn't done the system justice. He adored his home, even if it was now buried beneath the sea, yet the more he came to learn about the rest of his floating world, the more he understood how relatively quaint his isle had been, just another reason the ravens had been easy to overlook.

Today, the hummingbirds would learn the true strength of his people.

They would discover exactly how memorable a raven could be.

Embracing his fear and wearing it like a shield, Xander swept into the courtyard before the palace. He landed at a stride on the marble tiles, his boots loud as he stomped toward the door. Before he made it halfway across, a hum filled the air. Shadows flickered beneath the sun, whizzing overhead as bodies flooded in from the terraces. By the time he blinked, he was surrounded. Guards hovered in formation above the courtyard, each with an arrow trained precisely on him.

Don't act afraid, he silently determined.

Don't give them the satisfaction.

Be brave. Be bold.

Be yourself.

It was a point of pride that his steps didn't falter. Paying the display no mind, he continued on his path until he stood at the base of the short stack of stairs leading up to the wide veranda of columns and trees. Through it, the doors to the palace were just barely visible. The waterfalls sprayed water thunderously into the air. Xander cupped his hands around his lips and prayed someone would hear him over the noise.

"I am King Lysander Taetanus of the House of Whispers, and I've come for an audience with King Axos and Queen Odehlia of the House of Flight."

Then he waited.

The air thrummed with the movement of wings, but the hummingbirds remained in place, hovering menacingly above him. No doors opened. No emissaries appeared. Xander stood with his feet braced and his spine straight, prepared to stay there all day until he was acknowledged. In the end, it didn't take nearly so long.

A shout rang from an upper terrace.

A blurred figure hurtled through the foliage.

A gleam of silver brightened the sky.

Don't move, Xander thought. *Don't move.*

The unnamed hummingbird barreled toward him, the deadly intent in the attack obvious. But Xander was king of a foreign house. They might not welcome him, and they might not agree with him, but they wouldn't murder him. At least, he hoped not. Still, as his heart hammered in his chest, he couldn't deny that just this once it would have been nice to have a little of Lyana's impossible power, no matter how many times he'd preached for her to show restraint.

Don't move.

The hum of air through feathers and the ring of steel filled his ears, then silence. Xander didn't flinch. He simply swallowed, the skin of his throat grazing the edge of a blade as he stared into a furious face he recognized from the trials.

"Good morning, Prince Damien," he said, as nonchalantly as possible.

The prince sneered, his olive skin wrinkling as his iridescent violet wings ruffled. "What? No raven cry this time?"

Unfortunately not, Xander thought, fighting to keep his face blank as he struggled to recall everything Rafe had once told him of the prince. They'd fought during the trials, as all the heirs had. There had been some altercation during hand-to-hand combat, and he'd been dishonored during the welcome ball when Rafe interrupted his dance with Lyana. They'd never liked each other. All Xander remembered thinking at the time was that they sounded too similar for their own good. How would he play this if it were Rafe on the other side, throwing a tantrum?

He'd disengage.

Nothing would have infuriated his brother more.

"I didn't come to fight," Xander offered, keeping his tone even. "I came to speak to you and your family about the devastation about to befall your house. I came to help."

"We don't need help from a mage-lover like you," Prince Damien spat.

Before Xander could respond, the prince kicked him in the chest. He stumbled back but managed to keep to his feet. The hummingbird disappeared in a flash, moving too fast for normal eyes, and then hands shoved him from behind. Xander fell forward, dropping to his knees.

"Not so tough without your queen around to fight your

battles," the prince accused, loud enough for all those gathered to hear.

"I believe a battle requires an opponent," Xander said as he returned to his feet, brushing off his clothes. "And as I said before, I have no intention of fighting with you today."

The prince punched him in the stomach, and he doubled over with a groan. A fist slammed into his chest, and he flew back up. The swiping of legs left him on his ass.

"When I heard you lost your hand, I didn't think you'd also lost your spirit," the prince mocked, a low blow Xander should have expected. Even after a lifetime of similar jabs, it still stung. "What happened to the great warrior prince of the House of Whispers?"

"I grew up," Xander answered, unable to keep the simmering anger wholly from his tone. "Perhaps you should try it."

With a low growl, the prince grabbed Xander by the wrist and spun him so his wings slammed into the hummingbird's chest while his good hand twisted painfully behind his back. Prince Damien held a dagger to his throat, the point pinching his skin. "You cavort with mages, which is still punishable by death in the House of Flight. Give me one good reason why I shouldn't cut you right now."

"I'll give you three," Xander answered, his voice deathly calm. "One, your isle is going to fall whether you wish it or not, and I have the experience to ensure as many lives are saved as possible. Two, the gods are on my side, and if you murder me, I have no doubt retribution against your house will be swift. And three..." He paused to pointedly eye the guard around his right forearm, which he'd raised to his chest. As Cassi had so aptly predicted all those weeks ago, the prince hadn't bothered securing the limb he naively believed posed no risk. Now, he tensed upon noticing the sharp point hidden in the shadows of the metal. "The moment I turn my wrist, a blade will spring free, striking you in the throat. So if you want to kill me, kill me, but my blood won't be the only blood spilled today. The choice is yours. As I said before, I didn't come to fight."

Palm trees swayed on the palace verandas. Wings speedily beat. The waterfalls crashed. But the prince didn't move. The moment stretched, becoming two, then three. Bowstrings whined, pulled taut. Not a single arrow was loosed.

Xander had him.

They all knew it.

Still, they might have waited like that all day, the prince's pride too great to suffer such a wound, if two more figures hadn't shot from the palace terraces, descending in a *whoosh* of feathers and fine silks. The king landed first, his turquoise hummingbird wings carrying him faster to the fray. The queen, formerly of the House of Paradise, followed gracefully behind.

"King Axos, Queen Odehlia," Xander murmured cordially, as though their heir didn't have a blade pressed to his jugular. "So kind of you to join us. The prince and I were just getting reacquainted."

The king frowned and flicked his wrist. In a flash, the guards lining the courtyard vanished. Then he eyed his son. After a reluctant pause, the prince released Xander. They disentangled, each taking a moment to straighten his jacket.

"Tell me, King Lysander, what brings you to our home?" His voice was wary, the look in his dark eyes unsure. "We didn't send for you."

"No, you didn't, which is why if you ask me to leave right now, I'll go. But I believe that would be a mistake. I know relations are strained between our two houses, and my actions at the courtship trials are partially to blame for that, but I urge you to put the past behind us. Not for me. Not for you. But for your people. Change is coming. All I want to do is help."

"And where is Queen Lyana?" The king searched the clouds.

"The queen has been summoned by the gods, and though she wanted to be here, it was a call she couldn't afford to ignore."

"That's rather convenient."

"If you want proof of her power, write to King Dominic or Queen Zara, and they will tell you what they've witnessed. I didn't come to intimidate or boast. I came simply as I am to humbly offer aid."

The king and queen started, as though noticing for the first time that no other ravens filled the skies or the courtyard. He'd come alone. The tension in their stances softened.

"Queen Zara speaks highly of you," the king said, not a question, though it lingered just the same.

"As I always will of her, should anyone ask."

"You seem changed."

Gods alive. It took everything within him not to laugh. Rafe had certainly left an impression on people during his short stint at the trials, none of it very good. King Axos was now the second ruler to notice Xander's newfound composure. "You could say I'm a new man."

"We shall see." The king motioned behind him and a servant emerged from the palace carrying a tray full of glasses bubbling with hummingbird nectar. It was a wonder nothing spilled. "In the meantime, my son will show you the hospitality he failed to offer upon your arrival. Eurythes is god of the harvest, and we'd be remiss not to offer nourishment after your long journey. Take the afternoon to recover, then join us for dinner this evening and we'll listen to what you have to say."

The king and queen retreated into the palace as Prince Damien grabbed a drink and knocked his head back, downing the contents in one swallow.

"I should think you'd be thanking me," Xander murmured, drawing the prince's attention.

"For what?"

"Isn't it obvious?" Xander grinned, silently praying Lyana would forgive him for his next words. As he'd said, hummingbirds were quick to anger and even quicker to forget. Well, they'd done the fury portion. It was time to move on to forgiveness. "Had you matched with Lyana at the trials, you'd be her errant messenger boy instead of me."

A soft puff of air verging on laughter escaped the prince's lips. He took two more glasses from the tray and offered one to Xander, eying him as though aware of the aches already beginning to percolate. "It will help numb the pain."

Xander stifled his grimace. By nightfall, purple blotches would mark his skin, thanks to the prince. It wasn't an apology for the attack. Still, though, it was something. He took the nectar and brought it to his lips. The liquid burned on its way down, the local version quite a bit stronger than the drink he was familiar with, and he coughed.

"Not what you're used to?"

"Not exactly," Xander managed to say, his voice strained.

"Well, then, *King* Lysander." Prince Damien clinked his glass, a dimple digging into his cheek as his lips curved in an impish smile. "Welcome to the House of Flight."

34

LYANA

Deep in meditation, Lyana didn't sense the spirit racing toward her room until the door slammed with a loud *bang*. She and Rafe opened their eyes at the same time, his blue irises mirroring her shock. They were sitting cross-legged with their knees touching. He'd been immersed in his mental connection to the dragons, and she'd been steeped in her magic trying to access the rift. The slight body contact helped to keep them grounded—he knew she was safe, and she knew he wasn't doing anything heroically foolish.

"Wait!" an out-of-breath voice carried down the hall. "Wait! You can't— I'm supposed to—" Brighty slammed into the doorframe, a frown twisting her features as her chest heaved. "Magic alive, you people are fast! I tried to stop her, but—"

"It's all right," Lyana murmured, shifting her focus to the woman who'd charged into her room. "Welcome, Helen."

The raven started, forcibly pulling her gaze from where it had settled, on Rafe's fiery wings, to offer a stiff bow. "My queen." Within moments, her attention slid sideways again. Her voice was tight as, with a curt nod, she muttered, "Rafe."

He sighed. "I suppose Xander warned you."

"He did."

"And yet?"

The captain of the guards swallowed, fighting for composure. "It's a shock."

Outwardly, Rafe maintained his walls, but Lyana sensed his spirit clench, fighting an all-too-familiar pain, one buried so deeply he might never root it out. She reached across their laps to take his hand, and his fingers immediately tightened around hers. Helen watched on, her expression inscrutable. The wariness in her heart, though, was palpable.

"What brings you, Helen?" Lyana asked as she eased to her feet, pulling Rafe with her even as he tried to wriggle his hand free. She wouldn't let him run anymore. She was done hiding, and he had no reason to be ashamed. "Is Xander all right?"

"As far as I know, he's fine. He sent me here while he traveled to the House of Flight. Alone."

"The House of Flight?" Lyana scrunched her brows.

Beside her, Rafe tensed. "Alone?"

"It was his idea," the captain said, her reluctance obvious. "I'm to meet him with a set of guards as soon as I leave here."

"And where are those guards?" Lyana glanced quickly through the crystal wall, seeing nothing but frozen land stretched as far as the eye could see.

"Waiting in the House of Song for my return."

She released a heavy breath. Only a handful of people knew about the mages stationed here in the outskirts of the House of Peace, and Lyana wanted to keep it that way. Her people were opening to change, but a magical training ground, especially one outfitted with teachers smuggled up from the world below, would have been a bridge too far. Even Helen's discomfort was obvious.

"Have there been earthquakes?" she asked, turning back to the captain. "Why didn't he send word? I told him to communicate through Cassi."

"He waited, but she never came."

"She never..." Lyana trailed off, lifting her hand to her chin as she thought back. When was the last time she'd spoken to Cassi? Surely, it hadn't been that long. Yet her days in the House of Peace were a bit of a blur. Between the hours spent deep in her magic, and the brief breaks to monitor the progress of her army, and the lively dinners with the crew, and the quiet nights coaxing Rafe to sleep, time had passed more swiftly than she'd realized. Had Cassi visited her dreams at all in the past week?

No.

Unease made the hairs on the back of her neck rise. Lyana shuffled through her memories, back and back and back. When was the last time they'd met? It couldn't have been before the House of Paradise fell, could it? Cassi would have come after that, if for no other reason than to make sure her queen was alive. She would have checked in, unless something—or someone—had stopped her.

"What's wrong?" Rafe murmured, sensing her sudden fear.

"I have to find Captain Rokaro," Lyana announced, her pulse spiking. "Now."

"She's—" Brighty dove out of the way as Lyana raced toward the door, half running and half flying through the opening. "Oh, for magic's sake! Not again."

The words were lost to the winds stirred by her wings as she propelled forward with urgent speed, leaving the featherless mage far behind. Rafe followed, and Helen too, the three of them emerging from the royal quarters within moments. The truth was, Lyana didn't need help locating the older woman. A little spark of her magic was all she needed to sense the captain's spirit through walls of rock and crystal. Everyone was in the training field on the other side of the grounds. With a leap, she flew up and over the domed buildings, then landed at a run across the open snow.

"Captain!"

At the sound of her voice, half the mages in the field froze—the members of her army. At the sight of Helen, water, fire, and dirt dropped out of the sky with a sudden *whoosh*. Panic saturated the air and their magic drained away, the sparkles at their fingertips fading. They'd been sighted using magic.

Lyana didn't have time to soothe them. Instead, she marched to the single-winged hawk watching steadily with her arms crossed and an eyebrow raised.

The gods, they look so much alike, Lyana thought, a pang in her chest. There was no denying Cassi was a liar and a traitor, but despite everything, Lyana needed her—not just as a spy, but also as a friend.

"When's the last time you spoke to your daughter?"

The crew stopped dead the moment the question left her lips, their magic vanishing in the blink of an eye. As one, they turned to gape at their captain. For her part, the older woman just lifted her fingers to her forehead and smoothed out her frown lines with a sigh.

"Daughter?" Rafe spat. "Cassi is your daughter?"

"You didn't know?" Lyana spun to face him. How could he not know? Their mannerisms, their expressions. They were so similar. Yet the realization filled his normally clear eyes with tumultuous storm clouds.

"You said you didn't know anyone named Cassi," he accused, stepping forward. "You said—"

"Kasiandra is the name I gave her," the captain interjected in a tired tone. "And yes, she's my daughter, so the lot of you can shut your mouths before the cold air freezes them open. I had a whole life of my own before I became your captain and got roped into all your messes. I don't owe anyone any explanations, except maybe you…" She turned to Rafe. "I'll only say this once, so listen good. I'm sorry. When you landed on my ship, I knew you'd need someone to trust, and I knew that would never be me or any of my crew if you learned the truth. Maybe I should have told you. Maybe I did the right thing. There's no way to go back now, and everything else I ever told you was true. My king ordered me to catch a man falling from the sky, and that's what I did. The fact that it was my daughter who pushed you over the edge changes nothing."

"It changes something to me."

"Be angry if you want to be." Captain Rokaro shrugged, unfazed as the flames at Rafe's back strengthened in response to his fury. "Kasiandra is my daughter, and like me, she's done what she needed to do to survive. I won't fault her for it."

Rafe stared at the woman, his fingers curling into fists. She stared right back, expression open and somewhat sad as the breeze ruffled the fabrics entwined with her hair, highlighting that only one side of her face was framed by feathers. Their standoff was interrupted by a voice cutting across the silence.

"All right, I'm here—finally. Didn't anyone ever tell you it's rude to fly away in the middle of a conversation?" Brighty huffed as she trudged across the field. Everyone turned toward her, prompting her to stop where she stood. An almost comedic look of uncertainty passed over her features. "What? Did I grow a second head or something? What'd I miss?"

"Captain has a daughter," Archer offered casually.

Brighty started. "What?"

"And I think she's the one who cut off Rafe's wings," Jolt added.

"What?" The *photo'kine* spun so fast she risked whiplash.

"And apparently she's missing," Pyro said.

"Magic alive, you arrive five minutes late to the party, and—" She broke off to push her fingertips into her temples as her entire face scrunched. "Is that everything?"

"I think that about sums it up," Captain snapped, wiping the grins off all their faces. Lyana admired the woman's ability to reprimand so many at once, and by using nothing more than subtle intonation. Cassi might have been her only blood relation, but it was clear the ship ran like a family, the crew her unruly children. One word from her and they all shrank back, chagrinned. Those icy eyes turned on Lyana, but she wasn't afraid of reproach, because she, out of everyone here, was the only one who could feel the deep-rooted worry tangling the captain's spirit into knots. "And to answer your question, I haven't spoken to her in weeks. Why?"

Lyana's heart dropped. "The House of Flight started experiencing earthquakes, and she didn't come to tell me."

The captain pursed her lips.

"I haven't seen her since before the House of Paradise fell," Lyana continued, her pulse growing more rapid as she spoke. "It's not like her to go so long without communicating. I think—I think something's happened."

Captain Rokaro's expression darkened. Neither of them spoke, but a name passed between them just the same.

Malek.

He had Cassi's body. He had his *aethi'kine* magic. He was the only one in the world with the power to stop her spirit from reaching the world above.

"I'll save her," Lyana blurted.

"But the king—"

"Doesn't scare me." She took the older woman's hands in her own and held them to her chest as soothing magic flooded from her palms. The captain tensed, as though unused to the comforting touch of another human being. "He didn't kill her. He wouldn't dare, not while I'm still breathing. This is a ploy, probably to get to me—"

"It's working," Rafe interjected.

"Maybe." Lyana released the captain and turned to face him, hating the insecurity written in the tense clench of his teeth. "But I'm willing to take that chance."

For Cassi.

For the world.

The truth was this moment had been unavoidable from the start. Another isle had fallen, and a third would soon, yet Lyana was no closer to figuring out the mystery of the rift. More of those creatures would be coming, and eventually Rafe wouldn't be able to fight them off on his own. It didn't matter who the king of prophecy was, not really. Rafe was her protector. Malek was her teacher. And she needed them both to survive.

"I'm going to Da'Kin."

"I'm coming with you."

"I know." Lyana smiled and ran her fingers along the chiseled curve of Rafe's jaw. Golden magic seeped beneath his skin and silver swirls rose to meet it as he sank into her touch, lifting his palm to cover hers. "It's high time we face him together."

35

MALEK

"My liege!"

Malek looked up from his paperwork, annoyed by the interruption. There had been a slew of unexplainable deaths in recent weeks, in cities all across the seas, a puzzle that nagged to be solved. But if Viktor was here, it was important. His *aero'kine* knew better than to barge in unannounced. "What?"

"They're here."

No explanation was necessary. Malek dropped the report and stood. "Where?"

"Close," Viktor replied. "I sensed something cutting through the mist at rapid speed, too small to be a dragon based on the winds, but Isaak could feel flames. We don't have visual confirmation yet, but it's them. It must be."

"Alert Jacinta and Nyomi, and ready the rest of the mages. We'll only have one shot at taking them by surprise. I want you to concentrate on the raven, as planned. I'll wait here for Lyana alone."

"Yes, my liege."

"And Viktor?" His *aero'kine* stopped in the doorway, looking stoic the way he'd been taught. "Good work."

The barest twitch of lips was the only clue Viktor approved of the praise, at least to the outside observer, but Malek felt the thrill pass through his spirit. By the time his mage was gone, the king was already halfway to his balcony. Magic glittered around his palms as he gripped the metal banister and searched the gray expanse of the sky.

Where are you?

He'd been waiting for this moment for days, ever since he'd received the report from his *dormi'kine*. Lyana had moved into the House of Peace with her mages. She and the raven were inseparable. They knew the rumors. They believed them. He'd almost let Cassi go then, but it wasn't in his nature to admit defeat. Malek was the King Born in Fire. He knew it in his bones, and if she'd only just return to him, Lyana would see it too.

So he devised a plan to lure her back.

And now she was here.

A flash of white seized his breath. The trail of smoldering flames in her wake struck like a knife. His chest burned.

Come to me, he thought. *Come back to me.*

They were made for each other.

They were meant to be.

Two *aethi'kines* with the most powerful magic in the world. Two *aethi'kines* destined to heal the rift. Two *aethi'kines* able to understand each other in a way no one else ever could.

They were the saviors.

They were the chosen king and queen.

He retreated into his study and waited. Lyana arrived first, her ivory wings fluttering as she landed gently on his balcony—the space only big enough for one body. Already his dreary world felt brighter.

Come closer, he silently willed.

She listened, stepping cautiously into the room, her voice soft despite the hard emerald sheen in her gaze. “Malek.”

Now, he thought, and magic exploded across the skies.

36

RAFE

As Lyana disappeared into the castle, Rafe swooped to follow and landed hard on the stone balustrade. Something was wrong. Deep in his stomach, hunger panged. The air tasted of magic. A subtle prickle danced along his skin.

"Ly—"

A chain wrapped around his ankle, then pulled. The word died on his lips as he fell back, dropping out of the sky. Before he could speak or scream, he slammed into the cold waters of Da'Kin. Blue magic lit the dark depths. Liquid hands grabbed him from all sides, holding him down as he tried to swim. A strong current carried him deeper. White bubbles exploded from his wings as the fire and sea met in a wash of steam. He chased the pockets of air, dragging his hands and kicking his feet, searching for a way out.

A flash of green was his only warning as a plate of metal clamped around his mouth, molding to the curve of his chin as it wrapped around his skull—not meant to cut off air but sound. More chains plunged through the depths to secure his arms to his chest and his wings to his back. They wound him in a metal cocoon until every inch of his body was contained. Only then, with his chest burning, did his attackers finally let him up for air.

As soon as his face broke the surface, Rafe sucked a sharp breath through his nostrils. His coughs were caught by the muzzle, forcing him to swallow the water he spit up, the bile making his stomach turn. The *ferro'kine* deposited him on the rocks at the base of the castle, unmoved as he struggled against his binds. All the king's top mages were there. He recognized them from the warehouse, his few short minutes in their presence permanently carved like a scar across his memories. The water mage with slicked-back hair and golden eyes. The fire mage with wrinkled olive skin and a deceptively kind smile. The air mage with a lanky frame who seemed more likely to get blown over by a stray breeze than to command one. The light mage with hair the color of fire and eyes the same opal sheen as Brighty's, though not nearly as full of life. And of course, the metal mage with black hair and pale features as sharp as knives.

Rafe silently pleaded with them.

I'm not here to fight him. I'm not here to steal your prophecy. I'm not even here for the world. Please, I'm only here for her. To protect her. To keep her safe. Please, you have to release me.

They didn't get it.

They didn't understand.

They would soon.

Already, the two souls constantly alive in the back of his mind were racing closer. Craving gnawed at their insides, the pure instincts of a dragon. But fury simmered around the edges, undeniably human.

Rafe twisted his neck, fighting for one glance of the castle at his back. He thrashed on the rocks, unmindful of the jagged edges scraping his skin. Golden light emanated from the tallest spire, shining like a beacon through the fog, making his own longing surge. *Aethi'kine* power saturated the skies like the sweetest forbidden fruit, daring him to come and take a bite. That's what they were coming for. That's what they wanted.

"Lyana!" he tried to shout. "Lyana!"

Against the metal covering his lips, the name was little more than a muffled noise. The metal mage kicked him in the ribs.

"Quiet."

He glared at the woman.

"Not so tough without his raven cry," the water mage murmured, folding her arms across her chest as she tilted up her face. "How long does the king want us to wait?"

"Until we see the sign," Viktor murmured, his gaze on the balcony overhead. "I don't think he expected the fight to end so quickly."

It's not over, Rafe wanted to say. *It hasn't even begun.*

His bond with the creatures strengthened as they neared, closing in on Da'Kin. He could feel their wings beating, their hearts racing, their stomachs pining. On some level, he felt the same as them, the dragon in his soul crying out for a taste of the magic pouring from the top spire, such blatant power. Yet the human inside him felt something else entirely—dread.

"Let me go!"

The mages paid him and his garbled nonsense no mind.

"They're coming! They're almost here! Let me go!"

Nothing.

What do I do? How do I get out of this?

Already the scene played through his mind, of the shadow beast tearing through the open window and grabbing Lyana by the throat to drink her magic in. The battle would be over quickly, and with it, the world. None of the mages around him would even understand until the golden light winked out, never to be seen again.

He fought to jerk his arms free of the chains, his entire body trembling against the rocks. But it was useless. The green magic still glittering along the chains was binding. There was no way to muscle his way out of this.

Think, Rafe. Think.

What could get past metal? The sheet covering his lips was thin, so if he could just break through to his raven cry, to his voice… But how?

Fire.

Not his wings—they didn't burn hot enough—but there was another source of heat constantly churning deep inside his chest, one he'd been reluctant to use for the sheer monstrosity of it.

For Lyana, he would.

For the world.

Rafe sucked a long slow breath through his nose, letting his fury guide him. The volcanic pit deep inside spewed with repressed rage, ready to erupt. He didn't fight it. All the frustration, all the loathing, all the ugly parts of himself he was too afraid to face he now allowed to barrel up his throat and boil over. For the first time, he understood why dragons roared as they spit flames. The shout careened up his throat and spilled through his lips as a bubbling inferno.

The mages ignored him.

Rafe pushed, breathing in and roaring out, again and again and again, until he felt the metal band covering his mouth waver.

Come on. Come on.

In the back of his mind, two souls raced closer. Through the bond, he saw Da'Kin emerge from the fog, the groaning wood and slapping water, the maze of streets all leading to one central location. The castle loomed against the rocks, the top spire shining as brilliantly as the sun.

They were nearly here.

Come on!

Rafe screamed. The metal broke open and fire exploded across the rocks, singeing the mages. As one, they spun.

"Light up the skies!" Rafe shouted. There was no time to use his raven cry to free himself from the chains. He stared at the *photo'kine*, struggling to remember the man's name as he fueled every ounce of authority he could muster into his tone. "Kal! Light up the skies! Now!"

He didn't know if it was the panic in his voice, the command in his tone, or Kal's sheer instinct to follow an order, but white light cut through the mist and wrapped around the castle, chasing the shadows away.

A piercing howl sent a shiver down his spine. The mages whipped their faces toward the spot. A set of ebony wings beat helplessly within the glow, diving out of sight beyond the castle wall, back to the darkness.

"What was that?" The fire mage stepped forward, the blaze around his palm surging. "It's too small to be a dragon, but I sense—"

"It's like me," Rafe cut in, struggling to speak through the mangled metal muzzle still covering his lips. The *ferro'kine* didn't ease the binds, but the sheet covering his mouth peeled away, taking a layer of skin with it from where the melted metal had fused to his flesh. Rafe clenched his teeth against the pain, his magic already racing to heal the wounds.

"What do you mean?" she asked.

"They're half-dragon, like me."

"They?"

"There's a second, fueled by earth magic, somewhere close—"

Rafe cut off as the thunderous groan of splitting rock filled the air. Across the water, the wall collapsed in a heap of dust. Through the haze, the outline of dark green wings could only just be seen. Stones the size of men shot from the rubble, racing toward them.

"Viktor!"

A gust of wind blasted across the sky, blowing the boulders off course to crash against the cliffside. More came.

"Nyomi!"

Tendrils of water swerved like arms to swat the projectiles away, batting them down into the sea. The barrage continued. More of the wall collapsed. More rocks flew. The ground beneath them trembled as flecks of green magic soared across the distance.

"It's going to tear the castle down!"

"We need the king—"

"No," Rafe shouted, cutting the metal mage off. "Remember what happened on the ship? The king's magic is useless in this fight. I'm the only one who can fight them. Let me go, now! Let me go or all is lost!"

Fissures formed in the flattened rock, spidering out. The quaking intensified. Rafe rolled from side to side, still wrapped in the chains, as he stared at the *ferro'kine*. A stone crashed against the cliff, the pieces ricocheting in every direction as it exploded into a dozen deadly shards. One struck the *photo'kine*. He dropped and darkness descended.

"Let me go—now!"

The chains snapped, falling away in an instant. Rafe leapt up, taking to the sky as the ground ripped to pieces beneath his feet. A steady stream of *aethi'kine* magic still poured from the balcony, interrupted by the briefest ebony blip as the creature swept inside. Rafe dove after it, closing his wings tight to his back as he sailed through the opening to land on the rug at a roll.

"Lyana!"

She and the king were too deep in their magic to hear. Behind her ivory wings, shadows rippled. Black claws slipped around her throat.

"No!"

Rafe threw the broken strip of chain in his hand. The razor-sharp edge flashed gold, the metal catching the glow of her power before vanishing into darkness.

37

LYANA

Nails scraped across her neck as a cry filled her ear, jolting her from the fight with Malek. Lyana emerged from the throes of her power as the world came back into sharp focus.

"Move!" Rafe shouted as he ran toward her. "Move!"

She dove to the side. He barreled past her and collided into a body with a *smack*. Flame and shadow rolled across the floor, claws and hands and wings and limbs merging into one. The shadow beast was here. Before she could help, golden power enveloped her, dragging her backward across the room. Magic sizzling at her fingertips, she turned and struck back.

"Malek!"

He was too far gone to listen. His spirit thrummed with a crazed energy she'd never felt before, as though all his careful control had fled, leaving him unhinged.

"Malek, this is not the way—"

"Promise me you'll stay," he demanded again, repeating himself for the third time since her arrival. "I'm the King Born in Fire. You're the Queen Bred of Snow. We need to be together. We need to figure this out together. You can't live up there with him. You have to stay with me."

"I'm going to stay, Malek," she said, not using her power to fight him but to break through to him. "And so is Rafe. And the three of us are going to—"

"No!"

His power pushed against her back and she stumbled forward, her focus no longer fully on the battle with Malek but half-consumed by the fight raging on the other side of the room. Rafe gripped the shadow beast by the shoulders. The creature dug its claws into him, blood pooling around the edges of its talons. They circled, their wings pumping as they fought, neither strong enough to break the other's hold. The castle trembled. The earth shook. She didn't need to see the magic to know it was the work of the second creature, attacking from somewhere nearby. Only the strongest *geo'kine* magic could make a foundation of solid rock shift so precariously.

"Malek, this is bigger than you and me. Can't you see—"

"Nothing is bigger than you and me," he urged. "Nothing is greater than our cause."

"There are things you don't know—"

"I know the world depends on us."

"Malek, just listen!" she snapped. Her magic whipped across the room like a violent wind and smacked him in the cheek. Would he never learn to let others speak? Would he never understand that even the greatest king needed counsel? Would he never treat her as his equal?

"Lyana." He said her name like a broken man. "Lyana, please."

She wanted to throttle him. She wanted to comfort him.

A pain-filled grunt made her freeze. Rafe clutched his abdomen as blood spilled over his fingers. He wobbled on his feet, gritting his teeth before diving toward a spot of pure darkness. The shadow shifted, flitting away. Rafe fell to his knees. Lyana reached for the creature, but its soul burned. A yelp escaped her lips. In a blink, the creature disappeared, and one moment later, the golden magic filling the room winked out.

She spun. "Malek!"

It was too late. The creature clutched him by the throat, holding him so high his feet dangled two inches above the ground, his body thrashing. The dark eyes she'd so often seen stone-cold with control and full of storm clouds now flashed with the bright spark of something she never thought she'd see—fear. Power seeped from his spirit, sinking into the creature.

"Rafe!" she called, her desperation acute. "Rafe!"

He pushed off the ground, one hand clutching his stomach while the other reached for the sword across his back. His movements were sluggish, the gash in his side still gaping even as his silver magic raced to heal it. He stumbled forward unsteadily. There was no way he'd make it in time.

What can I do?

How can I fight it?

A letter opener sat on the edge of the desk, the edge sharp and pointed. Lyana gripped the spirit of the metal and flung the makeshift weapon across the room. It embedded itself in the creature's wrist. A roar shook the air and the black claw loosened. Malek dropped to the ground. Lyana retreated a step as a black wave swallowed the light, one even the golden glow of her magic couldn't penetrate. The walls and curtains and furniture disappeared, replaced with an abyss, as though she hovered in a starless night. Malek stood to her left and Rafe to her right, their spirits blazing in her mind's eye. A third shifted too quickly to follow. She went dizzy trying to trace the movement.

Fingers grabbed her braids and pulled. With a cry, she fell backward and landed hard on the ground. It was on her in an instant, sharp scales digging into her chest as the creature held her down with its knees. Claws snatched her wrists and the magic simmering at her fingertips dissolved into darkness. The beast drank in her magic, its spirit growing stronger and stronger with each passing moment. Her own muscles slackened. Her heartbeat slowed, as though her life force was draining into the beast along with her power.

Rafe slammed into them from the side, the flames along his wings flashing before he and the creature were swallowed by shadow. Grunts and cries filled the void. Her arms trembled as she pushed herself to a seated position, searching the deep ebony for some hint of the battle raging nearby. Unable to see, she could do nothing to help.

"Rafe!" she tried. "Rafe!"

A bellowing roar made her flinch.

Bright light flashed as the darkness receded. Rafe and the creature stood before the balcony, almost as though embracing. Both swayed, frozen in the moment. Lyana's heart pounded as she searched Rafe's body for a wound.

Is he hurt?

Is he injured?

The beast stepped back, and the sharp edge of steel caught the soft light flooding in from the outside. Rafe yanked his arms away and the sword slid free, covered in thick ebony sludge. No longer propped up by the blade, the creature slouched and clutched its stomach, beating its wings to remain upright. Darkness flooded from the leathery appendages, like smoke from a fire, blotting out the sky. Two onyx eyes stared at Rafe for a prolonged moment. Then, with a leap, it fled into the mist. The ground fell still as the second creature raced after it.

"They're gone," Rafe said with a relieved sigh. "For now."

"What are they?" Malek asked, his voice raspy. A red mark in the shape of a hand still colored the fair skin of his neck.

"You should know." Rafe sneered, his disgust evident. "After all, you almost turned me into one."

"They're soul-joined? But how? I didn't— You're the only—"

"The god stones," Lyana supplied as she struggled to stand, her legs still weak from the creature's brief but costly touch. Rafe came to her side immediately, wrapping his arm around her waist to help keep her upright. She leaned into his embrace. "The god stones are eggs. Whoever made the rift all those years ago somehow fused dragon eggs with human souls, and they've been maturing ever since, feeding off the power of the spell to strengthen their own magic. Every time a new one hatches, an isle falls. And that's why I'm here—why we're here. The world is running out of time."

Malek's gaze dropped to where Rafe's fingers dug into Lyana's hip, a frown furrowing his brows. If anything, Rafe's grip just tightened.

Men.

Lyana fought the urge to roll her eyes. "Look at me, Malek."

He did, and all his walls came down, leaving him exposed in a way he'd never been before. Right now, she wasn't talking to a king. She was talking to the lost little boy who'd been forced to grow up too quickly, forced to shoulder a burden so heavy it would have crushed anyone else. She was talking to a man who, above all else, was afraid to be abandoned again, especially as the one truth he'd always maintained as his guiding light flickered with uncertainty.

"I don't care who the King Born in Fire is."

He flinched.

"I don't care because it doesn't matter," she said, softening her tone as she stepped forward, bringing Rafe with her until she was close enough to also take Malek's hand. "The prophecy was written hundreds of years ago, yet you treat it as fact. Maybe one of you is the foretold king. Maybe neither of you are. We'll never know for sure, and I refuse to let a handful of pretty words decide my fate any longer. I need you to teach me, Malek. And we need Rafe to protect us. That's the only way to save the world. And despite everything, I know that's all you've ever wanted—to fell the sky, and seal the rift, and rid the world of dragons."

A war raged in his spirit. He didn't move or speak. He just stared at where her fingers entwined with his, pursing his lips as he fought to make sense of everything he'd ever believed and everything she'd told him. Just as he tightened his grip, the door to his study was flung open.

"My liege—" Nyomi stopped short upon seeing the three of them so close.

Malek ripped his hand from Lyana's grasp and turned to his mage, the stoic mask of the king back in place. "What?"

"Kal and Jacinta are injured. It's bad—"

"Where?"

"The rocks at the base of the castle, near the dock. We didn't want to move them."

"I'm on my way." He took a step forward, golden magic already bursting to life around his palm, then paused to glance over his shoulder.

"Go," Lyana mouthed.

A torn expression twisted his features. He turned back to his mage. "Take the queen to Kasiandra. Do exactly as she commands, even if it differs from my prior orders. Understood?"

"Yes, my liege."

He left without another word, but Lyana heard the unspoken message. He'd extended a peace offering, and for now that was enough. They followed the water mage down into the underbelly of the castle, through dank corridors and barely lit stairwells, and finally to a wooden door held shut by a thick iron bar. At Nyomi's signal, the *ferro'kine* stationed outside lifted the blockade. Nothing could have prepared Lyana for what waited inside.

Cassi lay trembling on a bed, easily twenty pounds thinner than the last time Lyana had seen her, all bones. Her eyes were closed, but she wasn't sleeping. Incoherent mumbles spilled from her lips as she twitched and jerked, her head thrashing from side to side. Deep purple bags stained her cheeks. Sweat covered every inch of her skin. A *cryo'kine* pressed frigid icicles to her brow, while a *pyro'kine* suspended a flame beneath her feet. The tortured cry of her soul nearly sent Lyana reeling.

"Stop!" she shouted, seizing the mages with her magic and practically flinging them from the room. The next thing she knew, she was on her knees, leaning over the bed with her hand pressed to Cassi's brow as her healing power poured into the owl. For the first time since learning the truth, Lyana didn't see a stranger or a traitor. All she saw was her friend.

Cassi's eyes fluttered open.

"Ana?" Her voice was barely audible, raw and scratchy, quivering with vulnerability. "Is that really you?"

"Shh, it's me," Lyana soothed, brushing her fingers over Cassi's forehead and into her hair. "I'm here. You can sleep now. I promise I won't leave you."

38

XANDER

For the first time in his life, Xander was well and truly drunk. And singing. Wait—was he singing? Yes, he was. The sound of his voice echoed off the vast halls of the hummingbird palace, slurred and nearly incoherent but definitely his.

"I know of a tavern not far from here, where the nectar flows from tier to tier. The hummingbirds flock from miles around. It's the best damn time, so fly right on down…"

He lingered on that last note, laughter stirring in the back of his throat as he and Prince Damien stumbled together over the marble floor. There was no way to know if he was holding the prince up, or if the prince was holding him up, but they each had an arm around the other's waist, their wings dragging as they followed a zigzag path toward the royal rooms.

"Have a sip, have two, and drown out your sorrows, say goodbye to your fears, they'll be there tomorrow. Seize the night with Eurythes' fine blessing, our god's on our side so stop second-guessing…"

They paused for the big finale. Damien threw back his head as he bellowed into the vines crisscrossing the ceiling above their heads. *"Now, drink and drink and drink—again! Now, drink and drink and drink till the end! Drink and drink and drink!"*

The room swam as Damien pushed him forward, possibly through a door, though there was no way to tell. Next thing he knew, he was in a seat with a new glass being shoved into his hand.

"No more," Xander protested. "I can't have anymore."

"Oh, raven lightweight," Damien jibed, throwing his own shot back.

"Your metabolism is five times faster than mine."

"Try ten."

"Exactly."

"You asked for a true hummingbird welcome. Well, this is a true hummingbird welcome."

"I think it's payback," Xander grumbled as he dropped his head into his hand. The floor and ceiling were spinning, so he couldn't tell which was up and which was down. Being seated made his stomach roil. The prince had been right about one thing, though—he couldn't feel the pain of his bruises at all. In fact, he feared his body might be numb. And for some reason, he wasn't sure he could feel his tongue. But could he ever feel his tongue? Or was it always this fat and heavy?

Tomorrow, he thought, cringing. *I'll feel everything and more tomorrow.*

"Sounds like you two had fun," a female voice chimed.

Xander rolled his head to the side. He would have attempted to stand and offer a formal bow, but he couldn't move his legs. Or his arms. Or anything, really. "Princess Coralee."

A grin curved her lips as she closed the book in her lap and uncurled her legs to rise from the window seat. Humor shone in her bronze eyes, but she didn't tease. She was too kind, or perhaps reserved, for that. Damien, on the other hand, was as loud and boastful as they came. As soon as his mate stood, he sped across the room, took her arms, and started twirling her around the room, a new song on his lips. They spun in a violet-and-amber blur, his wings moving far faster than hers. Whatever protests she made were quickly replaced by laughter.

Xander dropped his head back, smiling as he watched them. Strange to think that only months before she'd been his intended mate, until Lyana had changed the game. At the time, he'd thought Coralee would be his perfect match, but now? He wasn't so sure. They were both studious and polite, preferring books to people and quiet contemplation to raucous celebrations. How long would they have tiptoed around each other before forming a true connection? Months? Years? Maybe she'd needed someone like Damien to break her out of her shell. And maybe he needed someone who would throw him up against castle walls and question his every theory, someone who would pick apart his favorite books and force him to break into locked library rooms, someone who challenged him as he'd never been challenged before.

Black-and-white speckled owl wings filled his vision as his eyes slipped closed. Cassi's silver irises flashed with all the luminous mystery of the moon. She'd had many smiles, sometimes devious and sometimes teasing, though his favorite had been on the beach in that dream, her grin honest and true as they built a world full of wonder together. He could see her now, the silken brunette tendrils of her hair swirling in the breeze as she laughed and dipped her hands into a sea made of hummingbird nectar, the sun warm against her tawny skin.

"Xander?"

He glanced over his shoulder at the sound of her voice. "Cassi?"

"Your mind feels…strange."

The bookshelves behind her were familiar, a personal collection built over a lifetime, now buried beneath the sea. The leather armchair in which he sat was worn, molded perfectly to the contours of his body. The towering columns, gleaming white marble, and endless vegetation of the House of Flight were long gone. "We're in a dream."

"Right."

He sighed. "I thought maybe you were here."

"I am…" She trailed off, a groove digging into her brow. "Lyana sent me."

"You're too late. I already sent Helen."

"I know. Listen, a lot's happened, and— Are you sure you're all right?"

He wobbled unsteadily on his feet. If waking Xander couldn't move, did that mean dream Xander couldn't either? There was only one way to find out. He took a tentative step forward, spreading his wings for balance, then another and another. A grin pulled at his lips. "I'm walking."

"I can see that."

"Isn't it marvelous?" He spun to face her, and one foot caught on the other. His body was too slow to catch up to his mind, or maybe his mind was too slow to catch up to his body, or maybe it was all his mind since this was a dream. Regardless, he stumbled to the side and slammed into his desk. Cassi jumped forward to steady him.

"Are you…" Her lustrous eyes widened, sparkling with mirth. "Are you drunk?"

"Princes don't get drunk."

"Well, you're a king," she drawled, helping him reposition against the table so it propped him upright. "And you're definitely drunk."

Oh, right. He was a king now.

And an orphan.

And alone.

She stepped back, but he grabbed her hand, not letting go. "Do you know Rafe is the King Born in Fire?"

Cassi nodded slowly. "I do."

"I've been thinking..." It was his turn to trail off as he rubbed his thumb across the tips of her fingers, again and again, marveling at the smoothness of her skin. "If you never cut off his wings, he never would've fallen to the world below. And if he had never fallen, he never would've been soul-joined to a dragon. And if he were never soul-joined to a dragon, then he never would've become this king he now is. So, in an odd way, the horrible thing you did might have saved the world."

"Xander—"

"So I can't be mad at you anymore, can I?" he asked, lifting his face back to hers, remembering they were only a few inches apart. Her slightly parted lips were tantalizingly close. As if sensing his attention, she darted her tongue out, wetting them. His pulse spiked. "Not if you saved the world."

Shadows darkened her eyes. "You can be mad at me, Xander. You should be."

"Why?" He shrugged. "You're a liar, but now I'm a liar too. I'm lying to everyone in the realm, about the gods and magic and what Lyana's really doing. You thought about killing me, sure, but you didn't. The night my home fell into the sea, for a moment I thought about leaving you in that cell, but I didn't either. We're even."

"You're drunk," she said again, the word sounding like a protest as she slipped her hand from his. She didn't step back, though. The side of her thigh touched his, the small point of contact making his whole side burn. "You're talking nonsense."

"My mother used to say imbibing makes a man too honest. It was why she never drank. Rulers, she said, need to be able to deceive."

"Not you."

He sighed. "I'm not so sure. I've grown quite skilled at deception."

A snort slipped out. "You're the most honest person I know."

"You want to hear something honest?" His voice lowered to a

whisper. Unable to stop himself, he pressed his fingers to the bare skin of her arm, tracing a path from her wrist to her shoulder before letting his hand drop away. "I was worried when you didn't come."

She swallowed, loud enough he heard, but said nothing.

"You want to hear something even more honest?"

With a slow nod, she drew her lower lip between her teeth. All he wanted to do was use his mouth to lure it back out.

"I missed you."

"You're drunk," she murmured.

He arched a brow. "So?"

A moment passed, then two. Just as he started to lean in, she pulled back and turned her face to the side. Even in his stupor, the rejection stung. With a cough, he straightened his legs, forgetting how weak they felt as he gripped the table behind him to keep from falling.

"Maybe I should take a turn being honest," Cassi finally said into the silence. Lured by the sound, he lifted his face, along with his hope. She wrung her hands and took a deep breath, as though building her courage. "I want more than this for us."

His heart fell.

Of course she wanted more.

Of course she needed more than him.

"Xander," she murmured and took his hand, then his wrist, until all four of their arms were joined. "I want more than a drunken confession. I want to hear your forgiveness with my own ears. And for you to mean it with a sober mind. I want to touch you, the real you, and I want you to touch me, not in the stolen hours of a dream, but beneath the bright light of the sun. And that's partially why I'm here. Malek healed me, and Lyana is sending me back to the world above."

"You're healed?" He tightened his grip, unable to fight his smile.

As if it were infectious, her lips widened too. Yet something sad hovered at the edges of her eyes, a shadow dulling their shine. "I am."

"What's wrong—"

"Nothing." She shook her head. "Nothing's wrong, I promise. I'll explain another time, but for now, if you remember anything from this dream by the time you wake up, please try to remember this—I'm coming to the House of Flight as soon as I can. I'm coming to see you and to retrieve the diary."

"You're coming here?"

She laughed at his tone. "I am."

A new feeling overtook Xander, something wild, as if he were flying through open skies even as he stood, not so steadily, on his own two feet. He wanted to run. He wanted to jump. Deep in his chest, a knot burst, leaving him light and unburdened. There were more troubles than he could remember waiting for him outside of this dream, but right now, he was free.

For a moment, he thought of Damien sweeping across the room to pull Coralee into his arms, ignoring her protests as he spun her around.

Have a sip, have two, and drown out your sorrows, he thought, the tune playing in the back of his mind. *Say goodbye to your fears, they'll be there tomorrow.*

And they would.

Which meant he needed to make use of the night while he could. Xander took Cassi's hand and ran for the window, pulling her behind him.

"What—"

"Just come with me," he shouted. The glass disappeared and he dove through the opening. As the city below dissolved into a thousand glittering stars, they splashed into an onyx sea. A current of moonlight carried them deeper into this midnight world, the silver sheen dull compared to the light in her eyes, and they swam holding hands, as he rebuilt his dreams around them.

39

CASSI

The blistering winds in the open skies above the House of Peace were colder than Cassi remembered. She shivered, fighting the chill as she and Elias made their way across the icy tundra. The rolling hills of snow were painted in shades of pink, and a few eager stars already twinkled overhead.

"I see it!" he shouted, his excitement palpable. "There. Cassi, do you see it?"

A brilliant gold spot gleamed in the distance—the reflection of the dying sun on smooth crystal. A sense of dread panged in her chest. They'd reached the sky bridge.

"I see it," she called back.

"We're almost home!"

He sped ahead. Cassi let him, taking the opening to reach inside her jacket pocket and retrieve the vial given to her that morning by one of Malek's *agro'kines*. She unwrapped the cloth and emptied the elixir into its folds, careful not to breathe in the scent. Elias flapped his wings, his tan feathers glimmering as they caught the sun, and came to a stop at the base of the sky bridge. Heart in her throat, Cassi arched her wings back, an owl on the hunt.

"Cas—"

She slammed into him from behind, wrapping her arms and legs around him like talons, holding his limbs firmly to his torso. Elias stumbled forward in surprise. Before he could react, she pressed the cloth to his nose and mouth. Muffled protests spewed from his lips. Ever the warrior, he thrashed, trying to toss her off. Cassi clung to him, keeping her palm against his face as he jerked his head from side to side.

"I'm sorry," she murmured as his fight began to give. "I'm so sorry."

He'd been her protector all those weeks her body had been left to rot in Malek's dungeon. He'd tried to save her, and she'd tried to save him—which was exactly what she was doing now, she reminded herself. She was saving him from himself.

Unsteady on his feet, Elias stumbled left, and then right, teetering at the precipice of the cliffs. Cassi unlatched her legs from his waist and set them down as his body went slack. Keeping the cloth to his mouth, she slowly eased him to the ground until he lay still on the snow. Then she collapsed by his side and buried her face between her knees.

I'm sorry, she thought again. *Elias, I'm sorry.*

She thought she'd left her days of deception behind her. But this time, at least, it was a plan sanctioned by her queen.

"Cassi."

A breeze stirred her hair and two boots crunched on the ice, their owner casting a shadow across her lap. She didn't need to look up to know who it was. Luka's hand appeared in her field of vision, offering aid.

"I wasn't sure you'd come," she murmured as he pulled her to her feet. "I wasn't sure you'd remember."

People without magic didn't always remember her dream visits. It was one of the reasons she was desperately trying to forget her night with Xander a few days before, along with the hope she'd felt at the possibility of his forgiveness. Drunken minds were even more apt to forget. But Luka had been stone-cold sober when she'd paid him a visit yesterday evening, and thanks to Lyana, he now knew exactly who she was—no longer his first love, but a traitor. His illusions had been shattered weeks before, and Cassi had been avoiding him ever since.

"Well, I'm here," he muttered.

"Did you bring the supplies?"

"Let's get this over with."

His dark eyes were inscrutable as he slid the pack from his shoulders and wordlessly handed her a folded bundle of cloth. They unraveled it together, taking steps back, until the sling was stretched to its full length. Then they set it down and carefully rolled Elias into the center, careful not to crunch his wings. Once that was done, Luka handed her a warmer jacket—something she hadn't asked for but wasn't surprised he'd remembered to bring. The furs were smooth against her skin as she tied the openings shut, instantly feeling the chill in her bones lessen. Even though dark was quickly descending, she pulled the hood over her head, and he did the same with his. There was no way to hide her wings, but beneath the stars and at a quick glance, her coloring could be mistaken for a dove's.

"Did you find a safe place to hide him?" she asked cautiously. Luka had barely glanced at her, his focus on the immobile body of his best friend. A sad slant flattened his normally plush lips.

"Yes, an empty house near the edge of the city. Just follow me."

He took the front of the sling and buckled the straps around his shoulders. She did the same at the back. As one, they rose into the sky with Elias suspended between them. The sun had disappeared by the time they reached Sphaira, just as she'd planned, providing cover as they slinked into the city. Most of the population would be inside and out of the cold, and they'd never been a particularly vigilant house anyway, a fact Cassi had taken advantage of many times before. No one shouted an alarm as they stopped before a vacant crystal home and crept inside.

After they settled Elias on a bed, Cassi quickly closed the curtains. Luka emptied his bag, removing food, water, and finally a long length of chain. They both winced as the metal clinked shut around Elias's ankle, securing him to the heavy wooden frame.

Luka finally broke the silence. "What did you tell him?"

"Weeks ago, back before the raven isle fell, Lyana tried to explain the truth to him, about magic and the prophecy and the world beneath the mist, but he didn't believe her. He thought she was an agent of Vesevios. He wouldn't listen."

Luka nodded, unsurprised.

"So, this time around, we thought it best if we left the explanations to you. He thinks we escaped. I made sure the fight was convincing, but after what happened on the sky bridge, he'll be confused. You need to tell him what's going on. You need to make sure he believes you. Promise me, Luka, you won't let him go until you're sure he won't tell anyone what he saw beneath the mist. It could ruin everything."

"I promise," the prince murmured, his voice heavy. Not looking at her, he reached out and squeezed Elias's shoulder. His back shuddered as he drew a shaky breath. "Thank you, Cassi, for bringing him home."

"I couldn't leave him," she whispered as she took a spot on the opposite side of the bed. Maybe it would have been better for the world if he'd remained locked in Malek's dungeons, but after everything they'd been through, she couldn't abandon him. Cassi brushed her fingers across Elias's brow, smoothing out the wrinkles in his dark skin. "I wish I could stay."

"But duty calls?"

"Something like that."

"I'll stay, don't worry. I won't let him wake up alone."

"I know."

The thing she'd always loved most about Luka was his caring heart, maybe because it was the one thing Malek had never displayed in all their many years spent dreaming together. The dove prince, however, wore it proudly on his sleeve like a badge, a fact her own guarded heart admired.

"Are you headed to the raven quarters on the outer isle?"

"Yes."

"Good." He sighed and leaned back, letting go of his friend as he turned toward her, his expression all business. "We received word from the House of Song and the House of Prey. Both are expected to begin evacuations soon and asked for their guest quarters to be stocked with food. I imagine the ravens stationed on the House of Song will begin moving soon, too, so whatever army my sister is building out there, they need to move."

"So soon?" Cassi bit back a curse. "Have they experienced earthquakes?"

"Not yet, but word arrived from the House of Flight. The situation there is escalating quickly, so we asked the remaining royal families to begin evacuations and gather in Sphaira for us to discuss a course of action together. The Houses of Song and Prey agreed. The owls remain notably stubborn, as I'm sure is no surprise to you. They refuse to abandon the library."

No, she wasn't surprised, at his words or the slight jab. It was the least of her problems. "And where else should Lyana's mages go?"

"Back where they came from," he muttered.

Cassi frowned, staring at him hard.

"I know, I know. Don't even say it," he responded to her silent accusation. "Their magic is no different from Lyana's magic. I only meant they floated up from the Sea of Mist, so why don't they float right back down?"

They could, Cassi supposed, but Lyana had asked her to keep recruiting mages from the remaining houses. Visiting their dreams and convincing them to abandon their lives to join the ranks would be difficult enough, but asking them to travel beneath the mist? Impossible. No, Lyana's mages needed to stay close, no matter how much grief her mother's crew would give her.

"What about Sphaira?" she asked.

"What about it?"

"Could you find a few more empty houses, like this one?"

He sighed heavily, but a lifetime of dealing with her and Lyana made him perfectly aware it was futile to say no. "I could try."

"Thank you, Luka." She reached across the bed. He flinched at her touch, and she dropped his hand, retreating immediately. "It's late. I should go."

The mattress creaked as she shifted her weight, turning toward the door. Just as she eased to her feet, his voice stopped her.

"Was any of it real?"

A knot formed in her throat. She glanced over her shoulder, but he stared at the wall, refusing to meet her gaze, the tendons in his neck bulging.

"No one ever ordered me to be with you," she explained softly, forcing her voice to remain steady. "Everything I said, everything I did, I did because I wanted to. So yes, Luka. It might not have been fully honest, but it was real."

By the time she walked outside, the tear she'd been fighting finally fell, freezing upon her cheek in the cold night air. Cassi scrubbed it hastily away. She had no right to cry, and he had every right to question her. But she was tired, so tired, of facing the consequences of her actions. Had she done wrong? Yes. But it had come from a good place, as brutal and misguided as that was. She thought she'd been saving the world. Maybe she had been saving the world. Didn't that count for something?

There was only one person who'd never regarded her as a stranger, who knew all her secrets and never asked why, who never needed explanations and never demanded things she didn't want to give, and for the first time in fifteen years, that person was within reach.

Cassi kicked off the snow and raced into the sky. Time passed in a blur, the moonlit landscape shifting beneath her as she kept her focus on the horizon. Everyone was asleep by the time she reached the compound, but that didn't stop her. Cassi slipped inside one of the houses and sped down the shadowed halls until she reached the final door. Wood groaned loudly in the silence, and the woman on the bed jolted awake. Captain Rokaro sprang to a seated position, the colorful fabrics in her hair shifting around her shoulders as she turned toward the sound and froze.

Cassi swallowed nervously.

Her mother stood.

In all their years dreaming together, they'd never been particularly sentimental, both of them hardened by the difficult turns of their lives. But as the captain took a cautious step forward, her daughter did the same, and then they were running, until they crashed into each other's arms.

Xander could wait.

The diary could wait.

Lyana's army could wait.

But Cassi had waited long enough. As she buried her face into her mother's neck and breathed in the salty scent of her hair, the world and all its problems faded. At long last, she was home, and no one could take that away.

THE DIARY

Twenty-Eighth Day of the Fifth Moon

It is the morning of my wedding. My heart is at war, one side elation, one side fear. I feel torn down the middle. Last night, everything changed—and it will never be the same again.

Zavier and I were studying his magic as we have every evening for nearly four weeks, but the mood was different between us, more somber than usual. My thoughts drifted to my wedding, and I wondered if his did as well. Tomorrow night would be the first night we didn't meet in almost a full moon cycle. Would he miss me? I knew I would be thinking of him.

"Can I take you somewhere, Princess?" he asked into the silence.

I glanced up from the page I had been reading, curious. "Where?"

"Somewhere I haven't been since I was a boy. Somewhere safe."

"Of course."

His eyes flashed, sending a thrill through me. I put my book down and offered him my hand. We rose together, magic already sparking along his fingertips, tickling my skin. His brow furrowed as he concentrated on forming the rift, one he clearly had never formed before. The process was slower than for the rift to his mother's home, one he could form as easily as breathing, but his progress was showing. The magic yielded to his command, and before long, a seam formed in the aether. On the other side, there was nothing but inky darkness. I glanced at Zavier, but a small smile graced his lips, dissipating my fear. I trusted him, and he trusted this place, so I would too.

Still holding my hand, he led me through the door. We stepped into the thick shadow, my heart pounding, but when the magic of the rift disappeared and my eyes adjusted, I noticed the subtle shimmer of moonlight on stone. As I turned, the sight of endless trees greeted me. We were in a cave nestled in a mountainside.

"What is this place?" I asked.

Zavier turned to me with a full grin. "This isn't the place."

I could read the question in his eyes, so I nodded, not sure to what I was agreeing, but positive I didn't want to stop now. Gently, he folded me into his arms, and with the sweep of his wings, we were flying. I've never experienced anything as marvelous as drifting over the treetops, a canopy of stars above, the soft misty forests below, my head against his chest, his heart beating in my ear. Moonlight shimmering on a lake caught my eye, leaving no doubt as to our destination. Zavier started to descend, and the closer we flew, the more I noticed the subtle golden glow above the water, flickering like a thousand candles. We stopped by the shore and he set me down in the sand, close enough for me to feel the heat of his skin, but my gaze never left the wonder taking place across the skies.

"What are they?"

"They have many names—firebugs, moon beetles, lightning flies—but as a boy I called them sparklers."

"And how did you find them?"

"My father showed me," Zavier whispered, a heaviness in his voice I understood because I feel it in my own chest whenever I think of my

mother. We hadn't spoken much of his father, and the importance of this moment wasn't lost on me. "This was his favorite place in the world. He often spoke of escaping the city and living here, though my mother and I knew those were just dreams. But for a week every year around this time, while the firebugs were in mating above the waters, we'd come to experience a little bit of the wonder. I always used to think it looked a little like my magic, though my mother and father never understood. No one did. No one except you."

I turned to him then, watching the reflection in his gaze, the world retreating the longer I stared. "I have a confession to make."

The words left my lips before I could stop them. His head tilted, but he said nothing. I swallowed. It was too late to turn back.

"Before I ever met you, I saw your face in a vision. You were close," I murmured and stepped toward him, lifting my palm to his face. "And you held your hand against my cheek, like this. The way you looked at me in that moment, I knew you would become someone important in my life, and you have, Zavier, more than I think you understand."

"Princess," he said, voice strained.

"Please, Zavier, call me Mira."

"Mira," he whispered, and I shivered. He lifted his hand to mine and entwined our fingers as a look of pain passed over his face. "You are a princess. Tomorrow, you will be a queen."

"I'm a woman above all else."

His head melted into my palm as his eyes closed, but he said nothing. His wings widened, folding around us as though to hide us from the world. When he found my gaze again, his own was hooded with desire, such a deep green flecked with gold, as though the wild spirit of the forest were alive within them.

"I have so few choices left, Zavier," I continued, more brazen than I've ever felt in my life, and yet more at peace too. "Tomorrow, my choices narrow further still. But tonight is mine to do with what I will. There is a part of me I've never shared with anyone, and I can either let

it be taken by force, or I can give it freely to someone who I know will treat me well, someone who I've come to care more for than I ever thought possible. I choose the latter. I choose you. But I refuse to be another mage ruling by force, so you must choose me too."

He dropped his face so our foreheads touched, but stopped there. "We are from two different worlds."

"Yet here we are, together."

He sighed, his face inching closer so our noses grazed and our breath mingled in the space between our lips. I could feel the war raging inside his spirit, whether to give in to whatever this was between us or to run and save us both the heartbreak. It would be easier, yes, to pretend this was nothing, to walk away and be queen, and lead a single life with no double meaning; to be nothing more than a guard with a sword at his hip and no magic in his hands—but it would be infinitely more lonesome too.

He dropped the hand holding mine against his cheek, and my soul dropped with it, falling to the very tips of my toes. I thought he'd made a choice. I thought he meant goodbye. I was about to step away when he took me by the arms and pulled me close. I had just enough time to find his eyes for an instant before our lips touched and I melted into his embrace. We kissed as though it might be our only chance. I threw my arms around his neck, and he wrapped his around my back, his muscles holding me aloft as my legs went weak at the knees. His touch was like fire, leaving burning trails across my skin, his lips like tinder, feeding the flames. He found my throat, my collarbone, my naked shoulder, every inch of exposed skin, and when that ran out, he found the buttons at the back of my dress. I pulled the tie from his hair so it fell around his shoulders the way I'd imagined and dug my fingers through his waves, smiling as he groaned. His hands found their way to my thighs before lifting me. I wrapped my legs around him, and we sank together to the sand.

I fear I could fill all the remaining pages of this book with memories of this night—the sight of his bare skin in the moonlight, the feel of his feathers against my fingers, the sound of his sighs—but there are some things even I wish to keep private. So instead, I'll leave you with one image, of two bodies entangled on the shore, the starlight playing over their skin as they escaped the world together.

Avians do make love the way mages do.

But Zavier does it better than both.

Twenty-Ninth Day of the Fifth Moon

I am a queen. I am a wife. Most of all, I am tired.

The wedding ceremony felt long, but the evening that followed seemed endless. I don't wish to remember or record what happened inside my new husband's rooms—all I will say is I have never been as happy for the healing powers of aethi'kine magic as I was this morning when I was greeted at his door by Zavier and Mikhail. The bruises along my skin were gone. The wounds along my wrists and neck had vanished. I fear the scars lived inside my eyes, for there was no missing the way Zavier tensed the moment his gaze landed upon me, but I kept my face to the floor and let them escort me to the queen's quarters.

I'm here now, hiding in my mother's rooms.

Though I guess they're my rooms now.

Third Day of the Sixth Moon

Four more days have passed, and four more nights in my husband's rooms. I have learned a new trick all my years of possessing chrono'kine magic have never shown me—how to exist outside of time. When I step over that threshold, I seem to leave myself, my body an empty shell and my mind somewhere else, not coming back to the present until the next morning, when those hazel eyes find mine with equal parts fury and sorrow.

Zavier and I have not been able to meet.

It's too dangerous for him to spend significant amounts of time in my room during the day. A messenger might come. A maid. One of my husband's loyal advisors. The possibilities are endless and far too risky. Instead, we deal in stolen moments while we can—a desperate kiss when he brings in my breakfast, the barest brush of fingers as we pass in the hall, a longing gaze that always passes far too soon.

I spend my time alone reading, searching for things I can tell him about his magic and also researching my own. There are lessons my tutors used to teach that linger in the back of my thoughts, heavy and open ended. I remember them telling me I was not living up to my full potential, that I could be so much more powerful if I embraced my magic, if I guided it rather than allowing it to guide me. At the time, I thought I listened. I thought I tried. But now, I wonder. Did I want my father to underestimate me? To ignore me? To believe I was less than I was? Did I want the world to think the same? People like my husband and his mages?

Power always comes with a price.

As a girl, I wasn't willing to pay it. I preferred that the world thought me meek, that people left me alone, that I preserved what little freedom I could.

I'm a woman now.

And I can't help but think of the vision of my city burning, of that shadowy beast soaring across the skies, of that roar that shook the very foundations of the palace. The future is prodding me with snippets and scenes that don't make sense.

Maybe it's time I poke back.

Ninth Day of the Sixth Moon

I never understood what a gift it was to simply sleep in the arms of someone I know will never hurt me, to have our bodies flush, to feel the soothing beat of his heart against my back, to have his chin nestled upon my neck and his breath along my skin, to be able to close my eyes without fear of pain, to be at peace.

Zavier is always gone by the time I wake, but I long to know what it might be like to start the day that way too. Perhaps someday I will, though I doubt it is a future my magic will ever show me.

Eleventh Day of the Sixth Moon

I've been focusing on the image of the burning city, but my magic has given me nothing more, no matter how hard I concentrate. I did see something else, though—Bastiant with his spatio'kine, standing beside a large oval rock, a wicked smile on his lips as he pressed his palm to the gilded surface, his golden magic simmering at his fingers.

I don't know what it means.

When I told Zavier, he asked if it was time he learned how to make a spying window, a trick that uses his magic to make a one-way rift in space. I told him I would help him under one condition—he is never to use one when I am in my husband's rooms. It was the only time we've mentioned those nights, and his jaw clenched so tightly I feared his teeth might fuse together, but he agreed. I took his hand after that and pushed our books aside. They could wait another day. My yearning, however, could not.

Sixteenth Day of the Sixth Moon

We've started working on the spying window. I sit in my bedroom while Zavier remains out in the sitting room, attempting to draw the rift. So far, he hasn't been successful. I've seen through the opening. I've seen the white aura of his magic. I've felt his power in the air. But skills take time, and he'll master this one. I know he will.

In the meantime, I work on my magic too. If I close my eyes and focus my mind, I can feel it in a way I never have before, or perhaps never wanted to. The power is always there, deep inside my soul—a fathomless pool, calm on the surface and churning underneath. I am trying to learn how to draw it out, how to pull the chaos to the surface and force it to yield. My tutors used to tell me to control it, to bend it to my will, but time is not like water or earth or air or fire; even the aether is something that can be touched and felt. Time is beyond us all.

I'm starting to wonder what might happen if I free-dive into those depths. Maybe my power has never been about control, something I've never had in my life. Maybe it's about succumbing to the unknown. But I fear what I might lose in the process.

Twenty-Second Day of the Sixth Moon

Zavier tells me Mikhail has been acting differently of late, more distant, with secrets in his eyes. I wonder if it's my fault. He must know what goes on behind my door, why Zavier spends every night he can inside my rooms. He might be tired of covering for us, or afraid of what will happen to us all if we're caught, but Zavier thinks it is something more.

I know he doesn't want to spy on his friend, and yet I see the thought cross his eyes as we practice. Yesterday, he made a window I could not sense. At least, not at first. After a few moments, I felt the prickle of his power in the air, but it was something. If we're to spy on my husband, we'll need much more than that. His spatio'kine will be even more attuned than me to the sensation of magic carving through the air. But to spy on Mikhail, well, Zavier has the skills for that already. The dove would never sense his magic in the air—he can't. The one thing that divides them is the one thing that brings Zavier and me closer together.

He's being pulled in two different directions.

What will happen when the tension snaps?

First Day of the Seventh Moon

Life continues much the same, oscillating between pleasure and pain, between the man I've come to love and the one I've learned to loathe, between rebellion and duty.

I saw Bastiant again, this time with his spatio'kine beside an open rift that looked much like the one where my father was sent—nothing on the other side but barren lands, and orange skies, and onyx rock. I'm not sure what waits on the other side of that door, but I sense it has something to do with the beast I saw in the skies above my burning city. I think it must be from another world, and I believe I've seen a glimpse of that ghastly place.

I saw a woman, too, though I'm not sure who she is or what she means. I stepped out of my rooms and met Mikhail, only to see a stranger looking back. She had the same dark skin, but her eyes were bright green and the wings behind her back pure ivory. A smile graced her lips, as though she were on the precipice of a laugh, and then she was gone. Her spirit, however, lingered, staying with me long after the sight of her had passed. There was a kinship between us, as though maybe she, of all people, might understand me. Rebellion stirred inside her heart, a fierce independence and yearning, mixed with bright compassion. Is she his sister? His lover? His future child? His future mate? Do they have any connection at all?

I'm not sure.

But she's important.

I know she is.

Fifth Day of the Seventh Moon

Zavier did what he swore he wouldn't—he spied on his best friend. And then he came to my rooms to pace across my floor, a furrow in his brow and worry in his eyes.

Mikhail is planning a revolution.

He and a group of other avians are keeping a secret, one that could change everything—a child. Deep in the heart of the village where the birds of paradise live, they hide a little boy in an underground hovel, his wings little more than violet-and-ebony fluff. Zavier has been watching him, trying to understand why, and then he saw. The boy was playing with his keeper when the older man fell and hurt his wrist. The boy rushed over, a golden glow about his fingers, and sealed the wound.

He has healing magic.

He's an aethi'kine.

Zavier says Mikhail no longer trusts him, because of me probably, but he thinks it's more. He thinks it's because of his magic, because it's growing stronger day by day. I don't understand. All their hope lies in a little boy who might possess the most powerful magic of all, and yet he pushes away his best friend, a man who might be able to help more than any other. It's complicated, Zavier tells me, but the avians have learned not to trust mages. And though he's an avian, he's a mage first, with a power most of his people will never understand.

I asked if he'll confront him.

Zavier says that would only make Mikhail trust him less.

Eleventh Day of the Seventh Moon

We've spied on Bastiant, and as far as we can tell, neither he nor his mages were aware. They were in his council room, the most powerful mages in our entire kingdom all together discussing the business of the realm, and there Zavier and I were, in my room, watching it all.

We'll have to be careful, but with this power, we might be able to see what my husband has been up to, what that rock from my vision was, where that beast came from.

Maybe the city won't burn.

Maybe we can stop it.

Twentieth Day of the Seventh Moon

I must write this down quickly, so I don't forget a single detail. My magic whispers against my skin that this is important, that I must remember, that so much hangs on a single moment. Zavier and I spied on Bastiant again, and finally we caught him in the middle of something I know he would not want us to see.

We were in my rooms, late into the night. It took a moment for us to recognize the scene through the rift when Zavier first opened it, dark as it was, but after a moment the flickering torchlight cleared to reveal Bastiant and his spatio'kine. They were alone, deep in the dungeons, clearly doing something secretive or he would have had a photo'kine come to light the way. As it was, Bastiant held a torch, whose halo just barely showed what lay beyond. My eyes widened upon seeing the rock from my vision behind him, not gold this time, but a polished, obsidian oval. The more I stared, the more I realized there was not just one but six rocks, flashing all different colors as they caught the light—red, blue, green, yellow, ivory, and onyx. The colors of magic. I sensed the power even through the rift, pulsing all around him, invisible currents with a unique charge any mage can sense. All four elements were there, shades of earth and air and fire and water, and the black and white rocks had to be from light and dark magic. I didn't understand—magic can't be trapped or contained, at least not in crystal or stone but only in living things. How had he managed to fuse the power into these rocks? And why?

"After years of work, our quest is nearly complete," Bastiant said, his words as commanding as ever.

"Yes, my king."

Years. The word simmered in the back of my mind as my gaze turned to the rocks once more. He'd been working on this for years. Suddenly it became clear why he hadn't been interested in inheriting that fallen kingdom so long ago—whatever he was planning hadn't been ready. But by the time my father offered my hand in marriage, all the pieces were nearly in place—all except this last one, whatever it was.

"I've located our final specimen. He's in the city somewhere. I can sense his magic and his spirit—young and naive with no awareness of the true power he possesses. He's perfect and this opportunity might not come again."

"I understand, my king, but—"

"As soon as I find him, we will open one more rift."

"My king—"

"One more, and then all of this will be done."

"My king—"

"You object?"

"Of course not, my king. I have only a word of caution. Last time I opened the rift, the threads of space were unstable, as though something on the other side was fighting back. We know little of the beasts that live in that world, and I worry they have found a way to sense my magic and to see it coming. With every doorway I open, I fear we grow one step closer to losing the ability to close it."

"One more, Saven."

The spatio'kine nodded, though I didn't miss the way his throat tightened or the worried wrinkles crossing his brow.

"One more rift," Bastiant continued, a wicked glee alight in his eyes. "One more egg. And we will leave that world behind for good. Now, help me—"

Both men paused, their eyes lifting toward us. Zavier closed the spying window, his magic winking out immediately, leaving us alone in what felt like a thundering silence.

"Go," I whispered. "Go before he sees."

"What about—"

"I'll be fine. If they follow the threads of your magic, all they'll see here is me. Maybe they'll think it was a vision. But you must go, now, before they suspect you."

Zavier squeezed my fingers, but I pushed him away. There was no time for goodbyes, no time for anything at all. If the spatio'kine sensed his magic, if he followed it, they needed to find me here alone. It would take him a minute or two, but that was all the advantage we had.

Zavier swept away from the room.

My heart pounded as though it yearned to leap from my ribs and run after him. I forced a blank expression onto my face and pulled a book into my lap, leaning against my pillows as though reading. In truth, the words swam across the page, my mind a jumble, nothing but the conversation we'd overheard playing on and on in my head.

I lay there for an hour, mindlessly flipping pages, waiting for my husband to storm into my rooms, for the sounds of battle to filter through my door, for a scream, for a whisper, for anything. All I wanted to do was tear across my rooms and into the hall to make sure Zavier was there, still standing, still breathing, unharmed. But to do such a thing, especially if I were being watched, would only raise suspicion.

I fell asleep somehow and woke hours later to the sound of a tray being delivered to my sitting room. I ran to the door and threw it open, relief the sweetest pleasure as I looked upon Zavier's unharmed face. He couldn't afford to linger, so he nodded reassuringly, giving me a little smile, before retreating to his station outside the door. I've been on edge all day, but Bastiant treats me with the same disdain as always, acting no differently, and all I can hope is that his spatio'kine was unable to follow the threads they both felt the night before.

Now, as I sit here recording every detail I can recall, my thoughts have finally calmed enough to absorb what we overheard. Bastiant said he needed one more egg. Those things were not rocks. They were eggs. Eggs from another world. Eggs full of beasts…and magic.

Oh, aether, no!

My hands tremble at the very thought. I can hardly write this down, but he said he found the final specimen, here in this city. The only color I didn't see down in the shadows of that room was the gleaming gold of aethi'kine magic, the rock from my vision. But for those eggs to have our magic, to have human magic, it could only mean—

The boy.

The avian boy.

I'm nauseous at the very thought.

Bastiant wants to soul-join him to a beast.

40

LYANA

The edges of the rift stretched out like phantom fingers grabbing for more. Everything beyond was a barren void—not the sort formed by *umbra'kine* magic, marked by an absence of light, but something else, marked by the absence of life itself. There was no spirit for Lyana's magic to latch on to, no glimmer of rainbow colors swirling in the abyss, and every time she reached with her golden power, it simply disappeared into the chasm, as though swallowed by the nothingness. Worse still, with each passing day since the first egg had hatched, the poison spread, as if the rift were now the same as the creatures it produced, set to slowly consume the world.

Malek's magic merged with hers, poking and prodding at the boundary. He taught her and guided her, helping her center her power and stretch out her senses. They'd been at this for Lyana didn't know how long—days, maybe weeks—yet they were no closer to solving the riddle. Part of her feared they never would.

A bloodcurdling roar pulled her back to Da'Kin.

Lyana jumped to her feet. Shedding her meditative state, she ran for the balcony, Malek not far behind. Fire burned in the distance. A bubbling cloud of orange burst through the fog, swallowing an entire city square in the blaze. Two onyx wings, each as wide as a ship was long, carved through the inferno. An arrow shimmering with flecks of *ferro'kine* power cut across the sky to strike the beast. Spouts of water rose from the sea to douse the flames. Red glitter pulled at the heat. Fear and panic swelled in spirits across the city, rising like a tide, ready to crash. But there was something else too, subtler and easier to miss—hope. Lyana followed that feeling, looking to the right as one by one, more and more people's terror gave way to promise, the sensation spreading down an invisible line, as though following a path, and then she saw him.

Rafe soared over rooftops, his wings simmering with heat as he cut through the mist, a beacon even brighter than the dragon flames. As he raced by, spirits rose, one after another. She wished he could feel it, because he wouldn't believe her if she told him how much the people of Da'Kin glowed under his presence. But they did. The golden lights of their souls shone brighter and brighter as he flew overhead, hurtling fearlessly toward the dragon.

The beast froze as he neared.

Rafe didn't pause.

Arms held out, he slammed into the smoldering scales. Beneath his touch, the dragon retreated. A few pumps of its wings and it vanished, leaving the city behind. A cheer filled the air, not that Rafe noticed. He turned back toward the castle. Even from this distance, Lyana felt the grim determination flooding his spirit, and the exhaustion too.

How many beasts had he turned away since they'd arrived in Da'Kin? Five? Ten? And those were only the ones who made it close enough to cause damage. How many of them did he turn away without her knowing? How many minds was he living in all at once? How long could he keep this going?

"Lyana," Malek said, drawing her back to his study. "The danger has passed, and that's not our fight."

He was right, as usual. She sighed. "They just keep coming."

"As the rift widens, more dragons slip into our world."

"I know." She pulled herself from the balcony and stepped back into the room to face him. The deep purple bags under his eyes had faded slightly since her arrival, and his blond hair no longer hung in straggles. He was looking more and more like the composed king she remembered, cold and uncompromising. "But we both know it's more than that."

Malek's lips flattened into a thin line as awareness darkened his eyes. In all her former time spent in Da'Kin, the dragons had never come for the city like this, not with the unyielding force they displayed now, and they both knew why. Just as Rafe sent the beasts away, those two hybrid creatures sent them barreling back, again and again and again, commanding them from afar. And it made Lyana question just how much say the dragons had ever had over their actions, or if maybe they'd been led to this world by guiding hands all along.

"The only answer is to seal the rift," Malek finally said. "Before any more eggs hatch."

"And how do we do that?" she asked, hating the desperation in her tone, yet unable to hide it. Her doubts were showing—about herself, about him, about this prophecy. "We can't hold it. We can't touch it. No matter what we do, our magic won't stick. We've tried everything. We've—"

"What if we healed it?" he asked slowly.

She froze. "What?"

"When the House of Paradise fell, you said the only way you managed to slow the fall was by envisioning the land as something in need of healing." He rubbed his chin, his eyes glazing over as he retreated into his thoughts. "What if the rift is the same way?"

Lyana stepped closer, intrigued. "How do you mean?"

"We've been trying to fix it from the inside out, by grabbing the rift itself and whatever hides within the void, but what if we need to approach it from the outside in, as though it's a wound and our world is a body in need of healing? Instead of focusing on the rift, let's focus on something we already know how to work with—the spirit of our world. Maybe we can use that to push against the tear and stop it from spreading. The difference is subtle, but—"

"It might be everything." A grin spread on her lips, remembering him using those same words months before when teaching her about her magic. Back then, he had been telling her not to focus on the elements, but on the spirit around and within the elements. Maybe now the lesson was the same. Instead of forcing their magic into the rift, they needed to force the rift into their magic. They needed to fight defensively, a skill at which Lyana had never particularly excelled. "Let's try it."

They resumed their positions, sitting on the floor with legs crossed and facing each other. Lyana closed her eyes and sank into her power. The city and all its souls fell away, and the world dissolved into pure spirit. As if riding a current, she followed the path of Malek's magic until they arrived at the rift. Instead of reaching for the nothingness, she pushed her power into the lingering bit of spirit hovering at its edge, the last remaining vestiges of her world ready to be swallowed by the void. Together, they focused their healing might, sending wave after wave of magic into the earth. This deep in the power, Lyana lost all sense of time or place. She had no idea how long they pushed, or how much magic they used, but at long last, her mind weary and her body pushed to its limit, she felt the darkness of the rift recede—not a lot, hardly at all, but it was something.

Malek snapped them back to the present. "We did it."

She squeezed his fingers, her spirit soaring to match his. "We did."

"It wasn't fast enough."

"No."

"Or strong enough."

"No."

"Or permanent."

"No," Lyana agreed. Still, a smile tugged at her lips as she gave in to the optimism bubbling in her heart. "But it's a start."

He nodded, the grin on his lips making him look younger and handsomer than she could ever remember, as though all the storm clouds had briefly passed, and the weight on his shoulders had briefly lifted, revealing the man he might have been without them. "It's a start."

Her stomach rumbled, breaking the moment. His careful composure re-formed as he rolled to his feet and offered her a hand. Lyana took it, allowing him to help her. Outside, the sky was dark. Though it had felt like only minutes, hours had passed since the dragon attack.

"Go," he said, jutting his chin toward the door. "Eat something, sleep. We'll start again in the morning."

She gladly took the opening and retreated before the usual awkward air between them had the chance to descend. While absorbed in their magic or discussing the rift, they were fine. But if they sat too long in the real world, Lyana began to remember all the things he'd done, and he began to sense her disgust. It was easier to run. More cowardly, perhaps, than actually having the conversation, but what would that accomplish? She would yell. He wouldn't apologize. They'd be right back where they started, with him wanting more than she was willing to give. For the sake of the world, they had to work together. So until it was saved, the rest could wait.

When she opened the door to her bedroom, a soft orange glow permeated the darkness. All thoughts of Malek fled. Rafe lay curled on her bed, his body trembling as he hugged his knees to his chest. Unintelligible groans spilled from his lips as he winced in his sleep, if one could call what he did sleeping. Lyana thought it seemed more like succumbing to inevitable exhaustion, his body forcing rest upon him no matter how hard he fought to remain awake. She only saw him at night, and rarely at that. He was always zipping across the skies, chasing enemies both seen and unseen, or perched on the rooftop, his mind a million miles away. But she was grateful that when he finally did collapse, he always managed to first find his way here.

She sidled up to him now, curling her feet beneath her as she leaned against the headboard and spread her wings around them in a cocoon, careful not to touch the subtle flames burning along his. As though sensing her presence, he rolled closer. Lyana guided his head onto her lap and ran her fingers through his hair as her magic sank beneath his skin.

"Shh," she soothed, hating the grimace twisting his features. "I'm here."

"Ana?" he murmured, still half-asleep.

"Sleep, Rafe. I'll watch the skies. I'll wake you if anything comes near."

"They sent me visions." He shivered beneath her touch. Deep grooves carved into his brow as his eyes squeezed more firmly shut, as though trying to stave off the memory. "They slaughtered a whole ship of mages tonight, one by one by one. First the *ferro'kine*, then the *hydro'kine*, then the—" He broke off with a jerk as his entire body spasmed on the bed. "There was so much blood. So much pain. And I couldn't stop it."

"No one could have stopped it, Rafe."

"I could have, if I was there." He blinked and shifted his head, his blue eyes finding hers across the darkness, bloodshot and wide with horror. "They're baiting me. I know it. They want me to leave to give them the opening. They're killing them because of me—"

"No, Rafe," she murmured and cupped his cheek. "They're killing mages because it's what they do, and not even you could stop them. Go back to sleep, please. You need rest. And the visions won't come while I'm here."

He threaded his fingers through hers, holding on as if for dear life as his eyes slipped closed again. She ran her fingers down along his arm and across his back, then up into his hair, trying to calm him. Despite her own exhaustion, she dipped into her magic and wrapped it around him like a shield, so no foreign souls could push through. Eventually, his body fell still. Deep, even breaths lifted then lowered his chest. Lyana dropped her head back and stared into the fathomless fog visible through gently swaying curtains.

"I'll keep you safe, Aleksander," she whispered when she knew he wouldn't hear, his true name rolling off her tongue with a weight that made her heart burn. "I'll keep the monsters away. I promise."

41

CASSI

It was eerie to see empty air above the city of Abaelon. Cassi had visited the home of the hummingbirds many times before in her dreams. Their lush gardens and vivid blue skies had always been punctuated by the rapid movement of wings. Now, stillness permeated the streets. Palm trees swayed in the breeze, their fronds ruffling, and water ran through the aqueducts that were still standing, though many had collapsed into rubble, but there were no people. The City of Life was deserted, and it brought a chill to the back of her neck she couldn't quite shake.

Cassi landed in the palace courtyard, the scuffing of her boots loud. At long last, another soul appeared, zipping between the gleaming white columns. The hummingbird stopped before her and inclined his head in greeting.

"Welcome to the House of Flight," he said. "What brings you?"

"I'm here to see King Lysander Taetanus of the House of Whispers. Please tell him Cassi Sky wishes to speak to him as soon as possible."

"Very well."

As quickly as he came, he vanished, leaving Cassi alone once more. She shifted on her feet, surveying the damage to the buildings around her. Cracks marred the pristine white marble of the palace façade, fissuring up the columns and across the decorative trim. The tiles beneath her feet were broken and uneven. An entire building on the southern edge of the courtyard had crumbled. The earthquakes were worsening. It was only a matter of time before the next creature broke free.

"Cassi!"

Her heart leapt into her throat at the sound of his voice, but she remembered herself and dipped her head in a bow. "King Lysander."

He rolled his eyes, a slight grin on his lips. "Come on."

Cassi bounded up the steps and took the arm he offered. As soon as they touched, a thrill shot down her spine. Nervous flutters swarmed her insides. They hadn't seen each other in the flesh since the night the raven isle fell, and though she'd visited his dreams two more times since their drunken encounter, he hadn't mentioned a thing. They'd kept their conversation strictly to business, at least outwardly. Inwardly, though, her thoughts spun with questions. Did he remember? Was he embarrassed? Worse, did he have regrets?

"I'm sorry it took me so long to get here," she said, keeping her voice low as they walked arm in arm down the vast halls of the hummingbird palace. There was no telling who might be listening. "I meant to come sooner, but, well, you know."

"How's the…situation in the House of Peace?"

Situation. She snorted. "I'm not sure my mother will ever forgive me."

"That bad?"

"Let's just say I solved the problem of how to get the *guests* from one place to another, and in the eyes of my mother and her crew, it was little more than slaughter."

He laughed softly under his breath and shook his head. If he only knew. Thankfully, Luka had managed to find a few more empty houses in Sphaira to house Lyana's growing army. For the avians, the solution was simple—they'd fly under cover of night and slip into the crystal buildings unseen. Her mother's crew, however, had been a different story. Without wings, their trek across the barren tundra would have taken weeks, and out in the cold with limited supplies? Even with their magic, they never would have survived: Naturally, they'd been inclined to wipe their hands of this dying world above the clouds and return to the sea, especially now that some semblance of peace had been brokered with Malek—a temporary cease-fire, at the very least. But Lyana wanted them to keep training her mages, including the new recruits Cassi had managed to find among the refugees now living with the doves. The solution had been simple—a sled. There was only one problem. The only available source of wood was the ship her mother had attempted to camouflage beneath the snow.

The looks the crew had given her as the planks were stripped piece by piece could have slayed a dragon. Of course, Cassi had never been under the misguided notion that any of them actually liked her anyway. Brighty had made sure of that. The moment they'd met, the light mage had slapped her across the cheek, commenting, *That's for Rafe.* Then she'd offered a handshake: *And this is for Captain.* The rest of the crew had been much the same, minus the sting. They accepted her presence because of her mother, but their loyalties lay with their friend.

"So they've been safely moved?" Xander asked, drawing her back. "The raven guest quarters are clear?"

"Oh, they're gone all right," she muttered. "Along with most of my sanity." They'd used the sails to propel the sled across the vast icy landscape, making the trip in a handful of days. As soon as they'd reached Sphaira and snuck into the city with the help of shadow magic, she couldn't have taken to the skies fast enough. "Anyway, that's why I'm late."

"Did you happen to check if—"

"The ravens started evacuating the House of Song? The first few groups have already arrived on the outer isle of the House of Peace, led by Helen. We got out just in time. The guest quarters are filling up quickly, but Luka is working on a way to create more shelters to keep everyone safe from the cold."

"Thank you." He released a heavy breath. "Any updates from the other front?"

"More of the same. Rafe is being Rafe, running himself ragged. Lyana spends every waking moment deep in…conversation with the gods. She's getting closer to answers, but the process is slow."

"And how are you?"

Cassi snapped her head to the side, surprised to find concern in his lavender eyes. It was in moments like this, ones he probably didn't even notice, that his presence left her completely undone. Her throat went dry as her heart skipped a beat and she turned her face forward, fighting the blush threatening to crawl up her neck. No one ever asked her about herself. Not her mother. Not Lyana. Certainly not Rafe or Malek. She gave updates and she received new orders. She was a soldier. Yet Xander had a way of making her feel like a woman, seen in a way she'd never been seen before.

I'm better now that I'm here with you, she thought, not courageous enough to say the words out loud. "I'm alive."

"I hope that's not the current standard."

"It's more than some people can say."

He opened his mouth, then closed it with the shake of his head, as though thinking better of it. They reached a door. Cassi followed Xander inside and waited as he sealed the opening behind them, then circled the room. Like any guest room housed in a palace, its walls had ears. Like any smart ruler, Xander had already identified them.

"We're alone," he said after a few minutes.

"You're sure?"

"As much as I can be. Besides, I think the hummingbirds have more problems to deal with than worrying about my social life, or did you not notice the state of the city when you arrived? Damien hasn't even tried to force a drink on me in a week, which should tell you everything you need to know, not that I'd take him up on that offer ever again…" He shivered.

Cassi swallowed, trying to ignore the searing heat spiking in her chest.

It was the closest he'd come to mentioning that night, but he seemed completely unaware as he turned back to her, his expression lacking any hint of the anxiety currently coursing through her body, and said, "So, the diary."

"The diary," she repeated, forcing the words to come smoothly to her lips.

He reached inside his jacket, slid the small leather-bound book free, and offered it to her. Cassi flipped through the pages, breathing in the musty scent, still certain it held the promise of greatness. Xander moved into the spot by her side.

"You kept it with you all this time?" she asked.

"I was worried it might fall into the wrong hands."

An insincere undercurrent ran through his tone, drawing her attention. Cassi turned to the side, but Xander kept his focus on the open book. She couldn't fight the sense that he was hiding from her. "If not for you, it'd be buried beneath the sea right now."

"If not for you, it'd be safely housed within the archives." His mouth twitched with humor and she bumped him with her hip. Their feathers pressed together, hardly any space between them. His body heat saturated the air, making her warm in more ways than one, yet his gaze remained resolutely fixed on the page, all work and no play. "I know you said you're going to bring it to that mage in Da'Kin, the *skryr*, but can you read it at all?"

"No." She sighed and returned her attention to the diary. "At least, not all of it. Maybe someone can, but I wouldn't know where to start. Even in the world below, the ancient language is long dead. Only a few words survive, like this here. *Aethi'kine*." She pressed her finger to the parchment, pointing it out. As Xander leaned over her shoulder, his breath brushed her neck, making her nerves tingle with awareness. "That's our word for the magic Lyana has, and there are some other instances peppered across the pages. Whoever wrote this diary—and I'd guess from the loopy handwriting it was a woman—spent a lot of time close to powerful mages, or at least a lot of time writing about them, and the *skryr* should be able to unlock whatever memories still linger in the text. They could be useless, but I have a hunch her secrets are the exact ones we need."

"Well, you *are* the expert on secrets."

Cassi froze. All the warmth gathering beneath her skin turned to ice, burning her with the sting. It was all she needed to hear. Maybe he remembered their hours spent swimming through his glorious imagination, and maybe he didn't, but either way, forgiveness was off the table. Those seven biting words made his position absolutely clear.

She snapped the diary closed and stepped back.

"Cassi, I—"

"It's all right, Xander," she cut in, angling her face toward the floor, too worried he'd see her heart breaking the moment he looked into her eyes. After everything she'd done, she deserved to be punished. She knew that. But still, there were only so many cuts a girl could take before she bled out, and Cassi had all but reached her limit. "I should go."

"Wait."

"No, really," she continued quickly, ignoring his protest as she spun on her heels and made for the door. "I have what I came for, and if it's as important as I think, there's no more time to waste."

"Would you just—" He grabbed her arm to stop her. "Cassi."

"What?"

"Look at me."

The corners of her eyes burned. Already, she could feel the tears gathering. "No."

"Would you please just look at me? I don't want to say this to the back of your head."

"Say what?" She could almost hear his frown, his frustration tangible. Though her every instinct told her to run, she'd done enough running. Instead, she slowly spun. "What?"

"Cassi..." Her name turned into a sigh upon his lips and he took a step closer, reaching for her hand. Her breath hitched as he entwined their fingers. Against her palm, his pulse drummed, pounding just as quickly as hers. That alone gave her the strength to lift her chin. "Cassi, I—"

The floor jerked beneath them and they stumbled, falling together. He slammed her against the door, their bodies touching from chest to toe, but romance was the furthest thing on either of their minds as the palace walls groaned around them. The vibrations intensified, Cassi's teeth rattling as they coursed through her. The vase on a nearby table crashed against the tiles. Bits of marble rained from above as the ceiling split.

"It's not safe here," Xander said as he pushed off her and pumped his onyx wings. "Follow me."

They raced across the room and out onto the wide veranda covered in plants, then dove for the blue skies visible through the towering columns. Dust clouded the air above the city. Crashes and booms reverberated down the streets. To their left and right, hummingbirds spilled from the palace to escape the falling debris. Prince Damien hovered with a group of guards, his expression helpless, as though awaiting the inevitable. Her dread spiked.

"Xander," she whispered, jerking on the back of his coat. He glanced over his shoulder, his body already shifting toward the prince. "Catch me."

"What?"

"Catch me!"

She dove into her magic. The moment her wings stopped moving, her body plummeted toward the ground. Xander lunged for her, but she didn't have time to see if he caught her. As little more than spirit, she raced for the sacred nest, hoping she was wrong.

42

XANDER

"Cassi!"

Xander lurched as her body dropped from the sky and caught her in his arms. Limbs limp, she was too heavy to carry. With as much control as possible, he descended to the courtyard below and landed gently on the tiles. The ground shifted beneath them, rattling his bones. He hugged her torso to his chest as her legs shook haphazardly with the quakes. Her wings dragged behind her. He knew what she'd done and where she'd gone. A jolt of fear ran down his chest. "The gods, Cassi!"

It was too similar to the scene that had replayed so many times in his nightmares—Cassi lifeless as the House of Whispers sank beneath the sea, the water rising to pull her under as he watched stoically from above.

We saved her.

Lyana and I saved her.

Logically, he knew it was true. But his heart still hung on that brief moment when he had held her fate in his hands and felt torn. He'd never forgive himself for hesitating, just as he would never forgive himself now if anything happened to her before he'd had a chance to tell her the truth. He forgave her, as much as it was in his power to forgive the things she'd done. And more than that, he loved her—a fact he prayed Rafe would someday understand. After all, his brother knew better than most how uncontrollable the yearnings of the soul could be.

Gods alive, why did I say that foolish quip about secrets?

He'd ruined everything.

For weeks he'd been waiting for that exact moment—her body close enough for him to feel its heat, the sunlight streaming in from the veranda, not an ounce of hummingbird nectar on his tongue, everything just as she'd said she wanted, not a dream, but breathtakingly real. It had taken every ounce of his control not to blurt the confession the moment he saw her standing in the courtyard, the most beautiful thing he'd seen in weeks, her black-and-white wings shimmering like a mirage beneath the desert heat. Each step down the palace halls had been excruciatingly slow when all he'd wanted to do was race back to his rooms and tell her how he felt. Then they'd been there, and he'd been intoxicated by her nearness, the sweet floral scent of her hair, the smooth touch of her skin, the stunning sight of her smile. He'd lost his senses. It was the only explanation for how royally he'd messed things up.

Now she was gone. Her spirit was in the sacred nest where a monster might awaken at any moment, and only the gods knew if she'd return.

Please, Cassi. Come back this time. Please, come back.

"What happened?" Prince Damien asked, hovering a few feet above Xander. The air hummed with the rapid movement of his wings. "Is she hurt?"

"No. She— She—" Xander grappled for an excuse. "She fainted."

"Fainted?" Damien snorted and shook his head. "Owls. Take

them out of the library, and, well, you know…" He stared pointedly at Cassi. An urge to defend her tightened Xander's throat, but he held back. They had, after all, evacuated Princess Coralee the week before, when she'd passed out in the middle of an earthquake. Some owls, maybe, weren't made of stronger stuff, but Cassi was one of the toughest people he knew. "What was she doing here, anyway?"

"Bringing a message from Lyana."

"Oh, what news?"

Xander looked away to hide his wince. The gods, his mouth was getting him into trouble today. *What news? What news? Think…*

Cassi gasped in his arms.

"Thank Taetanos," he exclaimed, changing the subject as her eyes flickered open. All he saw in those molten silver depths was sympathy. She shook her head, the move so subtle anyone not perfectly attuned to her spirit might have missed it. His stomach flipped. The isle was falling. "Are you all right?" he said loudly, helping her sit up. "You fainted."

She wrinkled her nose. "I'm fine."

"Do you need help?" Prince Damien called. "I can take her ankles—"

"I'm fine!" Cassi repeated through gritted teeth.

The prince raised his brows toward Xander. "Touchy."

You don't know the half of it.

As Cassi jumped to her feet, the ground beneath them fell still. She and Xander shared a look. They knew exactly what it meant. The prince, however, dropped to the tiles beside them, joining their circle.

"That was a bad one," he remarked while staring at the palace, where three of the columns framing the front steps now lay in shambles.

"Damien," Xander said, his voice urgent. "Sound the alarm."

"What are you talking about? It just stopped."

"No!" He grabbed the hummingbird prince by the shoulder. "Listen to me. This is exactly how it happened in my home. Sound the alarm, now, while there's still—"

The isle plunged.

All three of them took to the sky as the ground gave way, their wings catching them before they fell. An unidentifiable scream pierced the air.

"Go!" Xander ordered the prince, pushing him toward his guards. Moments later, a horn blared, followed by another, then another, the call echoing across the city as more and more hummingbirds spilled out of their homes. He turned to Cassi. "What was it?"

"I didn't see it," she murmured, her voice almost drowned by the alarm. "I left as soon as the god stone started to crack. But it's blue, so it must have water magic."

"Is that bad?"

"Well, our friends are stationed in a city floating in the middle of the ocean, so it can't be good."

"We need to warn them. We need to—"

"You really don't feel it?" Cassi interrupted, her brows furrowed as she stared at him intently.

He shook his head. "Feel what?"

"Lyana's already here."

"Where?"

"Not *here*, here." She cast her gaze toward the cloudless blue overhead, then across the rooftops, at everything and nothing. "Her magic is everywhere, a golden glow more potent than the sun. She knows, Xander. She probably knew before we did."

"But that's—that's—"

"Impossible?" A smile flashed upon her lips. "You might want to remove that word from your vocabulary. Nothing's impossible, especially when magic is involved. I have to go."

His throat went dry. "Where?"

"To Da'Kin."

"Wait." He took her by the hand, stopping her, then dropped it as soon as he realized how familiar it might look to the hummingbirds hovering a small distance away. "If Lyana is using her magic, won't that be where the creatures are headed?"

"It's where I need to be." She offered an imploring look as she patted her jacket.

The diary. Of course, the diary. How could he have forgotten? The uncomfortable pinch of the binding against his chest had become so normal, he almost missed it. Somehow, the absence made Cassi seem even further away.

"Surely, it can wait a day," he tried to argue. "Maybe two."

"It's waited long enough."

"Cassi—" He broke off, unsure what to say. Now that she was here, flying before him, flesh and blood, her presence stirring a spark within like tinder to a flame, he didn't want her to leave. Not again. Part of him yearned to sweep her into his arms and kiss her the way he'd been longing to do in every one of their shared dreams. Part of him understood he was a king with a queen, and that an audience waited nearby. Part of him wished to take her by the hands and use whatever precious moments they had left to confess all the secret desires of his heart. Part of him realized such a gesture would be no different from a drunken confession, prompted by urgency and outside factors, when she wanted them to take their time.

In his torn silence, Cassi retreated.

"Whatever it is, it can wait," she muttered, glancing toward the hummingbirds to hide her fear—not of how the world crumbled before them, he knew, but of what he might say. She was wrong, though. For all her experience uncovering secrets, she failed to see the truth in his eyes. "I'll be back."

"Cassi—"

"Goodbye, Xander."

She fled, sparing a glance over her shoulder as she sped across the skies. The isle lurched beneath him, and his heart seemed to drop with it, tumbling from his chest to disappear into the chaos below. He watched, a sense of dread building under his skin as she shrank to nothing more than a black speck on the horizon.

What if they never got another chance?

What if that *was* their chance—and he blew it?

"It's really falling," Damien muttered, pulling Xander back to reality. The hummingbird prince hovered close by, a broken look in his normally proud eyes as he stared down at his home. The sight sobered Xander, reminding him of the gravity of their current situation. Cassi was right—she'd be back. They had time. He had to believe it.

"We should go meet your mother and father in the House of Peace," he told the prince, sympathy deepening his tone. The isle dropped again, another fifty feet this time. "There's nothing more we can do."

"I know."

"Damien."

"I know!" Tears pooled in the corners of the prince's eyes as he stared unblinkingly at the city growing smaller and smaller by the instant. "I know," he repeated, more softly this time. "But I need to see it. I need to watch it disappear."

Who was Xander to tell him no? When his isle had fallen, he'd clung to the stones like a dead man grasping for those final strains of life. The gods, he'd dropped all the way to the sea before finally letting go. The thought of Pylaeon slipping beneath those murky waters still cleaved like a chisel to the heart.

"All right."

He signaled for the guards to begin the long flight to Sphaira. The prince threw him a sidelong glance, surprise lining his features. Xander just nodded firmly.

They didn't speak anymore after that.

They didn't need to.

They simply watched in silence as the House of Flight sank into the mist, lush forests and vast deserts giving way to endless gray as the vapors swallowed the isle whole.

43

RAFE

"They're coming," Rafe announced. Not a soul beside him moved. The king's mages were practiced in the art of self-control, and their focus was absolute. He could hear a pin drop as they waited for instruction, a fact he begrudgingly respected. True, there was no love lost between them, but with Malek and Lyana deep in their magic, it had fallen on Rafe to lead them. "The shadow and earth creatures are approaching from the north. Kal, stay close and I'll tell you when. The water creature is moving more slowly but gaining speed. It's coming from the west. So far, no dragons, but I suspect that will change. I'd say we have five, ten minutes tops to prepare for their arrival. Go."

The mages dispersed. Spouts of water erupted near the western edge of Da'Kin, a symbol to the fighters stationed around the perimeter of the city. Shoots of green and black arched toward the northern edge. Horns blared, a signal for the rest of the citizens without magic to get to as safe a place indoors as possible. Unlike during the first attack, they were prepared.

Still, Rafe feared it wouldn't be enough.

He pressed his hands to the stone parapets as he studied the fog.

The view from atop the castle was the best in the city, but he didn't search with his eyes. Spirits lingered in the back of his thoughts, fueled by fire and hate, cutting closer. There was nothing Rafe could do to stop them, so he didn't waste his energy trying. The other souls, though, more animalistic and simmering with flames, were a battleground.

Stay away. He sent the warning down the bonds, along with images of dragons falling beneath swarms of magic and their hides being pierced by *ferro'kine*-directed arrows as they screeched in pain. *Don't come here today. Stay away. For your safety, for your protection, stay away.*

He could feel the creatures fighting back, urging the dragons to eat and destroy, their orders competing with his for space inside those beastly minds.

Go.

Leave.

Go.

Leave.

Back and forth they warred, a fight no one aside from him could see. The invisible combat would only last so long. They were getting closer…and closer…and—

They were here.

The water rippled, a pulse that grew larger as it approached. Whitecaps sloshed as the wave grew, as tall as a building—then twice that, maybe more. Nyomi sent her magic across the city, more a signal than anything else. Other streams of sapphire flecks rose to join it. The aura of sparkling blue crashed into the sea, holding back the rising tide. From deep within the murky water, a creature with cobalt scales burst forth, a cry upon its lips. Two serpentine shoots of water erupted from the surface and slammed into the outer edge of Da'Kin.

A thunderous *boom* from the other side of the city stole Rafe's attention. By the time he spun, nothing but dust clouds filled the fog. A moment later, another wooden building was blasted apart, green magic shimmering in the aftermath as the earthen creature ripped the city to shreds piece by piece. Already, the stones beneath him quaked as the air filled with subtle hints of magic. The king's *geo'kines* fought to keep the castle steady.

Where's the shadow?

Where is it?

Rafe gripped the stones, their scratching against his palms keeping him grounded as he searched the mental connection.

"There!" He pointed to the right. "Kal, there!"

A beam of pure white light arched over the rooftops, followed by a wail. The mages could handle the other two creatures, but the shadow beast was different—fast and quiet, easy to overlook and as sneaky as the coming night, slipping across the sky unseen while all eyes were drawn to the vivid sunset. Rafe needed complete focus to stick with it.

"There, again!"

The *photo'kine* obliged.

"Again!"

This time, Rafe vaulted over the rim of the castle. Wings carving through the air, he dove for the black silhouette currently writhing in the light. The creature swerved to escape. Rafe caught it by the shoulders and dug his fingers into razor-sharp scales, not caring if they cut deep wounds into his fragile skin. They wrestled together in the sky, neither letting go. Claws scraped his biceps, eliciting a hiss of pain. The creature's white teeth snapped with fury.

"Kal!" he shouted. "Now!"

His world went ivory. Rafe winced and closed his eyes, but it did little to stop the burn. Pure, potent energy bit into his skin. The monster thrashed in his arms, a cry of pain and frustration seeping from deep in its throat. Using the opening, Rafe swung the creature around and latched his arms around its chest, using its body as a shield. Kal's magic barreled into them. He turned his face away, protecting his eyes as he felt his flesh melt beneath the piercing glow. This was far different from the diluted balls Brighty used to light dark passages or the subtle beams she sometimes bounced between her fingers. This was the sun brought down to earth. Even his newfound affinity for fire couldn't save him from the burn.

Still, whatever he felt, the shadow monster felt tenfold.

Through the mental bond, Rafe could feel the creature's pain, an all-consuming ache as light ate into darkness, stripping its very essence away.

It's working.

The thought gave him the strength to keep fighting, to keep holding on despite the hurt. *Invinci* magic flowed through his veins, cooling the heat, but not fast enough. His fingers started to slip. The creature sensed the opening, jerking away. Rafe tightened his grip.

It's working. Come on, it's working.

A roar shattered his careful concentration. The *photo'kine* magic disappeared in a blink and the creature tore free of Rafe's arms. He spun to find the castle engulfed in a bubbling cloud of flames as a dragon descended from the fog. Isaak stood atop the stones with his arms outstretched, red magic surging up his arms to block the fire. It wouldn't be enough, not for everyone. Already, the acrid scent of burnt flesh carried on the wind. The mage had saved the king and queen, but in doing so, he'd left the rest to burn.

The dragon gripped the tallest spire in its talons and ripped the stones apart with a showering spray. Another inferno spilled through its lips, swathing the surrounding wall in a blanket of smoldering orange. Mages jumped into the canals to escape the flames. Forgetting the shadow monster, Rafe sped across the distance.

Leave. The command sped down the bond like an arrow toward a target. *Leave!*

The dragon didn't. It wouldn't.

Golden magic still poured from the open window in the middle of the castle, a beacon to draw hungry eyes, the potent scent of spirit making even Rafe's stomach rumble. He ignored the base instinct. The dragon roared at him in warning, but he wasn't afraid as the flames swept across the sky, surrounding him in a red-hot swarm. The fire sank into his wings and rolled harmlessly over his skin. Dragons couldn't hurt him anymore.

Leave!

Rafe put his palms against simmering scales and sent the order directly into the beast's skin. For some reason, with touch they couldn't ignore him. They cowered. Pumping its wings, the dragon retreated into the mist.

Heavy breaths spilled through Rafe's lips as he hovered for a moment. All around the city screams rose. Waves swallowed buildings whole. Stones and wood ripped apart. Somewhere in the darkness, the shadow beast lurked. And already Rafe sensed another dragon coming on the breeze.

They were losing.

If he didn't do something, they were going to fail.

But what?

A swiftly moving patch of darkness caught his eye. No time to think, Rafe raced for the monster, cutting it off at the pass as it made for Lyana. They slammed into each other just outside the balcony entrance, far too close for comfort. Without Kal's light magic, it wouldn't be so easy to keep the creature contained. Claws ripped down his arms, shredding flesh. Anger barreled into his thoughts. It was all Rafe could do to hold on, his body screaming at him for pushing too far. Even his *invinci* power couldn't keep up with the injuries. Blood loss made his grip go weak. The demon kicked him in the chest, tearing free.

An explosion of pain shocked him still.

It's not mine, Rafe realized, whipping his head to the side. It was one of the creatures. The shadow sensed it too, its head swiveling between the castle and the city, clearly torn. It had an opening, but the creatures were a unit somehow. After spending so much time in the spell together, hundreds of years incubating in the same magic, they cared more for each other than for a human desire like revenge. Those black eyes found Rafe's, churning with an even deeper truth—time was on its side. In a few more weeks, there would be four of them, and what would the world do then?

Dread dug into his chest like talons.

The shadow beast fled and Rafe fell from the sky, collapsing onto the castle roof as his body finally gave out. He lifted his face just in time to see the three creatures disappearing into the fog together, the earthen one being carried aloft by the other two, its left wing bent and misshapen. He dropped his head back and closed his eyes. For a few minutes, he did nothing but breathe as silver magic coursed through him.

Time, he thought. *We're running out of time.*

"I'm going, Malek."

"Lyana—"

"Those people deserve our help, too. I'm going, and there's nothing you can do to stop me."

Rafe groaned and rolled to his feet as two familiar voices carried on the breeze. He already knew what they were arguing about. He'd expected it, which was why he'd taken those few precious moments to heal while he could. Two ivory wings appeared beneath him, catching the wind. Rafe leapt off the roof, ignoring his aching muscles, and raced after her.

44

MALEK

In all his years spent spying on the avians, Malek had been envious of many things—their endless food supply, their fruitful isles, their cloudless skies, their freedom. But he'd never craved flight, not in the way he did at that moment, watching Lyana and Rafe soar away, her wings as white as snow, his rippling with fire, the pair of them cutting across the skies like prophecy brought to life.

He'd never felt so weighed down, his heart sinking as though pulled by an anchor to the bottom of the sea. All around him, spirits mourned, reaching out in pain, pleading with him to be healed. His city burned. His people suffered.

Did she really think he didn't feel it?

Did she really think he didn't want to help them?

Of course he did. But there was a difference between a want and a need. He *wanted* to heal everyone in Da'Kin. He *needed* to concentrate on the mages first, and the strongest ones at that, if they were to have any chance at fending off the next attack. When would she understand that? When would she see?

Let them go, he thought viciously, a sneer working its way across his lips. *Let them run off to help the masses. Let the people have their symbols of hope. And I'll stay right here where I've always been, alone and unafraid to do what must be done.*

"My liege." The voice of his fire mage cut through the silence.

Malek abandoned the balcony and marched back inside. "Where are they?"

"Follow me."

They ran through the castle halls as fast as their feet could carry them and emerged on the roof. Malek fought a cough, wincing as the scent of burnt flesh filled his nose. All around him, mages moaned. He went to Kal first, his chest tightening as he walked by Jacinta's charred body to kneel beside the *photo'kine*. This wasn't about who he cared for the most—it was about whose magic the world most required. And against the shadow creature, it was Kal's, bar none.

One by one, Malek healed his mages, moving from the roof to the rocks surrounding the castle to the wall and then beyond, to the garrisons stationed throughout the city, and finally, to the front line. The people didn't cheer at the sight of him the way they had for Lyana as she walked among the wreckage, but he didn't need their praise. The role of king was a thankless one, built of difficult decisions few would ever understand—not even, it seemed, his queen.

"My liege."

Jacinta found him in his study hours later, long after the rest of the castle had gone to sleep. He leaned over a map of Da'Kin, searching the winding canals as though they held all the answers he craved: how to fight these monsters, how to seal the rift, how to carry out the prophecy before everything was lost.

"Initial damage reports came back while I was gone," he said, not looking up as she came to stand beside him, her attention also on the map. "At first light, I need you to lead the rebuilding efforts. The pipes were shattered, here and here and here, cutting off fresh water to nearly a third of the city. They need to be restored as quickly as possible. People can live without homes and with little food, but without water they won't survive."

"Yes, my liege."

"I also want you to gather a team to work on crafting more fire shields. The mesh blanket the raven carries—every mage in the castle guard should have one on hand for the next time a dragon attacks. The work will be tedious, but worth the effort."

"Done, my liege."

"Good."

He expected her to leave as swiftly as she came, but she hesitated. Malek gave her his full attention. The planes of her face were as sharp as ever, the flat line of her ebony bangs against pale skin, the point of her chin, the angular cut of her cheekbones. Her spirit, however, wavered, flimsy and uncertain in a way his *ferro'kine* rarely was.

"Jacinta?"

She swallowed, her guard momentarily dropping to reveal the fear in her eyes. "Do you know what creature will come next?"

There were only three elements and three isles left before the *aethi'kine* creature in the House of Peace emerged—fire in the House of Song, air in the House of Prey, or light in the House of Wisdom. Two of those they could handle. One, they couldn't. When the light dragon awoke, it would be faster than the shadow creature, too fast maybe for his *umbra'kines* to catch, moving with the speed of light itself. He didn't know how they would stop it from getting to him or Lyana, but they would. To save the world, they'd find a way.

"No," he answered honestly. "But whatever it is, we'll fight it, the same way we always have, because we have no choice but to win."

"Of course." Doubt flashed across her spirit, at odds with her firm response. It was the first time he'd ever felt her question their victory.

"Have I ever led you astray, Jacinta?"

"No, my liege."

"Then hear me now. The world will be saved because I will do whatever it takes to save it, the same way I've always done. If you believe in nothing else, believe in that. Now go, get some sleep. Your work begins again at dawn."

As he watched her leave, he thought, and not for the first time, how relieved he was that none of his mages could sense his heart the way he could theirs. If they did, they would know he was just as terrified as the rest of them, just as unsure. The truth was he had no idea what he was doing or who he even was anymore, let alone whether he would save the world. But he would never stop fighting.

So while his queen slept peacefully in the arms of another man, her soul at ease in a way it had never been with him, Malek remained at his desk. He wrote orders and crafted plans, solving the problems at hand while trying to ignore the nagging question of what the future would bring.

45

XANDER

The last time Xander had flown down the grand entrance to the crystal palace, he'd been hiding—behind a mask, behind his brother, behind a glove. Now, he was laid bare. The king of a lost kingdom. The raven without a hand. The man whose most valuable possession was the conviction in his heart. Strange that he was less afraid than he'd ever been before.

"King Lysander," a dove called out in greeting as he flew into the central atrium of the domed structure. "They're waiting for you."

Xander's gaze slid over the messenger and swept across the sun-filled room. The mosaic floor sparkled with a reflection of the scene visible through the crystals overhead, as though the sky were both above and below, leaving the doves wrapped in their god's loving arms. The space was empty now, but if he closed his eyes he could still see the platforms circling the outer edge, each one bathed in the colors of its house, a decadent display of might. The courtship trials seemed a lifetime ago. Had it truly only been a matter of months since Lyana had shocked them all and flown across the atrium to kneel before him? The *thwack* of his mask falling gracelessly to the floor still echoed across the shocked silence, loud within his memories. How, in such a short amount of time, had the prince who'd once cowered before them become the king from whom they all waited to hear?

His mother would have been proud.

The thought brought a slight smile to his lips as he finally turned toward the dove standing patiently by the entrance. "Please, show me where."

The man led him to the highest level of the palace, where a set of brilliant golden doors were being held open by two guards with ashen wings, then through them to a meeting room near the front of the royal chambers. The rest of the kings and queens were already there waiting. The room fell silent as he entered.

"Apologies for the delay," Xander said as he took his seat at the far end of the table where a wooden chair upholstered in black leather stood empty. The matching one to his left would remain that way. "I received an update from the queen."

The royals around him shifted audibly, the rustle of silks loud over the silence. The dove king was the first to speak, concern visible in his warm brown eyes. "Will she not be joining us?"

"Unfortunately not."

Worried glances were exchanged across the table. Xander tried to ignore them as he brought a new round of lies to his lips, a cover story he and Cassi had worked on the night before. By the time she'd made it to Da'Kin, the city had been in shambles. The sector where the *skryr* lived had been blasted apart, leaving the man's whereabouts in question. Rafe and Lyana were both alive but frustrated, no closer to figuring out how to slow or stop the rift spell from unraveling. Cassi hadn't even told her friend she was in the city when she visited her dreams. She'd been too worried her presence would only be a distraction.

"Lyana managed to save the House of Flight from complete ruin, much the same as she did the House of Paradise. The isle still stands, surrounded by water now instead of air, and though Abaelon has suffered great damage, it will someday be home to the hummingbirds again."

King Axos and Queen Odehlia shared a glance, relief palpable in the space between them. With the way the queen's arm shifted, Xander guessed she'd grabbed her mate's hand under the table. It almost made him wish he could have someone there beside him, to share in the fear and the pain, but especially in the victories. Lyana, extraordinary as she was, would never be that woman. At least not to him.

"And what of the remaining isles?" a sharp voice to his left asked.

Xander turned toward the eagle king. "Vesevios gains strength at a speed even the gods had not predicted, so they will not release her from her prayers. We don't know which isle will be next to fall, but whichever it is, we will be prepared."

"And when it's this isle?" the man asked, not relenting so easily. He was, after all, a hunter through and through. "What will we do then? When there is nowhere left to run?"

All eyes returned to Xander. Once, the very idea would have intimidated him. Now, he'd faced death, he'd faced a dragon, he'd faced betrayals so deep he thought he might not recover, he'd faced the end of everything he'd ever known—and still he'd survived. A few kings and queens with an inflated sense of self-worth no longer scared him. "If you think acting in the best interests of your people and moving them to the safest place possible is running, then I think you've been flying across your open plains chasing buffalo for too long."

The eagle king sneered.

Xander continued before he had a chance to interrupt. "And to answer your question, we will fight. If Vesevios sends his dragons, we will fight them. And if he sends his flames, we will fight that. And if he tries to trick us, we will fight his lies, just as we've started to do now by stopping the executions of our mages. They will help us when the day comes, just as Lyana will be there when she is needed most, to save our world from complete ruin. So no, she is not here now, but don't mistake that to mean she is cowering in fear. Every moment she spends fortifying her power is a moment she spends fighting for us."

In the wake of his words, silence lingered. Xander used the pause to meet each and every eye turned on him now. Some looked on in doubt such as the King of the House of Prey, some in solidarity such as the Queen of the House of Paradise, and some in gratitude such as the King of the House of Peace, whose daughter had yet again become the talk of the kingdoms. Then his focus shifted to the two empty seats next to Lyana's, their leathers the rich amber of the House of Wisdom.

"Now," Xander said, "where are the owls?"

"They refuse to abandon the libraries of Rynthos," Queen Zara said, her tone tired.

"Did anyone explain to them that evacuating as many people and volumes as possible in the time they have left wouldn't be *abandoning the library*?"

"Yes."

"And that the books will survive the fall far better than their citizens will?"

"Yes."

"And that the isle will fall, regardless of whether they stubbornly remain behind to protect it?"

"Yes," she answered more softly this time. "They understand that is what you believe."

Xander sighed as he rubbed the bridge of his nose with his fingers. "It's not what I believe. It's what will happen."

"They believe that if they display enough faith, Meteria will save them."

He ground his teeth. Faith in the gods had always been

something he prized, but there was a difference between faith and folly. The owls, for all their intelligence, were choosing the latter. "Was this communicated through letters?"

"We sent emissaries while you were in the House of Flight. They were unsuccessful."

"Who did you send?"

"Myself and the Queen of the House of Peace."

Xander bit back a curse. After spending so many hours in close conversation with her before the House of Paradise fell, he knew Queen Zara was as convincing as they came. If the owls had ignored not only her but also Aethios's queen, then who would they listen to?

Me.

His heart sank as he looked into the queen's dark brown eyes, her solemn expression only confirming the truth. He'd convinced the House of Song. He'd convinced the House of Paradise. He'd convinced the House of Flight. Now he would need to convince the House of Wisdom too. "I'll leave tomorrow. There are some matters I must attend to for the ravens first, and then I will try my best to convince the owls to see the one thing they so pride themselves on —reason."

"Very well," the dove king said, no surprise in his voice. They'd all known exactly where this meeting would lead. "Now, onto the other matters at hand…"

Xander half listened as they continued down the agenda, reviewing the evacuations, the food stores, the housing requirements, the crowds, and the many other challenges that came with merging the people from seven thriving houses into one, especially on an isle made almost entirely of ice. In the back of his mind, though, he thought of what Cassi had told him in his dreams the night before, while they'd sat by the warm fire in his now-drowned study, the flames casting her in an orange glow, illuminating her already luminous features.

Do they know which house will be next? he'd asked.

Not yet. I just pray it won't be the House of Wisdom.

Why?

When she turned to face him, he'd expected to see memories of their time spent together in the library reflected in her eyes, something warm and nostalgic, a bright light fluttering across those silver depths. Instead, he saw iron. *Because the god stone in the House of Wisdom is made of light magic, and when that creature hatches, we're doomed. It'll be even faster than the shadow beast, and if they work together, I don't know how Rafe will stop them from getting to Lyana.*

Just thinking about the conversation made his shoulders writhe, a discomfort that stayed with him the rest of the day, throughout the remainder of the meeting and during his flight back to the raven quarters nestled in the city of Sphaira. He was greeted by Helen, who waited with folded arms and a frown just inside the door.

"What news?" she asked.

He shrugged out of his furs, already growing overheated now that he was back inside. "I leave for the House of Wisdom come morning."

She snarled. "You're leaving again? Your people need you."

"They have you—"

"No," she interrupted, unmindful of rank or protocol, a fact that under normal circumstances would have brought a smile to his lips. "You're not traveling without me or a personal guard again."

"I won't put raven lives in danger."

"We're already in danger!"

"Be that as it may," he said as he walked past her, positive she would follow as he made for his room, his stomach already rumbling for a meal. "This is the safest place for you right now, and the owls would never harm me. I'll be perfectly safe—"

"Then why can't I come?"

He turned and stared at her, one hand on the door. "Helen."

"My king."

With one brow raised, she practically dared him to speak. The woman was small but exasperating at times, though he couldn't get too angry. She was, after all, acting out of misguided loyalty and a deep-rooted fear for his life.

"I'll be all right," he murmured, his rigid stance relaxing.

"Now, where have I heard that before?"

"And am I not standing before you, alive and well?"

"If you keep flying heedlessly into danger, one of these days you won't be."

A smile spread his lips. "Are you admitting you miss the prince who spent all his hours alone with his books? I thought you were the one who told my mother it would be good for me to get out more."

She snorted, the tension easing from her frame. With a sigh, she glanced to the left and to the right, disgust curling her lips. "Where are the servants? I'll tell the kitchen to bring refreshments, then I'll gather the advisors. I'm presuming we have a long night of planning ahead."

"We do."

He shut the door as she left, resisting the urge to collapse against it. Exhaustion almost overwhelmed him, but it was something a leader didn't have the luxury of feeling, not in times such as these. If he were being honest, another emotion weighed down his bones, one that was more difficult to face, so his feet dragged as he crossed the room.

Unease.

Knots tightened his shoulders. His insides twisted in coils. Pressure pushed on his chest, making it difficult to breathe.

Doomed. Cassi's voice played on repeat in his mind. *We're doomed.*

Given their luck, he had no doubt which house would be the

next to fall, and the knowledge did nothing to ease his fears. The libraries of Rynthos were one of the most majestic places he could imagine, bathed in soft amber light, humming with the subtle *swish* of wings, filled with the musty scent of vast knowledge, an untapped land just waiting to be explored. Yet when he pictured them now, he imagined the stone canopy overhead and the porous walls, a newfound claustrophobia drying his throat.

I can do this.

I'll convince them.

The affirmations did little to assuage the fear that, come morning, he'd be soaring directly into the belly of the beast. And this time, he might not make it out alive.

46

CASSI

Cassi landed on the ship at full speed, her boots slamming into the planks with such force they shook. "By order of the king, don't you dare lower those sails one more inch."

The captain arched a brow. He was young for such a position of power, his skin hardly weathered, which meant his magic was undoubtedly strong. Muddled green eyes cast her a dubious look, his expression just as hard as she expected from someone who'd spent his life crossing these dangerous seas. "Do you have papers?"

"There wasn't time." And technically, she wasn't here under Malek's orders. But if she had consulted him, she knew exactly where he'd stand. "There's a man on your ship I need to speak with."

The captain frowned and signaled to his first mate. The creak of wood and ropes told her everything. Cassi reached out and gripped the wheel. "I said, don't lower the sails another inch."

"Or what?" the captain drawled. "No papers, no proof. And the only people on my ship are my crew."

"Oh, really?" A fiendish smile widened her lips as her wings spread menacingly. "Not even the man I watched you smuggle on board last night, foolishly believing you were alone? I'd expected more from the captain of a dragon-hunting ship. You, of all people, should know someone is always watching. The king has eyes everywhere."

He slowly perused her wings. By the time his gaze settled back on her face, it was sharp with realization. "You're a *dormi'kine*."

"I have business with the *skryr*."

He hesitated, but only for a moment, before nodding to someone behind her. Boots stomped on wood then a door opened, the planks groaning. Cassi turned slowly so as not to appear too eager—superiority was her only source of control on this ship. Inside, though, her nerves fluttered.

The *skryr* had been a surprisingly difficult man to track down, especially considering she'd spent much of her youth hovering in the back corners of his shop, using her magic to watch him work. His spirit was slippery. She'd never quite caught the scent of it, the flavor shifting and changing with each new object his magic touched, as though bits of the souls lingering in those items leaked into his. By the time she'd arrived in Da'Kin a few days before, the city had been in chaos. His shop was located in one of the sectors blown apart by the earthen creature, nothing left but wood shards floating in the canals. It had taken hours of scouring the city to even catch the hint of his name on the breeze, something about money and a debt owed, which was when she'd realized he was on the run. She'd spent the next few nights searching the ships, but in truth, dumb luck was the only reason she'd stumbled upon his being smuggled onto this ship in the early hours just before dawn. She'd been on her way to the ship docked two streets down when she saw a hooded figure creeping through the mist, just suspicious enough to pique her interest.

He wore the same cloak now as two sailors dragged him up the steps, one holding each arm, though it hardly seemed necessary. The man was ancient, his skin covered in wrinkles and his white hair swirling in the breeze. A sneeze would have knocked him over.

"You can't, please," he begged as they carried him on deck. "He'll kill me."

"Not on my watch," Cassi interrupted as she pumped her wings twice to sail over the rail and land on the main deck.

The *skryr* whipped his head in her direction. "Who are you?"

"A person who is very much invested in keeping you alive," she answered truthfully, signaling for the two sailors to release him. "And in Da'Kin."

"I can't stay here."

"We don't have time to go anywhere else."

His thick white eyebrows knitted together, intelligence churning in the depths of his hazel eyes. "Who sent you?"

"The king."

If he was surprised, he didn't show it. "Can you guarantee my safety?"

"Look at the world." She scoffed. "I can't even guarantee my own safety. But I can promise this—if you don't come with me, I'll never stop looking for you, and there's nowhere you can run where my magic won't find you."

"Very well then, *dormi'kine*." The words came out sounding like a sigh. Clearly, it wasn't the first time in his long life he'd been threatened. "But first I need proof of your connection to the king."

"I don't have papers."

A sly grin crept across his face. "That's not the sort of proof I require."

Cassi swallowed. Guarding her secrets had long been her way of life. Freely offering them to a stranger went against every fiber of her being. Still, she reached for the dagger at her hip and offered it to the mage. Of all her possessions, it held the strongest connection to her spirit. After all, what was it she'd told Xander all those weeks ago?

Your weapon is your best friend.

The *skryr* snatched the blade from her hands. As soon as his pale skin touched the metal, bronze sparks circled his flesh. His hazel eyes glittered with his magic, and his expression went blank as he sank into a world where no one else could follow. Cassi's heart pounded in her chest.

What was he seeing?

What parts of herself had she given away?

What would he know?

A few minutes passed in silence before the power fizzled. With a blink, he returned to the present. She snatched the dagger from his palm and slid it back into its sheath. He looked up at her slowly, his head tilting to the side as though he was seeing her in a new light.

"Well?"

"Lead the way, Kasiandra."

A shiver rippled down her spine, but she tried her best to ignore it as she ushered the old man off the ship.

"Stay close and keep your hood low," she whispered. "With any luck, people will be too focused on my wings to even notice the man walking slowly before me."

He nodded and retreated farther into the cloth. Cassi mumbled directions, letting him set the pace. It was early, but the docks already bustled with life. People gawked as she passed by. The occasional single-winged avian, such as her mother, was a rare enough sight in the world below, but one with two working wings? That was unheard of. If Malek didn't know she was in the city, he soon would. Though she doubted he would tell Lyana, if for no other reason than to keep her focused on him.

By the time they reached the inn, she was eager to get inside. Her mother had given her a purse full of coin before she'd left

Sphaira, and she'd been renting a room since her arrival. The *skryr* didn't lower his hood until they closed the door behind them.

"What did you see?" she asked, the words practically shooting from her lips the moment they were alone.

"You don't work for the king," he said—a statement, not a question.

"Not anymore."

"But you want to save the world."

"More than anything."

Her answer must have reassured him because the angles of his face softened. "I saw your last clear memory of the king. You were yelling at him, threatening that you were going to tell the queen who the real King Born in Fire was, a fact I've recently suspected myself."

He'd seen the dream when she confronted Malek, before he'd healed her and tortured her and kept her locked in his dungeons. Disgust curled her lip. "I didn't think your magic worked so quickly. I used to come to your shop and watch you. It took hours for you to glean information."

"On a grand scale, yes," he explained as he dropped onto the edge of her bed with a grunt, his old body giving out. Cassi pulled a chair over from the other side of the room to sit beside him. "If I'm trying to absorb all the information an object can offer, it can take hours, days, even weeks to learn every secret the soul housed inside has to give. But I was just looking for a single moment, and thus directed, my power works quickly."

Suspicion needled at the back of her mind. "What else did you see?"

"Why do you ask?" A delighted sparkle lit his weary eyes.

"Call it a hunch."

"I guess someone who's spent their life learning other people's secrets would recognize a half-truth when it's offered. Let me see it."

She frowned. "What?"

"My girl," he murmured, his voice amused. "The diary. I saw you take it from the library of the owls. I sensed your spirit sing as soon as your fingers grazed the leather binding. You want to know what it says, and with any luck, I can tell you."

Cassi reached inside her jacket, then paused. "What makes you so eager all of a sudden?"

"Is it so incredible to think you're not the only one interested in saving our world?"

"In my experience, altruism doesn't rank high on the list of human motivations."

"It's what drives *you*."

She flinched as though struck. It was the sort of compliment she might have paid Xander, not the sort reserved for people like her—people who lied to their best friends and betrayed nearly everyone who had ever been kind to them.

"Perhaps you'll understand this more, then," the *skryr* continued. "Curiosity. You believe the answers to all the questions that have ever plagued our world might rest in that book, and I've touched many compelling objects in my life, but I've never touched one as powerful as that. Or maybe my reasoning is even more banal. I don't want to die, not before I've seen the blue sky beyond the fog or felt the sun warm my cheeks. Everyone who lives in Da'Kin can see the time of prophecy is drawing near. If my actions can tip the scale—if they can grant me a few more years—I'm sure as magic going to take them."

All three were convincing reasons, yet Cassi still didn't quite believe him. Regardless, she had no choice. She needed his magic, a fact he clearly knew. And he needed her, to keep him alive if nothing else.

"Who were you running from?"

"A woman came to my shop about a month ago with a trinket

she said belonged to her father. I realized too late it belonged to one of the most powerful mages in the city, and now I know a secret of his he very much wants to keep quiet. If I tell you what it is, he'll want to silence you as well."

Now, *that* she believed. Cassi shook her head. It didn't matter anyway. "What sort of mage?"

"An *umbra'kine*."

She wrinkled her nose. Shadow mages could be sneaky bastards. "Does he have access to a dreamwalker?"

"Not that I'm aware of."

"Good. I'll need to know more if I'm to keep us both safe, but it can wait." She tightened her fingers around the leather book pressed against her chest and slid it free. "The diary can't. I want to know who it belonged to, what it says, and everything it can tell us about the prophecy, and I want to know now."

"Answers such as those will take time."

"In case you haven't looked outside recently, time is the one thing we don't have. Da'Kin burns. The dragons are multiplying. The rift is weakening. And in a few weeks—" Cassi broke off as the words caught in the back of her throat. An earthquake had struck the House of Wisdom the day before. The light creature would soon be here, and when that happened…she didn't know. Just the thought sent a hot rush of fear into her veins, not only for their world but also for Xander, now living among the owls. "In a few weeks, there may be nothing left."

The *skryr* lowered his gaze to the book in her hands, then lifted it back to her face, the hint of a challenge in his eyes. "Then I suggest you let me get to work."

She extended the diary.

He snatched it, his magic bursting from his fingertips before they even touched leather. A bronze halo exploded from his palms, lighting the room in a glittering haze. His eyes rolled to the back of his head and he collapsed on the bed, his body twitching. Cassi jumped to her feet to help, then froze. Breath passed evenly through his lips. No strain tightened his features. He was alive yet removed, a sensation she understood better than most. So she sat back down and propped her feet beside him, doing the only thing she could—waiting to hear what secrets he'd reveal.

THE DIARY

Twenty-Third Day of the Seventh Moon

I told Zavier my fears—about the dragon eggs, about the aethi'kine avian boy, about what Bastiant intends to do. We both agreed that whatever his plan is, it can't be good. He's going to talk to Mikhail, but I fear the dove's reaction when he learns Zavier has been spying on him. Will he believe us? Will he think we work for my husband? Will he trust us?

And if he doesn't, what then?

Twenty-Fourth Day of the Seventh Moon

We told Mikhail that Bastiant knows of the boy and is looking for him. I can't tell if he was grateful or furious, though I fear the answer lies somewhere in between. Something has changed between him and Zavier. I don't think their relationship will ever be the same. But he says the avians will take the boy from the city and hide him in a place where my husband will never find him, at least not until he's old enough to understand the power in his skin.

I fear no such place exists.

Fourth Day of the Eighth Moon

Bastiant has been acting oddly peaceful of late. I worry he's coming closer and closer to discovering the location of the boy. He hasn't called me to his rooms. He seems to have no idea I even exist. When I see him, his eyes are glazed over, as though they're staring into another world, perhaps the one he is on the cusp of creating.

I'm doing everything I can to stop it.

Zavier spies on Bastiant as often as he can, quick peeks, there and gone too swiftly to merit suspicion. We haven't caught him in a private meeting again. For my part, I try to search the future, but my magic remains as stubborn as ever, almost willing me to give in, to surrender, to let it sweep me away. But Zavier and I are the only ones who can uncover my husband's plans. What would happen if I lost myself to the power? To the future? What if time carried me away and never let me return to the present?

No.

I won't let the magic take me—not yet.

Instead, I'll make do with the snippets I've received, small moments in time that form a puzzle I'm no closer to solving. I saw the girl again, a dove like I thought, with ivory wings and dark skin. This time, her palm glittered with aethi'kine magic. Where is she? Is she alive? Is she the one Bastiant will take? I fear she is far away—her clothes too regal and her smile too free to be an avian of this world.

I saw a man too, with pale skin and blue eyes. He has wings, though I can't quite determine which kind. At first, they seemed black as night, the obsidian silk of a raven. But just before the vision ended, they shifted, flashing with orange and changing shape, too fuzzy for me to see clearly. He had magic, though I didn't see what. It was more a feeling of power, similar to his spirit, which was torn and broken yet with unwavering strength beneath it all.

I've seen flashes of the future too. The beasts will come, unless I can stop them, and if they do, my city won't be the only one to burn. They spew fire with each breath. They are difficult to kill, with thick scaled hides and expansive leathery wings. I foresee a battle in the skies above a gleaming city I don't recognize. The air glitters with magic and burns with flames. I see avians and mages alike, but I can't tell if they fight each other or if they fight together. And I can't tell which side wins. There is too much death, too much destruction.

Is this the future my husband races toward?

Does he even understand the game he is playing?

I believe he does.

Worse still, I believe he doesn't care.

Fifteenth Day of the Eighth Moon

More visions. More desolation. More despair. Why can't the future show me things I truly want to see? Happiness. Love. Light. Is that too much to hope for?

Seventeenth Day of the Eighth Moon

Part of my prayer was answered. I saw the girl and boy in a vision again, but this time they were together, their faces close, their gazes yearning, their bodies pulled toward each other as though by strings. Ash fell all around them, or maybe it was snow, I couldn't quite tell, though the orange glow of flames flickered clearly across their faces. What struck me the most was their spirits. The connection between their souls was so absolute I could feel it across time. They are lovers, and yet all I see for them when I look into their future is pain.

I hope I'm wrong.

I hope it with everything I have.

The vision so affected me, even hours later, that I couldn't shake the image of their desperate faces or the sensation of their breaking hearts.

Odd that after so many pictures of death and decay, of blood and gore, of screams and snarls, it is the sight of love that has left me undone. When Zavier came to my room that night, I crumbled into his arms. After all the nights I've spent in his room, my husband has yet to break me, but these forlorn lovers in a faraway future have touched me deeply. Perhaps I see myself in them—myself and Zavier. Perhaps I want us all to have the happy endings we crave.

Zavier held me until my tears had passed, not demanding answers, simply providing solace. Then I kissed him with a fervor I didn't need to explain, one he felt too. Even without chrono'kine magic, he can sense time slipping away from us, from the world. We'll take advantage of whatever stolen moments we have left.

Twenty-First Day of the Eighth Moon

I fear the tides have shifted. My husband leaves in the morning, though he refuses to tell me where he's going. In my heart, I already know.

He's found the boy.

Our time is up.

Twenty-Fourth Day of the Eighth Moon

Mikhail came to us in a panic. The boy is gone, as I suspected.

Without my husband home, any pretense of covering our tracks is finished. I know the avians would never rat out one of their own, even if he is cavorting with the enemy, and Bastiant's advisors practically ignore me, just as my meek persona allows. We spy for him day and night. We've seen the boy, but they don't seem to be bringing him back to the palace. They're going somewhere else. The avians sent a team to try to retrieve the boy, but all it did was anger my husband and cause ten more to lose their lives.

Aethi'kine magic is unbeatable.

So how in the world are we going to stop him? Won't my magic show me that? What use is seeing the future if I've no way to stop the worst from happening? I wonder if it's time to succumb to the future's alluring pull, but my gut tells me not yet.

So I wait, and watch, as helpless as I've ever been.

Twenty-Sixth Day of the Eighth Moon

The world is ended.

I know it.

We were too late, too weak, too unprepared, too outmatched, too everything. And my husband was too. The enemy is here, and it is unlike any enemy I've ever seen before. Zavier and I are the only people alive who bore witness to the downfall of man, so I will record it here, in the hopes that history won't be lost like all things to time.

By the time Zavier formed the spying window this morning, Bastiant's spatio'kine had already opened the rift and disappeared inside it. My husband stood in the middle of a clearing, staring at it, his hand wrapped around the boy's forearm, gold magic glittering around them like a cage. I don't know why they opened the rift in the woods instead of coming back home—perhaps to keep other mages from sensing the magic, perhaps to keep the other eggs safely away in case something went awry. Either way, against my husband's magic there was nothing Zavier or I could do but watch. So we did, studying the rift for any change. Minutes passed. It could have been an hour. I know not. My eyes grew dry. My fingers ached from clutching Zavier's hand. We both jolted when we finally saw movement.

The spatio'kine tore through the rift rolling an egg before him, the surface a mix of black and red, speckled with flecks of yellow and as smooth as the others I'd seen. His eyes were wide with fear and his clothes were in tatters, shredded and burned, still smoldering as he swatted at the edge of his jacket, leaving embers in his wake.

"It's coming!" he shouted. "It's coming!"

"Close the rift," Bastiant ordered.

His power rushed across the distance to wrap around the egg and pull it toward him. As soon as he laid a palm on the curved surface, a smile I fear will haunt my nightmares spread across his face. The boy cried, but there was no way to fight. Bastiant's magic shifted, wrapping around the boy he held with one hand and the egg he touched with the other.

The soul joining had begun.

Behind him, the spatio'kine struggled to undo his weave, the threads of space growing slippery in his hands, weak and injured as he was. With every passing moment, his back hunched closer and closer to the ground. He wobbled on unsteady feet, his knees trembling as he swayed.

My husband didn't notice or didn't care. He was too deep in his power, seeing not the world but the two souls he intended to fuse. The egg shifted from black to gold, again and again, magic shimmering over its surface. The boy's transformation was more gruesome. His skin bubbled with scales, wings flashed at his back, and claws hovered over his fingertips. When he tried to shout, the bright spark of a flame erupted from his lips instead. With my husband still clutching his forearm, the boy eventually succumbed to the pain, dropping to the ground as though dead, but he wasn't. He had a worse fate in store.

"My king!" the spatio'kine screamed.

Bastiant was beyond hearing. The boy and the egg oscillated in spirit faster and faster, becoming little more than two blurs, until finally, with a gasp, my husband released them and stepped back. His magic dispersed.

"My king! You need to heal me. I need—"

The spatio'kine dropped to his knees, clutching his stomach and he bent over in pain, a groan escaping his lips instead. Bastiant didn't bother to turn around. His gaze was fixed on the boy and the egg, watching their spirits battle for control.

"What's happening?" Zavier asked by my side.

He was an avian. His body had waged this war once, but he'd been too young to remember, and he'd probably never borne witness to the change the way I had by my father's side. "Their souls are battling for dominance. Only one will win—the boy or the beast."

"How will we know who does?"

"Whichever body is left at the end is the winner," I explained, silently urging the boy to fight this otherworldly creature, to be the more powerful soul. When avians got their wings, the human soul was almost always more powerful than the bird's. We're the more intelligent beings with more commanding minds and a stronger sense of self to pull us through. There were some casualties, of course, but not many. These beasts were different, though. There was no telling what they were capable of, and as I stared at the twitching body of the little boy, I feared the spirit residing in that egg, even if not fully developed, was the stronger of the two.

My fears were confirmed moments later.

An explosion of energy knocked Bastiant back. Zavier and I turned away from his rift as a bright light flashed, temporarily blinding our eyes. By the time my vision returned, it was done. The boy was gone. My husband stood beside a gleaming golden egg, his covetous palm pressed against the surface, a victorious look in his eyes. It was my vision come to life.

"My king!" the spatio'kine screamed again.

Bastiant turned, annoyance twisting his features. "What—"

His words were cut off by a bubbling wave of fire barreling through the rift. Before the blast swallowed him, I saw my husband lift his hand, aethi'kine magic already rising to the defense. When the flames cleared, he was unharmed. I could not say the same for his spatio'kine. The man's skin was black, flaking from his face and his arms, melted in some places and charred in others. Breath hardly stirred his chest. A pained wheeze escaped his lips. Bastiant sighed and knelt beside his mage, sinking his healing magic into the man's skin. For a moment, I thought maybe that would be it.

Then a beast flew through the rift.

It was immense, far larger than I realized even in my visions, its jaw the same size as Bastiant's entire body. He had barely enough time to shift the focus of his magic before the thing was upon him, fire tearing from its throat as its claws reached for his head. Those expansive wings pumped with such force the leaves ripped free from the surrounding trees. When it roared, even Zavier and I flinched where we sat safely in the palace.

Aethi'kine magic wrapped around the beast, encircling it in a web of glittering gold. I waited for it to fly back through the rift, to be gone from our world, to succumb to my husband's will.

It didn't.

Bastiant stumbled back with his hands outstretched as he sank all his focus into his magic. A grimace slowly spread across his face as more and more time passed. The beast took the onslaught head-on, flapping its wings and stomping its feet, getting no closer to my husband but going no farther away either. The more I watched, the more awed I became, realizing that even Bastiant's magic wasn't enough to hold this beast at bay. My husband stumbled and fell. His skin began to bubble in spots, as though melting from the inside out. I'd seen this once before, in a vision of my father—the vision of his death. I'd wondered at the time what could burn an aethi'kine, and now I knew. This beast and the incomprehensible power residing in its skin.

As my husband weakened, the beast strengthened, as though it absorbed his magic and took his power for itself. My gaze dropped away from the battle nearing its end to the golden egg sitting on the ground. If that was a beast without human magic, I could only imagine what sort of demon Bastiant had birthed with his power—part beast, part aethi'kine, the strongest of two worlds united into one unfathomable monster.

We needed to close the rift.

We needed to close it with that egg safely on the other side.

"Zavier, he's going to lose." I clutched his hand, unable to look

away even as the horror of it all fought to steal the words from my lips. "They're going to die."

"I know."

"We need to close the rift."

"Not we, Mira."

I turned to him with a protest on my lips, but it was too late. His hazel eyes were already hardened by determination and laced with apology, a combination that tore the breath from my chest. All I could manage was a soft, "No."

"I love you," he whispered.

Then he fell through his rift and sealed it behind him.

I waited, unmoving, for what felt like an eternity, uncaring as my muscles grew stiff, my mind's eye not in my room, but still watching those horrors unfold. Horrors the man who had come to mean everything to me had just chosen to face without me. I knew there was little I could've done to help—my magic was useless in battle, my body even more so—but the not knowing was excruciating.

Zavier came tumbling into my room in a flash of white magic. The egg rolled across my carpet as a scream tore from his throat. I spun just in time to see a cloud of flame barreling toward me before the rift sealed, and it was gone, nothing but a cloud of quickly disappearing smoke. We sat in silence for a moment, except for his ragged breathing, as my gaze shifted to the golden egg gleaming in the candlelight.

"What happened?" I murmured softly.

"I couldn't close it," he said, his tone rough, his eyes hollow with a despair I will remember for the rest of my days. "I tried, Mira. I did everything I could, but it wouldn't let me close it. I don't know why. I'm not trained well enough to understand why. Perhaps because it's another mage's rift. Perhaps the very foundations of that world fight me. Perhaps these beasts do. I know not, but I know I couldn't close it. And I couldn't let them have that thing either."

I nodded, closing my eyes as visions of fire and ash flickered, so many burning cities, so many screaming people. Then I looked at him again. "Them?"

"Another flew through while I was there. I took to the sky and they followed, but I was faster through the thick terrain of the forest, spaces too narrow for their bodies to fit. I led them away then doubled back, getting to the egg just fast enough to make a rift back home and toss us both through."

"We need to destroy it—"

"No," he cut in, placing his hand gently over mine. "Not yet. I think I know what your husband intended to do with them now that I've felt one. His spatio'kine was going to use them as anchors, just as we do living people, for some sort of rift. I know not what, but I pray we can use them to close the one he left open."

"How?"

"I'm not sure. But I promise, Mira, somehow I'll find out."

"I know you will," I said as I closed the distance between us and pulled him into my arms, letting him collapse against my chest as we held each other tight. I pressed my lips to his cheeks, his brow, his hair, murmuring over and over, "I know you will, my love. I know it."

Hours later, we finally moved the egg to where the others remained hidden, stashing it away. We need to take advantage of the next few days, before people begin to suspect my husband's absence for exactly what it is. We will read as much as we can, diving into the most advanced practices of spatio'kine magic ever recorded, and someday Zavier will understand it.

I know he will.

I believe in him with everything I have.

He'll save us.

Second Day of the Ninth Moon

Zavier and I have searched and searched and searched for information on using items as anchors for spatio'kine magic, but we've found nothing. There's got to be a way, something we can use to close the rift. We must keep looking, and we will.

In the meantime, the rift grows.

We spied on the spot, and instead of only two, there were at least two dozen of the beasts that we could see. The once-small door of the rift was now wide enough to easily fit a pair of them through, and the forest around them burned, the skies filling with smoke and ash. They came for their eggs, but now I fear they stay for the richness of our world, a paradise compared to the barren wasteland they left behind. The very earth grows black beneath them, devoid of life, as though they've sucked it into their skin the same way that beast absorbed Bastiant's magic. I fear for the spirit sewn into every fiber of our lands—I fear they will devour it.

Fourth Day of the Ninth Moon

The beasts have come to my city. I don't know how they found us, but they're here. Our mages took them down before too much damage was done, but the battle has only just begun. I know it in my soul.

Seventh Day of the Ninth Moon

Hummingbirds arrived this morning from two of our neighboring kingdoms. The beasts have attacked their cities as well.

I wonder if they're drawn to the magic.

I wonder if they consume it like food.

I wonder a lot about the eggs stashed deep beneath this castle, pulsing with a power this world has never seen. Are they a beacon? Will they be our saving grace or our doom?

Tenth Day of the Ninth Moon

More beasts came, and more hummingbirds too.

Unlike with humans, elemental magic seems to be the most effective against them—puncturing them with metal, burning them with light, dousing them in water. I believe they're drawn to all magic, but they don't absorb it the way they did my husband's power. Maybe they aren't smart enough to know the difference. Maybe animal instinct prevents them from knowing any better. Either way, the most powerful mages in our world, the aethi'kine kings and queens, have been rendered useless in the war to claim it. Spirit magic seems to lure them most of all, and I've already heard of another king falling.

Zavier says the avians are planning to leave now that word of my husband's disappearance has spread. They're fleeing to another kingdom with an aethi'kine still in power, but he won't go with them. His mother begged, but she doesn't understand. It's not about him choosing me. It's about him choosing the world over his own wants and his own desires. It's about his noble heart.

He won't leave the eggs.

He's determined to figure out how to use them.

Sixteenth Day of the Ninth Moon

As I look outside, my city is burning. Twelve more beasts came in a pack, and there were heavy casualties as we tried to fight them. Some of our most powerful mages are gone—the best of them, killed; the worst of them, fled. Most who are left have no magic or a weak amount. When the beasts come back, I don't know how we'll stop them.

Twenty-First Day of the Ninth Moon

We haven't heard from the other kingdoms in days—no hummingbirds carrying messages, no visitors, nothing. Zavier and I peered through spying windows, but it's hard to discern the truth. Other cities burn like ours. Did their mages go into hiding? Will that help or hurt? Half of the skies were free of avians, which makes me think too many of our aethi'kine monarchs attempted to battle the beasts and paid dearly.

I'm slowly losing my best friend. Zavier doesn't sleep. He hardly speaks. He spends all hours of the day in the library, and no one stops him, because the world has gone insane. The advisors are gone, the avians too. It's just the people outside the palace walls who stay, desperate for aid, though there is nothing I can do to help them.

Twenty-Third Day of the Ninth Moon

More beasts came. They reached the palace, burning the throne room just as my visions showed me. Zavier and I had no choice but to flee as the walls crumbled around us. We barely reached the eggs in time to push them through a rift before the walls caved in.

Now I sit beside the spot where we first made love, the moonlight my only guide as I scrawl across this page, one precious bottle of ink left before my words run dry. Nearly a full moon cycle has passed since my husband opened the rift and the beasts first came. One moon cycle. Who would have thought the end of the world would be so swift? Hardly a blink in time? I see flashes of the future, and I know it will take far, far longer to save it.

Eighth Day of the Tenth Moon

We live on the run now, jumping through rifts from place to place, always on the edge of annihilation. The eggs are a beacon, something within them calling out to the beasts no matter what we do. I think it might be more than just magic—I think it's the creatures my husband made, alive in there, growing nearer and nearer to hatching with each passing day. They don't want to be around us. They know, somehow, that we mean them harm. But the beasts will protect them as their own. The beasts will keep them safe long enough for them to destroy us.

Seventeenth Day of the Tenth Moon

There is no good news. Every time we look to the other cities, they are drenched in fire. Mages have dispersed throughout the kingdoms. The avians stick to the high mountains and rugged terrains where the mages aren't likely to travel, hoping to remain under the radar and safe. The beasts grow in numbers, more and more of them flooding the rift with each passing day. The forest is gone, nothing but ebony dirt beneath their claws, burned away, its spirit devoured. I begin to wonder if the world they came from was not the first they've wrecked, and if ours is just another in their path of destruction.

Twenty-Second Day of the Tenth Moon

We are running out of time.

We are running out of time, and I know what I must do, though I hate it with every ounce of my being.

The future calls.

I must find the strength to let it take me.

Twenty-Ninth Day of the Tenth Moon

This is my last entry for I don't know how long, perhaps ever. I thought my hands would tremble. I thought I would be afraid. But I'm not. My head is clear. It's time. So many lives have been lost, so many homes destroyed. I owe it to these people to do what only I can do—to look through time for the answers.

Zavier and I returned to our forest. Though the firebugs were gone, the stars still shone down upon our final hours together. It's hard to believe I have known him less than a year, when it feels as though I couldn't exist without him by my side, as though our souls are so entwined one would not survive without the other. We lay on the sand, every ounce of our bodies and spirits bared for the other to see. It was then, his hand on my cheek and his body above me, his hair falling in waves around his face and his hazel eyes fiercely set on mine, that my first vision came to life. The sight reassured me. We were always meant to be here in this moment together. We were destined for it, which meant somewhere out there, the aether had a plan, and someday, we would see.

"You are my favorite future," I whispered later as I lay in his arms.

"You are my forever," he answered, his strong hands gently caressing my skin. "And no matter how far you travel, I will always bring you back to me."

I hope he can.

I hope he will.

My ink is running low, and I must save some, just in case his words hold true. I pray this is not the end of me, but if it is, I can see no better way to go than carrying the fate of my world in my heart. As soon as I put this quill down, I will sink into my magic and let it carry me away. I will venture into horizons unknown.

Aether be with you.

Goodbye.

47

LYANA

With a gasp, Lyana jolted awake. The hairs on her arms stood. A current lit the air, simmering with power—the devouring might of the rift. The nothingness reached for her, all-encompassing and without end, devoid and barren, trying to pull her under. Heart pounding in her chest, she turned to the balcony just in time to see Rafe land on the stones, his flaming wings bright against the dark night. He pushed through the gauzy curtain with wide eyes and strode into her room. Flicking her fingers, she tamed the fire left in his wake. It was a testament to his panic that he'd let the fabric burn in the first place, his control a tenuous thing.

"It's happening."

"It can't be." She rose from the bed and rushed to him before putting her hand to his arm to still his trembling. "It's only been two weeks since the earthquakes began in the House of Wisdom. It's too soon."

"I know," he said, his voice rough. "But it is. Somehow, it's happening. I can feel the creature waking up. I can feel its mind unfurling. I can feel the others celebrating, the eager glee rushing through their spirits."

"But the owls, they've hardly evacuated. They won't suspect—" Lyana broke off. A lightning bolt zipped down her chest, shocking her to her core as she realized the true source of Rafe's fear. Not the end of the world, but the end of one of the few people in this world who mattered to him. "Xander."

"He's still there." Rafe's voice was small. Fractures spread across his bright blue eyes, as though he were breaking right in front of her. "He's still there, and I can't go to him."

She wanted to tell him to leave, to fly, but the words caught in her throat. All Rafe had ever wanted was to set her free, and now she was the one holding him hostage. He had to stay—the world needed him to stay. She and Malek couldn't fight those creatures on their own.

"The owls live underground. What if— What if—"

"Stop." She took him by the hands. "Nothing is going to happen to Xander, do you hear me? I'll catch the isle. I won't let it sink into the sea. I'll give him the time he needs to escape."

"What if there is no time?" His voice wavered as he turned toward the balcony, his features strained. "They're excited. I can *feel* it. And when the light creature hatches, when it's here—"

"You'll make time, Rafe. Gather the mages. Prepare them for battle. Sound the alarms. Do whatever you need to do, just give me as much time as you can." She brought their cupped hands to her lips and kissed his fingers softly. "For Xander, for me, for the world, you'll find a way."

He dropped his forehead to hers as a shudder passed through him. "Ana."

"Don't," she whispered, taking a moment to breathe in his presence, to memorize what it felt like to have him so close. "Don't say goodbye."

"But—"

"Not like this, Rafe." She held his gaze across the narrow space between them. "Please, not like this. We're going to win. You're going to fight those monsters. I'm going to seal the rift. We're going to save the world. And after we do, you can come find me and tell me all the things you want to say right now—not because it's the end, but because it's the beginning. Our beginning. Can you promise me that?"

He lifted his hand to her face and ran his thumb across her lower lip, the fire in his eyes just as hot as the sparks igniting along her skin. "I promise."

Lyana shifted her face to the side and kissed his palm. The touch was supposed to be brief, but her mouth lingered, hungry for him. Rafe went still as she peppered a trail of kisses down the center of his hand, only stopping once she met the soft skin of his wrist. His scorching pulse drummed rapidly against her lips, making hers race to meet it. Fire lit his blood and her tongue darted out before she could stop it, stoking the flame. Rafe gasped, a strangled sound. With her tongue still against him, Lyana looked up. Passion filled his hooded gaze, the sort that had always lingered between them, daring her to come closer.

She knew the world was ending.

She knew every second was precious.

But more than anything, she knew she would spend the rest of her life, however long it was, regretting this moment if she didn't rise on her toes, close the distance between them, and taste him one last time.

They crashed together as though fate itself had provided a little shove. Rafe growled into her mouth and slid his hand behind the back of her neck, pulling her closer. She moved her arms up his chest and dug her fingers into his hair, angling her face to the side to deepen their kiss. Bodies melded from chest to toe, they fit as though made for one another. His skin blazed. The fire along his wings flared. But it didn't burn her. It stirred something inside her, thawing every hesitation. Warmth pooled in her belly, spreading out along her limbs until she tingled with the heat.

A roar tore across the sky, a reminder of the stakes.

"Go," she mumbled against his lips, but Rafe wouldn't. Not yet. His grip tightened as he reclaimed her mouth. The subtle pull on her braids was more pleasure than pain as he arched her neck up and devoured her protests. Lyana melted against him, the heat of his touch burning through her once more, stimulating every inch of her body. His tongue moved with the precision of a blade, and she met him strike for strike, hungry and demanding.

Another roar pierced the heady drug of their passion.

With a cry, Lyana pulled away.

This time, Rafe let her.

"Go," she whispered, her voice one breath from breaking. Their panting filled the silence as he held her gaze for one more second, time stretching like the final note of a song, lingering even after it was over. She blinked, and he was gone.

Tears stung her eyes, but she willed them away as she ran for the door, ignoring the scorching in her chest, no longer sweet but scathing. Fire burned the back of her throat, worsening every time she tried to draw breath, threatening to break free as a sob. By the time she threw open the door to Malek's study, her heart seemed lost to the flames.

"I felt it," he said, not looking up from the papers strewn across his desk. She knew he'd be awake. "But it's too soon."

"It's not."

At her grave tone, he lifted his head. "What?"

"Rafe felt the beast awaken. It's time."

"It can't be—"

"It is."

Malek jumped to his feet and raced across the room. She let him pull her to their usual spot and dropped beside him on the floor, her muscles giving out as a helplessness she couldn't fight took over. They weren't ready. Not yet. No matter what she'd told Rafe, in this room, with Malek, she stared the truth in the face. How many hours had they sat in this very position, funneling their magic into the rift? They'd made progress, but not enough. It took days to push the rift back what felt like the smallest inch, yet somehow they needed to close it, now, before all was lost.

"Lyana!" Malek snapped. "Focus."

She was focused. For the first time, she was seeing things clearly. *But only on the day when the sky does fall, will be revealed the one who will save you all.* The one. Not the two. Not the king and queen. The one.

They were going to fail. Maybe they were always meant to fail. They couldn't close the rift. They didn't know how. But in the little time they had left, before the creatures came to claim them, she could still fight to save the world—not its dirt and stones and sea, but its people, their hope the only thing more powerful than magic.

"We need to help the House of Wisdom."

"There's no time. We need to go to the rift—"

"No, Malek." Every wilted bone in her body turned to steel, hardening her back into the weapon she knew she was. Time and time again, she'd done as he'd asked. Now he would bend to her iron will. "I need to save the isle."

"Land can be replaced—"

"But not lives. Xander is there. He—"

"Isn't worth the world."

"He *is* the world. Don't you see that, Malek?" Lyana took his hands, letting their magic simmer together as she searched the depths of his slate eyes for a crack, just one glimpse of the man underneath the mantle. "Rafe will need him to keep fighting, to keep going, after we're gone. And the people will need Rafe to keep their faith alive. The rift won't be closed tonight. We both know it, and it's time to stop lying to ourselves. But that doesn't mean the battle is over. We've been looking at this all wrong. The skies have been falling. Your cities have been burning. And we've been ignoring it. We've been too deep in our magic to pay attention. But you can't save the world by abandoning the people you love most, whether it be a city full of owls somewhere high above the clouds, a city full of mages floating in the middle of the sea, or a single man whose love will give our greatest champion a reason to continue living. We can't waste time pushing the rift back another useless inch, not when we can use it to save what matters most—lives. We need to fight for them. *I* need to fight for them, and I need you to fight with me, for however long we have left. Just this once, Malek, I need you to hear me. I need you to trust me."

He opened his mouth, but no sound came out.

Golden magic swelled, spilling through the open balcony into the sky. He stared at her through the haze of their power, his neck muscles strained, his lips flat, his brows set in a hard line even as his soul wavered. A breeze swept in from the outside, loosening a blond lock of hair so it fell over his forehead—and just like that, his carefully crafted walls came undone. All the fear he tried to hide, all the uncertainty, all the loneliness and pain bubbled to the surface as his spirit cried out to her for healing, for help. Her grip on his fingers tightened, as though somehow if she just held on with enough force, she could reach the person he kept hidden deep within. It was just the two of them in this room, and outside the world was dying. He didn't have to carry the burden alone.

She was here.

She was with him.

"Please, Malek," Lyana whispered, willing him to listen. "Please, just trust me."

48

XANDER

The ground fell still. In the absence of groaning stone, an eerie silence settled over Rynthos. Dust clouded the air, swirling with the steady flutter of wings. Fissures snaked across the cavern ceiling. Two of the library columns had crumbled to the ground, leaving vast piles of rubble and books scattered across the streets. Soft cries grew louder, becoming shouts and screams as the shock wore off.

That was bad, Xander thought as he studied the aftermath. *That was far worse than it should have been this early on.*

"King Lysander!"

He spun to find a messenger hovering behind him, garbed in the amber silks of the royal house. Though her speckled brown wings beat steadily, the wringing of her hands gave her anxiousness away.

It's about time, he thought wryly. He'd been in the city for two weeks and King Sylas had yet to summon him. Oh, they'd spoken, of course, but only when Xander managed to chase the man down the halls demanding an audience. If the king was finally calling on him, maybe he'd begun to see reason, and none too soon. Xander had been planning to leave come morning. The ravens needed him alive, and even the promise of so many untapped books had done little to assuage his claustrophobia. This visit to the House of Wisdom had been nothing like his last one, lacking all the previous marvel and awe, leaving an emptiness behind. He couldn't help but wonder if the absence of a certain person by his side made all the difference.

"King Sylas requests your presence in the throne room immed…" The messenger's voice trailed off as her jaw fell open, a look of wonder in her eyes. Gasps rose from the ground below, followed by cheers. The single awe-filled word that fell from her lips made his heart stop beating. "Meteria."

Xander spun.

A being as bright as the sun emerged from the rubble. The light emanating from its pores was nearly blinding. All Xander could decipher was the subtle movement of wings within the glow before he had to look away. Dark spots danced across his vision as a sinking feeling twisted his gut. *No.*

It was too soon.

They weren't ready. He wasn't ready.

"Meteria!" The shouts rose. "Meteria will save us!"

No, she won't. Nothing can save us now.

"Get out!" he shouted as loudly as he could, refusing to let the despair blackening his soul win. He wouldn't stop fighting. He couldn't. "Get out while you still can!"

No one listened.

No one heard.

Every face in Rynthos was turned toward the radiant figure slowly rising higher and higher over the city, pulled like moths to a flame, trapped by their reverence. If he didn't know better, he would have been sucked in too, but all Xander saw in that pure, pulsing ivory was their doom. He turned toward the exit, shouting as he soared above the streets.

"Get out! Get out!"

The seconds ticked on, stretching like a bowstring, the tension mounting in the air as he watched them, and they watched it, and it hovered in place, waiting like a notched arrow for a target.

"Get out!"

Snap!

The creature flew across the air with the speed of a shooting star and disappeared into the entrance of the tunnel leading to the open skies above. Xander chased after it, but he already knew he would be too late. Before he even made it halfway across the city, the House of Wisdom plummeted. He dove with it, all too aware of the yawning ceiling overhead even with his focus securely latched on the dark opening of the exit. The isle fell still. He couldn't gauge how far they'd dropped, but it didn't matter. This was only the beginning.

"Get out," he shouted. "Get to the sky!"

Once more, the city dropped.

Xander plunged, nearly slamming into a building as the isle suddenly steadied. Screams reverberated off the walls, echoing eerily across the cavern. The air turned to chaos, nothing but a mass of beating wings as the owls took flight. But there was nowhere to go, nowhere to run. As one, they raced for the tunnel. Feathers slapped his legs. A foot slammed into his head. Wings muddied his view, mixing with the dusty air until he could neither see nor breathe. Owls were solitary creatures. They were hunters. They didn't think like a flock. They fought for themselves, pushing and shoving to get one extra inch closer. They were more broadly built and faster flyers. Xander quickly fell behind.

No. He pushed his way through the throng. *I need to see Rafe. I need to make sure he knows I love him. And I need to see Cassi. I need to tell her all the things I never got to say. I need to tell Lyana the people believe in her. I need to lead the ravens through the coming war. I need to get out. I need— I need—*

The isle fell.

In the mess, Xander didn't notice until it was too late. He collapsed his wings to his back, colliding with feathers and limbs as he dropped. It wasn't fast enough. Something hard struck the back of his skull. Stars burst across his vision, and he vanished into darkness.

49

RAFE

They arrived in a pack—black, blue, and green wings sifting through the fog as half a dozen dragons flew at their backs. Rafe's throat ran dry at the sight. Instead of charging the castle, they circled Da'Kin, spewing fire in a flaming arch across the sky. The people ran in fear until the streets and canals stood empty, leaving an eerie silence broken only by shattering roars, each one making the air itself tremble.

The creatures weren't hiding anymore, and they weren't rushing, which begged the question of what exactly they *were* doing. Every time he faced them, their strategy grew more sophisticated, as though the human parts deep inside of them were finally waking up.

He didn't like it.

They were strong enough as is.

"Get ready," Rafe said to the mages standing at attention by his side, the king's most prized warriors. Still, he could smell their fear.

Kal leaned closer. "What are they doing?"

"I'm not sure." Rafe frowned, pushing on the mental connection, but their minds were blocked. He could sense them there, but he couldn't break into their thoughts or their communication with each other. All he knew was that the light creature was coming. Its spirit was still unguarded and open as it raced eagerly across the sky. "Just be ready."

As one, the creatures dove, green and black disappearing into the city and blue slipping beneath the sea. The dragons flew up, vanishing into the mist. Magic shot into the air as the mages stationed across Da'Kin readied themselves. They waited, the rainbow display growing brighter and brighter with each passing second. Rafe's stomach tightened with hunger, the power calling out to the dragon in his soul.

That's when he finally understood.

"The mages!" he shouted. "We have to warn them!"

It was too late.

Ripples tore through the canals as water barraged the streets, wave after wave pounding the ships stationed along the edge, their masts tipping precariously to the side even as *hydro'kines* attempted to calm the swells. Green magic lit the skies and an entire building blasted apart, sending the mages inside it flying. On the other side of the city, a swathe of darkness swallowed a garrison whole. One by one, the colorful sparks of magic died out, first red, then blue, then yellow, until there was nothing left but shadow. Eventually that faded too, leaving an empty wooden building creaking along the canals, no sign of movement or life. He didn't want to know what scene was now painted within those walls.

"We have to help!"

Rafe's scream was lost to the roaring as the dragons descended, diving toward the city like comets falling from the skies. They crushed buildings beneath their flaming bodies, then burned the rubble to smithereens.

"We have to do something," he tried again.

Fingers gripped his arm firmly. Jacinta stood by his side, her expression strained as she stared out at the city. "We stay with the king and queen."

"They're ripping our army to shreds."

"Our mages were trained for this."

"No one was trained for *this*."

Ferro'kine magic pulled at the buttons on his jacket, forcing him to turn from the scene. Her deep brown eyes regarded him sternly. "That's what they want—don't you see? They want you to leave the king and queen unguarded."

Rafe clenched his teeth, torn between his instincts and his intellect. The longer the creatures stalled, the more time Lyana had to save the House of Wisdom. It would give Xander a better shot at survival. It would give the world a fighting chance. But with each passing second, the mages of Da'Kin were rapidly disappearing, and what would happen when no one was left? Surely that only made them weaker. They might win today, but what would they do the next time a dragon showed up? The next time those creatures came? How long would they last then?

"I'm going after the shadow creature."

"Alone?" Kal interrupted.

Jacinta tightened her hold on his arm. "Rafe—"

"Stay here and keep an eye out for the other two. You know how to fight them. And keep your fire shields close. I'll be back as soon as I can."

"Rafe!"

He was already airborne, flying toward the black cloud around a nearby garrison. Shrouded in darkness, he couldn't see where he was going, but he could hear the screams and he could feel the savage apathy of the shadow monster. One by one, the mages were struck down, their magic fading from his senses. With his hands outstretched, Rafe searched for a window or a door, any way to get inside, the fire in his wings providing the briefest hint of light. His fingers touched glass and he punched through the surface, not caring when warm blood trickled down his forearm.

"Fight me!" he shouted as he forced his way through the tight opening of the window. "Face me!"

Wicked delight lit the creature's soul. In a flash it was there, too quickly for Rafe to react. Claws dug into his abdomen as he flew back, the pain searing as his jacket quickly got soaked with blood. Beneath his skin, magic flared, rushing to the spot. Talons scraped down his spine, but he caught the scream behind clenched teeth and rolled, kicking out with his feet. They connected. A hiss sounded to his left. Rafe gripped the raven dagger at his waist, the gift from Xander, and dove toward the spot. His hands brushed sharp scales and he plunged the blade blindly in the dark.

The shadows receded.

The creature was right next to him, gripping the hilt of the blade lodged in its shoulder. Its head snapped up as its magic vanished, leaving it exposed. Before Rafe had time to attack, the demon rushed him. Ebony wings thrashing, it gripped Rafe by the jacket and flew across the room to slam his back into the wall. The flames caught dry wood and fire ignited.

"Get out!" Rafe shouted, for the first time noticing the crimson splashes and splatters on the walls. Bodies littered the floor. "If anyone's alive, get out now!"

Sharp claws reached for his throat and he went for the dagger, twisting it then ripping it free. With a howl, the creature dropped him. Rafe took the opening and dug his shoulder into the beast's chest. They fell to the floor, a mess of scales and wings as the fire blazed brighter around them. Smoke drew a haze across the room. Crackling and grunts filled the silence as they wrestled, unbothered by the heat. No matter how the creature cut him, he healed, but Rafe couldn't say the same for it. If he could just get an opening, one fatal blow was all it would take. One good strike.

The house exploded.

Water tore through the floorboards, launching Rafe and the creature up through the burning ceiling and into the sky. As the torrent encircled him, the shadow beast broke free. He tried to follow, but the liquid wrapped around him like chains. Blue sparks cut across the stream. Just as quickly, the gushing spew vanished and he fell through the fog until his wings caught the air. High atop the castle, Nyomi's glowing fingers spun. By her side, Kal sent a beam of pure light across the sky. It missed.

Where is it? Where is it?

Rafe pulled on the bond at the back of his mind, sensing something to his right. A moving sliver of darkness caught his eye and he raced for the spot.

Watch me, Kal. Watch me.

The *photo'kine* must have sensed his call because the next moment, a blinding ivory wave stole his sight. Pain stung at the back of his thoughts as his ears filled with a wail. Rafe surged ahead, his *invinci* magic providing a cooling relief as the energy bit into his exposed skin. His hand found an ankle. The creature kicked him away. Rafe pumped his wings, stretching his arm as far as it could go. His fingers brushed scales—

Something slammed into him from the side.

Arms enveloped his waist as talons dug into his back. Together they crashed into the streets below, slamming hard against the moist wooden planks. Rafe expected to find darkness, but when he opened his eyes, they burned from the glow.

The light creature was here.

It charged, on him in a heartbeat. Rafe closed his eyes, the glare still so bright his world turned red, and blindly reached out with his hands. Claws slashed his shoulder, then his stomach. Hands gripped him by the waist and tossed him. Rafe rolled over the ground, his wings crunching painfully. Teeth dug into his calf and pulled. He screamed as his flesh split. The attacks came too fast for him to think. Magic rushed beneath his skin, but he feared it might not be enough. The scent of copper filled his nose as he rolled in a pool of his own blood, the liquid sticky against his hands. More gurgled in the back of his throat. Rafe coughed, tasting iron.

The shadow beast had never left him so outmatched.

Why? Why?

Realization dawned—because he himself was part shadow.

No time to think, Rafe reached deep inside, remembering the bird still housed within his soul, and released his raven cry. The magic spilled from his lips and flooded into the world. A wail sounded. The blinding light dimmed enough for Rafe to slip open his eyes. The white creature gripped its ears, shaking its head as his raven power fuddled its mind. The only way to fight light was with darkness, and he released his cry again, uncaring of who else might be caught in its path. The beast before him was the only thing that mattered and the more Rafe pushed his raven magic into the world, the more it faltered, whipping its head from side to side, its distress funneling through the bond.

Pushing off on all fours, Rafe staggered forward. The creature shifted its wings, but so confused, it couldn't fly. The darkness stole its thoughts and its control. It stumbled and dropped to its knees along the street, ivory scales staining red with Rafe's blood, still pooled below. He reached for the twin blades strapped to his back, cursing his magic for reacting so slowly as his muscles screamed at him to rest.

But he couldn't.

There was no time.

With each step he released a new cry, the sound stretching across the sky. Any moment, the shadow monster would come to save its brethren, and he couldn't fight them both. Rafe limped closer, only stopping when the creature was within reach of his swords. A hilt in each hand, he crossed the metal in an *x*. Then, in one swift move, he slashed with all the strength he could muster.

The bond was the first thing to sever. Next went the head,

sliding slowly from the creature's shoulders to hit the ground with a *thunk*. And last, the body, falling lifelessly to the side. Ivory liquid spilled across the wooden planks, turning the blood on the streets pink as they mixed. In the back of his thoughts, the other creatures wailed.

Rafe smiled.

I guess they can be killed, after all.

He swayed and dropped his sword points to the ground to keep from falling, taking a few precious moments to breathe as his magic coursed through him. When he finally looked up, the castle was gone. No golden power lit the skies, no rainbow sparks. The center of Da'Kin was a raging swarm of shadow.

50

LYANA

Magic pulsed from Lyana's body as she fought to keep the House of Wisdom from slipping beneath the sea. The jagged cliffs on the underside of the isle transformed into open wounds her *aethi'kine* power sought to heal. The sands along the ocean floor rose and hardened. Inch by inch, the home of the owls settled back into the earth from which it had once been ripped, reconnecting as though it'd never been separated in the first place. The sensation calmed her soul, as though finally she was doing something right, something worthy, and that was when the realization hit.

Healing. Of course, healing.

It was written in the prophecy. It had been there all along.

Together they will heal that which we broke.

All this time, they'd been thinking of saving the isles and closing the rift as two separate things—to Lyana, the first a far-off dream, and to Malek, nothing but a distraction. Yet the ideas were the same. They were connected. The spell holding the isles aloft was the spell keeping the rift contained, and one couldn't be fixed without the other. That was why her magic was useless against the growing void, why it was taking her and Malek so long to push back the abyss. The isles were the rift and the rift was the isles, and in order to save the world they had to first put it back together. That was her role. That was her job. To *heal.* According to the prophecy, someone else would come to defeat the dragons, to save them all, but only after the sky fell. Not just a handful of isles, but all of them.

The House of Peace.

Aethios's god stone was the keystone holding the spell together and keeping the rift at the bottom of the sea. As long as it remained in the sky, the world would never heal. That barren void, that poisonous abyss, would keep spreading. But if she returned the isle to its rightful place, if she lifted the rift from the depths, if she stopped the bleeding, maybe the rest of the puzzle would fall into place.

I have to go to Sphaira.

There was a reason Lyana had been born a dove. A reason she'd been raised in the halls of the crystal palace, granted access to the sacred nest by birth. A reason she'd been given an adventurous spirit, spending her youth learning how to sneak into and out of her home. And this was it. She could *feel* it, as though the very spirit of the world were urging her down this path, urging her to carry on, to take this leap of faith, to believe her wings and will would be there to catch her. Everything in her life had been leading to this moment, this decision, and all she had to do was make it.

I'm ready.

Lyana withdrew from her magic, praying she'd done enough to save Xander, but there was no time to waste. Not for him. Not for Rafe. Not even for herself. Now that she knew what she was meant to do, she couldn't delay another moment. Not if it risked the world.

She opened her eyes to pitch black.

A claw wrapped around her throat and the golden power flooding her veins simply vanished. Sharp talons dug into her skin as the fingers squeezed, cutting off air. She tried to scream, to alert Malek, but no sound escaped her lips. Gripping the slick scales, she pushed the creature away, but without her magic she was weak. The shadows around her receded, until an onyx arm slipped into view, then a chest, then a head. She kicked and squirmed, but the grip around her throat was as unbreakable as iron. Its arm didn't even budge. Darkness swirled in a vortex around them as the creature pulled her closer, opening its mouth so its ivory teeth gleamed against black lips. Her throat burned. Those bottomless eyes stared into hers, almost as though it wanted to watch the life leave her, something vengeful about their obsidian gleam.

Movement caught her eye.

A silver sword carved through the spinning shadow. Her vision started to spot. The creature leaned closer, hissing. As it shifted its head to the side, Rafe stepped free of the darkness. Her heart leapt in her throat, but Lyana willed her face to remain still lest she give him away. He lifted his finger to his lips, signaling silence, then arched his sword overhead.

As the blade came slashing down, the shadow creature tossed her aside and spun. It caught the metal edge in its palm, seemingly unconcerned as the weapon sliced through its scales. Rafe pulled back and attacked again. Lyana didn't see if his blade struck true. The world descended into darkness again, leaving her blind. Grunts and hisses echoed across the void. As much as she wanted to help, she had to trust that Rafe could handle this fight himself.

"Malek!" Lyana called through the black. "Malek!"

He didn't answer.

Diving into her magic, she reached for his spirit. He was close. He was alive, just too deep in his own power to hear her call. Lyana crawled across the floor on her hands and knees, using his soul as a guide as she crossed over the rug, not stopping until her fingers found a warm body. She shook him by the shoulders.

"Malek! Come back. Malek!"

A gasp escaped his lips as the magic flooding from his spirit drew back. She knew the moment he opened his eyes because his soul flashed with panic. "Lyana?"

"I'm here," she answered, skimming her hand down his arm until she found his fingers. "I'm right here."

"What's going on? Where—"

"The shadow creature is here. Rafe is fighting it. We don't have much—"

The darkness vanished, but there was no time to turn around and see why. Malek's stormy eyes regarded her fiercely, as though he knew she had more to say. The battle at her back might as well have been in a different realm for all the regard he gave it. There was no fear in his spirit, only iron determination as he tightened his grip on her palm.

"I know what to do, Malek," she said. "We have to get to Sphaira. We have to return all the isles to their rightful place upon the sea and lift the rift from the ocean floor. We have to heal the world. That's the only way to save it."

"But the spell, the rift—"

"I know," she cut in. "I know it sounds crazy. The spell is the only thing keeping us from complete ruin, but it's keeping us from victory too. I can't explain how I know. I just do."

His sandy brows drew together, carving a deep groove above the bridge of his nose. "If we do this, the *aethi'kine* creature will be freed."

"I know."

"And yet you're certain?"

He'd trusted her enough to send his magic to the House of Wisdom instead of the rift. Somehow, he would trust her enough to do this too. "It's the only—"

A mangled cry stole her voice.

Lyana spun.

Rafe stood with his back to her in the opening of the balcony.

One of his wings was bent in half, the bone shattered as the leathery expanse dragged along the floor. The shadow creature stood behind him. For the first time, she noticed the deep maroon stains upon his clothes. How many wounds had his magic healed? How many still bled? He swayed on unsteady feet, fighting to keep his balance. It was no use. The creature shoved and Rafe stumbled through the door. His hips hit the stone rail and his body tumbled over the side.

"Rafe!" she screamed, her magic already chasing after him.

The shadow creature stepped in its path, absorbing the golden glow within its onyx scales. With a hiss, she retreated, the merest touch of its soul burning her to the core.

"Rafe…" she whimpered.

Even if he did hear, he wasn't coming to save her. Not this time. The shadow creature raced across the room, a claw outstretched. Lyana winced and closed her eyes.

The strike never landed.

"Go!" Malek screamed.

Tendrils of his golden magic wrapped around the shadow creature and held it in a vicelike grip. He grunted, denying the scream surging up his throat. Lyana whipped around to face him, a protest rising to her lips.

"Malek, you can't—"

"Go, Lyana," he ordered. The peach skin of his face was already turning red. As she watched, a boil bubbled along his neck, his flesh burning from the inside out. The tips of his fingers blackened. Wavy blond locks dropped to the floor as his scalp melted. "I can't hold them for long. Go! Now! You're the Queen Bred of Snow and you're going to save the world. So, leave! Fly! And don't you dare waste time looking back."

She did waste a moment, but just one to memorize the faith and trust shining in his eyes like the sun after a storm. Then she turned and flapped her wings as she took to the sky.

51

CASSI

The *skryr* lay still as the world outside their window burned. Cassi had hardly left the room in two weeks, except to scavenge food from the tavern downstairs. He'd nearly reached the end of the diary—and she'd been right. It *was* important. The author was the prophetess herself, and her memories told the story of the end of everything, or maybe the beginning, depending on how one looked at it.

Come on. Come on.

Cassi's knee bounced, making the floor squeak, as she stared at the *skryr*'s impassive expression. Bronze magic glittered around his fingertips and simmered in the air above his body. There was no telling how soon he'd wake. Sometimes he spent a few hours deep in his power. Sometimes it was only minutes. This time, he'd been asleep for nearly a day. They'd eaten a quick lunch together the afternoon before as he described the chaos of the dragons flooding through the rift, the mages scattering, and the avians hiding; all while the prophetess and the riftmaker shuffled the eggs around, trying to avoid detection. They'd shared one final night together before she bid farewell to her sanity and let her *chrono'kine* magic consume her.

And that was the last Cassi had heard.

As soon as the *skryr* had finished eating, he'd reached for the diary, ready to uncover its end. There was only a single entry left, not overly long and hastily scribbled, the writing messier and heavy handed. Foolishly, she'd thought it wouldn't take long. But the man had been deep in his power for hours, and the memories stored within those final pages must have been vast indeed, because he showed no signs of waking anytime soon.

Oh, come on!

Cassi flicked her gaze to the window again. Fire danced across the rooftops of Da'Kin. A roar split the sky, rattling the glasses on the bedside table. The room bounced, the building unsteady as the tides below shifted unnaturally, a rising and falling that could only be caused by magic. A battle was clearly taking place outside the inn. It was against her nature to sit and hide, to do nothing, but this final diary entry held the key to everything. Cassi didn't know how she knew—instinct, a gut feeling, sheer hope—but she did.

Still, the wait was killing her.

She twiddled her thumbs. She counted the floorboards running parallel across the room. She traced the cracks in the plaster walls. She closed her eyes, trying to recall the lullaby her mother used to sing, something about foggy seas and the soft whipping of sails as the magic guided her home. Just when she was about to give in and slip into her spirit body to figure out what exactly was going on outside, *aethi'kine* power lit the skies.

Cassi jumped to her feet and ran to the window.

Golden sparks stood bright against the fog, dazzling as they rushed in steady streams toward the dragons torching the city. The magic wrapped around the beasts and they froze, moving nothing but their wings as they hovered in midair. The shadow creature emerged from the tallest spire of the castle, surrounded in a metallic glow. Its ebony wings pushed slowly through the haze, as if facing strong winds. Two more creatures rose from the rooftops, also fighting against the magic.

No.

No.

No.

Cassi threw open the glass and leaned her head out, trying to taste the spirit in the air. A breeze ruffled her hair, carrying the scent closer.

Malek, she realized. *It's Malek.*

Relief washed through her, followed by something she'd never expected—grief. It cut sharp and deep, stealing the breath from her lungs as she pictured him alone in that tower, his flesh burning, his body dropping, his power flooding out to the world in one final act of stubborn control. The man had tortured and abused her. He'd been her greatest dream and her worst nightmare, her first love and her fiercest rival, her dearest friend and her diabolical king. And now he was dying. Cassi didn't know where Lyana had gone, or what had happened to Rafe, or why Malek had chosen this fate, but she knew enough to understand that the dragons were killing him, and, for the world, he was letting them.

"I have to go."

The words spilled out before she could stop them. Unlike in the world above, where each window was crafted for access, the one in this inn was too small for her body, let alone her wings, to squeeze through. Heart thumping, she spun, the world blurring as her thoughts rushed too fast to process. The *skryr* lay still on the bed, his bronze magic flowing. The fate of the world might very well rest on his remaining alive, but she couldn't sit in this room any longer. Not when Malek—not when he—

Cassi scrawled a hasty note explaining she'd be back, in case he woke before her return, and then she took the stairs two at a time. Distantly, she recognized that if the dragons were trying to chase

Lyana across the skies, the danger was over for Da'Kin. As soon as that golden power winked out, they'd be gone. Still, she grabbed the innkeeper by the collar on her way out.

"If you let anything happen to the man in my room upstairs, I'll end you. I'm one of the king's *dormi'kines*, and now that I know the scent of your soul, there's nowhere in all the skies or the seas where I wouldn't find you. No one goes into his room. No one comes out. Deliver his meals to the door and keep your mouth shut. I'll be back."

She ran.

Emerging from the cramped first-floor tavern, Cassi spread her wings and took to the sky, no longer worried who might see. Her singular focus was on getting to that tower before—before—

Just before.

As she flew across the city, the *aethi'kine* power on the wind faltered. The golden beams flickered. The dragons and creatures roared, fighting against its hold. Just as she crossed over the castle wall, it faded entirely. In a blink, the beasts disappeared into the mist.

No!

Cassi swept into Malek's study, her heart fortified against what she'd find inside, but nothing could have prepared her for this. He lay crumpled on the floor, unrecognizable. His fingers had melted down to the bone. Boils covered his neck. His exposed flesh was raw and running like hot wax. A dusting of blond hair surrounded him, the tendrils rising into the air as her feathers caused a draft. His scalp was bloody and bald. He shivered, his body in pure shock.

Her breath hitched. She froze, unsure whether to run to him or turn away. He'd always loomed like some sort of invincible god in the back of her thoughts, but now, at the end, she realized he was just as human as the rest of them.

"Malek?"

He flinched on the floor.

Cassi broke and dashed across the room before falling to her knees beside him. Oh, what she wouldn't give for Lyana's healing touch, to ease his pain if nothing else. As it was, she hovered her hands above his broken body, unsure if touching him would help or hurt.

"Malek, I'm here," she whispered. "You're not alone."

"R— R— R—"

"It's okay," she soothed. "You don't have to say anything. You don't—"

"Rafe," he wheezed, the name more breath than voice, but she heard.

"Rafe? What about Rafe? Did he leave with Lyana? Where'd they go?"

"B— B— Bring…"

Footsteps sounded behind her. Cassi glanced over her shoulder, finding Jacinta in the doorway with wide eyes, horror written across her normally severe features. Tears already streamed down her cheeks, but the flow strengthened at the sight of her king, as though this were the confirmation she'd been dreading.

"Is Rafe here?" Cassi asked, but Jacinta showed no signs of hearing as she stared unblinkingly at Malek. Cassi tried again, more loudly. "Jacinta! Is Rafe here?"

"What? Rafe?"

"He just told me to bring Rafe. Is he here? In Da'Kin? I thought Lyana must have left. Why isn't he with her?"

"I don't—" The metal mage broke off, shaking her head. "I'm not—"

"Listen to me," Cassi interrupted, unused to seeing the woman so helpless. But Malek had been her world, her entire belief system, and now he was moments from his end. "There isn't much time. I know you loved the king and I know you believed in him, so snap out of it and heed his final wishes. Rafe is close. He's got to be. Find him and bring him here immediately. Go!"

The mage took off running.

Cassi turned back to Malek and watched him tremble on the rug, still not sure if she should touch him—or if she could. After everything he'd done to her, she thought she'd be cheering when he finally found his demise. She thought she would ache to deliver the last blow. She thought she'd feel free. Instead, the burden sat heavy at the back of her throat, a tight knot robbing her of her voice as a burning sensation needled at her eyes. Looking at him now, she didn't see the king who'd coldly stolen her sky, who'd commanded her to murder and lie, who'd whispered in her ear as he forced his mages to torture her awake. She saw the boy who'd run with her through fields of wildflowers under a purple sky, who'd drawn rainbows across her dreams and made it rain candy, who'd held her hand on the grass while they studied sugar-spun clouds and shared secrets no one else would understand—about their parents, their fears, and the world they would build together.

His hand found hers and clutched it with surprising strength. She tried to ignore how hot his skin felt, how it squelched when they touched, and the blood that ran down her fingers.

"R— R—"

"Jacinta will find him," Cassi said. "They'll bring him."

"No," he said with sudden clarity, his throat raspy and his breath short, but his voice somehow carrying strength. "King."

"King?"

"Rafe. King," he repeated, more adamant.

Cassi exhaled softly, the realization somehow making her heart hurt for him more. No one, not even Malek, deserved to find his entire life a lie right at its very end. "Rafe is the king. He's the King Born in Fire."

"He. Lyana. Sphaira."

The words were broken and cracked, but she understood. "He needs to go after Lyana. She went to Sphaira."

He nodded, coughing as his body convulsed. "I—tried—"

"You did, Malek," she urged, squeezing his fingers even if it caused him pain, because he had to understand. In the end, when it mattered most, he'd given up everything to save the world. "You held them. She got away. And Rafe will be here any moment. I'll tell him what you said. He'll protect her. He'll keep her safe. And because of you, they'll see the prophecy through."

His hand went limp in her lap. The edges of his burned lips twitched into the ghost of a smile. When he opened his eyes to look at her, they were the same as she remembered, as tumultuous and deep as the sea, a vast pool she could lose herself within. But there was a difference too. They were open and honest, too aged to belong to the boy of her youth, more like a glance of the man she'd always hoped he might become.

"You," he said, his voice losing vigor as his body grew slack. "Dreams. F— F—"

Your dreams have always been my favorites.

It wasn't an apology, but she'd never expected one from him. In truth, she wouldn't have believed it if he'd offered one. He wasn't sorry. As long as the world was safe, even at his end, he would never be sorry for the things he'd done or the people he'd hurt. So maybe he didn't deserve what she was about to do, or maybe he did, she wasn't sure, but she knew she'd always regret it if she remained silent. Whether she felt this way or not, she hoped one day she would, and by then, it would be too late to tell him.

"I forgive you," Cassi murmured, keeping hold of his hand as she said the words she so longed to hear from everyone she'd ever wronged, all the friends and lovers and even enemies she prayed would someday understand why she'd done the things she'd done—that, whether right or wrong, her actions had all been in the name of saving the world, same as her king's. "I forgive you, Malek. For everything."

He tensed and then relaxed against the floor.

Voices carried down the hall, then the heavy shuffling of boots. A group of mages stomped into the room, moving as one while flames simmered between them. It took a moment for her to recognize the body draped over their arms and the leathery wing dragging across the floor. Isaak stood at the front, drawing Rafe's fire into his arms to keep it from burning the others.

"We found him unconscious on the rocks," the fire mage hastened to explain. "We don't know how or why—"

"Drop him here, now," Cassi ordered, indicating the spot next to Malek. The king had known Rafe was injured. He'd known Rafe had fallen. And he'd held on with everything he had so, with these last few breaths, he could save him.

Cassi took Malek's lifeless arm and placed it on Rafe's chest.

For a moment, nothing happened.

She feared they'd been too late.

Then a golden wave burst from his palm and enveloped Rafe. The air prickled with the power, nearly pushing Cassi over with the force. The magic was as ferocious as it was brief, disappearing in a blink. Malek's arm slid to the floor. His head lolled to the side. Next to him, Rafe jolted awake and jumped to his feet.

"Lyana!"

"She's gone," Cassi said, then swallowed the knot in her throat as she rushed to stand. "She went to Sphaira. I don't know why, and the creatures went after her. Malek bought her some time, but I'm not sure how much. You have to go, Rafe. Now. You're the King Born in Fire and she needs you."

"I—" He broke off, his gaze dropping to the body at his feet, then shifting to the window before settling back on Cassi. A pained expression pulled at his features. "Xander's in trouble. He was in the House of Wisdom when it fell, and I'm not sure if Lyana was able to settle the isle in time. Please, Cassi, go to him. Make sure he's all right. Do this for me, and everything between us will be even. Save him, and nothing else matters."

"I will."

Without another word, Rafe took off. A heavy silence followed his departure, the mages at her back and the king at her feet now looming in the quiet. Cassi turned, meeting the eyes of Malek's closest advisors. Jacinta. Isaak. Nyomi. Kal. Viktor. The people she had spent most of her life studying, envying, sometimes hating, because they got to see him in the light. To them, she was little more than a name he sometimes spoke, just another *dormi'kine*, one of many, yet they watched her expectantly now, as though she might hold the answers.

She didn't, not even close.

But she did have a lifetime's worth of knowledge of pretending.

"The king is dead," she told them, not harshly but honestly, because it was the sort of thing one needed to hear to believe. "And with his dying breaths, he proclaimed Rafe the King Born in Fire. The world might end tomorrow for all I know, but until it does, we need to do everything we can to continue the fight. There's no time to mourn. He wouldn't want that. Instead, go out into the city and do what you can to help. Rebuild. Regroup. Send a team to the Salty Clam Inn. The *skryr* is in a room on the top floor, at the end of the hall on your left. Protect him at all costs, and make sure he doesn't try to run. As soon as I get back, I need to speak with him."

"Where are you going?" Nyomi asked, stepping forward.

"To keep my promise," she said, already arching for the sky. Xander's name whispered through her thoughts, louder and louder with each passing second. He was in danger, and she would go to him. Not for Rafe, but for herself. "There's a raven out there who needs me."

52

LYANA

The crystal city was just as she remembered, gleaming beneath a sun-drenched sky, a symbol of hope and peace and light. Soon it would be bathed in fire. Fur-clad doves soared across the glittering rooftops, not a care in the world. Before long, they would cower in fear.

Lyana swallowed the tightness in her throat, unable to imagine her childhood home surrounded by fog and flames. But she knew what she'd brought by coming here. She knew what followed her on the wind. Time was the only thing on her side. The quicker she acted, the quicker it would all be over and the quicker the people of both worlds would be safe.

With that in mind, she dove for the nondescript dome on the northern edge of the city, fighting a chill as the cool air rushed over her body. Her clothes had been made for humidity and heat, and the cold was already nipping at her bones. When she landed on packed snow, her toes immediately prickled with the sting.

I miss my boots.

The thought was so silly it almost made her laugh. But she did. She missed her boots, and her furs, and all the other things that reminded her of home. Never in a million years would she have thought she'd be returning like this—sneaking into her own house to bring about its ruin.

Lyana threw open the door.

"What—" The guard stationed inside immediately jumped to his feet. Upon seeing her, he froze, confusion twisting his features. "Princess Lyana. I mean, Your Majesty."

He sank into a deep bow, his tawny wings spreading wide as a sign of respect.

"Please, don't," she said and stepped forward, her heart jerking wildly. She was about to end the only world he'd ever known. She didn't deserve his admiration.

The guard stood. "What are you doing here? The king and queen will—"

"No," Lyana interrupted. Invisible to him, her golden magic took hold of the spirit glittering inside his chest. Though he didn't move, fear flashed in his russet eyes. Swallowing back her disgust, she pushed on, aware that with every wasted moment her head start was disappearing. "I know you don't understand, and I'm sorry for that, but no one can know I'm here. So I need you to go out that door and fly until you reach the very end of the House of Peace, until there is nothing but open skies beneath you, and only then can you even think about coming back. Go, now."

He left, heeding her orders.

The command would wear off, probably by the time he reached the sky bridge, but by then the fighting would have already started.

Lyana shut the door behind him and ran down the tunnel, keeping her wings tight to her back in the cramped corridor. She knew every inch of the secret passage. Even in the dark, her steps didn't falter. The last time she'd been there was on the dawn of the courtship trials, when she and Cassi had snuck out of the palace to spy on the arriving houses. Little had she known then what fate had in store for them. That morning had changed her life. But here, now, racing toward her destiny, Lyana had the sense that everything had happened exactly as it was supposed to, as though guided by the gods' own hands.

She reached the end of the passage and pressed her palms to the trapdoor, searching for the latch. At this time of the day, the palace should be quiet, not much activity except for servants shuffling between the rooms. Still, she cringed when the *click* reverberated through the silence and slowly eased the door open a crack. Wielding her magic, she stretched out with her senses, feeling for all the souls currently fluttering across the crystal dome.

Leave the main atrium.

Don't turn back.

Get inside a room, lock the door, and stay there until the danger has passed.

The order was subtle enough that it would seem innate to most, only appearing strange as it started to wear off and they wondered why they'd locked themselves away. By then, the dragons would be here, and they'd have far more to worry about.

She waited a few moments for the gentle rustling of feathers to fade, then strode into the main atrium. A deep breath filled her lungs at the sight of her home, overwhelming in its midafternoon glory. The sun cast a dazzling glow upon the mosaic floor, so from floor to ceiling the might of Aethios shone through. Lyana drew on that strength as she soared to the entrance of the sacred nest. Normally, the door, towering thirty feet high, would be too heavy for a single person to move, but with her magic she gripped the spirit of the wood and it glided silently open, just far enough for a single dove to slip through. A resounding *thud* echoed across the stones as it slid closed, loud despite the chirping of birds and the rustling of leaves. At the end of the hall, just behind the ornate gilded gate, a priestess waited in flowing ivory robes, almost as though she'd known Lyana would come. The trees beyond were backlit by the golden glow of the god stone hiding within.

"Open the gate," Lyana commanded, her magic giving the words weight.

The priestess complied, slipping a key from around her neck and inserting it into the lock. The bars swung open, and Lyana stepped inside.

"Now close it," she ordered, guilt coiling inside her at treating one of Aethios's chosen with such little respect. But there was no time. The power of the stone thrummed from the center of the nest, urging her closer, calling out to her the way it always had. "Find the other priests and priestesses, and lock yourselves in your sleeping quarters. Don't return to the sacred grove until I say you can. It's not safe."

As the priestess disappeared around the perimeter of the large room, Lyana stepped between the trees. Leaves crunched under her feet as doves cooed overhead, their gentle calls almost like a blessing. Warm light streamed through the branches, a mix of the sun and the stone, sparkling with the hint of magic. The pulsing in the air drew her in, luring her closer as her heartbeat shifted to the same rhythm.

There, in the very center of the sacred nest, waited the brilliant golden egg she'd been looking for. It hung suspended in the air, oozing power. Deep in her spirit vision, she no longer viewed the stone as an emblem of her god. Now it was the center of the rift spell. Threads unspooled from the orb in a spectrum of rainbow weaves, some dim, some blinding, all burning with power. Letting her hands hover above the smooth metallic surface, Lyana felt connected to it all. The rift waiting thirty thousand feet below, drowning beneath the sea. The remaining stones keeping the House of Song and House of Prey afloat. Even the creatures, no longer connected to the spell but still connected to the beings housed within the eggs, just waiting to hatch. She could feel them racing closer. She could feel the *aethi'kine* creature pulling them in. They were a part of this, just as much as she was. Everything was connected. The isles. The rift. Their souls. It was a vast puzzle she was on the verge of solving.

Yet she hesitated.

What if I'm wrong?

Blood pounded in her ears as her fingers twitched a mere inch above the egg. The *aethi'kine* power seeping from inside wrapped around her, telling her not to stop, to keep down this path, to give in. Was it Aethios? Was it the creature? Was it her own intuition? There was no way to be sure. It was a leap of faith, a belief in the prophecy and in herself, a trust that despite all her faults, she knew what she was doing. Love had always guided her—a love for adventure, a love for the world, a love for its people—and that love had led her here.

People were dying. Their souls called out to her for aid.

The world was suffering. Even now, the black abyss at the center of the rift claimed more and more of its beautiful spirit.

The unknown was calling, and she had no choice but to answer.

Aethios, be with me.

Lyana swallowed and took a deep breath as she lowered her fingers to the stone. *Aethi'kine* power rushed through her like a windstorm unleashed. Her body snapped back even as her palms remained stuck to the surface, connected to the power in a way she couldn't control. Her magic fled from her spirit, draining into the egg. The trees disappeared. The doves vanished. The grove fell away. Her vision ran gold as the glittering power pulled her under. There was no way to fight, no way to stop. All she could do was spread her spirit wings and fly as the torrent carried her forward.

53

BRIGHTY

"Put 'er there, Sparky," Brighty said as she lifted her hand toward the young *photo'kine* sitting across from her on the floor. The perfectly controlled white orb hovering between them vanished in a blink as the girl leaned forward and slapped her palm into Brighty's, a self-conscious smile on her lips.

Oh, for magic's sake, Brighty internally cursed as her chest warmed at the contact. *Not this again.*

She'd told herself she was done taking in strays. Ever since Rafe had abandoned them to fly directly into the path of constant danger, she'd been in a state of emotional upheaval, oscillating between worrying over his safety and ruing the day he'd been born. It was exhausting. Honestly, fighting dragons was less draining than this constant gnawing fear that came with caring about people. Brighty was over it.

And yet, when a girl with deep mocha feathers speckled with copper highlights walked into their guest cottage, her eagle wings too large for her gangly little frame, Brighty had taken one look into her pearlescent eyes and caved. The mark of a *photo'kine* was too obvious to ignore. Under Captain's sharp, scrutinizing gaze, she'd mumbled a begrudging, "Fine," and stomped across the room to welcome their newest recruit. That had been about a week and a half ago, and already the girl had needled her way into her heart.

What in magic's name is happening to me?

She was hiding in the middle of a city full of powerful avians who loathed magic. She was living on an isle hovering fifteen thousand feet above the sea and ready to drop. She was pretty certain the world was in the process of ending. Now was *not* the time to turn soft.

"All right, all right," she grumbled, her grouchy tone wiping the girl's smile right off. *That's more like it.* "It's a start, but don't get too cocky. You're a long way from lighting a dragon's ass on—"

"Language!" Captain interrupted.

Brighty jolted and glanced over her shoulder. The woman missed nothing. "Sorry, Cap."

Honestly, she'd heard worse by the time she was five. Then again, not everyone grew up running wild along the docks of Da'Kin.

"How's the training going?"

"Great!" Sparky chirped. Oh, the enthusiasm of youth.

Brighty frowned. "It's going."

"Let me see."

"All right…" Brighty trailed off as she scanned the room. They'd painted the crystals black in this central atrium of the building to keep out any peeping eyes, so the magic glowed vividly despite the midday hour. Sparks of every color danced about the shadows as Pyro worked with her group of fire mages, and Leech his trio of earth mages, and Archer his two *ferro'kines*. Spout was no longer allowed in here with her buckets of water after she'd sprayed the entire room during a sneezing fit—twice! Her set of *hydro'kines* was relegated to their own space down the hall. No *electro'kines* had stepped forward, so Jolt was usually the one surveying the progress, though Captain must have taken over. Her air mages were huddled in the corner following Patch's lead, just Brighty's luck.

"There."

She pointed to a glass lantern on the floor by Pyro and her fire mages. The wick wasn't lit, and the container was a perfect test of control. Too much light and it would shatter. Too little and the glow would die out. Just enough and a wonderfully self-sustaining ball of energy should be able to live inside there for a few hours.

"Let's see if you can set some mage light from a distance."

The girl nodded and scrunched her face in concentration, every ounce of her tiny body straining with the effort. Brighty snorted softly because, magic help her, it was endearing. Captain caught her eye, a subtle questioning arch to her brow. Brighty wrinkled her nose and turned her focus to the beam of light racing across the room.

Too much.

Too much!

She winced before the glass even cracked, anticipating the explosion. When the lantern shattered, a blast of power cut through the air, so forceful it stole Brighty's breath, and every mage in the room froze.

"I didn't—" Sparky sputtered. "I mean, was that—"

"Shh!"

Brighty held up her finger, demanding silence as the magic simmered across the dark and a subtle golden sheen lit the room. *Aethi'kine* magic. Here. This was bad. This was—

The ground shook violently and Brighty stumbled to find her balance. Rustling feathers filled the silence as the avians around her used their wings to steady themselves. Archer and Jolt dropped to their knees. Captain took off running.

"Stay!" Brighty ordered her apprentice, then raced to follow, pushing through the door already closing behind Captain Rokaro. If she were anyone else, the shocking switch from darkness to full sun would have blinded her or stung her eyes, but light was her magic. A gasp escaped her lips just before the captain's as the two of them took in the view through the crystals.

Dragons.

From their location at the edge of the city, the house had an uninterrupted view of the barren tundra beyond. Every other day, it had been filled with nothing but ice, rock, and clear, open skies. Now flames sparked on the horizon as six beastly bodies rushed toward them. In the mist, they never would have seen them coming. But up here where clouds were rare and the blue was endless, there was no mistaking the sight.

"The queen?" Brighty asked.

"It must be," Captain confirmed, not glancing away from the danger soaring steadily closer. "They're coming after her."

Brighty tried to ignore the rapid thumping of her pulse as she asked her next question. "And Rafe?"

"I don't—"

"Is that him?" Patch interrupted them in a deep voice.

Without turning, Brighty sensed the rest of the crew squeezing into the small corner bedroom, the shuffling of their boots and the whisper of their sighs easy to recognize, every sound unique and familiar. She squinted to get a better look at the dark spot flying just ahead of the dragons. Horror widened her eyes.

"That's not Rafe."

"How do you—"

"There are three of them, look. It's not Rafe. It's those things." Fire burned her veins, so hot for a second she was sure Pyro must have been playing a prank. But she wasn't. The inferno came from within, a flood of panic.

"If he's not there," Jolt muttered slowly, "where is he?"

"With the queen, I'm sure," Captain interjected, her normal authority frighteningly absent. "He must be."

"What if he's not?" Brighty gulped as a sick foreboding twisted her intestines in a knot worthy of the worst storm. Logically, she knew that she and Rafe were just friends. There was no cosmic connection tying them together. There was no thread of fate woven through their souls. And yet, in that moment, she just *knew* he was in trouble. She couldn't explain it. The understanding came like a punch to the gut, stealing her breath. He was in trouble, and she had to help the only way she knew how. "We have to stop them."

"Brighty." Captain grabbed her arm, catching her before she even realized she was turning toward the door.

"Think about this," Archer cut in, worry sharpening his normally carefree voice. "We're in a city full of avians who despise mages. Even with our magic, they're stronger and well trained, not to mention they currently outnumber us by, I don't know, a thousand to one. You'd have to be crazy to—"

"Maybe I am," she snapped and wrenched her arm free, taking a moment to meet the eyes of her crew. "Maybe I am crazy to think none of that will matter with a herd of dragons breathing down our necks. Maybe I am crazy to think they might fight with us rather than get burned alive. Maybe I am. But I'd rather be called crazy than a coward."

"If the king and queen are here," Captain interjected, her tone meant to soothe the tension, "they must have a plan—"

"Are you kidding me? This is Rafe we're talking about. Of course he doesn't have a bloody plan."

"She's got a point, Cap," Pyro muttered.

Brighty spared a moment to look outside. The dragons had already closed half the distance between them. The creatures flew even faster. In a matter of minutes, they'd be here.

"We don't have time for this." She back to her crew. "We've spent our lives hunting dragons, and I, for one, am not about to stop now. Join me or don't—I really don't care. Those creatures will tear this city apart, and us with it. I won't sit around and watch it happen when I can fight the bastards instead."

With that, she tore through the stunned crew, not entirely sure when she'd become such an upstanding person, yet certain Rafe was somehow to blame. A hiss slid through her lips when she reached the outdoors. It was freezing, as she knew it would be, but with all this sunshine and clear skies, the frigid bite came as a shock every time. She never thought she'd long for the fog, but she did. At least down there upon the sea she didn't have to listen to the incessant chattering of her own teeth.

A roar broke through her complaining. Brighty ran around the side of the building and skidded to a halt as six raging dragons barreled down on her. Archer was right. This was idiotic. This was crazy. What in magic's name could one dragon-hunting crew and a team of novice mages do against this? What could she do out here by herself?

Dammit. I've got to try.

Bracing herself for what was to come, Brighty squared her shoulders and sent the most powerful beam she could gather across the vacant tundra. In an explosion of brilliant white, her magic and the dragons crashed together. Roars filled the air. Fire and light ricocheted across the sky. One of the creatures howled.

The black one, she thought, eying it through the radiant display. *Of course. The one made of shadow.*

Brighty homed in on the spot, shooting another blast of power at the creature. It jerked backward as her magic slammed into it, crippled by the light.

She didn't relent.

The dragons soared closer. The ground shook as *geo'kine* magic painted the air green. The snow around her melted and condensed into a slithering tendril rearing to strike. She didn't care. She kept her magic trained on the shadow creature, not letting up as it fought to escape her hold, body twitching within the center of her pure, unfiltered light. If she could just do this, if she could just stop one of them, maybe it would make a difference.

The group was a hundred feet away, then fifty, then twenty. One of the dragons arched its head, fire bubbling visibly at the back of its throat. Brighty winced.

This is going to hurt, she thought as flames barreled from its snout, the sound of its fury rattling her bones. *This is why I told myself not to care about people. Caring makes you do crazy, idiotic, noble things that will only get you killed.*

Yet she didn't try to run.

She didn't try to save herself.

She let her power flood out in waves, determined to fight until the very end, only turning away when the heat of the blaze was close enough to burn her skin.

The pain never came.

Red sparks flew past her face and caught the inferno before it struck. Then blue ones raced by, grappling with the shoot of water aimed at her torso. Then green. Then yellow. Then purple, until a rainbow lit the skies.

The shock must have been written on her face because Jolt ran over and nudged her with her hip. "You didn't really think we'd let you die, did you?"

Sort of? Maybe?

"All right," Captain shouted. "*Pyro'kines* on the dragons. *Hydro'kines* on the blue creature. *Geo'kines* on the green one. Brighty, I want you on the black one. Everyone else, do what you can to help. If you have wings, use them. If you're under the age of eighteen, get the hell inside. And for the love of all the gods, someone find an alarm or a horn or something to alert the avian soldiers, because we can't win this fight alone."

They scattered, little more than a handful of ragtag sailors and two dozen novice mages with wings, but they were the queen's army and they were all this world had left. So somehow, they'd bloody well find a way to save it.

54

RAFE

Rafe couldn't believe his eyes as Sphaira slipped into view. Nearly a dozen dragons darkened the skies, but he'd expected those. What he'd never anticipated was the flood of magic reflecting off the crystal domes and bursting through smoke. What he'd never dared imagine was the sight of avians and mages working together to fight a common enemy. Yet as he neared, the truth was undeniable.

While flocks of birds from every house concentrated on fighting the dragons with swords and spears, a small set of *pyro'kines* raced between them, stopping the flames and taming the fires. *Aero'kines* stirred the winds, sending the beasts off balance so their attacks went astray. Two concentrated auras of blue and green rose from opposite ends of the city, what he could only imagine were water and earth mages fighting the two hybrid creatures. While Da'Kin had been drowning beneath the onslaught, somehow Sphaira was holding on. Maybe because it was a city built of crystal instead of wood. Maybe because its soldiers now had both wings and magic. Maybe because the sight lines were clear so high above the fog. Rafe didn't know, but he was proud—until he noticed one being was absent.

Where is it? Where is it?

The shadow creature was missing, and the realization sent a pang of dread down Rafe's spine. If it had already reached the stone, they were doomed. Lyana couldn't fight it on her own. Yet a golden gleam still emanated from the palace looming in the center of the city, and though the isle was dropping, the pace was almost too slow to notice, gradual and controlled. She was alive. She had to be, which meant there was still time.

All right, Taetanos, you vicious bastard. Fate stole my family. It took my wings. It turned me into a dragon. For once in my gods-damned life, you owe me a win.

Help me find it.

Help me save her.

The breeze shifted direction and a billowing plume of smoke brushed to the side, unmasking the black figure hiding in the darkness. Rafe dove for the spot, cutting through the air with all the speed he could muster.

Thank you.

Thank you.

Before he got there, a brilliant white beam slammed into the creature, eliciting a wail. Rafe followed the path to its owner and a laugh barked through his lips, easing the tension in his shoulders. Brighty, of course it was Brighty, but not on her own two feet. The raven *agro'kine*, Amara, had created a harness made of vines. As her obsidian wings carved a path through the sky, Brighty hung below her like a fish in a net, one hand gripping the leafy stalks for dear life while the other blasted magic at the monster. Unlike in the mist, it couldn't simply meld into the shadows and disappear. Up here, surrounded by glistening translucent stone, compact ivory snow, and radiant noon sunshine, its onyx scales stood starkly out.

The creature dove for the nearest ash cloud to take refuge in the soot.

"About bloody time you got here!" Brighty shouted.

"Where's the queen?"

"Hell if I know—ahh!"

A high-pitched scream tore through her lips as Amara swooped in a sharp arc to the right. The blood rushed from Brighty's face and her fingers tightened around the vines. With gritted teeth, she sent another flash of magic into the dark. The creature howled.

"We have to find a way to kill it," he yelled.

Despite the urgency of the situation, she found the time to offer him a pointed glare. "Well, magic alive, Rafe! What do you think I'm doing?"

"I just have to get close enough to sever its head. We need a plan."

"By all means, take your time!"

She was right. He needed to act fast. An onyx wing sifted through the ash and Rafe dove, hastily shouting over his shoulder, "Wait for my signal!"

Soot stung his eyes as he flew into the smoke. Darkness stole his sight. He didn't need it. Using the bond at the back of his mind as a guide, Rafe slammed into the shadow demon. They grappled, scales and skin clashing. He went for its wings and bent them backward as he hugged the creature to his chest, clenching his fingers in an iron grip. Carrying both their weights, he soared back into the daylight.

"Now!"

"Now what?"

"Your magic!"

"But Rafe—"

"Now!"

Energy pierced from all sides, stinging his skin. The creature in his arms thrashed as a wail spilled from its lips. Rafe clutched it tightly, ignoring the pain as his magic rushed to heal the burns. Hugging his wings to his back, he dropped from the sky with the creature. They landed hard against the ice. A bone in his forearm snapped. The creature's wings crunched. Rafe dug a knee into its chest as he dragged his uninjured arm free from where it was stuck between snow and scales, and reached for his dagger. The demon got a hand free. Talons dug into his wrist as fingers wrapped around his arm. They wrestled while Brighty's magic raged. On top, Rafe took the brunt of the beam and the tough hide of his wings smoldered. Already depleted from the fight within the mist, his magic struggled to keep up with the demand. As though sensing the weakness, the shadow beast roared, flashing teeth. In a burst of strength, it flung Rafe across the snow and retreated.

"No!"

The creature disappeared behind a wall of blinding ivory, one of its onyx wings dragging in the snow. On his hands and knees, Rafe geared up for another attack, preparing to launch himself across the ice. Something wrapped around his ankles and tugged him backward.

"You idiot! *That* was your plan?"

Rafe came to a stop at Brighty's feet, the vine around his leg retreating under Amara's command. "I almost had it!" he said, jumping to his feet. "It's injured. Just let me—"

"I almost bloody killed you!" Brighty snapped and grabbed his shoulder, surprisingly efficient at holding him back despite their size difference. "Only you could come up with such a ridiculous, self-sacrificing, self-mutilating—ugh! Did it ever occur to you that just because you have healing magic doesn't mean you need to use it?"

No.

It hadn't.

"Well, what do you want me to do?"

"Go find Captain and Archer."

"Why?"

"Because your plan sucked, and I obviously came up with something better."

"But the creature! It—"

"I've got it," she said, her exasperation at an all-time high as she nudged her chin toward where her magic still beamed over the wide city street. Through the shimmering ivory, he could only just make out the dark outline of a body. "I'm using the reflection off the crystals to form a light cage. As long as it's grounded, this should hold it, but I'd rather not test that theory." Even as she said it, a cloud of darkness rose from the center of the light, pushing against her barrier. A sneer flitted across her lips. "Bring me Captain and Archer. Now!"

Rafe took to the sky, casting a single glance below as Brighty sent another wave of power to combat the shadow, light and dark warring for dominance. She would hold it. She was too damn stubborn not to.

Shifting his focus to the battle raging in the city, Rafe searched for the telltale haze of *aero'kine* magic. Streaks of it raced across the breeze, plowing into the dragons, but only two of those yellow flows started from the ground. One would be Patch, the other Captain. He took a gamble, arching left toward the closer target.

An arrow whizzed by his ear.

What the…?

Another whistled through the air and he dove to escape it. A spear came next, narrowly missing his shoulder.

My wings, he realized, catching sight of the flaming scales in his peripheral vision. *My gods-damned wings.*

"I'm not—" he tried to shout, stopping abruptly to escape the volley of three arrows sailing in his direction. A magic-laced gust of wind whooshed by, blowing the weapons off course.

"He's one of us, you blasted fools!" Captain stood below with her arms raised as the colorful fabrics of her hair danced wildly around her face. He'd been an idiot for not realizing she was Cassi's mother. The look in her icy blue eyes was just as lethal as the one he'd seen on her daughter's face, but luckily, this time it wasn't turned on him. "He's the King Born in Fire!"

"Vesevios is the only king of fire they understand," Rafe said as he landed by her side.

Captain spared him a glance, a frown on her lips. "What are you doing here? You're going to get yourself killed. Find the queen."

"We need to deal with the shadow creature first. Brighty has it trapped. She told me to find you and Archer."

"Archer?"

He nodded.

Grooves dug into her weathered skin. "He's helping with the dragons. I don't know where."

"I'll find him. Can you get to Brighty?"

Captain raised a brow in his direction and a wind tunnel funneled down from the sky, wrapping them both in whipping gales. Shaking his head, Rafe stepped out of the tornado just as her feet began to lift from the snow. Sticking low to the ground this time, he launched into the air and searched the city for the pine-green sparks of *ferro'kine* magic.

There.

There.

There.

None of those trails led back to the ground. Lyana's army had grown in the weeks they'd been beneath the mist. At least a dozen, maybe two, mages with wings raced across the sky, openly using their power in a display he never thought he would live to see. They were a long way from those hours in the cave when he and Lyana had first met, magic creating a deep trust between two strangers who'd only known fear.

"Rafe! Watch out!"

He spun just in time to see a flash of green redirect the spear two feet from lodging into his spine. Magic his people could deal with, or at least tolerate, but a man with dragon wings was apparently beyond their comprehension.

Just my luck.

"Archer!" Rafe dove toward the sound of the man's voice, searching for him in the nearby streets and finding him crouched behind a crumbling crystal wall. "Brighty needs you—"

No sooner had the words left his mouth than a chain shot up from Archer's feet. The bottom end wrapped around his waist as Rafe snatched the top piece and lifted the man into the air. A swirling storm of white and black ballooned across the northern edge of the city. Taking the most direct path, Rafe flew past three dragon fights and swerved around the palace, the warm glow of Lyana's magic bringing a brief sense of peace among the chaos. Shoots of green darted by his face as Archer watched his back, redirecting any wayward arrows his own people volleyed toward him. By the time they returned to Brighty, sweat dripped down her brow. She didn't spare them a glance, keeping her focus on the battle of light and shadow.

"Archer," she said through gritted teeth, "do you remember what we did to that *cryo'kine* who attacked Jolt a few years back?"

"Hell, yes."

"Good. You ready, Captain?"

"I'm ready."

"Rafe, when I say so, you better put those swords you're always carrying around to good use, or I might just have Archer stab you with them. All right, everyone—now!"

A blinding flash of white made Rafe's vision spot. Just as quickly, the glow disappeared and the raging black-and-white storm winked out. The creature stood in the center of the street, its dark scales stark against the icy cityscape. One of its onyx wings dragged along the ground, the bones shattered from their earlier fall. Before it could run, chains shot through the air and wrapped around its hands and ankles. They tightened. It dropped to its knees, struggling with the binds. Captain ran across the snow. Shadows exploded from the creature's mouth, flowing out in a smoky plume that enveloped them whole. Only the subtle glow of Archer's magic broke up the spreading wave of darkness. Rafe jumped forward, but Brighty held him back.

"Wait."

"But Captain—"

"Wait," she repeated more firmly.

Nothing happened.

The shadows spread until the darkness nearly spilled over his toes.

"Brighty—"

He broke off as the smoke abruptly vanished. Captain stood with her palms against the creature's face, her fingers glowing yellow as they covered its nose and mouth. The shadow monster froze, its eyes wide as though it were in shock.

"Now!"

Brighty shoved him from behind and Rafe charged, his wings and feet propelling him across the snow. He gripped one of his swords with both hands, the leather soft and worn. Captain watched him approach, waiting until the blade arced over his shoulder before jerking out of the way. The creature inhaled sharply, its throat expanding as it gulped down air. Rafe slashed toward the mark. His sword flashed, catching the sunlight, and then a gush of black blood splattered into the sky as he lopped the creature's head clear off.

Two down, he thought as the lifeless black scales collapsed, spilling ebony sludge across the snow. *Five to go.*

"How'd you do that?" Rafe asked, turning from the carnage as the remaining creatures wailed in the back of his thoughts.

"I stole the air from its lungs," Captain explained as she wiped an onyx dollop from her cheek. The spots along her clothes wouldn't be so easy to remove. "It's a nasty little trick, and it can only be done from close range, but it's effective. A normal human would've been dead long before your sword reached it."

"Rafe!" The shrill edge to Brighty's shout sent his heart racing. "We might have a problem…"

He spun. Over her shoulder, a firestorm sped toward the city, the bubbling orange blaze charging like the sun unleashed. But Brighty's wide eyes were pointed in the other direction. He pivoted. A brilliant, billowing ball of yellow swept across the barren tundra. Two bonds he hadn't even noticed burned brighter in the back of his mind. The fire creature and the air creature were here, which meant there was only one more left to hatch—the *aethi'kine* creature.

The light of the sun dimmed. Rafe looked up to find a haze creeping across previously clear skies. The upper layer of the mist was starting to swallow the House of Peace. They were running out of time.

"Go." Captain met his gaze, the same realization flaring in her eyes. "We can handle them. Get to the queen."

55

LYANA

The end was near. As the *aethi'kine* egg and the rift moved closer together, the world was healing. With every inch the isle dropped, the barren void receded, its poison shrinking beneath the deluge of power flowing through Lyana's body, not all of it hers. The creature was helping her somehow, its magic passing through her spirit the same way it passed through the priests' and priestesses', using her as a conduit for an immeasurable source of life.

The spell was crumbling.

It wouldn't be long now.

Through the creature, Lyana felt the other hatchlings, two more just arrived, two lost, their souls still some sort of moving anchor for a magic she couldn't begin to understand. Beneath her palms, the surface of the egg rippled as the being within began to force its way out. The moment the rift returned to its natural spot, the creature would break free.

Lyana knew it.

And she knew exactly what to do.

No panic sped her heart. No fear constricted her throat. No

hesitation clenched her gut. She was clear. This was what she'd been born to do. Did she want more time? Of course. Yet she'd lived long enough to explore not one but two worlds. She'd loved. She'd laughed. Her days had been full, her faith had been strong, and whatever came next, she believed her gods would see her through. They'd chosen her. They wouldn't abandon her now.

A brief image of Malek in his final moments flashed.

His reddening skin. The boils. His charred fingers.

She refused to be afraid.

"Ana!"

Rafe's voice pulled her from the magic. Golden light flooded the sacred nest, whipping through the trees like a godly wind. Leaves rustled. Branches snapped. There was no sign of the doves or the sky or the world beyond these crystal walls. Saturated power swirled around her in a storm. With gritted teeth, Rafe pumped his wings, taking one forceful step at a time, his feet skidding back even as he fought to move forward.

"I'm here!"

"Ana!"

He pushed with renewed vigor, moving until his face no longer hid behind a translucent golden sheen but was close enough for his blue eyes to pierce. They touched her straight to her soul. He was her partner. Her destiny. Her king. And he would do this for her, not because the world depended on it, but because she asked. For him, it had always been that simple.

"The air and fire creatures are here," he called across the chaos, still struggling for another inch. "The mages are spread thin. I don't know how long we can hold them."

"Don't," she said softly.

He scrunched his brows. "Don't what?"

"Don't hold them, Rafe. Don't let anyone else die. Let them come."

"But, Ana—"

"Please, Rafe. Let them come."

Realization passed over his features, leaving him slack-jawed. He looked up, then side to side, then at the egg hovering beneath her hands. A frown flitted across his lips and he shook his head. His wings dropped just enough to send him stumbling back before he regained his footing.

"Ana."

"Rafe, listen—"

"You're setting it free." He spoke the words as though they were a foreign language, too unfamiliar to be believed. "It's excited. It's eager. It's…helping you."

"Rafe—"

"You can't," he urged, his muscles flexing as he stood his ground. "You can't let that thing out into the world."

"I'm not."

"But—"

"I'm not," she repeated more firmly. "I know what I have to do. Bring the creatures here. I need them close when the moment comes."

This time, as his understanding dawned, not a fraction of him moved. Pain exploded in his spirit, strong enough to make her wince, even as he remained frightfully still. The throbbing pounded at her soul, the sort that couldn't be healed. Heat burned in the back of her throat, a flaming knot. Her eyes stung. They looked at each other across the billowing *aethi'kine* power, part of the madness, yet removed in their own private world.

He didn't argue.

He didn't try to change her mind.

He didn't hold her back.

The connection between them burned as bright as ever, two hearts and two minds formed into one. A king of fire. A queen of snow. Two equals bound by trust.

"Tell me," he whispered.

So she did.

56

RAFE

The fog was thick enough to block out the sun when Rafe emerged from the palace, his heart like stone, his mind determined, his soul unflinching. Orange glows flared through the gray as dragons continued to blast fire across the skies. This deep in the mist, he found it impossible to tell who was winning. Wings and weapons flashed through the haze. Magic flared. The dragons pushed both pain and pleasure down the bond, while the creatures simmered with savage wildness. They fought with abandon to reach the *aethi'kine* leader calling them close, and now he was about to give them what they wanted.

Rafe flew toward the earth creature first, shouting when he got close to the *geo'kines* struggling to keep the beast contained, "The queen has a plan. Stop fighting. Release the creature and concentrate on the dragons. This will all be over soon."

They listened.

He went to the water creature next, then the fire creature. Both times, he thought the crew might question his order—first Spout, then Pyro—but they didn't. He was the King Born in Fire and they'd been told all their lives to heed his command.

The air creature was last.

When he told the *aero'kines* to let it be, Captain's voice cut across the madness, her magic still flaring on the wind. "Have you lost your gods-damned mind?"

"The queen has a plan."

"What plan?"

He landed beside her on the ice and put a hand to her shoulder, drawing her gaze as he spoke, no give in his tone. "The queen has a plan."

She narrowed her eyes, concern flashing, but lowered her arms. In a blink, the air creature fled toward the palace. Rafe moved to follow, but Captain Rokaro took hold of his forearm. "What's the plan, Rafe?"

"You'll understand soon."

"Rafe—"

Panic sharpened her tone, a fear he'd never heard in her voice before, but he snapped his wrist free. "I have to go."

He took to the skies, where even if she'd wanted to, she couldn't follow, at least not quickly enough to keep pace with his wings. A numb feeling settled on his heart as he raced for the palace. The creatures were already there. They'd broken their way inside. He could feel their spirits wrapped up in the *aethi'kine* magic tearing the sacred nest apart, the swirling vortex too thick to push their way through. They stopped trying. Lyana was no longer a concern. Instead, excitement lit their minds—their leader, the most powerful among them, was almost here.

"Rafe!"

He ignored the shout as he flew over the towering main door of the palace, now little more than shards of wood in a heap upon the ground, and into the entrance hall.

"Rafe!"

Though months had passed, as he approached the main atrium he could see it as it had been during the trials, clear as day, with

Lyana upon the main dais, a vision in flowing ivory silks, metallic embroidery and jewels twinkling, her wings tucked demurely behind her back, her pearlescent feathers forming a mask to shroud her face. He remembered kneeling before her and taking her hand in his, the feel of her soft skin too familiar to ignore, the mischievous curve of her lips giving her away as he placed the coal upon her palm. The moment she crushed the rock to reveal a diamond, with Taetanos's laughter ringing in his ears, his fate had been sealed. Yet he wouldn't change it, any of it, except to carve out more time with her.

"Magic alive—Rafe!"

A beam of pure energy slammed into him from behind, sending him to the floor in surprise. He skidded across the mosaic tiles before coming to a stop beside the wreckage of the door to the sacred nest, now just another pile of broken wood. Brighty's footsteps echoed loudly across the crystal stones in the entrance hall as she ran closer.

"Don't do it, Rafe," she called across the distance. "Whatever asinine thing you're planning, don't do it."

He ignored her and pumped his wings to soar easily through the door. Another beam of light magic narrowly missed him as he flew deeper into the hall. The golden gate at the end was mangled, the metal door crushed in, and beyond there was nothing but a solid wall of swirling *aethi'kine* might. Somewhere at its center, Lyana battled alone.

That wouldn't be her end.

It couldn't be.

"Rafe!"

He anticipated the attack this time and dove to land in a roll along the floor. Before she could make another move, he jumped to his feet and slipped through the door, already calling upon the inferno constantly simmering deep in his lungs. Gripping the metal bars in his hands, Rafe finally met Brighty's gaze. Flames barreled through his lips, shrouding her face in the angry blaze as the metal weakened and warped.

"Rafe! Rafe!"

He fused the mangled door back to its frame just in time for her to slam furiously into it. The barrier held. Brighty hissed when her fingers touched the bars and snatched her hands back, the metal too hot to touch.

"Don't do this, Rafe," she whispered, her voice uneven. "I don't even know what you're going to do, but I can tell from the look on your face I won't like it. So please, don't do it."

"I'm sorry," he said, a knot rising in his throat as he noticed the liquid pooling in her eyes. "But I have to."

"Why? It's the queen's magic. It's her fight. You've sacrificed enough."

"Have I?" he asked, dark laughter upon his lips as he glanced over his shoulder, unable to see through the pulsing magic at his back, then back at Brighty. "Lyana is about to give everything she has to save the world. Don't you think she deserves to know there's at least one person in that world willing to give everything he has to save her?"

Brighty swallowed, for once at a loss for words. In that split second of silence, the ground shuddered. His heart dropped. The isle had reached the sea. His time was almost up.

"I have to go."

"Rafe," she said, not so much a plea as a surrender.

He didn't say goodbye. He couldn't. Besides, that wasn't their style. Instead, he reached through the bars to wipe the tear from her cheek and offered her a lopsided grin. Then he turned and stepped into the storm.

Aethi'kine power rushed him from all sides.

Rafe forced his way through the madness, taking one labored step at a time. His wings beat, propelling him forward as he stumbled to keep his balance. Though he could see nothing through the churning golden haze, he knew exactly where to find her. The creature called to him through the bond, urging him closer. The other four were near. They moved as a unit, inch by inch, until the egg came into view. Though it still hung in midair, a crack ran up its center. In the empty space below, a brilliant white line pulsed, growing taller with each passing moment. The blue, green, red, and yellow creatures stood at each corner, circling Lyana. Rafe pushed past them, grinding his teeth as power slammed into his chest and he fought his way forward.

He wouldn't leave her alone.

He refused to.

With a defiant yell, he crossed the distance between them and placed his hands over hers on the god stone. Her brilliant emerald eyes popped open in surprise.

"Rafe. What are you doing here? I told you to leave. I told you—"

"I'm not going anywhere."

"But—"

"You started this by saving my life. I'm going to finish it by saving yours."

Lyana opened her mouth to challenge him, then paused, her brows falling as the fight left her. He'd done as she'd asked. Now it was her turn to let him fly free. This was his choice to make, and there was nowhere else he'd rather be. Rafe threaded their fingers together, creating a pattern of light and dark against the golden egg, two halves of one whole. Her braids swirled around her face. Her feathers fluttered in the invisible breeze. She'd always been as radiant as a queen, even in the damp dark of that long-ago cave, dressed in rags with a dusting of soot along her umber cheeks. His fate had been sealed the moment he'd woken to find her face across the fire, the sparkle of wonder in her gaze touching something deep within his soul, making him feel seen. Even now, she glittered.

More fractures splintered across the egg. The ivory glow by their feet intensified. The magic spinning around them sped.

"It's almost time," she whispered.

"I'm ready."

A silver glow lit his hands as he brought his power to the surface. Golden sparks sank beneath his skin. They held on to each other in that sacred place, their magic dancing, their spirits joined, their bodies connected in every way possible.

The pressure in the room built.

The air grew too full to breathe.

Lyana rasped, her focus turning inward as she prepared for this one final move. If he could just take some of the burden, she might survive. The blinding shine of the rift pierced the egg as they merged. Rafe reached for the bonds in the back of his mind, throwing them wide open, removing all his guards as he clutched for the creatures' souls.

Go, he thought.

Go.

Go.

Go.

The tension pulled taut.

All at once, it snapped. The stone broke open. Lyana grasped the *aethi'kine* creature with her magic, a burning cry upon her lips. He latched on to the others with his mind, using sheer will to overpower them. White and gold flashed. The magic imploded, caving in on itself. There was no time to run, no time to get away. The swirling storm of power collapsed, sucking them into the void.

"Rafe!"

"Ana!"

She clutched his fingers. He grasped hers. They were floating, flying, racing through oblivion together.

57

XANDER

The cool kiss of water woke Xander. His head throbbed and the world spun as he opened his eyes, awareness coming slowly. Gentle trickling filled his ears, then cries and screams, then the grating groan of stone, and suddenly it all came rushing back. The House of Wisdom had fallen, taking him with it.

The gods!

Xander jumped to his feet. His clothes were soaked and sticking to him like a second skin. A stream rushed over his toes, flowing up to his ankles. Unlike his home when it fell, the ground didn't sway or bobble in the sea. It was steady. But the rocks were porous, and the city lay deep underground. If he didn't get out, he'd drown. It was only a matter of time.

Heart lurching, he spun. The air was alive with the flurry of wings. People pounded at the ceiling. They circled, zipping this way and that, like bugs in a jar, fighting inevitable suffocation. Where the dark opening of the tunnel should have been, there was nothing but a mound of collapsed rubble. Owls dug at the stones, flinging them away, but for every one that was removed, two more slid into place. Liquid seeped through the cracks, flowing faster with each passing second. The barrier acted like a dam, keeping them alive even as it killed them.

They were stuck.

They were trapped.

I won't let it end like this.

His vision spotting and his skull pounding, Xander took to the air and surveyed the masses for the telltale flash of amber silks.

There.

"King Sylas!" he shouted, but the name died on his lips as he neared.

The king wasn't moving. He lay sprawled across the castle courtyard, the wall beside him crumbled, his forehead stained red. The queen knelt over him, her body trembling as her warm honey wings spread wide, trying to shield him from view. Prince Nico and his mate stood to the side, grief-stricken as they clung to one another. Guards stood around the family in a protective ring, though the rest of the owls seemed too busy trying to escape to even notice their fallen king. When Xander landed in the circle, no one tried to stop him.

"What happened?"

"The wall," Prince Nico said, his voice thick.

"Is he breathing?"

The prince could only shake his head.

Heaviness pulled at Xander's heart. He understood this specific hurt rather well—he'd felt it twice before. And though he longed to give the family space to mourn, this was the sacrifice that being royal exacted. Private pain had to wait. Their people needed them.

"I'm sorry for your loss, truly I am, but we need to find a way out of here."

Prince Nico nodded, his warm brown eyes glazed and unseeing.

Xander put a hand to his shoulder. "The tunnel collapsed. Is there another way out of the city? A secret passage? Air holes? Anything?"

"I— I don't—" The prince shook his head, unable to speak as he turned back to his father, his gaze growing distant once more.

"There are air passages, but they're too narrow to fit a body, and they're blocked by metal bars above and below," the princess said softly, studying Xander over her mate's bowed spine. "I don't know of any way out except the tunnel. I'm sorry."

He glanced toward the queen, but before he could even speak her name, a wail spilled from her lips and her body began to shake anew. If she knew anything, she was beyond telling him—she and the prince both.

If the tunnel was the only way…

If there were no air holes…

If there was no backup exit…

The ceiling overhead shone copper in the firelight as shadows danced along the layers of sediment. Cracks marred the once-smooth surface. Stalactites that had been dry for centuries now glistened with an ominous sheen. Many of the vast columns holding the cave aloft still stood, though an area on the northern side had fared worse than most. Three of the library's pillars had fallen, all right next to each other, and dust clouded the air as loose boulders ground together, fighting the downward pull. That was the way out, but he'd need help.

He'd need magic.

Dark humor made Xander's lips twitch. Of course it came down to this. The very thing his people had spent their lives persecuting was the only thing that might save them, if—and it was a big if—he could find someone willing to step forward.

"Is there a horn?" Xander blurted, asking everyone and no one, his mind racing. "Is there an alarm, some way to cut through the chaos?"

Silence greeted him. The princess watched him uncertainly. The prince and queen hadn't even heard. The guards shifted their weight but maintained their positions, unsure whom to obey.

Xander took a deep breath and strengthened his tone. "Is there—"

"Yes." One of the guards broke rank and stepped forward, a clear tremor in his voice, from fear or sadness Xander didn't know. "It's built into the castle."

"Go now and use it. I need to get the people's attention."

The guard spared a glance at his leaders, then took to the sky. Xander followed, searching for a prominent spot where he'd be seen from every vantage point in the city. The top of the castle would have to do. He landed on the tallest spire, watching owls dash across the sky, their panic thickening the air. His voice alone would never catch their attention. Where was the horn? This had to work. This—

The stones beneath his feet vibrated. His heart skipped a beat, worry tightening his throat, but it wasn't another earthquake. A low hum coursed through the air, almost like a mournful cry. No one listened. No one stopped. Suddenly, the sound ballooned. The brassy note blared into a bellowing call that reverberated across the cavern, bouncing off stone, crashing and booming. A ringing filled his ears as a quiver coursed down his spine.

One by one, the owls dropped from the skies. He couldn't tell if it was obedience or if they simply couldn't fly with the sound waves thrumming through the air. The cacophony of feathers died away. The city grew still. The droning of the horn gradually faded, the echoes lingering in the silence left in its wake.

"People of Rynthos!" Xander shouted across the quiet. No one paid him any mind—a foreign king, a raven, an outsider. He cupped his hands around his mouth and infused an authority he wasn't entirely sure he felt into his next words. "People of Rynthos, listen to me if you want to make it out of the city alive!"

Faces turned. The hairs at the back of his neck rose, an

awareness of being at the center of something. It was a feeling he'd often run from, preferring the solitude of his books and the quiet halls of the castle, comfortable staying at home on the isle he knew rather than dreaming of the world beyond. But that fear had changed. Someone needed to step up, to lead, and Xander could be that person—not just for the ravens, but for his world.

"I know you're scared. I am too—of what's happening to our homes, of never seeing the sky again, of the unknown. But we've been a people guided by fear for far too long. We let it cage us in. We let it suffocate us. And we've lived so safely in our prison, we stopped seeing it for what it was. The bars no longer keep our enemies out, they hold us in, and I say no more. There is someone in this room right now who can save us, someone with a power given by the gods, a power we scorned and cast aside because we were afraid—but they are afraid too. Every day, they live in terror that their secret will be found out, that their life will be forfeit, that their loved ones will be left alone, and for what? Vesevios's greatest power is the one we've given him—the fear we hold in our hearts and our minds. But now here we are, at the end of everything, our homes fallen into the Sea of Mist and the god stones failing us, yet where is he? Together, we are stronger than he can ever be. United, we can overcome. So I beg of you, please, let it go. Step out of the cage. Don't be afraid of what you don't understand. Accept it. Embrace it, here and now. And if you are that person in the crowd with the magic to help us escape, please, in the name of all the gods, reveal yourself. I know you've been wronged, and though the past can never be undone, we can move forward, together, to a new future."

Xander breathed deeply, his heart pounding in his chest as he waited. The city was utterly silent, nothing except the trickle of water, reminding all of them that time wasn't on their side. No wings moved. No voice called. With each passing moment, the air tightened like a vice around his throat.

Please. Please.

Someone was out there, he knew it. Lyana had found mages among the citizens of all the other houses, and Rynthos would be no different. He just needed to convince them it was safe, not in the dark hours of night as she had done, but right now, with everyone watching.

"Please," he shouted again. "For all our sakes—"

"No!"

The shout cut across the rooftops, a woman's voice, high pitched with terror. Xander jerked his head to the side in time to see someone rise from the streets, their wings beating fast and their flight erratic. A moment later, he realized why—it was a boy. He was small, his feathers little more than fluff, but as he soared across the city, he seemed more courageous than any grown man Xander had ever known. Behind him, being held back by two owls, his mother cried, tears glistening on her cheeks as her whimpers carried softly through the quiet.

"I can help," the boy said as he landed on the castle spire. "I want to help."

"Thank you," Xander said as he knelt to meet the boy at eye level. He took the child's hand and held it to his chest, overcome by the sight of such innocent bravery. "What is your magic?"

The boy pulled his bottom lip into his mouth as his brows furrowed, the first flicker of uncertainty flashing in his gray eyes. But there was a stubborn determination in them too, one that almost reminded Xander of Cassi. He lifted his hand, the slightest tremor to his fingers as he waved them sideways. The water saturating the fibers of Xander's shirt sprang free of the threads, then floated for a moment in the air before dropping to the stones like rain. A collective gasp filled the cavern.

He was a water mage.

A feeling of defeat carved a hole in Xander's chest, but he lifted his hand to the boy's cheek, keeping a warm smile on his face. "That was amazing."

And it was. It just wasn't the type of magic they needed.

But maybe the boy could hold back the flood in the tunnel. Maybe it would give them enough time to dig through the debris. Lyana and Rafe knew where he was. Maybe a delay was all they needed. A group of mages might already be on their way. For all he knew, they might already be aboveground, trying to break their way in. Maybe—

"I can help."

The words were softly spoken, the voice deep and aged, but they rang loudly across the city, carried along by whispers. A man took to the air, his focus not on Xander but on the boy, as though the sight of such courage had left him in awe. Though his skin was wrinkled and his hair peppered gray, he flew with strength and precision before landing on the castle in a proud stance, his chin tipped defiantly.

"I can move the earth," he said, then swallowed, his shoulders wilting slightly, though it was hard to tell if the weight was being lifted or made heavier. Turning away from Xander, he scanned the skyline of his home, taking a moment to memorize it as though it might be his last chance. With a resigned breath, he glanced back at Xander. "That's what you're looking for, right? I might be able to collapse part of the ceiling."

"There's a section—"

"The northern edge, I agree. As soon as it's been cleared of people, I'll do my best to form an opening. And you..." He paused and took the boy by the shoulders. "Return to your mother and never scare her like that again."

"But I—"

"You're brave," the man said, "far braver than most, especially me. And you've already done the most important thing—you stepped forward when no one else would. But now it's time to step back and stay safe. I'll take it from here."

He nudged the boy between his wing joints, prompting him to leave. Then he beat his own wings, stirring the air.

"I hope you meant what you said," the mage whispered, all his focus on the stone overhead. The words, though, were for Xander. "I'm an old man. I've lived my life. But that boy deserves a future. Remember that when all this is over."

"I will," he promised, but the man was already gone. "All right," Xander shouted, returning to the task at hand. "We need to clear out the northern section of the library."

The owls listened. Under his guidance, they scattered to safer locations. Anyone who couldn't fly was given aid, until the area was clear. Then, as one, they watched the mage stand alone beneath the cracked ceiling and save them. A day before, he would have been their nightmare. Now he was a hero. Chunk after chunk of the cavern gave way, falling with unnatural control toward the ground. When the cracks along a different part of the ceiling began to spread, he sealed them. When a nearby column swayed, he steadied it. The power was invisible yet undeniable, especially as a rush of cool, fresh air swept in, tasting of freedom.

The mage went through the opening first to make sure it was safe. When he returned, the city began to empty—not in a mad rush but, as Xander bid, in a controlled and orderly fashion, until he was the last soul left. Alone in the quiet, he surveyed the vast columns filled with books, the entrances to the archival tunnels, the winding streets. Someday he prayed Rynthos would thrive again, not as a secret underground world, but out in the open for all to enjoy. Right then and there, he promised he would live to see the revival, not just here, but across all the houses now left desolate upon the sea.

Xander would save them.

He would build a new world, one where his brother could stand by his side, and Lyana could be free, and Cassi could be his. The isles were falling. Magic was everywhere. The old ways were over, and to them, he bid good riddance. It was long past time to change the rules. Together, they'd create brand-new ones, better ones, built on love instead of fear, the way the gods had always intended.

With that promise in his heart, he finally flew through the gaping hole and into the thick fog. He'd told the people to make for Sphaira, yet as he emerged into the mist, a flutter at the back of his neck pulled his gaze from the vast gray overhead. A figure stood by the rim of the crater, shrouded in the haze, little more than a dark outline, yet his heart skipped a beat. He recognized the bend of her wings and the curve of her hips. He knew the silhouette of her face. What was she doing here?

Xander landed on the rocky ground, closing the distance between them. Cassi remained frozen as he neared. With each step, the fog dissipated, revealing why. Tears spilled from her eyes, drawing sharp lines down her mud-stained cheeks. Her arms were brown up to the elbows. Her clothes were caked in dirt. Blood coated her fingers, the nails cracked and broken, her skin covered in scrapes, as though she'd literally dug her way out of an early grave.

"What happened?" He ran to her and took her by the hand. "Who did this to you?"

"No one," she whispered. Her lips trembled as she spoke. Her silver eyes were wide with shock. "I— I— Rafe told me to come save you, so I did, but the tunnel had caved in, and then I saw you facedown on the street. I tried to touch your mind, but I couldn't. I thought— I thought—"

Her voice cracked, and in that broken sound, he realized the truth. She hadn't dug her way out of anywhere. She'd been trying to dig her way in, to get to him, to save him.

Xander pressed her hand to his chest, so she could feel his heart beating. "I was knocked unconscious during the fall, but I'm fine, Cassi. I'm alive."

"You're alive," she repeated, as though afraid it wasn't true.

"I'm right here."

Light filled her eyes, a glow so bright the mist receded, and she flung herself into his arms. He caught her around the waist and held her to his chest. She trembled against him, crying with relief as she buried her face into his neck. Xander held her, acutely aware that he never wanted to let go. Though she had said she wanted sunshine and unhurried words, that wasn't their life. Their life was here, now, enshrouded in fog and covered in grime as the world ended all around them. Their life was a countdown. Every moment was precious, and he wouldn't waste another one. There was no perfect. This was perfect—her arms wrapped around his neck and her laughter in his ears, her body pressed tight to his and her warmth sinking into his skin.

Any moment they were together was the right moment, so he pressed his nose into her hair, his lips skimming over the soft skin of her neck, and whispered, "I love you."

Cassi jerked back and dropped her feet to the ground as she searched his eyes for the truth. He lifted his hand to her cheek.

"I wanted to tell you before. I wanted to tell you so many times, but—"

The words were lost as she gripped the back of his head and pulled his face down to hers. Their mouths came together in a searing kiss that he felt all the way to his toes. She'd been right. This was so much better than a dream, a moment worth waiting for, because the heat running through his blood was real and the sighs in his ear were hers and they were touching each other with an honesty only the waking world could provide. His movements were a bit awkward, hers were a bit aggressive, yet he wouldn't change a thing. She tugged at his hair and nipped his bottom lip. He slid his arm around the small of her back, pulling her closer as they stumbled over the uneven dirt. The world faded. It could have ended right then and there, and he didn't think he'd notice. As his head grew light and their breathing turned ragged, he didn't want to stop, not even to come up for air. He wanted to live in this small pocket of infinity with her.

The boulder on the ground, however, had other plans.

Xander's toe caught the rock and he tripped, falling forward as his wings flapped to catch him. Cassi wasn't so lucky. Her less agile owl wings unfurled a moment too late and she smacked butt first into the soil. By the time Xander landed on his knee at her side, an apology surging up his throat, laughter was already spilling from her lips. She hugged herself around the middle and let her head fall back, succumbing to her joy. Curious relief replaced the panic and he exhaled heavily, not sure if he'd ever seen her so happy. Her mirth was infectious, and it brought a grin to his lips despite the reality of their situation. The world was ending. Their homes were still falling into the sea. Their way of life was over. But within so much darkness, he supposed the only way to keep going was to follow the light.

"Cassi?"

She reached up, gripped him by the shirt, and pulled him to the ground. In one smooth roll, she'd pinned him to the dirt. Chest to chest, she leaned over him and ran her fingers slowly through his hair, pulling her bottom lip between her teeth as if to hide her grin.

"I love you, too, Xander."

While he was still caught in his surprise, she pecked his lips and jumped to her feet. He shook his head to clear the emotional whiplash, aware of the secret flashing in her silver eyes, and gradually rose to standing. "What do you know that I don't know?"

"It's over," she whispered giddily.

He furrowed his brow. "What do you mean?"

"It's over, Xander. The war. The battle. The end times. It's over. I felt it a little while ago. Lyana went to Sphaira, and Rafe went after her, and they must have figured out what to do, because the spell holding the rift has unraveled. The prophecy is realized. The world is saved. It's done."

"It's done?"

"We have time, Xander. As much time as we want," she murmured and stepped closer, entwining their fingers.

Her features softened, as though a weight had lifted from her spirit, leaving her reborn. Her walls were gone. There were no more lies, no more fears, no more impossible choices tearing her in two. This was Cassi, the real Cassi, full of life and joy, a woman set free.

"Let's go," she bade, pulling him toward the sky. "Everybody's waiting."

58

CASSI

In all her years spent sneaking into and out of the crystal palace, Cassi had never soared toward Sphaira with such joy in her heart. It was over. The battle she'd been waiting for her entire life and the war she'd sacrificed everything to win were finally over. She didn't know how Lyana had done it. When last they'd spoken, she and Malek had been no closer to figuring out how to seal the rift. But the House of Peace now rested in the sea. The sky had fallen. The spell was unmade. Cassi knew her best friend, she knew her queen—there was no way Lyana would have let the prophecy fail. She'd seen it through. She'd succeeded.

They'd won.

And yet, an eerie feeling crept down her spine as crystal domes appeared through the dense fog. In the sparkling sun, the skyline had always glittered majestically, the jewel of the kingdom. Now, the sight of so much ice and gray made it feel strangely ghostlike, a shadow of its former glory. A mix of distant cries and groaning filled the air. Doves sifted through the mist, their wings blending in with the monotony, while the injured called out from below.

Rubble littered the streets. Some fires still burned, though not nearly as badly as in Da'Kin. The dragons were long gone. Why, then, weren't the people rejoicing?

"It's too quiet," Xander said from her left, a frown upon his lips. "Something's wrong."

Cassi swallowed as her chest tightened. "Their home just fell into the sea. People are scared and injured. We should have expected this somberness."

"Maybe," he murmured noncommittally as he surveyed the streets. "But where's Lyana? I would've thought..."

That she'd be out healing the weak?

That she'd be out calming their fears?

Cassi had thought so too.

"She must be at the palace. Come on."

When they arrived, the front entrance was smashed beyond recognition, the grand door nothing more than a pile of wood among the ice. Mist infiltrated the hall beyond, shrouding the view. They glided through the opening, moving at a hesitant pace, both worried about what they'd find, yet neither willing to give that fear life.

"Who are you?" The voice boomed across the haze, and Cassi recognized it immediately—Lyana's father, the King of the House of Peace. "Where did you come from? And for the last time, what have you done with my daughter?"

"Nothing."

Cold dread dripped down Cassi's throat as the defiant response echoed through the atrium, the softly spoken word reverberating across the silence until it gained a life of its own.

No.

She raced ahead, forgetting about Xander, forgetting about Lyana and Rafe, forgetting about everything except the sudden fear twisting her insides. Captain Rokaro knelt on the colorful mosaic floor in the heart of the dove palace, her arms bound behind her back, her single caramel wing arched high, a proud tilt to her chin. By her side, three of her crew sat in chains—Brighty, Leech, and Spout. Jolt lay sprawled on the floor before them, an arrow in her shoulder as blood leaked across the tiles, her whimpers the only sign she was alive. A troop of guards surrounded them, weapons drawn, and across the perimeter of the atrium, the royal families of all the houses watched. Cassi landed at a run.

"Stop!" Her shout cut across the room like a blade. Heads turned, none faster than her mother's, those colorful fabrics swirling as she snapped her face to the side. Fear flashed deep in her icy irises —a warning.

It came too late.

Two spears blocked Cassi's path. She ran into them, folding in half as hands grabbed her arms. Glancing from left to right, she recognized the faces of the two guards holding her, but couldn't recall their names. Still, they must have known her, the best friend of the former princess. Yet when she tried to shrug them off, they only dug their fingers in deeper.

"What are you doing? Let go!"

"What is the meaning of this?" Xander boomed, exuding authority as he came to a regal stop by her side, his wings rippling like liquid obsidian, his jaw set and his expression strong. "Unhand her now."

"Not so fast," Lyana's father ordered. He'd always been jovial and kind, a bit of a pushover when it came to his daughter. At that moment, Cassi didn't recognize him. The man had been like a father to her, but his gaze slid over her as if she were dirt, his brown eyes as cold as his home.

Luka stood by his side, his jaw set, his face purposefully turned away. Still, she couldn't keep his name from rolling out of her lips like a plea.

"Luka?"

"Cassi Sky," the dove king said, no warmth in his tone, no hint that she'd grown up in his halls beneath his watchful eye, regarded as family. "Were you or were you not born beneath the mist?"

She swallowed, her mouth going dry. "I— I—"

"Were you or were you not sent to my house to spy on my family?"

"Luka," she begged. He closed his eyes and held them shut for just a moment too long. The truth hit her like a smack to the face, making her flinch. He'd been the one to give her up. Her mother would have died before spilling her secrets—the crew, too, out of nothing but stubborn loyalty—but for his sister, Luka would do anything. "You know the truth," she beseeched. "Luka, you know—"

"Are you or are you not an agent of Vesevios?"

"I'm not," she cried, turning back to the king. "I swear to you, I'm not."

"Then tell me where my daughter is."

"I thought she was here," Cassi whispered, confused.

She glanced about the atrium as though Lyana might jump out from behind someone's shoulders at any moment, revealing this to be one of her many ill-timed jokes, the mischief of their youth returning now that the world was safe and she was home. But no one moved. The room was filled with familiar faces, kings and queens she'd spent her life watching, yet none of them knew her. None would speak for her.

"I thought she was with you," Cassi insisted.

Xander stepped forward. "This is ridiculous."

Of course he would defend her, but the last thing she wanted to do was pull him into her mess. Cassi tried to catch his eye, to call him off, but he pointedly ignored her, the move telling. He knew exactly how stupid he was being and how thin of a line he walked. He simply didn't care.

"Stay out of this, raven king," Lyana's father demanded, as if stealing the words from Cassi's lips.

Yet Xander remained unfazed. "Lyana is my queen. If something happened to her, it is entirely my business. I demand to know what's going on."

"My daughter was last seen entering the sacred nest by one of our priestesses," the dove king explained, his gaze still firmly on Cassi, suspicion gleaming like the edge of a blade. "Witnesses then saw a man with dragon wings follow her inside, trailed by *that* woman." He pointed to Brighty, who curled her lip in response. "No one has seen either of them since. He was an agent of Vesevios, that much is clear, and he was working with these outsiders, these creatures from the mist. They protected him from our attacks. They helped him get into the palace. They used magic—"

"We used magic to save your bloody asses," Brighty snapped with a sneer. "Or did you conveniently forget—"

A palm slapped her cheek, the blow loud enough to cause an echo. She didn't cry out. She just stared daggers at the king as a gag was forced into her mouth.

Cassi hardly noticed.

No one has seen either of them since. The sentence played on repeat in her mind. *No one has seen either of them since.* They'd been in the nest. They'd been with the egg. They'd touched the rift. And no one had seen either of them since.

No!

She inhaled sharply, meeting Brighty's gaze. Her opal eyes were wet with unshed tears, grief pulling at the edges. Cassi looked at her mother. The captain set her jaw in a hard line and slowly shook her head.

No.

It couldn't be.

Panic coursed through her like a firestorm, setting her every nerve aflame. Cassi didn't know where she found the strength, but she tore free of the guards and unfurled her wings, slamming her feathers into their faces as she took to the air. Shouts followed her. Arrows too. A yellow-laced gust of wind pushed the weapons aside, and then a searing light flashed across the atrium. Cassi had lived in these halls long enough to know where to go without needing to see, and she swept blindly through the open doorway to the sacred nest, aware the doves would be right on her heels. Her owl wings were faster, and she used her predatory grace to carve a quick path down the hall. The golden gate was sealed, but Cassi slammed into it feetfirst, flying at top speed. The door tore off its hinges and fell inward, not truly built to keep people out but rather to keep the birds in. She tumbled inside and sprinted past the trees, not slowing, not stopping, until she reached the center of the grove, where she fell to her knees, a cry on her lips.

The god stone lay open in two parts on the floor. In the space between the shells, a radiant white line hovered in the air, vibrating with a power Cassi didn't understand.

The rift.

It wasn't closed. It wasn't gone.

It was still here.

Hands grabbed her by the feathers and jerked her backward. Cassi didn't have any fight left. Her body went limp as they tied ropes around her wrists and ankles. She slid into her spirit form and let them take her, not bothering to follow when they carried her away.

Please be here, she prayed. *Please be somewhere.*

Lyana's spirit had always tasted of pure life, simmering with energy and magic, bubbling with enthusiasm and power, like the warmest brush of the sun, her soul glowing with a light all its own. Cassi searched for that feeling now, pushing her magic to the limit, but she was flying in a void, nothing on either side but darkness. If

Lyana were alive, if she were anywhere in this world, Cassi would have felt her.

She didn't.

The queen was gone. The king, too. And there was only one place they could have traveled—through the rift.

THE DIARY

Date Unknown

Zavier tells me it's been weeks since my last entry, and he has lost track of time. I know no time. I am every time at once. It is a struggle to write this. Even now, the words wobble across the page, the parchment growing aged and withered to my eyes—

But I am here.

I am now, whatever now is.

With his hand on my skin, I'm more grounded in the present. When he is gone, I float in oblivion, the world a blur around me as futures oscillate across my vision, a thousand different possibilities alive at once, always changing, always shifting. But I have learned there are some things that never change—some people who are meant to live and meant to meet, whose faces never fade and never alter, the only solid points in my ever-flowing world.

I have seen how the world ends.

And I have seen how it is put back together again.

Zavier urges me to write it down, now while I'm having a lucid moment and there is still some ink left, so it is recorded in case the worst happens to us, allowing someone else to carry on the message and keep hope alive. Together, we will come up with something shorter, a poem or a prayer, something people will be able to remember, a lullaby to be passed down from generation to generation, until the chosen ones arrive.

But I'm ahead of myself already. Here, in this time, the rift is still open, and the beasts still roam free, claiming the lands for themselves. There is enough magic on this side of the peninsula to keep them distracted, but soon they'll venture over the mountains and across the seas to other lands. We must stop them before they do. And we will. I've seen it.

Zavier will create a rift spell the likes of which this world has never seen. I have told him how to do it, and he is ready. The eggs will be our anchors, and we will use the magic within them, part beast and part man, to seal shut the entrance to the other world. For a long time, the tight bind of the weave will keep them from hatching, though eventually, Zavier's magic will weaken, and the monsters will be freed from this cage. I've seen that too. I've—

I'm supposed to go in order.

What a strange concept—order doesn't exist to me anymore.

The rift will split the land as the anchors rise into the designated positions, a complicated diamond pattern that will last longer than any other design. The avians will claim the skies. The magic in the aethi'kine egg will be sewn into the rift, and they will be able to siphon power from it to keep their kind alive. But the cost will be immense. They will discover that magic weakens the careful balance Zavier will weave, and they will banish it from their lands—all in possession of magic will die. Mikhail will be their king, and he will see this order through. He will forget that Zavier's power created this new kingdom of peace and prosperity. He will forget the priests they claim to be of their gods are really low-level spirit mages who can help channel the aethi'kine power from the rift for the soul fusions. He will forget who the real enemy is, and so will his people.

But the world below will remember.

I will make them remember.

The early days will be rough. Most of the land will be torn apart by the creation of the rift weave, and what's left will be little more than barren rock and endless sea. But some of the mages will survive, and they will lead the rest through. As the weave weakens, they will be the gatekeepers protecting the rest of the world from the beasts. They will become the hunters instead of the hunted.

And so it will be for a long time, one land above and one below, both isolated from the realms beyond and the people living in ignorance of how close to destruction their world teeters—until the saviors come. They are a dove princess and a raven warrior, two lovers always torn asunder, one with the magic to heal the world and the other, oh, I hate to even write his fate. He will be the only of his kind, and I have not seen far enough to know if it will destroy him. Perhaps I don't want to look. In a battle of fire and snow, they will save the world. At least, that is what they and their people will think.

But it won't be so.

They will delay the inevitable, yes, and will have played their parts, but there is another face I see across the ages, always with perfect clarity. Her skin is freckled. Her hair is as blonde as corn stalks. Her honey eyes are as fierce as the noon rays of the sun. She is a spatio'kine, the first of her kind in hundreds of years, born on the other side of the great mountains, and she will be the one to finally seal the rift.

At least, I pray she will.

I have not seen the end. Time is a fickle master, and it keeps secrets even from me, but I know enough to know the fate of everyone lies in her.

If anyone is reading this, please, I pray you find her.

Find her and find salvation.

Find her and be free.

ABOUT THE AUTHOR

Bestselling author Kaitlyn Davis writes young adult fantasy novels under the name Kaitlyn Davis and contemporary romance novels under the name Kay Marie.

Always blessed with an overactive imagination, Kaitlyn has been writing ever since she picked up her first crayon and is overjoyed to share her work with the world. When she's not daydreaming, typing stories, or getting lost in fictional worlds, Kaitlyn can be found indulging in some puppy videos, watching a little too much television, or spending time with her family.

Connect with the Author Online:

Website: KaitlynDavisBooks.com
Facebook: Facebook.com/KaitlynDavisBooks
Instagram: @KaitlynDavisBooks
TikTok: @KaitlynDavisBooks
Twitter: @DavisKaitlyn
Goodreads: Goodreads.com/Kaitlyn_Davis
Bookbub: @KaitlynDavis

CPSIA information can be obtained
at www.ICGtesting.com
Printed in the USA
LVHW081940030621
689284LV00013B/200/J